Blood Brothers

A novel by

Sebati Edward Mafate

"Blood Brothers," by Sebati Edward Mafate. ISBN 978-1-63868-089-5 (softcover); 978-1-63868-090-1 (eBook).

Published 2022 by Virtualbookworm.com Publishing Inc., P.O. Box 9949, College Station, TX , 77842, US.

For two men who had a positive impact in my life, and have since gone to be with the Lord: Paul Fletcher and Don Perfectpicture Johnson.

BOOK ONE

CHAPTER 1

The Okavango Delta, North-Western Botswana,
October 1988.

THE OKAVANGO SWAMPS, the largest inland delta in
the world at the northwestern part of Botswana, is a
breathtaking beauty, a paradise on earth that has drawn
tourists from every corner of the globe. It originates as
a perennial river from Angola, which once it reaches
Botswana breaks into twisting waterways spreading
like tentacles covered by papyrus and reeds, forming
numerous islands in its wake.

Because of its never-ending supply of water, the
area is a natural habitat for all kinds of wildlife found
on the African continent and has since been declared a
national game reserve. Now, because of where it is
located close to at least four international borders with
Angola in the northwest, Zambia in the north,
Zimbabwe further east, and Namibia due southwest—
as well as a healthy population of elephant and rhino
whose tusks fetch a fortune in the illicit ivory trade—
the area has been from time immemorial a target-rich
environment for poachers.

With the rapid decline of the elephant population in East Africa, the poachers began drifting south to countries like Botswana and Zimbabwe, and their methods became more and more sophisticated. In neighboring Zimbabwe, where then-President Robert Gabriel Mugabe had issued a directive that was unequivocal in that poachers would be killed on sight, their anti-poaching unit was staffed with ex-guerrilla fighters of the famous 'Chimurenga War' that had liberated their nation, and were thus well versed with the art of 'bush war' and guerilla warfare. They were more than a match for the poachers, which meant that for now at least, Zimbabwe was left alone.

With South Africa much further south, this left Botswana in their sights. For many years, the protectors of these magnificent creatures were no match for the elusive, well-armed, and well-trained poachers. In the process, many good men, elephants, and rhinos had been killed, with the poachers retreating across the border into either Angola or Zambia via the Caprivi Strip. Aside from taking a toll on the local game rangers, who were poorly armed to begin with, the situation was fast getting out of hand. Suddenly the depletion of these wonderful creatures, just as it had happened in East Africa, was a very distinct possibility.

At the urging of the President of Botswana, who was at the time Lt. General Seretse Khama Ian Khama, a nature enthusiast himself, a resolution was passed in Parliament the purpose of which was backed even by the opposition parties, in a rare show of political unity. An anti-poaching unit comprised of army personnel with Special Forces training would be established to protect these animals. The threat to the national wildlife, the elephants and rhinos in particular, needed to be confronted head-on. Tourism was a source of national revenue, and if that was not protected, the end of tourism to Botswana, or its rapid decline, would deal a very crushing blow to the nation.

One such unit, a platoon of these specially trained men and members of the Botswana Defense Force, was hidden and lying in wait somewhere on the outskirts of the Okavango Delta under the cover of thick bushes that stretched for miles in every direction. There were eight of them in all. In addition to their army fatigues, they were clad in ghillie suits designed to resemble background environment such as bush, shrubs, and savanna. They were crouched in a semicircular arrangement.

Their leader, a young lieutenant named Frederick 'Freddy' Motang, was issuing last-minute instructions. Apart from being the well-trained Special Forces type, these men were members of the elite and vaunted Anti-Poaching Unit. The special wing of the military was founded specifically to hunt, kill, and when necessary capture these poachers who were slowly but steadily illegally crossing the border into the country and killing their beloved elephants and rhinos. Since it became known that the poachers themselves were well-armed, and more disturbing that a growing number of them possessed military training and would not hesitate to kill if threatened, the President, with the blessing of Parliament and his cabinet, decided to act by involving the military with a directive that they were to shoot to kill.

The poachers in this particular case were an organized unit with criminal ties to organized crime in the Far East. The leader of this band of rustlers was a ruthless ex-military combatant of Angola's UNITA (The National Union for The Total Independence Of Angola) named Molo Sahili. Many times the anti-poaching unit had crossed paths with this bandit, and on those many occasions it had cost the lives of very good men, with Sahili not for the first time escaping the carefully laid trap that was meant for him.

On this particular bright early morning, Lieutenant Motang was determined to put an end to Sahili's reign of terror. Through its network of spies and informants that stretched across the border, the army had learned that Sahili and his merry band of men had set up camp not too far from where this particular platoon was planning its assault.

"I repeat," Lieutenant Motang said after looking at the men crouched on one knee around him. "Try and get him alive if you can, but kill him if faced with no other options. Am I understood?"

"Yes, sir!" the soldiers answered in unison quietly yet firmly, as if fearing if they responded any louder, their voices would carry over to the enemy encampment less than two miles away.

Motang looked at them again. They were all good men, the best of the best, which was why they were chosen for this particular mission. Also with them that morning, but a few feet away from the crouched men, was a white man with curly blond hair, an American named Paul McDaniels. He had a certain lean, athletic quality about him—broad shoulders, thin waist, developed legs, all three parts in balance, and a very handsome face to boot.

In his early thirties and a nature enthusiast who shot documentary films for National Geographic, he had on his shoulder a large commercial video camera, and to his side as always was his trusted tracker, sometimes soundman, and boom operator—a Bushman named Xaraga. He was quietly filming the entire event, something that seemed to displease the lieutenant and his men, as they once in a while gave him disapproving looks. This, for all Motang knew, was an extremely dangerous mission with too many moving parts that could go wrong at any moment, and the last thing the lieutenant wanted was to be babysitting two civilians when the stuff hit the fan.

After pushing that particular thought out of his mind, Lieutenant Motang faced his men again. There was an unmistakable tension etched on their faces. They were all good men, the lieutenant knew, but none of them had ever experienced real combat before. Granted, they were not taking on an enemy fort manned with combatants who also had Special Forces training, but a bunch of armed poachers. Still, these men knew all too well there was always a real chance of a gunfight that could end up with one or more of them taking a bullet – even a well-placed one in between the eyes.

However, what concerned the young lieutenant more than anything was the presence of the American man crouched on one knee a few yards back, and his most trusted guide. The Bushman whom Motang had come to know as 'Sam' when introductions were made, simply because the white man could not pronounce the man's given name, had suspected that that was a name the white man had come up for him.

Paul Wesley McDaniels, a nature aficionado and filmmaker, was from Altadena, California. His wife had first came to Botswana ten years earlier with him for what was supposed to have been a short assignment for National Geographic about a particular pack of wild dogs that they were to follow and film from birth to an age where they began hunting. The couple had instead fallen in love with the country and its natural habitat, whose beauty defied explanation, so they decided to make Botswana their permanent home—so much such that, to prove their intent, they decided to naturalize as Botswana citizens.

The process was long and arduous, but in the end extremely rewarding, which explained in no small part why he was here on this very secret exploit to take down not just the troublesome poachers, but the head of the Mamba, that being the scar-faced Sahili. A man who had proven time and time again to be almost untouchable over the years. Years that left many carcasses of elephants and rhinos strewn about the African wild.

Motang focused his gaze on McDaniels and his aide, and the American could see the disapproval in the young lieutenant's eyes.

"You know my stance," Motang said at last after a long pause. "Personally, I would never allow a civilian on an exploit like this one, but my orders come from the very top."

The poaching of elephants in Botswana had become a hot topic, and with the news spreading all over the world, it was not the kind of attention this nation the size of France, also known as the 'Beacon of Africa' because of her stable political environment, needed.

The government needed to show the international community that they cared for their wildlife, and that they were ready to fight fire with fire. In other words, they needed a brave filmmaker to document the taking down of one of these batches of poachers, particularly the ruthless Sahili. When approached with the idea through one of the president's personal advisers, Paul McDaniels did not balk at the chance to film something so daring. It was just the type of thing that his employers, National Geographic, would kill for.

"I understand, Lieutenant Motang," Paul McDaniels nodded. "But just know that I want that scumbag just as bad. And don't worry, I won't be in your way. I just want to catch every piece of the action on this." He smiled as he patted the video camera on his shoulder.

The American was disheveled and ruggedly handsome with an easy smile. He had not shaved in a while and his hair was unkempt, revealing a man who spent most of his time outdoors, frequently under the blistering African sun. The young lieutenant eyed the small man crouched next to McDaniels, as if seeing him for the first time, even though introductions had been made earlier.

"And who's he again?" he asked, pointing at the small man.

Without turning, but flashing a smile that revealed a perfect set of teeth, McDaniels said, "Like I mentioned earlier, Lieutenant, his name is hard to pronounce. It has a clicking sound, as is common among his people, but to me he's Sam – my assistant and also master tracker."

Motang studied the small man again. His hair was short and unkempt with lines that revealed the scalp beneath, his light skin was wrinkled with deep lines, which put him in his late fifties, but the lieutenant knew that he also could be way off in his estimation. The San, better known as the Bushmen, lived a nomadic life and had done so since the stone age. Coupled with that, many of their kinfolk and perhaps even Sam himself were not born in hospitals where records of their birthdates could be kept. It was almost impossible to guess their true age.

Xaraga, Sam to the rest, was dressed in a pair of faded jeans that had holes at the knees and were cut at the bottom, the lieutenant could tell, so he could fit perfectly in them. He also wore a faded t-shirt of some unknown football club that had been washed so many times, the lettering in front was all but obliterated.

Upon making these observations, the lieutenant nodded and said, "Yes, so I hear."

He turned to his men, who though still crouched on one knee in a semicircular arrangement were now facing outward and on high alert, their weapons at the ready as they scoured the surroundings, all of them keenly aware of every sound in the surrounding forest. Not that they expected an ambush of some sort, but their years of training had kicked in. They were ready. It was time to confront the enemy.

The lieutenant turned around again, and with a subtle nod to his men, they all stood up as one, their American-made AR 15 machine guns at the ready, locked and loaded the safety off, the only safety being their trigger fingers. One of his men had a high-power, specially calibrated Sniper Rifle.

Without another word, Motang lifted his left hand and spread all five fingers, and his men spread in different directions and vanished like forest spirits in the surrounding woods, their ghillie camouflage suits making them appear as if they were part of the surrounding bush. It was as amazing as it was breathtaking to witness. The lieutenant had instructed Daniel and his tracker to wait exactly ten minutes before they could follow suit, and the American did as instructed. As the minutes slowly ticked by, he kept glancing at his watch ever so anxiously. By the seventh minute he could not bear it any longer.

"Let's go," he said to Sam as he switched on the camera and placed it on his shoulder.

Silently, the small man led the way but he was careful, as he had been taught a long time ago in such situations, to stay out of the camera frame. The two men trudged along quietly as they followed the general direction the soldiers took, while at the same time making certain that they do not stir their quarry as to their presence. With the Bushman in the lead, even though he could barely see far ahead, McDaniels knew they were headed in the right direction. These small people of the desert could track anything and anyone. The American had come to realize that a long time ago.

As they got closer, in Paul McDaniels' estimation, Sam the Bushman began slowing down, crouching, looking up ahead of him and around before stealthily making his way ahead. They were getting close to the enemy encampment, McDaniels could sense it as he felt the adrenaline surge through his veins.

"How far?" he whispered at Sam as he slowly panned his camera slightly to the left and then to the right. At times he would catch his master tracker in his frame, but he was not unduly worried, all this could be fixed in the editing room. For now, the ultimate prize lay ahead.

"Shhhh!" the small man admonished as he turned and placed his index finger on his lips. He did that with an intensity that told the American they were closing in on the target.

CHAPTER 2

THE ENCAMPMENT, which had since become the *defacto* base of operation for the poachers, was well hidden. It was deep in the ancient forest, and for a long time its location had not been known. There had been rumors about this hideout, but in spite of many efforts to locate it, that included foot and aerial searches, none of them bore fruit. And the elephants kept being killed. These particular poachers operated with a level of stealth and sophistication never seen before, leaving the authorities baffled.

This went on for months until the authorities caught a break in a series of unlikely events, in a place far from the swamps at the village town of Maun. As it turned out, Sahili and his brigands needed supplies while in hiding and taking down elephants and rhinos at a rate never seen or heard of before. The person who was assigned that particular errand was a young man named Patrick Lefatshe, a local well-known petty thief who had been recruited by Sahili and his cohorts for this particular task.

At least twice a month, he would drive the 41 miles from the edge of the delta to Maun in his off-road 4X4 Toyota Hilux. Now, on this particular excursion, he was to stock up as many goods as possible, which included mealie-meal, tomatoes, cooking oil, salt (lots of it to help preserve the meats), flower, paraffin for the portable stoves used for cooking, and lamps, but most important of all, 3D batteries for the handy radio and walkie-talkies— something they could never have enough of.

To make a long story short, a kleptomaniac through and through if there ever was one with sticky fingers he could never stop from wandering, Patrick was arrested for trying to walk out of the Cash Bazaar Store with a pack of batteries without paying for them. This in spite of being warned on several occasions not to draw any kind of attention to himself. On being interrogated by the police who had been called to the scene by the store owners, this young man who, due to some prior misdemeanors was actually on probation and facing two years in prison, told a very strange story.

In fact, Patrick Lefatshe became a gift to the authorities that kept on giving. At first the police thought that the young man was high from sniffing glue, a substance he was known to abuse as a kid, when he told them that he knew the poachers' hideout, their mode of operation, and their leader, Molo Sahili. It took a while, but finally he was able to convince them that he possessed this knowledge, because he had been recruited by one of Sahili's top men to be one to get supplies when needed and since he was a local, he could blend in with ease. Add to that, he was also instructed to keep his eyes and ears open when in town to find out if the law was closing in on their operation or not.

The ultimate act that convinced the police that Patrick Lefatshe was who he claimed to be, was when he led them to his truck, which was fitted with a canopy above its bed and all the supplies needed by the brigands. It galled Patrick to know that possibly the poaching operation was exposed, because he just could not control his urge to steal, especially after being warned not to bring attention to himself—and this over a pack of cheap batteries, of all things.

A plan was quickly put into play. Patrick was told to continue as if nothing had happened. He headed back to the delta with one of the policemen, a constable, following him. Now, to get to the encampment located due east of the delta, he had to cross the river by hiring a local boatman and two more to help him carry the goods by walking the five and a half miles to the bivouac. The helpers, including the boatmen, were all undercover policemen. It did not take long for the poachers' hideout to be finally, and at long last, located. As soon as all the intelligence was gathered, it was swiftly and quietly passed on to the army, who in turn rallied the Anti-Poaching Unit, a unit that consisted of men with Special Forces training.

CHAPTER 3

THE POACHERS' ENCAMPMENT was in a small clearing in the middle of the forest. It was so well hidden that it was little wonder it could not be found, and the situation would have most likely remained had it not been for the lucky break that came about because of Lefatshe's arrest, who incidentally was told to make himself scarce a day before the raid went down and to sin no more.

At the corner of the clearing was a primus stove with breakfast already cooking, and one of the poachers was tending to the frying pan. There were trophies from animals killed, but most importantly, in a hidden corner was a pile of neatly arranged elephant tusks, ready to be transported for the second phase of the operation.

Among the men moving around and apparently preparing to leave was a muscular man in his early to mid-thirties with a glossy scar that ran from the right side of his face to his upper lip, which at times gave him a sardonic smile when he looked at something for a while or engaged in deep thought. Molo Sahili. And just like the rest of his men, strapped on his shoulder was the ubiquitous Russian-made AK47, the staple of violence and revolution on the continent and the world over.

For Sahili and his men, these were weapons they were ready to use in case they encountered the enemy. For their prey, the elephants, they employed a very large gun that was always kept in its case until the time to use it came. It was the American-made Beretta fifty-caliber BMG armor piercing incendiary that could split open the head of a bull elephant at a distance of up to one mile.

They had gathered all they needed, and even though Sahili would have liked to stay a little longer and in the process kill four more bulls as an added bonus, some gut instinct, a voice at the back of his mind, told him that he had pushed his luck far enough. It was time to pack up and leave.

"Okay, quickly," the scar-faced man said to two of his men close by who, like him, were armed with AK47s. "We should have been on our way before dawn."

The younger of the two men he had been talking to, Moses, who appeared to be in his mid-20's, looked at his boss, before turning to point at the loot they had painstakingly acquired over the past two months, constantly evading anti-poaching units who were now on high alert, and at times barely missed being spotted by the skin of their teeth.

"Sahili," Moses said. "Are you sure the goods will be safe here?"

To Moses, the tusks, particularly this much, represented untold riches in the young man's imagination that was becoming more and more inflamed with every day that passed.

For an answer, Sahili smiled and walked over to where the pile of ivory lay, and from behind it pulled a net that was hidden all along from the rest of his men until now, and with it concealed the neat pile of tusks. The net was green and covered with artificial leaves attached to it that in no time made it look like part of the forest, rendering it harder to detect. Moses was impressed, and so was the other man with him who had been silent all along. His name was James.

"Ingenious," James said with a smile. His brow then furrowed as he thought of something. "But that hides it even from us. How are the others going to find it?" Before Sahili could give an answer he continued, "They can't afford to waste time looking for it, especially if they're getting here by helicopter. Our window for a successful pick up is just a few minutes," he cautioned.

That familiar sardonic smile from Sahili flashed again as he raised his hand. In it was a compact Global Positioning Device, better known as a GPS.

"They already have the exact location, down to the last coordinate," he said with a triumphant smug on his face.

The two younger men's eyes bulged indicating that they were visibly astonished.

"You sure as hell think of everything, don't you, Sahili?" James said smiling as he shook his head, totally impressed.

"I try," Sahili said with feigned modesty. "This has got to be the biggest score ever," he promised, even though he knew they would not even get a fraction of the spoils after all was said and done. He was going to give them just enough to want more with a promise of much more to come, and if they kept asking for more he would just silence them with a bullet to the head. He did not like complications. After all, these men meant nothing to him. They were just cannon fodder, totally dispensable. He could recruit another batch of men for fifty Pula per head in no time and be back in business as early as next month.

"We're going to retire on this one, so there's no way I can mess this up," Sahili continued, and James was completely reassured.

"I see," James said.

"Now you know," Sahili said. "We need to clear out within the next twenty minutes."

Sahili then looked around the encampment. At least eight men were accounted for. They were hastily packing their belongings in their rucksacks and began hiding the other animal remains, clearing up the campsite in such a way that it looked as if no major activity had taken place. The men were so quick and so thorough that it was obvious that they had done this type of thing so many times that it had become second nature to them.

"Where is Ntemwa?" Sahili asked.

John Ntemwa was his adjutant, his right-hand man, someone he relied on heavily. The only man he could trust in this crooked business, and that was saying a lot.

"Oh, he's around somewhere," James said as he packed his rucksack.

"And Patrick?" Sahili inquired.

"Don't you remember, Sahili?" James said without looking up from his backpack. It was packed to capacity, and he was forcing some clothing items into every little crevice he could find. "He said he had to head back to the village after dropping off the supplies because he found out that his mother is ill."

It was then Sahili understood what had been bothering him all morning as he knit his brow in perplexity – the absence of Patrick Lefatshe. The local boy from Maun had been recruited a few months ago by none other than his *aide-de-camp* John Ntemwa. There was no need to suspect treachery from him or any of his men, as they all had been fully vetted, but the absence of Patrick soon after he arrived from his monthly errand was cause for concern. None of his men had ever done this, asked for permission to visit an ailing parent while in the middle of an operation. Somewhere in the pit of his stomach, something gave way as a wave of misgivings assailed him.

***

Unbeknownst to Sahili and his men was the fact that all their movements and activities were being caught on camera at that moment, as Paul McDaniels and his small assistant filmed them from a well-hidden vantage spot right at the edge of the clearing, as close to the action as they would dare. There was no sign of the soldiers as the small man led McDaniels slowly, cautiously, but surely to the encampment.

After looking around, and making certain that nobody was lurking nearby, McDaniels turned the camera on one more time, adjusted the focus, and began filming. Under ideal circumstances, he would have attached the boom pole and mike covered with a fur Rycote windjammer windscreen, then have Sam capture the sound like he always did on regular productions. This was certainly not one of them. It was not staged or rehearsed, it was the real deal. And for all intents and purposes could turn out to be extremely dangerous. Of the two men, the only one who seemed to sense the possible peril was Sam.

"Mister McDaniels," the small man whispered. "I think this is good and close enough."

Sam had found a nice spot within a thicket that was a little over thirty feet from the edge of the campsite. However, Sam's warning was definitely falling on deaf ears, it seemed. Paul McDaniels was like a kid on

Christmas morning opening presents, while his tracker was crouched on his heels a few feet behind his boss.

"Sam," he whispered excitedly, breaking his own statute of keeping his mouth shut. "This is totally cool, man. Absolutely National Geographic material."

Sam merely grunted his approval, praying for the hour to pass so they may return to safety. Some sixth sense, a virtue, and instinct very prevalent among his people told him that something was not right.

As he gazed at the American, he could hear him mumbling to himself with what the small man could attribute to excitement. White people could be strange sometimes, Sam Xaraga had long since decided. Why couldn't this man realize that the danger in the air was almost palpable, to a point of reaching out and touching it?

"Sam," he heard the American hiss again. "We got them!"

We? Sam wondered.

As he leaned forward to pick up what his boss was saying next, a very tall, dark, strongly built man who looked to be in his late 20s suddenly and quietly emerged from the clump of thickets directly behind Sam the Bushman and Paul McDaniels like a forest sprite. He immediately froze at seeing both intruders at a place where they were not supposed to be. It was John Ntemwa! He had earlier excused himself from the hideout to go and perform his morning ritual of relieving himself, and was apparently on his way back when he stumbled on the two men, one of them a white man, he quickly realized, who had a large camera on his shoulder and was filming incessantly the activities of the campsite.

This could not be good, Ntemwa realized. Their leader, the great Molo Sahili, had warned them about the presence of these foreigners, the so-called 'Nature

Conservationists' who claimed to come to Africa to save the animals and Africa from Africans, when really they were publicity hounds who were nothing but hell-bent on making a name for themselves. And here was one of them and his sidekick.

Ntemwa had to think fast. He could quietly backtrack, head to the camp from another direction, and notify Sahili of his discovery in a way that would not tip the white man and his friend that they were onto them. Or, he could deal with the situation right there and then, quietly and yet effectively. Without further hesitation, he decided on the latter. He would never get another opportunity like the one that had just presented itself.

Slowly and silently, he crouched on one knee as he methodically placed the machine gun that had been dangling from his left shoulder on the ground. Then in one fluid, clearly practiced move, and without even taking his eyes away from the two unsuspecting men, John Ntemwa reached with his right hand to the small of his back, and from its sheath pulled out an oversized hunting knife. The razor-sharp blade was so broad that it glinted from the rays of the early morning sun that penetrated in single beams through the foliage behind him.

His heart fluttered so wildly with acute anticipation and excitement that for a second, he feared that his two would-be victims would hear it. Ntemwa tried to will his heart to beat at a much steadier pace as he slowly crept toward Sam, who was still so engrossed in what his master was doing that he ignored the hunter's 'sixth sense' common among his people from time immemorial that told him that something was stirring behind him.

In no time, John Ntemwa was directly behind the small man. He quickly covered his mouth with his massive left palm to prevent him from shouting a warning to his master, and then in one swift motion with his right hand, sliced Sam's neck with the sharp blade, so razor-jagged that it sank deep, severing arteries, veins, and was stopped only by the deep neck bones and cartilage from going any deeper. Bright red blood gushed from the severed neck like a broken pipe with multiple holes in it, and Ntemwa was forced to hold him tight as Sam's body first jerked violently, and then began flopping like a fish on dry land. Ntemwa held fast with his powerful arms as he gritted his teeth, feeling the spasms that were violent at first, and then began to lose strength until their power dissipated and finally stopped. He then lowered what was left of the smaller man's head to the ground. Sam Xaraga was dead as a doornail.

Ntemwa did not bother to wipe the blood from the blade as he crept toward his next quarry, Paul McDaniels. He did this by placing his heel first on the ground and then the ball of his foot, to make certain that he did not step on a dry twig, leaf, or any such thing whose crackling sound was definitely going to give his advantage away.

A smile crept from the corner of the brigand's mouth in anticipation of this high profile kill. It was going to be a doozy, another trophy to add to his kill ratio—and this would be the head of a white man, a stupid one who could not keep his pointy nose out of things that did not concern him.

Meanwhile, Paul McDaniels sensed movement behind him.

"Shhhh! Sam, we gotta get this right, man," he said but immediately froze for less than a fraction of a second. Something was not right – very wrong, in fact. Sam Xaraga *never* made a sound, he quickly realized.

Especially in situations like these where silence was paramount.

With his camera still on his shoulder, Paul McDaniels turned just in time to see a very tall and dark-skinned man closing in on him, brandishing a blood stained knife. Instinctively, and without even looking at where he last saw Sam, the American knew right away that his most trusted tracker, friend, and sometime confidante for the past five years was dead. The sorrow and grief would come later and hit him in waves, he knew. Right now it was about dealing with this immediate threat to his life.

He straightaway tossed the still running camera to the side, and in one swift motion, while still on his knees, parried Ntemwa's outstretched arm to the side. With his palm stretched in a karate chop, hit the inside of Ntemwa's wrist so hard that he was forced to let go of his knife.

On the other hand, McDaniels' super-quick response was enough to cause the poacher to hesitate in surprise. It was now obvious, even to him at that split moment, to realize that the white man had very acute battle instincts and was trained to react quickly to surprises. And at that moment of uncertainty after he disarmed him was more than enough time for McDaniels to grab both of Ntemwa's hands, fall on his back and as both legs shot up, strike Ntemwa on the belly, keep his feet there. Using his back as a pivot, he executed a perfect overhead throw.

For a while, it looked as if John Ntemwa was suspended in the air and spun end over end, for a good ten seconds it seemed, before he landed on his back with a loud thud. The fall emptied his lungs of oxygen, and Ntemwa wriggled on the ground for a while, eyes popped out, mouth open and gasping for air like a fish.

"Hahaha!" Paul McDaniels laughed mirthlessly. "I'm the nightmare your mama warned you about."

In spite of it all, the brigand recovered quickly and had the presence of mind to roll to where he had dropped his knife, which he quickly picked up as he sprang to his feet to face the American, once again brandishing his knife but still showing the aftereffects of the fall, for he was still gasping for air.

"Ahhh! Now you die, stupid white man!" The bravado that had momentarily deserted him was back now that he was armed again. In his mind, he had underestimated the white man and he was not going to do that again.

He then lunged at Paul, knife first, and the latter simply swerved to the side, and in the process, revealing by the way he moved that he was an exponent of the martial arts. This was then followed by a flurry of well-aimed strikes that consisted of punches, and kicks. He began by disarming the poacher with ease and this time made sure that the knife was far from Ntemwa's reach, before clinically cutting him down to size. In a few seconds, it was all over. Even Ntemwa, in spite of himself, was shocked at the speed and quickness by which his opponent had taken him down.

With his foot on Ntemwa's throat, hard enough to subdue him but not cut off his air supply, the American hissed, "How many more out there?" He pointed at the direction where Ntemwa had come. "I said how many more?" He exerted more pressure as he pressed down his foot even harder on the man's throat.

Part of him was telling him to crush the poacher's larynx and put him out of his misery as he fought hard to control the rage that was building up in his chest. This man, this animal, had brutally killed his friend, he thought as he fought back stinging tears. As he turned to look at the small man's body, which lay sprawled on the forest floor, the bright red arterial blood still gushing from his severed neck and eyes wide staring at nothing, he registered the shock that had flashed through them the moment his life was swiftly and ferociously taken from him. The anger surged even more through Paul McDaniels' entire body, it took an incredible amount of willpower and training to keep his body from shaking.

At the moment Paul McDaniels turned to face his fallen tracker, the pressure on Ntemwa's throat eased, and the poacher was able to extricate his neck, albeit briefly—but long enough to shout a warning as loud as he could under the circumstances.

"Sahili!" he screamed. "Ambush! Ambush! A …"

And then all hell broke loose.

CHAPTER 4

THE DESPERATE SCREAMS FROM THE POACHER were heard by Sahili and the rest of his cohorts. They were also heard by Lieutenant Frederick 'Freddy' Motang and his men, who were at the opposite end of the camp as they advanced in a rapid infantry crawl, their ghillie suits blending perfectly with the surroundings, that the only thing that gave them away to an astute observer would be their movement.

The young lieutenant swore under his breath. This was exactly what he had feared all along and why he had vociferously protested the American's participation in this operation – or anyone not of his platoon, for that matter. Now a well-planned assault had been compromised before it even started. During his Special Forces training under the Israelis, the lieutenant had been told that operations rarely work out as planned, there was always an 'X Factor,' the unknown. This was why these elite soldiers were taught to adapt, improvise, and continue on the fly, in a manner of speaking. They were taught to 'think on their feet.' But what just happened was something that could have been avoided if the American and his Bushman friend had not been included in this operation. However, orders were orders.

"Dammit," he spat. "The stupid white man has let our presence be known." The lieutenant gave the signal via his lip mike, and the men stopped their crawl at once but remained still on the ground.

Motang activated his lip mike again and spoke into it.

"Modojwa!" he called.

The diminutive Christopher 'Mapeni' Modojwa was the platoon's sniper. It was believed by those who knew him, and those who had seen him in action, that he was the best in the business. He was perched and well hidden, as previously arranged, on one of the highest branches of a thickly leafed Mimosa tree about one hundred meters away from the camp, where he had a bird's eye view of everything within a mile radius.

"Yes, sir!" The sniper's voice crackled in his earpiece.

"Engage the enemy at will, but spare Sahili if you can. I repeat, engage the enemy at will, but spare Sahili if you can. We need to do everything in our power to take him alive."

"Yes, sir!" was the crisp response from the well-concealed sniper.

It didn't take long for Motang to hear screams of horror from the camp as Modojwa began his onslaught.

"Two hostiles down, lieutenant. I repeat, two hostiles down," the sniper's steady voice crackled again in the lieutenant's earpiece along with those of the rest of his men.

"Give them hell, Modojwa!"

"Yes, sir."

***

Sahili, just like the rest of his men, froze when he heard the terrifying scream he immediately recognized as that of John Ntemwa. And then in less time it took for his brain to relate the signal to his limbs to aim his weapon at where he believed the danger lay, the face of one of his men directly in front of him literally exploded, accompanied by a pink mist of flesh, blood, and bone. A heavy caliber bullet, most certainly from a well-hidden sniper, had entered the back of his head and left an insulting, gaping hole in place of what once used to be the man's face.

Before Sahili could make sense of what was going on, another one of his men fell to the earth. There was now absolutely no doubt in his mind – their hideout had been discovered. And the hidden enemy was picking them out one at a time like they were target practice. Out of sheer panic, the remainder of his men sent volley after volley of machine gun fire into the surrounding bush, even though they had absolutely no idea from which direction the attack came. For all they knew, they were completely surrounded, and after a while they knew it would come down to two unpleasant choices – death or surrender.

In the ensuing confusion, Sahili saw his chance. Grateful for the reprieve, he turned and ran in the opposite direction from where he believed most of the enemy fire was coming.

Upon seeing the poacher vanish through a clump of bushes, Motang yelled in his mouthpiece: "Madisa! Mogapi! … Don't let him get away!"

The two young soldiers, who looked to be in their early twenties and still dressed in their ghillie suits, immediately sprang to their feet, automatic rifles in hand, and gave chase in an all-out attempt to overtake the fleeing fugitive. However, Sahili, a better sprinter apparently, was swiftly increasing the distance between them with ease.

From where he was, Paul McDaniels saw all this unfold and quickly incapacitated Ntemwa by cold-cocking him with a blow to the temple. He felt the anger in his chest.

"Son of a bitch!" he spat and then immediately joined the chase.

On seeing this, and the fact that the white man was unarmed and going after a known ruthless killer, Lieutenant Motang was horrified.

"Goodness gracious … McDaniels, nooo!" he screamed.

He never liked losing a man on his watch, like any good platoon leader. But if it happened to one of his men, God forbid, it was a possibility they signed up for, something that could be expected. The killing of a civilian, on the other hand, and a white man for that matter who happened to be an international celebrity in the preservation of animals, could have serious political ramifications. The outcry would be deafening. Forget the fact that the white man knew exactly what he was getting into and had been warned time and again that he could be harmed if things went south. None of that mattered if Paul McDaniels was killed. Lieutenant Freddy Motang would be the one who'd take the fall—unfair of course, but unfortunately that was the nature of the world they lived in.

As if on cue, the fleeing Sahili turned around, leveled his AK-47 at the soldiers giving chase, and fired a volley at full automatic. By this time, the forest had opened up into a field with many wet patches on the eastern side of the swamps. Mogapi gasped, pitched forward, and fell to the earth as a bullet hit his chest and another hit Madisa in the shoulder. With both men down, this left an unarmed McDaniels, who upon seeing the two men fall, actually accelerated, hurtling along after the rustler at incredible speed.

His anger fueled at the image of his tracker with a slit throat, and now the two young soldiers he just saw go down under a hail of desperate gunfire, Paul gritted his teeth as he willed his powerful legs to move even faster. *No!* This bandit, this brigand Molo Sahili had to go down, one way or the other. The American, a superb athlete to begin with, began cutting the distance between them, even though the running was quite cumbersome for both men because of the periodic muddy bogs on the surface.

Sahili, on realizing that the American was closing in, increased his speed, and showed that he was more adept at this particular landscape than his pursuer. All of a sudden he was dodging bushes and quagmire with more than uncanny dexterity as the wet patches became more and more consistent. The same could not be said for Paul McDaniels as the surface of the landscape changed. He began to constantly stumble, but his determination kept him going. Even a baboon in a tree he ran past seemed to take note as he watched the two humans speed past.

McDaniels saw his quarry slow down and immediately knew what was coming next. He took cover by hitting the wet and muddy ground belly-first, and barely seconds later a burst of machine gun fire issued an almost deafening blast that echoed in the distance. On seeing the white man on the ground, Sahili smiled, assumed the proper stance, leveled his weapon, and squeezed the trigger again. There was an audible click, followed by another and yet another, indicating that the banana-shaped magazine was empty.

On realizing that Sahili had run out of ammunition, Paul McDaniels seized the moment, and in an instant he was on his feet. With all his might and as fast as his powerful legs could carry him, he raced toward the master poacher who by now was fumbling with his weapon by disconnecting the magazine, turning it around, and jamming it back into the body of the gun, the way an AK-47 assault rifle is reloaded.

By the time he was about to level the firearm at the oncoming McDaniels, he was too late. With one powerful, well-aimed, front flying snap kick at the weapon which sent it flying harmlessly into the air and over Sahili's head, instantly disarming him, McDaniels, a martial arts expert who trained constantly and a former national champion in his younger days, delivered yet another kick. This time it was a roundhouse kick to the head, which Sahili, himself, no pushover, tried to parry with his forearm. However, the force of the kick was so much that he staggered backward and was about to fall, but somehow managed to grab hold of McDaniels' shirt. In so doing, he dragged him on his way down with both of them falling into the reeds of a nearby wet patch.

They rolled in the mud, wrestling, each trying to gain the upper hand as their muscles took the strain. After a brief moment, both men struggled to their feet. They were both muddy and at first fought awkwardly, but in the end Paul McDaniels' martial arts prowess— and the fact that he trained hard at least twice a day if he was not engaged in a project, and ran five miles each early morning—proved to be the difference. Even though it must be said that Sahili held his own against his skilled opponent. He had, after all, been a guerilla fighter with the UNITA forces under General Jonas Malheiro Savimbi, and was consequently trained in the art of unarmed combat. However, because he lacked the training discipline that the American possessed in spades, he began to tire as Paul grew stronger as the fight progressed.

Upon seeing his opponent beginning to fade, McDaniels delivered a series of rabbit punches to the face, stomach, and chest, crowned by a blood-curdling *Kiai*, the war cry synonymous with martial arts that was accompanied by a flying front double snap kick. It found its mark and was followed by a vicious but well-placed back kick to the chest that sent the brigand flying a good five feet to land on his back as he gasped for air.

McDaniels delivered the *coup de grace* when Sahili was about to sit up. The American, who was hovering over the clearly beaten man, struck him with a karate chop, better known as the *shuto* strike, at the back of his neck. This was enough to put him out of commission for a good thirty seconds or so. When he opened his eyes, he found himself staring into the dark, menacing holes of the muzzles of at least five or six AR-15 automatic machine guns.

The soldiers had closed in and had watched the fight with astonishment. They were totally mesmerized at the fighting skill displayed by the American, especially the young lieutenant. His respect for the documentarian grew tenfold – never had he seen anything so spectacular. He had taken Paul McDaniels as nothing but a soft filmmaker who would have pee running down his leg at the sight of physical confrontation. Yes, the man had a very good and discernable physique, but that could come from pumping iron and doing pushups consistently. The idea that the man could be a skilled fighter to boot never even crossed his mind.

"Make a move," he snarled at Sahili. "And you're dead. You hear me, you filthy swine? Oh, you're going to look really pretty in a prison cell, you bastard, that ugly scar notwithstanding," the young lieutenant taunted.

His trigger finger was itching, the safety off, and in spite of himself, his training, his discipline, and the warrior code that was instilled in him that there was no honor in killing an unarmed prisoner totally at his mercy, Lieutenant Freddy Motang was willing, and even praying that Sahili make one wrong move so he could end it right there and then. It would avoid the circus of a trial which was sure to follow with the notorious poacher involved.

The rustler smiled sardonically, his scar making him look even more sinister, and spat at the lieutenant's feet. His spittle was filled with blood and accompanied by a couple of teeth, thanks to the blows that were delivered in quick succession to the face and side of the head by McDaniels.

"We both know that I will never see the inside of one of your prisons." He said this with a calm confidence that seemed to have unnerved the young lieutenant.

Instead, Motang scoffed and said, "Hahaha, we shall see about that, Sahili. This time we have you dead to rights. We've got you cold."

One of the soldiers walked up to Sahili and roughly forced him to his feet. He had a pair of handcuffs dangling from one hand, and with them cuffed him from behind. Prodding with his AR-15, still fitted with a silencer, he made him walk back toward the camp. He had been one of the two men who had been instructed to move as close to the poachers' encampment as possible and try to cull the herd by silently eliminating one after another to reduce the threat their size brought to bear, with the diminutive sniper, Christopher 'Mapeni' Modojwa providing much-needed cover. This carefully orchestrated plan had been inadvertently foiled by McDaniels, of course, but the American had more than made up for that mistake in a way that none of them could have thought possible.

Motang walked up to Paul. The American was away from the rest, facing south, hunched over, hands on his knees as he caught his breath. It was obvious that the chase over the unfamiliar, unwieldy territory and the ensuing fight had taken a lot out of him. In spite of overpowering him, Sahili had been a formidable opponent unlike any he had faced in a very long time. There was a newfound respect in the young lieutenant's eyes.

"Are you okay, McDaniels?" the lieutenant wanted to know as he placed a hand on the back of the other man and bent at his waist as he peered into the mud-stained face

"I'm okay, Lieutenant."

"That was very fine work you did," Motang said.

"Thanks, Lieutenant," McDaniels said. He was still breathing hard but recovering rapidly. "It was my pleasure," he continued as he finally stood to his full height. The man stood a little over six feet and thus towered over the younger muscular man.

"I'm curious, though," Motang said as they trudged behind the others who were marching Sahili forward and in no way treating him with kid gloves. They hated these men who poached on their wildlife with seeming impunity, and if it were up to them would have preferred to line them all up, their leader Sahili included, and summarily execute them. However, unfortunately powerful people way above their pay grade were calling the shots on this particular mission, and those orders had to be followed to the letter.

"What?" McDaniels asked, finally catching his breath.

"Where did you learn all that stuff?"

"What stuff?"

"That Bruce Lee, Crouching Tiger Hidden Dragon stuff?"

Paul McDaniels smiled as his gaze took upon a faraway look, thinking of his brother Sean Kane McDaniels, whom he had not seen in over seven years.

"I had a great teacher."

CHAPTER 5

BACK AT WHAT USED TO BE the poachers' hideout, the situation was under control. The remaining poachers who had not been killed, including John Ntemwa, had surrendered, handcuffed, and made to sit on the ground next to one another. Their leader, Molo Sahili, who was eyeing Paul McDaniels with unabashed hatred, was also made to sit with his men. In Sahili's mind, the American documentary filmmaker was responsible for his capture and the death of three of his men, who were lying at the other end of the small clearing, their bodies covered with a bloodstained white cloth.

An army medic was tending to the two young soldiers, Kennedy Madisa and Boikanyo Mogapi. Lieutenant Motang had radioed for help, and a chopper that had been on standby for just such a situation had been given their exact coordinates, and was expected any moment. Of the two wounded men, it was Madisa, who had taken a bullet to the top right side of his chest, which needed immediate attention. He was conscious, stable, but a little delirious thanks in no small part to the morphine that had been administered to him earlier. However, the medic was certain his life was not in danger as long as he reached a hospital bed within the next four hours.

Boikanyo Mogapi was shot in the right shoulder and was now bandaged, his arm was in a blue sling, but the medic had warned that there may be some nerve damage. That was for the doctors to determine, and if it was the case, he would have to undergo at least a month of physical therapy. Xaraga, otherwise known as Sam, Paul McDaniels' tracker, was also covered with a white cloth away from the other bodies. He, unfortunately, had been the only casualty.

Again, Paul McDaniels was forced to push his sorrow aside for now as he retrieved the camera from a clump of bushes where he had hidden it before chasing after Sahili and resumed filming. He did so first with the surroundings before slowly panning the camera from one end to another as an establishing shot, and offered a somewhat somber narrative from the cuff before he focused his attention on the leader of this elite anti-poaching unit that had finally captured the most notorious of all the poachers to have ever crossed from the north, northwest, and northeast of Botswana.

Paul McDaniels was in professional mode now as he got a makeup kit from the side pocket of his camera bag and lightly touched up the lieutenant's face. This, he explained to his subject, was meant to eliminate the shadows from under his eyes. After he was done, he asked the lieutenant to look to the side and not directly at the camera, but train his focus on an object and keep it there as he gave his narrative. After McDaniels slated the shot and explained what was going on, he instructed Lieutenant Frederick 'Freddy' Motang to relax and speak naturally. And since he did not have a sound person, McDaniels asked one of the soldiers to operate the boom pole by placing the windjammer-covered microphone just above the lieutenant's head, but out of frame. Normally this would have been Sam Xaraga's job.

At first the young lieutenant was nervous, fumbling his words a bit, which would have been hilarious under different circumstances. But the death of Paul McDaniels' tracker had cast a dark spell on what should have been a momentous event. However, after a few gaffes here and there, Lieutenant Motang was able to get the hang of it. Not long after that he was on a roll, revealing the fact that he was indeed a natural performer, orator, and spellbinding storyteller. A few times McDaniels had to suppress a smile. The man was a natural.

Motang continued by saying, "Our intel informed us that this particular band of poachers has devised an even more sophisticated method of collecting these tusks from the elephants and rhinos they've killed."

"What kind of sophisticated method?" McDaniels asked, even though he knew the answer. He was asking for the benefit of the millions of viewers around the world who were certain to watch this the moment it was shot, edited, scored, color-corrected, and then submitted to his employers.

For an answer, Lieutenant Motang held up a device that he had confiscated from Sahili, and McDaniels zoomed in for a close-up as the young lieutenant continued his narrative.

"This," he said, "is a GPS tracking device. It pinpoints the exact location where the tusks are hidden, which happens to be right here at this location. A helicopter painted to look like one of ours, up to the specific make and model, is set to come and pick up the loot."

Now this was news to the American. He had not been read in on this, so he paid even closer attention to the lieutenant.

"Painted to look like one of yours?" the American asked in disbelief. This meant these poachers operated at a level of complexity never seen or heard of before. It was clear that the bandits were backed by some profoundly serious high rollers.

"Yes, Mr. McDaniels, painted like a military chopper. You see, as you probably know, this is a National Game Reserve, a restricted area. Unless by prior arrangement, only the military is allowed to fly and land in this area, so by using a helicopter that looks like one of ours, their accomplices can fly in and out uninhibited. Except now, they don't know that we're on to them." He paused, looked around, and then returned his focus to a bushy shrub off-camera that he used to keep from looking directly at the camera lens.

"One thing you've got to realize," he continued, "is that these poachers have gotten pretty ingenious and very brazen. You will be amazed as to what lengths they will go to kill our beautiful creatures just to satisfy their greed."

The lieutenant at that moment glanced at Sahili, who was still seated on the ground with his hands cuffed behind his back. Paul McDaniels was in time to pan the camera at the poacher, and then back to his main subject, who reminded him of a young Cassius Clay before he became Muhammad Ali. In that brief moment, he was able to capture the glare the soldier gave the bound poacher. It was not rehearsed, coached, or directed. It was pure and real, and the American had caught it all on tape. It was what people in the business called 'the money shot.' Again, Paul McDaniels suppressed a smile, but the image of Sam with his slit throat managed to erase such thoughts. He needed to stay focused. This documentary would go far in bringing his killers to justice.

"And this animal here," Lieutenant Motang almost spat at the brigand. "Is the head of this brutal organization. He's very cunning and elusive, this Sahili is. Twice we've crossed paths, and twice it has caused the lives of good men. Now, I'm going to personally see to it that this filth is put away for good. Already there's been one killing that happened today that we can add to his string of murders. Granted, he did not physically perform the murder, but he was an accessory nonetheless. However, I'll leave it to the magistrate to sort it out."

"I see," McDaniels nodded.

For the first time, Lieutenant Freddy Motang looked straight into the lens of the camera that was pointed at him. He then turned slightly to look at Sahili, who gave that sardonic and at the same time menacing smile, before he turned to face McDaniels, and then past the camera. Yet again, it was a telling shot.

"No, you don't see, Mr. McDaniels," he said at last. "There is more to it than that. When elephants were almost depleted in east Africa, these scum migrated down south. Our local game rangers could not cope with this kind of opposition, because unlike them these, poachers were armed with some of the most sophisticated weapons on the market today. In other words, they were bringing heavy fire into the fight, which is why the army was forced to intervene. Our directive from the Commander in Chief is to shoot on sight. However in this instance, we had to get this man, Molo Sahili, alive. The rest of the gang are just cannon fodder, men that can be replaced without breaking a sweat, because they come cheap. In order to defeat this syndicate, the head of the Mamba has to be crushed."

Just when Paul Luke Wesley McDaniels was about to open his mouth and ask another question, the lazy *whoppity-whop* of an approaching helicopter could be heard. That was enough to break the spell and send Motang and his men into action.

"That's them," he said, rousing his men into action. "Take cover and be ready."

As the bodies were hidden and the prisoners dragged into the surrounding bushes with the speed and efficiency known only to Special Forces type, Sahili saw his opportunity to say something that had been brewing from the basin of his stomach.

"You're a dead man, McDaniels, you hear me … dead!" he screamed. The hatred in his voice was so intense that tears flowed down his cheeks.

"Someone gag that fool!" the lieutenant shouted as the sound from the approaching chopper grew louder while his men scampered for cover, ready to lay their trap.

Sahili, however, would not be denied his chance to spew his vitriol. "I swear to God, McDaniels, you're just a white imperialist poking your nose into African affairs, and that's going to cost you big," he threatened. He spoke with a diction that showed there had been better days before a life of crime.

"Shut up!" the young lieutenant fumed as he all but slapped the brigand. "I did not know that thieves could express themselves so eloquently. What stopped you from embarking on a more honest trade?"

Sahili ignored him and instead focused his ire on the American. In his mind, it was the documentarian Paul Luke McDaniels who was responsible for his capture.

"You're a dead man, McDaniels!" he shouted again.

McDaniels, on the other hand, continued filming the entire proceedings, now from a well-hidden position with affected unconcern, as if he had heard none of the bandit's threats.

"Shut him up, Private," Lieutenant Motang ordered one of his men.

The private, one Emmanuel Butale, still clad in his ghillie suit like the rest save for their leader, was more than eager to perform the task and would have executed none other with greater enthusiasm. He rushed at the poacher, duct tape in hand, and just to remind him who really was in charge slapped Sahili across his blabbering mouth before he covered it with a piece of silver duct tape. And since the poacher was cuffed behind his back, all he could do was watch helplessly. Like the rest, he was then dragged into the nearby bushes and shoved to the ground. Molo Sahili, feeling totally emasculated, could only watch as his well-planned heist shattered into tiny pieces.

"That should do it, sir," Private Butale announced and immediately took cover with the other soldiers. The helicopter was getting ready to circle around the rendezvous point as previously arranged before finally landing.

CHAPTER 6

MOMENTS LATER, A BELL HELICOPTER in military colors was hovering above the clearing. The rotor wash swayed branches, twigs, and kicked up dust. The pilot began descending, totally unaware that the jaws of the lion were about to clamp. As the helicopter made its final descent, even from his hiding place Lieutenant Freddy Motang had a hard time believing this was not one of his, but in fact a very convincing replica meant to fool anyone who even attempted to take a closer look, let alone a cursory one.

As the scene unfolded, the lieutenant was forced to ask himself some very tough questions. Did this syndicate end with Sahili? Or did it go much, much, higher than that? Obviously, this type of planning, even acquiring a million-dollar, battle-specific Bell military helicopter meant that someone, or certain individuals with serious purse strings, were calling the shots. It would be up to the higher-ups to force that information out of Sahili. Just as quickly as those thoughts had come, Motang was able to push them aside and focus on the task at hand.

The platoon once again took strategic positions around the encampment. One of them was brandishing a rocket launcher that was aimed at the fake army chopper, with specific orders to take the bird down if it attempted to escape. The two wounded soldiers, Kennedy Madisa and Boikanyo Mogapi, had since been evacuated to a safer spot a mile south, where a real army helicopter was en route to transport the two men to the nearest hospital, which was in Maun. The helicopter itself was equipped with state-of-the-art medical equipment, staffed with a medical doctor, who happened to be Pakistani, and two female nurses. This meant that the critically wounded Madisa would be further stabilized on the way to the hospital.

Meanwhile, the phony military chopper drifted to the left and then to the right before finally landing. The rotors were still running, and the rotor wash caused the branches and the long grass around the camp to sway even more violently. It remained that way for a while and was immediately apparent to the watchers that whoever was in that helicopter was making sure there were no unwanted surprises, other than the loot waiting for them. By now, Sahili and his gang were supposed to be miles away, making their escape toward the closest border near the Caprivi Strip, and ultimately to safety. They'd planned to wait a month or so before returning and picking up where they left off.

The side door of the huge Bell finally slid open, and a disheveled-looking man, clearly not the military type, let alone Special Forces, jumped out from the door and landed on the ground a good three feet below, followed by another. They were so sure of their situation that they foolishly came out unarmed. In spite of that, they appeared to be slightly nervous as they looked around. The two men were not expecting an ambush necessarily, but seemed to be overwhelmed by the overall serenity of the area—that and the fact that they were in the midst of conducting a daring heist.

As soon as they realized there was nothing out of the ordinary they needed to be concerned about, one of the men, who was tall and so dark that his skin tone looked blue, pulled out a walkie-talkie and brought it to his mouth. By no coincidence, his name was Blackie, and looked to be in his mid-thirties.

"Alpha, this is Blackie, come in please," he said after pressing the button on the side of the device.

An unintelligible response crackled from the communication device.

"All's clear. We've located the inventory and are about to transport it on the magic carpet to you … over."

He waited for the scratchy response that also seemed to suggest that perhaps it would be a good idea to stay off the air. There was a chance that their chatter could be picked up by the wrong party.

Blackie then said into the walkie-talkie, "That's a copy, Alpha. We're also aware that time is of the essence and we will stay off the air. The camouflage was good by the way, over and out."

Following this, the dark-skinned man consulted a handheld GPS for a moment, and then looked at the three other men who had also come out of the chopper, waiting for instructions on what to do next. As soon as the GPS was fired up and able to connect with the satellite some two hundred miles above Earth, he was able to pinpoint exactly where the tusks that had been hidden by Sahili for him to find.

"Over there," he said, pointing ahead while he consulted the coordinates on the small screen. "Now quick, we have less than ten minutes to get it all loaded and get out of here."

At least eight sets of eager eyes, including that of the documentary filmmaker, followed the activities of these men with keen interest. Many times, Paul McDaniels had to fight one surge after another of utmost euphoria. He could not help but wonder how much all this would be worth to the networks. It just so happened that on this particular project, he was a freelancer. He was not contracted to National Geographic as he had been with previous assignments, which meant he could sell the finished product to the highest bidder, and then there was possible syndication with other networks. The sky was indeed the limit. He again fought to stay focused on the mission at hand, which clearly was no easy task as he adjusted the zoom lens on his camera to catch the action as it unfolded from his hidden place.

Motang, McDaniels, and the rest of the men watched as Blackie, who seemed to have a flair for the dramatic, paused for a few seconds longer within the clump of bushes, and forcefully yanked the camouflage netting that covered the neatly piled tusks. The three men behind him gasped with astonishment and then simultaneously let out a cry of controlled, greedy joy.

Each of the three men had been promised a tusk, and to them that spoke of untold riches, money they'd never see even if they worked two lifetimes in their current menial jobs. What they did not know was that after this assignment, they were to be quickly and quietly disposed of. The holes at their destination, somewhere in the Caprivi Strip forest, were already dug for them to vanish without a trace forever.

Following their initial shock, for the booty was much larger than they expected, they began loading the tusks into the waiting helicopter. The rotors were still spinning, but not as rapidly as before, and each time as they deposited the batch into the cargo compartment, they instinctively stooped as if avoiding having their heads chopped off. This right here was the crux of the military's case. They had to catch them in the act, and that was in actual possession of the ivory and moving it as they were at that very moment. And what was even better was that they had it all on tape. No defense lawyer, if it got that far, could get around that.

CHAPTER 7

AS BLACKIE AND HIS MEN were loading the final batch, Lieutenant Motang let out a loud whoop into his mouthpiece, rallying his men into action. And in less time than it took to think, Blackie, his men, and the chopper were surrounded by camouflaged soldiers pointing their machine guns at them. One of Motang's men ran into the helicopter to secure the pilot before he took off.

Not that it would have mattered, because a rocket launcher was aimed at it, and the bird would have been blown out of the sky at the first attempt at escaping. In any case, an intact helicopter used to make it look like one used by the army was another nail in Sahili's coffin to make sure that he was locked up for a significant amount of time behind bars. The noose was certainly tightening around the notorious poacher's neck, no doubt.

"Freeze! Stay where you are, and don't even lift a finger!" Lieutenant Motang ordered. The directive was unnecessary. The criminals knew the jig was up.

First it was Blackie who raised his hands slowly, totally flabbergasted. He was followed slowly by the other three men. This was supposed to have been an easy pick-up and go, conducted in complete secrecy. It was now clear that somewhere, somehow, their operation had been compromised.

In no time, Blackie and his men, including the pilot, who happened to be a retired Australian aviator for one of that nation's foremost airlines, were all handcuffed and made to sit with the rest of the captives. They were all downcast, except of course their leader, who never stopped throwing daggers at the American with his eyes. In his mind, Paul McDaniels and only Paul McDaniels was to blame for his capture. White people, as far as he was concerned, could never keep out of affairs deemed African.

After the bandits were made to sit in a single line next to one another, McDaniels continued filming, and once again Lieutenant Motang was the centerpiece of his production, as he panned the camera right back at him.

"What's next, Lieutenant Motang?" Paul Luke McDaniels, again in professional mode, prompted.

The engine of the helicopter had been killed earlier on, and after the pilot's weak attempt at declaring his innocence he was told to shut up and subsequently cuffed behind his back, just like Sahili and his men. Two of the soldiers went inside and made certain that there was nobody else hiding within the chopper. The presence of the Aussie, who told them his name was Charles Pearce, showed just how far-reaching the tentacles of the poachers' syndicate were.

"We've radioed the base commander," Motang answered. "Two choppers are on their way here, one for us and the other for the prisoners."

McDaniels fired another question, "And what's going to happen to them—the prisoners that is?"

He knew full well what awaited the pilferers, Motang knew he knew, but appearances had to be kept. All this 'Q and A' was for the benefit of a future audience worldwide, so the Special Forces man played along as best as he could as he pretended to give the question some thought. McDaniels loved it – the man was a natural.

"They will be arraigned first by the local magistrate. However, since there was a murder involved, this is a case that will most certainly end up at the nation's High Court in Lobatse. But trust me, if it were up to me, these animals would never see the light of day ever again. Lock them up and throw the key."

Paul McDaniels nodded thoughtfully. He now had a pair of headphones that were attached to the camera and was catching the diction free of static. He then adjusted the frame so it had Motang in close-up.

"I suppose it's safe to say *Operation Swift* has been a total success, wouldn't you, Lieutenant Motang?" he smiled.

"Yes, Mr. McDaniels, *Operation Swift* was a success," he agreed. The young lieutenant had wanted to add, '*except that we lost your tracker in the process,*' but then thought better of it. No need to add salt to the wound of a man who was turning him into a movie star, albeit through a documentary – almost every child's dream much less one born bred in what was regarded as a sub-Saharan backwater.

"Do you see a promotion on the horizon for this splendid work you and your men did today?"

Now, this was from left field and the lieutenant had not expected it, so he smiled rather bashfully for the very first time since this operation began.

"Well, that's up to the commander, Paul, but believe me no rank would ever satisfy me more than seeing that these poachers who continuously butcher our animals are done away with once and for all."

McDaniels nodded again, and at that moment, the sound of two more approaching helicopters could be heard. Paul and the lieutenant exchanged a knowing glance that was followed by a brief smile. The birds had been expected. It was time to wrap this thing up and head back home. All this time though, even after the poachers had been captured, the deadly sniper, Christopher 'Mapeni' Modojwa had not moved from his hidden position up in a tree, keeping an eye on things. It was time even for him to emerge from his hiding place.

CHAPTER 8

THE FOLLOWING MORNING, PAUL MCDANIELS was on his way back to his ranch, which was about 20 miles (about 32 kilometers) southwest of the village town, Maun. The previous day after Sahili and his men were captured had been a very hectic one. The moment the two helicopters landed at the military base, they were handed over to the local police and transported to the precinct under heavy escort. They were not going to take any undue chances, given that they were dealing with an exceedingly high-profile criminal and his gang of ruffians.

Since the small man, Sam Xaraga, McDaniels' tracker had been murdered, the American's written statement and sworn affidavit was needed, and so was that of Lieutenant Frederick 'Freddy' Motang. The lieutenant's situation had to be handled differently, though. He was an army officer, after all, and that of a Special Warfare outfit, so it had to be handled by the military police since he fell under their jurisdiction. Sensitive information was at play and would have to be handled as such, like for example how they found out about Sahili's hideout. Such information could not be handled by anyone outside the military, and thus a sanitized version of his statement would be given if and when this thing went to trial in a civilian court.

It was a little after midnight when Paul McDaniels was finally free to go home. He felt too exhausted to drive that night and instead loaded his gear in the canopy of his Toyota Land Cruiser, then checked in at Riley's Hotel for the night and went straight to bed. But before he did, he called his wife Natalie to let her know he would not be coming home until the next morning. She said she understood. After all, she would have accompanied him if she was not nearing the full term of her pregnancy.

While on the drive home, the American had a chance to reflect on what had happened in the last 48 hours. The mad dash to insert himself into Motang's operation after word had leaked to him that the notorious Sahili and his gang had been spotted. He remembered the excitement he felt when he made preparations to film the takedown, and the inevitable guilt he felt for inadvertently causing the death of his master tracker.

No matter how he sliced it, he had led Sam the Bushman into the vices of death. Paul McDaniels was very much aware of the danger this particular mission entailed, and his ambition had cost a man his life. The guilt hit hard. He had made the necessary funeral arrangements, Sam was going to be buried according to tradition prevalent among his people, and with full rites. A generous trust fund had been established that was to take care of his family and his children's schooling. He also had plans to dedicate the production of Sahili's capture to the small man's memory. It was the least he could do, he believed, but the guilt still remained. Only time, and lots of it, would help to alleviate that, as it was known to be the 'healer' of all things.

The view immediately changed as the Land Cruiser negotiated an upward slope, and when it began its gradual descent, the McDaniels ranch was visible in the valley below. It was a view Paul McDaniels never grew tired of. A sight that kept him in this country the size of Texas he now called home, and boy did he love coming home!

The magnificent countryside landscape from here was like a framed picture of a shot taken of a Chateau in the valley of the Swiss Alps during the summer months. Like all others, the main house at the center of the property was thatch-roofed, and the five-bedroom home was surrounded by nicely manicured lawn that from a distance looked like a well-kept carpet. On the south side of the house was a fenced garden, which was laden with citrus trees and rich vegetable plots with ornamental shrubs and rosebuds. It was Natalie McDaniels' beloved garden.

On the west side, behind the house, were several brick rondavels that were also electrified, using electricity tapped from a generator. These were the servants' and ranch hands' homes they shared with their respective families. Beyond the rondavels, and as far as the eye could see on all sides were areas of bush and savanna. The well that supplied the residents with water and irrigation was situated somewhere in that wilderness, about a mile and a half from the property. Next to the well was a large tank that was on a partition that stood well over 25 feet (a little over 7 meters) from the ground.

As the Land Cruiser approached the gate, the dirt road turned to concrete stones that made a crunching sound as the tires made contact. The American drove through the open gate just as the front door to the main house flung open. And like it did all the time, the sight of his beautiful wife made the breath catch in his throat.

Her long blond hair was slightly wavy and reached just under her shoulders. She was wearing a light, long sleeveless summer dress that went all the way to her ankles. Her protruding belly was visible from where he was, and for that magic moment, the capture of Molo Sahili and the death of his tracker were instantly forgotten. Natalie McDaniels was an exceptionally beautiful woman, her pregnancy notwithstanding. If anything, it seemed to add a glow to her face that he had never seen before, which somehow added vivacity to it. She was smiling widely, he noticed, and was waving at the same time, her bright white teeth sparkling in the late morning rise of an enchanting African sun.

He stopped on the beautiful driver's curve in front of the house and immediately jumped out of the car with athletic grace and into his wife's waiting arms. She was in her late twenties but looked more like a vivacious teenager straight out of a high school yearbook.

"Oh, so good to see you, babe. You've been gone two days and I was getting a bit worried," she said after they exchanged a long and passionate kiss like two love-struck adolescents.

Paul said, "I missed you too babe." And instinctively his eyes lit up as he shifted his gaze to her belly. He took a small step backward and bent to place his right ear on her stomach. "Did you miss me too, old buddy? Gosh, I can't wait to meet him."

"How do you know it's a him?" Natalie stepped back, hands on her waist and her brow twisted in mock anger.

"I can just feel it, that's all," he said with a smile as he pulled her closer. "But I'll love whoever comes out of the oven, whether it's him or her."

Changing the subject, Natalie looked into her husband's face for a moment and then said, "You look beat, baby, how did it go?"

The other shoe was about to fall, he knew, because he had not told her about Sam Xaraga. The gentle, graceful, San who had been their tracker for years.

"Not too good," he sighed as he led her into the house. This was the part of the conversation they could not have standing up.

The equipment, including the VHS tapes containing all the footage and then some, was still in the Land Cruiser. He would deal with it later.

"Oh?" Natalie wondered.

"Yeah, we got them all, and I filmed everything. After a few editing tweaks and scoring, we should get a good price from *NG*, but I'll leave all that to Kevin."

Kevin Armstrong was their agent based in the United Kingdom, who handled the sales of their work to various television and cable networks the world over, with National Geographic and the Cable TV program *Animal TV* being their biggest clients. The previous year alone, the couple had netted close to half a million US dollars, meaning that at this rate they would save over ten million dollars in five short years, which was more than enough to retire on and maintain a comfortable living for their family.

"That's wonderful, darling, but why was it not so good?"

He sighed again, in a way stalling as he helped her sit on the loveseat in the well-furnished living room. This was going to be the most difficult part, he knew, as he pulled a chair, sat directly in front of her and held both her hands in his and looked his beautiful wife in the eyes.

"Babe, I'm sorry to have to tell you this," he began solemnly. "Sam was killed during the operation."

She gasped, and immediately her big beautiful blue eyes welled with tears. Paul bent forward to catch her in case she fell, but there was no need as Natalie quickly recovered and composed herself.

"Oh my God, Paul!" she said softly. "How was he killed?"

"He was ambushed by one of the poachers."

"Does his family know?"

"Yes, I believe someone has been assigned to get in touch with them," he said.

He went on to describe in glowing detail how the whole thing went down, leaving nothing out, including the part he may have played in hastening Sam Xaraga's death by not listening to his instincts, right up to the capture, arrest, and booking of all the poachers at the local police station in Maun and their imminent transport to the maximum security prison in Gaborone.

After he was done, they both sat in silence for a while before she said, "Okay, sweetheart, I will have Naledi prepare your bath as I fix you something to eat."

She got up and headed to the kitchen, which was to the right of where they were seated in the living room.

"How is she holding up?" Paul asked. He had long given up asking his wife to take it easy with the chores, as she needed rest, but Natalie would not be deterred.

"Naledi? Oh, much better, thank God, she isn't complaining much about the dizziness and fatigue anymore. I suppose she's come to realize that that's the norm in these situations."

Naledi Moletsane was the McDaniels' young, petite, and beautiful Motswana maid who had been in their household for the past three years, and just like Natalie McDaniels was almost at her full term of pregnancy with her first. In fact, it was even speculated that the two had probably conceived at almost the exact same moment. As of yet, the father of the soon-to-be mother's child was unknown to the couple, but Paul had made some discreet inquiries and was at the moment trying to verify a few facts.

A popular music group from South Africa, Naledi's favorite it turned out, had come to perform at a trendy Maun amphitheater, an event that lasted for almost a week. Upon hearing of the impending extravaganza, the beautiful young maid girl begged the McDaniels couple for this once-in-a-lifetime opportunity, as she put it, to go and watch her favorite group perform live.

Not only did the McDaniels agree—after all she was a dutiful and conscientious worker—but Paul gave her some extra cash and even offered to drive her to the village town a day before the concert, which turned out to be a festival as other bands, both local and from South Africa, had joined the show. She was a native of the village, so accommodation was not going to be a problem.

However, like most 'groupies' the world over, Naledi readily availed herself to one of the band members, a striking young man who had caught her eye among the thousand screaming fans and invited her to his room after the show, following which their assignations became a regular occurrence the rest of the week. It went on like that until the group left for South Africa, and then a few weeks later Naledi discovered that she was pregnant. This was almost nine months ago.

"Maybe she should get more rest," Paul suggested. "I'll prepare the bath myself. Have you had any luck finding a replacement?"

"Yes, she arrives today. Her name is Nchadi."

"N-who?"

"Nchadi," his wife smiled as she had time to practice and muster the pronouncing of the unusual name. "It took me a day to say the name perfectly."

Her husband smiled. Their fluency of the local language, Setswana, was a little past the rudimentary stage, but they were getting better with each day that passed.

CHAPTER 9

A WHILE LATER, PAUL MCDANIELS, bathed, clean, and shaved, was relaxed and stretched out on his living room couch, remote control in hand and watching a video cassette tape of an old feature film while Natalie was in the kitchen preparing his meal. The aroma that filled the room only intensified the hunger pangs in his stomach.

The nicely furnished living room was one of his favorite rooms in the house. It was, like the rest of the home, well-kept and nicely decorated. There were lots of beautiful indoor plants that revealed the fact that the McDaniels were indeed nature lovers and people who loved the outdoors. Next to the television was a gigantic shelf with neat rows of videos, many of them from National Geographic, The Animal Channel, and copies of productions they themselves had done.

On top of the shelf and along the brick fireplace mantel was an array of framed photographs, medals, and trophies from his martial arts tournament days. There was also a black-and-white photograph of a younger Paul McDaniels proudly hoisting a trophy, smiling goofily at the camera with a legend at the bottom that read '*The Ed Parker Karate Tournament, Long Beach California.*'

There were several pictures of an older blond white man also clad in the traditional white karate uniform, complete with a black belt strapped on his waist. It was his older brother, Sean Kane McDaniels. There was yet another framed picture of the two of them as kids, and another of them much older, but this one had them dressed in their karate *gis*.

The most significant however, was one of Sean Kane that looked to have been taken recently. In this one, the older McDaniels was grinning excitedly at the camera. It was clear that the reason was in the way he was dressed. He had on a black cassock with a white collar that distinctly revealed aside from being an avid martial artist, he was also a man of the cloth – a man of God. And by the look of it, it seemed like the calling had come later in life and not too long ago, for that matter.

Another picture, an earlier one, revealed that he had also once been a member of the United States Armed Forces, the Navy most likely, which specialized in special warfare better known as the SEALS. In this one, he was dressed in a neatly starched uniform with dark sunglasses that covered his face and posed proudly next to an Army Jeep. Upon catching a glimpse of this one in particular, Paul smiled as he thought of his brother. It had been a little over seven years since he last saw him, and he missed him.

As if reading his mind, Natalie interrupted his thoughts by saying, "Oh, he called last night."

She was standing by the doorway of the dining room, holding a tray of breakfast, and had paused for moment to follow his gaze, noticing that her husband had been absent-mindedly gawking at the pictures while he lay on the couch – something he always caught himself doing whenever he was relaxed.

"Oh yeah? Did he, now?" Paul asked as he sat up straight to face his wife.

With the way the telephone exchange was, especially in this remote area of the country, receiving an overseas call out here in the boonies from his brother was always a treat.

"Yes," she said as she placed the tray on the coffee table next to him. There was a plate of bacon and eggs over easy - just the way he loved them. Black toast with butter and jam, black coffee, and a tall glass of freshly squeezed orange juice minus the seeds. The oranges had been picked from the garden earlier that morning. Natalie knew her husband was a heavy eater, especially in the morning, because he said it gave him an entire day to burn it.

"What's he up to? And thanks, darling," he said as he eyed his breakfast, ready to attack as he got the fork and knife that were placed on the side of the breakfast tray.

"Enjoying his crusade. He just came back from a devotional in Eugene, Oregon, and now he's headed to Texas."

Paul McDaniels just nodded at the revelation. His brother had been an astute martial arts practitioner. Even after graduating from the University of California at Berkeley with a degree in Mechanical Engineering after serving in the military, during which time he saw active combat during the first Gulf War, and working for Synergy Company in the Bay Area, he still found the time and energy somehow to open and run two martial arts training studios, known as '*dojos.*' This soon grew to six more schools, and in no time, he was earning enough of a living from the schools to quit his day job and concentrate mainly on his art.

Within a short space of time, Sean Kane McDaniels became one of the foremost martial arts instructors in the state of California. And with that mantle on his head, it didn't take long for Hollywood to come knocking at his door. He was offered roles in first what was known in the industry as 'B movies,' and then later studio-backed motion pictures, all of which he turned down because he always stated that the limelight was for certain people and he was absolutely not one of them.

He did, however, hire himself out on the technical aspect of the business, from fight choreography to providing extras in scenes that required fights in bars, warehouses, and other such locations which action movies could never do without. Then suddenly and without warning, all this changed when Sean Kane McDaniels had an epiphany of some kind. 'An awakening' was what he called it when he decided to become a man of the cloth.

The older McDaniels surprised many when he sold all his martial arts schools and become a full-time minister at a local church. Even though he wore a cloth and collar, fed the poor and needy around the world, and helped build churches and schools in the remote corners of the globe, his martial arts skills and teachings were never far behind. He was known for performing his famed flying spin kick dressed in his cassock and collar to the amazement of many, and the delight of the children he met while on these worldly excursions.

"Excuse me, Mr. McDaniels," a soft feminine voice broke his reverie.

He looked up from his breakfast plate, a fork with a piece of bacon pierced in it halfway to his mouth. His wife had momentarily left the room, so he was alone eating his meal before being interrupted.

"Yes, Naledi?"

"Mister McDaniels, please excuse me, I was not aware that you were back otherwise I would have had your bath ready. I'm really sorry, sir," the beautiful young woman said as she looked at the floor in embarrassment.

Her movements were slower now as her huge belly protruded from her small frame. Paul was already used to her formality and had since given up trying to have her address him simply as 'Paul' as opposed to 'Mr. McDaniels.' However, what concerned him most was her condition.

"That's okay, Naledi." He smiled at the young woman who he and his wife really adored. "And besides, you should be resting and not up and about. Natalie tells me that someone should be here later today to take over your chores until you're back on your feet," he assured her.

The young woman smiled submissively and said, "You mean Nchadi, sir, I actually recommended her to madame."

At that moment Natalie reentered the living room and sat back on the couch next to her husband, after wiping her hands with a kitchen towel she placed on the coffee table next to her husband's breakfast tray.

"We appreciate that, Naledi," Paul said again. "But from now on, no more working, is that understood?"

"Yes sir," she bowed politely.

"Any contractions yet?" Natalie asked with a smile, in spite of herself.

"Yes, but they're slightly mild so far."

"So are mine," Natalie McDaniels said as she patted her own extended belly gently.

Paul gestured for Naledi to take a seat opposite them. She did as asked, her legs tight together and her hands on her lap. Her face was slightly averted. Eye contact with these people, particularly since they were white, was something she found difficult to do in spite of having worked for them for over three years.

He looked at the beautiful young Motswana woman again and smiled. Like his wife, she was wearing a long summer maternity dress.

"Looks like both of you might be having your babies at the time. How cool will that be?" Paul said as he smiled widely. The dimples on his cheeks were more pronounced whenever he did that. "Have you come up with any names?"

Naledi's face brightened as she straightened up and smiled proudly and said, "Yes sir. Dumisani if it is a boy and Karabo if it turns out to be a girl. How about you, madame?" She smiled at Natalie.

The couple exchanged a quick glance, and before his wife could answer, Paul was quick to say, "Since we know it's gonna be a boy, we've decided to name him Sasha?"

Men! Naledi thought to herself but dared not put a voice to it.

Not to be denied, though, Natalie added, "And Jennifer LeAnn McDaniels if it's a girl."

They looked at each other again, two people madly in love with one another, clearly what the other woman in front of them did not have and very much envied them for. Naledi saw this as her cue to leave. So, she got up slowly, ready to take up Paul McDaniels on his offer.

"Okay Mr. and Mrs. McDaniels, I think it is time for me to go and lie down," Naledi said as she suppressed a yawn and sheepishly smiled at the couple who were still caught up in the magic of staring into each other's eyes.

Instinctively, she stooped to pick up the breakfast tray, but Paul immediately stopped her.

"No, let me, Naledi, please. You go on ahead and rest."

She thanked him yet again and politely left the room. The couple was quiet for a while, each occupied by their thoughts, which as it turned out were along the same lines.

"Has she told you who the father of her child is?" Paul asked his wife.

"No," Natalie replied in deep thought suddenly as if wondering if she did have that information or not. "However, I suspect it's that South African fella who was a member of that band that came to perform at that jazz and pop festival almost a year ago at the amphitheater in Maun."

Paul nodded thoughtfully, as yet not willing to reveal to his wife that she had probably hit the nail on the head. He was never one to gossip about people, especially in matters deemed private and personal.

"That would probably explain the name Dumisani," Natalie continued.

What they did know, but would rather not say out loud, was that the father, whoever he was, was probably gone forever. Naledi, like many women her age, would end up being a single mother, raising an illegitimate child all on her own. The McDaniels were going to help in any way they could, but in the end, it would be Naledi and her baby all alone without a father to take care of that child.

CHAPTER 10

THE FATIGUE OF THE LAST FEW DAYS and the guilt of losing his master tracker in such a brutal way began to take its toll on Paul Luke McDaniels, and for a man like him there could be only one remedy, and that was a full-blown Spartan workout that would realign him, so to speak. He also knew that to sequester himself for the next two months or so editing the footage he had shot, he needed to have a clear mind.

That is why one morning, two days later, he was in his backyard where a bag was hanging from a tree, hard at work, punching and kicking at the bag like a man possessed. His well-chiseled torso was bare, and his square protuberant chest heaved back and forth as rivulets of sweat flowed down his body and onto the ground. It did not take long for his limbs to feel as heavy as lead, his lungs burning, but he fought through the pain, determined to exorcise the guilt and pain he felt in his heart over the death of his tracker and personal friend, not forgetting the role he'd unintentionally played in hastening his demise. Why didn't he feel that murderer creep up behind him? Why didn't he 'smell' him before it was too late? Too many questions, Paul McDaniels knew, but no answers, not now maybe not ever.

This went on until he was interrupted by a young dark woman who looked to be in her late teens or early 20s. The disturbance made him pause, hunch over for a second and in a way grateful for the reprieve with his hands on his knees for a few seconds, before he stood up straight and raised his hands in the air as he filled his lungs with the much-needed oxygen. As the blood began flowing more to his brain, he took a look at his stopwatch. He had been at it for a good two hours.

He finally shifted his gaze to the young woman, who stood nervously a few feet away. Paul was certain that he had not seen her before until then. From the nervous look on her face, he was almost certain that she had some kind of urgent message for him.

"Eh, and who might you be?" he finally asked. His breathing was now finally under control.

"I'm Nchadi Molefe sir, the new maid, here to help until Naledi is well again."

"Oh yeah that's right," Paul grinned. "And what seems to be the problem Nchadi?"

The white man's kind demeanor instantly put the young maid at ease.

"It's Mrs. McDaniels, sir. I think she's about to have the baby."

The news had a very sobering effect on the American, instantly taking away any little desire left to continue with his workout.

"Oh my God! It's time," he said quickly, immediately ready to bolt.

He was about to do just that when Nchadi's voice again froze him in his tracks.

"Sir?"

"Yes?"

"And Naledi too," she added quickly.

This bit of news jolted him, for that was unexpected, not at least for another week or so.

"Naledi?" Paul was incredulous. "She isn't supposed to go into labor until next week at the very least," he said more to himself, but now was not the time to second-guess things. He had two women possibly in labor who needed him now more than anyone else in the world. "Where is Steven? I sure as hell could use his help right now."

Steven Selepe was the McDaniels' ever reliable ranch hand.

"Who?" Nchadi wanted to know with genuine confusion on her face.

"Steven, the ranch hand," Paul said as he quickly put on his t-shirt, not even bothering to wipe the sweat off his face and upper body. The man was obviously in a hurry.

"Oh, Mr. Selepe," Nchadi said as she quickly put it together. "I heard he's at the water hole fixing the pump."

"Well, go get him," he ordered.

"Where's the waterhole?"

Paul McDaniels was about to lose it but immediately caught himself. The girl was still new to the place. Getting angry with her over things he thought she should know by now could prove to be counterproductive – especially now when Natalie and possibly Naledi needed him like never before.

He pointed northward and said, "Follow that path, Nchadi, it will lead you straight to him. Tell him to stop whatever he's doing and get his ass over here."

"His ass?" Nchadi asked, genuinely confused.

"Just tell him to get here as quickly as he can." It did not need to be any more complicated than that.

Without another word, and thankfully another question, Nchadi turned and ran off to do as instructed, while Paul took off in the opposite direction and entered the main house via the kitchen door that faced Natalie's garden.

While still inside the kitchen, Paul called out to his wife, "Babe, where are you?"

"We're in the living room, honey," he heard his wife respond.

Inside the living room, he saw Natalie on her knees, one hand on her belly and the other gently patting a wet rag on Naledi's forehead. On witnessing this, there was suddenly concern on her husband's handsome face.

"Are you alright?" he asked as he slowly and gently helped her to her feet and parked her on the comfortable couch.

"I'm fine, darling, it's just that the contractions came fast and without warning," she said almost apologetically.

The American turned his attention to Naledi, who was lying on the clean carpet, a velvet cushion under her head and knees, her eyes glazed. She did not look well at all, and at the moment appeared to be barely conscious.

"What about her?" Paul asked as a sudden wave of misgivings assailed him fast and furious.

"Same thing," Natalie said. "However, it seems as if she can barely handle hers and keeps drifting in and out of consciousness. We must hurry." There was a slight note of alarm in her voice that spurned Paul into taking action a split second later.

"You're right," Paul agreed. "We've got to get going right now." He was already reaching for his car keys that were on the coffee table, and Natalie and her maid's bags were always packed and ready under the table for exactly such a moment.

Natalie looked at her husband, a bit surprised, and asked, "Aren't you going to wait for Steven?"

"Too late for that. Can you walk without help?"

"Yes."

"Good, head on out to the car. I'll carry Naledi," he said.

"How long until we get to the hospital?"

Paul answered by saying, "Well, it won't be fast, at least not on the bumpy dirt road, so we're looking at a little less than an hour tops."

Natalie sighed as she slowly got up. She was obviously more worried about her maid's wellbeing than her own. Naledi had quickly and suddenly began developing contractions that had kept spiraling her in and out of consciousness as they intensified. Fortunately, the Land Cruiser, which they used on their many adventures and filming, was the conversion type fitted for the outdoors and their line of work.

The back canopy had been turned into a living space, with a stove, fridge, and a bed. And the ever-conscientious Steven Selepe had cleaned the inside and outside to a point that it looked and smelled new. Paul and Natalie's filming and camping gear had also been dusted and stored away in various compartments of the off-road vehicle, ready for the next venture, even the refrigerator had been replenished with fresh supplies. All this, Steven Selepe did without being told. God bless him! Paul made a mental note to give him a nice Christmas bonus when the festive season arrived.

A little later, the Land Cruiser was racing along the dirt road toward Maun. In spite of her own circumstances, Natalie was seated next to her maid, who was now lying on the bed, holding her hand, and constantly whispering encouragements at the beautiful young woman. Paul, on the other hand, was tense at the wheel. He kept glancing at the rearview mirror at the two women as if he was afraid they'd vanish into thin air at any moment.

"Her contractions are coming pretty fast, babe," Natalie said from the back. "How long until we get there?"

"Not too long," Paul reassured her. "How is she?"

"Not very good," was the solemn response from his wife.

Natalie shifted further on the bed to a more comfortable position as she held on to Naledi's hand, her back now resting on the cabinet of the kitchenette. Her maid's head was resting on her lap, which in itself was no easy task since Natalie's own extended belly was in the way. With Naledi barely conscious, her shrieks were a little less audible, as now the contractions were coming one after another in rapid succession. And with heroic resolve, trying hard to ignore her own contractions, Natalie McDaniels kept patting the young woman on the forehead with the cold rag.

Some twenty-five minutes later, the Land Cruiser hit the first tarmac of the village town of Maun, and the American kicked the vehicle into high gear and sped toward Maun General Hospital.

Maun, dubbed the 'Tourist Capital' of Botswana has one of the largest and well-equipped hospitals in the land. Located at the bank of the great Thamalakane River, it is large enough to cater to the 55,784 inhabitants of the village town and its visitors. The Land Cruiser almost hit the wall near the entrance of the emergency room, and the outdoor vehicle, very common in this area, was barely turned off before McDaniels, showing remarkable athletic grace, jumped out of the car and was out like a shot.

"Can we get a doctor out here, please?" the American yelled as he burst through the double glass door and into the hospital's long corridor.

The fact that it was a panicked white man doing the yelling in a land where, for the most part, Caucasians were held in high regard, let alone a village town, this display certainly got everyone's attention and sparked them into action. In record time, two trolleys were procured, and the two pregnant women were rushed to the maternity ward. It seemed, from what Paul McDaniels could tell, there were some complications with Naledi's pregnancy, because the doctor immediately ordered that an IV be inserted in a vein inside her left elbow. At the very least it meant she was dehydrated. Knowing that he would hear from the doctor or nurse at some point, he retired to the waiting room where he anticipated to be for a while.

CHAPTER 11

ALONE AND WITH NOTHING to keep him company except his thoughts, Paul waited for what he estimated to have been two and a half hours before the door to the waiting room opened, and in stepped a young-looking, light-skinned Motswana doctor whose stoic face revealed nothing. On seeing him enter the room, the American sprang to his feet in anticipation of the news the man actually had.

"Mr. McDaniels?" the young doctor asked, his face revealing nothing like a carved wooden figure.

"Yes?"

The doctor's arm stretched out for a handshake, and the two men shook hands. He was still dressed in his medical scrubs complete with a perforated paper hat that covered his hair. This meant that he had come straight from the operating room.

"I'm Doctor Henry Mokwadi," he said. "Pleased to meet you."

"Likewise, Doctor … how are they?" McDaniels wanted to know, almost getting the queer feeling that the doctor was in a way stalling.

"Your wife and baby are fine, Mr. McDaniels." He then let out a sigh that betrayed his features. "But I'm afraid we lost Naledi during …"

Suddenly the room came in and out of focus and things started spinning as Paul felt his legs weaken and lose power. For a moment it looked as if he was going to collapse as his face turned instantly pale. The young doctor saw this and rushed to his aid as he quickly helped him to the chair he had been sitting on earlier.

"I'm really sorry, Mr. McDaniels. Believe me, we tried everything we possibly could."

It took a while to process all this. Two people he knew very well and were in a way close to him were dead in the same week. First it was his tracker and now his maid. Seated now, he had his head buried in his powerful hands.

"And what about her baby?" Paul asked without looking up, because he dreaded the answer the doctor was going to give him that Naledi's baby was dead too. The American could only take so much, he thought.

"The baby is fine and healthy, Mr. McDaniels."

Paul looked up at him. The doctor could read the question in the other man's eyes before it was asked.

"Oh, and it's a boy just like yours. Your wife informed us that the young lady's wish was to name him Dumisani."

"Yes … it's true," he confirmed, still shaking his head in disbelief. He still could not comprehend how this could have happened, and could not reconcile the fact that the once vivacious and full-of-life maid, before her pregnancy, was gone forever, leaving a baby who will never know her. With that in mind, there was only one thing he and Natalie could do.

"Can I see them now?" Paul asked. He did not even want to think of yet another funeral arrangement at this moment. That sad fact was far from his mind.

"Of course," Dr. Mokwadi said, leading the way.

As he got up to follow the young doctor, hot tears trickled down his cheeks, which he quickly wiped with the back of his hand. When the two men got to the door of what Paul assumed was Natalie's private ward, Dr. Mokwadi paused, nodded, and then slowly opened the door and ushered the filmmaker into the room.

***

Natalie McDaniels was in bed, tucked neatly and fast asleep. However, what caused her husband's breath to catch were the two brand newborn babies feeding on each one of her breasts, their eyes shut. One was white and the other was black. The sight was breathtaking. It was the most beautiful thing he had ever seen in his life. He wished he had brought his camera from the car to capture this incredible moment. Natalie's arms were both protectively around the babies. The gesture alone said it all – *these are my babies, you so much as touch them, or look at them funny, and they'll never find your body*.

Upon taking in all this, Dr. Mokwadi finally smiled in spite of the fact that he had lost a patient, and left the room.

"Have one of the nurses page me if you need me," the doctor said over his shoulder as he reached for the door.

"Will do, Doctor," Paul said without turning, obviously still mesmerized by the scene before him. He wiped his eyes again.

He slowly walked toward the bed and its enchanting sight. Paul then looked at his wife and the newborn babies. They were so beautiful. He remained transfixed for what to him seemed like hours, when in fact it was close to three minutes. It was a sight he never wanted to forget for as long as he lived. The babies and their mother looked peaceful and serene.

When he couldn't bear it any longer, he gently placed an open palm on his wife's forehead. It was warm.

Natalie's eyes slowly fluttered open. She offered a weak smile when she realized it was her husband, now one of the three most important men in her life. It had been a difficult pregnancy for both women, but unfortunately the other had succumbed during labor.

"Hello, Mom," Paul said softly.

"Hello, Dad." How he loved the sound of that!

Their eyes turned to the two sleeping bundles of joy - the recent tragedy forgotten for now. A life had been lost, but two new souls had come in return.

"They are beautiful," Paul said softly, not wanting to wake the babies up.

"Yes," his wife agreed as she unconsciously held the babies tighter, but not so much as to make them uncomfortable. It was just a lioness protecting her cubs.

Paul looked at the beautiful black baby and nodded before saying, "He is ours now. He's a McDaniels."

"Yes," Natalie agreed. "They'll be brothers."

"Blood brothers," Paul McDaniels accentuated as he spread his arms and hugged his new family. The new parents thought of Naledi Moletsane and both wept albeit briefly. They both knew that to honor her memory they'd have to raise this child as they would their own, afford him opportunities his mother never had and much more—but most importantly, give him a last name and a belonging he would be proud of. They believed in their heart of hearts that Naledi would have wanted it no other way if she had a chance.

CHAPTER 12

Lobatse, Botswana – Six Months later.

ONE CAN NEVER REFER TO LOBATSE, a town back in 1988 before it became a city much later, forty-seven miles south of the capital city Gaborone, without thinking about the nation's supreme center of justice – the Lobatse High Court. For those who have lived in that town or still do, the Lobatse High Court is a serious monument of sorts, for obvious reasons. Located among the blue gum trees very common in that area of the town, the pristine white courtrooms and the newer ones that are visible from the main road that runs through Lobatse provide cover for judicial sages who crafted and delivered a number of famous decisions in the country's jurisprudence.

This was where the trial of the notorious poacher Molo Sahili and his cohorts was held. It had been all over the news and on the streets, people at taxi ranks, bus stations, beer halls, and gossiping men and women talked of nothing else. Each time the exploits of the infamous poacher were exaggerated with each retelling. There were claims that he had killed over a thousand elephants and rhinos. It was even suggested by some that while doing so, soldiers sent to apprehend him were killed in the hundreds. Others even went so far as to say he was under the spell of a powerful witch doctor, who could make him vanish into thin air, which was why he had avoided capture all these years, and on and on the stories and urban legends went.

Thus, it was little wonder that the courtroom was packed to the brim from day one. However, in spite of these stories, the prosecution team assigned to the case were rather surprised by the legal firepower brought to bear by Sahili. There was a renowned criminal law firm in Gaborone, the firm of Drake Moribame, Michael Moruti, and Associates. They had defended and won more high-profile murder and white-collar crimes than any law firm in the nation put together. Plus, they did not come cheap. So, how could a brigand like Sahili afford them? Especially the services of Drake Moribame Esq., dubbed by many as 'The Magician' and 'The Legal Gymnast,' among his many monikers, because of his ability to perform magic in the courtroom by creating reasonable doubt, even in cases considered to be 'slam dunks' by the opposing counsel.

This was the question the head prosecutor John Balebetse and his team asked themselves, which was why, on the strength of this, they felt the need to dig deeper. Throwing the vast resources of the state at this inconsistency, they found out that the source of Sahili's defense fund originated in the Far East. Very wealthy businessmen who happened to be Chinese, South Korean, and Taiwanese, no doubt the people who funded the poacher's exploits. Little wonder, Balebetse and his team realized, since the brigands carried arms and ammunition that could rival that of a small but well-organized militia.

However, despite all this, the evidence against Sahili and his gang was so damning that even Drake Moribame's so-called courtroom magic failed him. The poacher had been caught red-handed, and what's worse, his crime had been captured on tape—at least the part where Sahili and one of his men, later to be identified as James Kopane were discussing how the tusks were going to be picked up.

Paul McDaniels flew in from Maun to Lobatse to testify for the prosecution. Upon taking the stand, he was first asked to identify some of the footage he had shot and was being shown to the court. This the American did flawlessly, especially after a white portable screen was procured, and on it the film was played, with the filmmaker offering his narration in the process. All told, he was a very damaging witness to the defense. Paul, on the other hand, was eager to get his testimony on the record, and the sooner that was done the better. He was anxious to get back to Natalie and the boys, Sasha and Dumisani, the latter who had been legally adopted and was now officially Dumisani Peter McDaniels. The boys were almost seven months old and proving to be a handful, but the kind every proud parent can never get enough of.

Next on the stand was Lieutenant Freddy Motang, and he further nailed the lid on Sahili's ivory casket shut. Despite the withering artillery fired at him by a now desperate lawyer, Drake Moribame, the Special Forces lieutenant held tough on the witness stand. It was at this point when many of Sahili's codefendants decided to jump ship and offer testimony, most of it unsolicited, against their leader with the hope that they could be given a lighter sentence in return.

In the end, Molo Sahili was found guilty on all counts except the death of Sam, known to the court by his legal name Xaraga Xau. The prosecutor, John Balebetse, piled on the charge even though it had been John Ntemwa who had performed the deed of slitting the tracker's throat. Ntemwa's head had been slightly grazed by a bullet during the commotion. However, here, Moribame was able to argue almost convincingly that even if causation were to be a factor, then Paul McDaniel shared some of the blame.

In the end, the famed attorney's courtroom 'gymnastics' failed him this time and his client was found guilty.

Upon issuing his sentence, the Honorable Chief Justice Kabelo Richard Kavindama stated that Molo Sahili was a 'menace not only to the country's wildlife and the nation's pride, but to society as well …' and was given a prison sentence, effective immediately, of twenty-two years. The rest of his crew received sentences ranging from three to twelve years. The pilot of the getaway helicopter, the Australian Charles Pearce, tendered a passionate and tearful plea in mitigation stating that he knew nothing of Sahili's activities and that all he had been, was just a simple pilot hired to fly the helicopter from point A to B. and that was it. The judge did not buy it and was sentenced to four years in prison, following which the Aussie was led out of the courtroom in chains, sobbing like a little girl. He knew very well that an African prison, especially for a white man with soft features like his, was definitely not a place to endure for a day, let alone four years.

Molo Sahili's trial and ultimate conviction marked the finality of a very painful chapter in the nation's all-out fight against wanton murder and the poaching of elephants and rhinos. Surely there were many Sahilis out there, and this punishment was meant as a warning to embryonic poachers and those yet to be caught that the jig was up. The directive was clear as it was unequivocal – you mess with our wildlife and you will suffer the consequences.

Some human rights activists the world over protested what they perceived to be a very harsh sentence by Judge Kavindama, and voiced their concerns whenever there was a TV camera or microphone to perform to, but the government's stance was unyielding with the support of nature enthusiasts and filmmakers like Paul McDaniels, as well as many like him who saw firsthand what was being done to these magnificent beasts.

Animals like elephants and the white rhino were on the verge of extinction, and unless those very so-called human rights activists and others like them perched on their ethical high horses wanted future generations to see these creatures in captivity in far-off lands, and not in their natural habitat, the fight to protect them would never end and would continue until the bastards got it in their thick heads that it was time they sought another trade that did not involve killing animals.

Paul McDaniels could not have been any more pleased with the outcome of the Sahili trial, and the flight back to Maun was indeed a very pleasant one. To cap the occasion, he even ordered a bottle of Champagne that he happily shared with some of his fellow passengers. McDaniels had other reasons to be gratified. The Molo Sahili verdict, he knew, marked the perfect ending to his documentary. And when he got home, he went straight to his dark editing room to put the finishing touches to it. A month later, his finished product was broadcast on the Discovery Channel, BBC, CNN, Al Jazeera, and many other major networks the world over.

***

The reviews were positive across the board, and the documentary went into syndication on TV stations in Australia, Singapore, Hong Kong, and many other countries, making the McDaniels quite wealthy because the royalty checks were in abundance and came in daily, and would continue doing so for at least the next ten years. An American film production company known for making highly successful and profitable feature films, and associated with one of the five major Hollywood studios, bought the film rights to the story after a bitter bidding war with two other rival production companies, in the process padding the McDaniels coffers even further. There was also an interesting narrative along the way—a major Hollywood star was slated to play Molo Sahili in the proposed feature film.

All this good fortune afforded Paul and Natalie McDaniels more time to spend with the boys, who by the way were growing like weeds. They traveled the world with the now-toddling boys, who were inseparable and behaved more like identical twins, starting with the United States, and places like the United Kingdom, Israel, Egypt, the Bahamas, the Cayman Islands, Tahiti, Malta, and so on.

In many instances, because the McDaniels' documentary 'The Elephant And His Enemy' had brought awareness to the vexing problem of elephant and rhino poachers in Botswana, Paul McDaniels as the expert on the subject was invited to speaking at events the world over. Whenever he could, he was almost always accompanied by his family.

When he was back in Botswana, he continued with his profession of filming animals in the wild, albeit not with the zest and zeal he once had now that money for as long as he lived would not be a problem. This gave him even more time with his family, especially the boys. When they were old enough, he took them camping, fishing, and even on many of his nature shoots. By the time they were nine years of age, he began in earnest to pass on his expertise of the martial arts so that by age 15, Dumisani and Sasha were both first-degree black belts.

Life went on this way until after a while, Molo Sahili, who was serving his sentence at the maximum prison in Gaborone became a distant and fast-fading memory. What was even more gratifying was that the poaching problem, it seemed, at least for now, was under control and everyone was happy.

BOOK TWO

CHAPTER 13

PRESENT DAY.

THE VILLAGE OF MAUN had in a short period of twenty-plus years become a town that had an eclectic mix of modern buildings and native huts. Being a gateway to the Okavango Swamps, this was the last stop for the tourists headed to that modern-day Garden of Eden, and the first stop when coming back. As a result, the tourists with their foreign money were a big boon to the local community and economy. There were many paved roads as a result, just as there were dusty roads and huts that stayed true to the one-time village's past.

The great Thamalakane River cuts through the village, and running alongside the winding river is a paved road. On one sunny Saturday morning, an old but well-maintained Toyota Land Cruiser was traveling along this road and slowly drove into the parking lot of an exotic-looking hotel – the Sedia Riverside Hotel. Thousands of tourists pass through this area and many like it that have made the place known now as the 'Tourism Capital' of Botswana.

The Land Cruiser was dusty and muddy, reflecting the fact that the occupants had been engaged in outdoor activity for quite some time. As soon as the vehicle stopped, after easing into a parking spot on the right side of the main entrance, two tall, handsome young men with distinctive athletic gaits stepped out of it. The driver, Sasha McDaniels, came out first. And the other young man who was riding shotgun was black, and he was Dumisani McDaniels.

Just like his brother, he too was good-looking with dreadlocks long enough to tie up into a ponytail at the back of his head. They were both wearing matching khaki shirts and pants, unkempt with equally identical sunglasses. They looked as if they had been outdoors for a while, which in fact they had been. The two brothers had gone out camping the week before, something they did regularly, which was why their clothes were crumpled and dirty, and were planning on stopping for a quick cold beer that always felt good after their time in the wild before they headed home to the renowned McDaniels Ranch. Even in light of the rapid developments with a populace upside of fifty thousand, home was still several miles away, south of the outskirts of the 'Tourist Capital' of the nation.

Sasha removed his sunglasses, revealing sparkling blue eyes in an extremely handsome face, and appreciated the building before him that had a long thatched veranda at the side that faced the river. He smiled at his brother, who was just as good-looking and happened to be black. Perhaps it was because they grew up together, but the two never seemed to notice that difference.

"I sure could use a cold one, Dumi, how about you?" Sasha asked.

"Isn't that why we're here, dummy?" Dumisani shot back, smiling.

Like typical brothers, the two liked ribbing one another at every chance, and perhaps because they were raised by two American parents who spoke to them in English and rarely in the native language, which of course they could all speak fluently, Dumisani, just like Sasha had adopted a speech pattern very similar to that of his brother and their parents. It was not exactly American English, but it had a bit of the nuances expected of children born to foreign parents.

"Good idea," Sasha smiled.

"One or two for me, at least. I can't wait to get back home and jump into a hot bath, we've been out in the boonies for way too long," Dumisani said as he, like his brother, used his hands to dust his clothes.

Dumisani reached into his left pocket and with his fingers felt the last two Percocets. He had injured his back while engaged in a rigorous training regimen that involved weightlifting a few months earlier. Without properly warming up, he bent to pick up a set of barbells and had not assumed the proper stance required when doing so. He suffered a near slip disc that required that he refrain from strenuous activity for at least three months, and to help deal with the pain, the doctor had prescribed Percocet. An extraordinarily strong painkiller that was also highly addictive, and unfortunately the young man had gotten hooked, but so far was doing a particularly good job of hiding that problem from those close to him.

That is why he suggested having one or two beers, because he knew that at least one of those and a beer would have him giddy with euphoria. Unbeknownst to the young man at the time was that this was to become a profoundly serious problem. Add to that, it was a growing epidemic the world over, particularly in the

United States, in what came to be known as the opioid crisis.

After deciding that they were reasonably presentable, the brothers headed to the entrance of the hotel, and on the way, they walked past four American make Halley-Davidson motorcycles that were parked side by side. Sasha paused briefly to admire the bikes and smiled at the same time, wondering whom they belonged to.

Sasha then looked at his brother and noticed the somewhat troubled look on his face.

"What is it about this place you don't like Dumi? Please don't tell me you feel out of place," he teased as he playfully punched his brother on his massive shoulder.

"No, I just hate being stared at all the time."

As brothers from two different races, Sasha and Dumisani McDaniels, almost inseparable to begin with, were always the center of attention. Every resident in Maun knew their story, or so it seemed. A poor maid dying while giving birth, and as fate would have it, her employer was also giving birth to her first child in the next room but survives and then adopts the suddenly orphaned baby. Orphaned, because the natural father was unknown then and unknown since.

**

The Sedia Riverside Hotel bar was beautifully designed with a long, shiny mahogany counter with a thatched shade above it, and also a veranda shaded by a thatched roof that overlooked the winding Thamalakane River. It was semi-dark, spacious, and almost always crowded, mainly with tourists either on their way to the Okavango Swamps and its many campsites, or on their way back. There were a good number of these people who had come as tourists initially but then fell in love with this village town and had taken up permanent residency.

Today, on this bright Saturday African summer morning, the place was packed as usual with almost all of the patrons white. Some were seated on barstools at the long counter, and others at the round tables in the room, and at the outside veranda that overlooked the great seasonal river. The brothers paused briefly at the entrance as they took in the scene. They soon thereafter became the center of attention, which bothered them not at all. They were used to it.

Their gaze instantly settled on three beautiful young women whom the brothers instantly pegged to be American tourists. They looked to be college students no doubt. The three women also noticed them and giggled as they followed the two young men with their eyes as they made their way to the long bar counter. It also happened that there were two empty tall barstools just waiting to be sat on. The bartender whom they knew very well, was a local young man, Bashi Mogomotsi, who instantly flashed a wide smile. He had bright white teeth that were more pronounced in his very dark face. It was also obvious that Sasha and Dumisani were regulars at this establishment.

"Ahh! Mr. Sasha and Dumisani, what can I get you?" The bartender grinned again, showing those sparkling white teeth.

"The usual," Sasha said. "Two club sodas with lime."

"Sure thing, Mr. Sasha, right away," Bashi the bartender said.

"Just Sasha," Dumisani said with a straight face.

"Excuse me?" the bartender said as he quickly turned to face the brothers. Bashi had veered to get the required drinks.

Then in Setswana, Dumisani said to Bashi, "I don't know why you try to keep trying to impress him just because he's white."

The brothers were fond of razzing one another, and those who knew them well knew that this was what made them who they were. What made them unique.

"I... I ..." Bashi was embarrassed as he struggled to come up with what to say.

However, Sasha came to his rescue by saying in perfect Setswana and without an accent, "Ahhh ... don't mind him, Bashi, he's just jealous because you were brought up well, my friend."

Dumisani shook his head, smiling, and said, "Anyway, enough of this ass-kissing, and for a change make mine a Castle Lager."

Bashi was taken aback by this. For a long time, even though a regular at the place, Dumisani had sworn off alcohol.

"Wow, what's the occasion, Dumi?" he asked as he pushed a bowl full of roasted ground nuts and then served both brothers their drinks in frosted mugs.

"Nothing," Dumisani said as he cracked open a shell and popped two loose nuts into his mouth.

"Well," Sasha McDaniels said as he raised his glass in toast, "My brother Dumi finally got accepted at the Pasadena Art Center to study journalism and video production."

He said this a bit loudly, and his brother had to wonder if he was doing it for the benefit of the three tourist women they had spotted on their way in. Dumisani also noticed from his peripheral vision that ladies had been gawking at them, and were doing a poor job hiding the fact—or were they?

He looked at his brother and said, "You make it sound as if it was a struggle." Indeed it had been, and to the bartender he said, "Besides, you know this brother of mine can't keep his mouth shut. With a big mouth like that you wonder what would happen if he took a drink, God help us."

He laughed and playfully punched Sasha on his equally muscular shoulder. The McDaniels brothers were in peak shape, and it showed.

There were four other white men seated a few tables away with frothing glasses of beer at a table in front of them, and it was easy to peg them as Afrikaners. South African whites, also known as Boers. Men raised from birth in Apartheid South Africa who thought because of their skin tone, they were superior to those of a different hue. They had immigrated to Botswana a few years earlier with their families due to the change in the political climate in the country of their birth.

Even though the laws of their adopted country forbade the practice of their prejudice which was indoctrinated at birth, that did not mean that they were the type of people who would not break such laws if given the chance. That meant the presence of Dumisani in particular, since he was the only black person other than Bashi, who was a bartender and thus did not matter, really irked them. He would become a target of their suppressed rage at the laws of this damn country, peaceful as it was.

To add insult to injury, three of the four young men, Stefan Vorster, Chad Viljeon, and Franz Potgeiter, had tried putting the moves on the American girls and had been summarily rebuffed. This left the fourth man, Andre van De Merwe, the odd man out. However, upon witnessing the total humiliation experienced by his friends, he dared not even try and was content to just sit back and enjoy his drinks. All men were in their mid to late twenties and in spite of having girlfriends, whom they willfully left behind, they thought the beautiful young tourists would be easy pickings.

After all, this was their favorite hunting ground. Whenever they got lucky with a lonely female tourist not well versed with the country and eager to make friends, one of them would strike up a conversation, insist on picking up the tab, and if things went well as they normally did, book a room right there at the hotel and get busy. Now, the fact that at least two of the women, especially the very pretty one with dark hair and exotic features, seemed to be paying Dumisani McDaniels the most attention, and the latter seemingly nonchalant about the whole thing made them all the more incensed.

"That's the McDaniels brothers," Franz Potgeiter said. Like his friends, he had that thick and distinct Afrikaner accent that was hard to miss.

Andre Van der Merwe raised his thick bushy eyebrows and said, "Brothers? What do you mean, brothers?"

"As in real brothers," Franz nodded.

"Same father and mother?" Stefan Vorster asked, perplexed.

"Yep," Franz answered before Van der Merwe could.

Stefan, his face ruddy and red like his bull neck because of too much alcohol and exposure to the Botswana heat nine months out of the year shook his head and said, "Blood brothers, my ass. More like a couple of freaks to me, that's all."

He was intentionally loud, and his friend winced as he furtively looked around to see if anyone else heard him.

"Shhhh!" Franz hissed between gritted teeth. "They'll hear you, man, cool it."

"So?"

"Well," Franz said, barely above a whisper. "They may be a couple of freaks, but I hear they're pretty good with their hands and feet, won a couple of major tournaments too – especially the white one."

It was true, the McDaniels brothers had participated in tournaments far and wide, even representing Botswana in regional championships that featured neighboring countries that included South Africa, Namibia, Zimbabwe, Mozambique, and Swaziland. In fact, Sasha McDaniels, arguably the slightly better of the two brothers when it came to full contact, no-holds-barred *kumite*, reached the semifinal match at the All Africa Championship Games held in Egypt, but narrowly lost to eventual champion Sizwe Ryan Biko from South Africa.

So, when Franz Potgeiter pointed out that the brothers were 'good with their hands and feet,' he was absolutely accurate in his observation. The brothers were both advanced third *dan* (or third degree, as it is sometimes referred to) black belts, indoctrinated in the martial arts from the moment they could walk. This made total sense, of course, because their father, Paul McDaniels, was a sixth *dan* black belt and also their *Sensei* or teacher.

That knowledge had been passed to Paul from his brother, Sean Kane McDaniels, now an ordained minister who still practiced as hard as he did when he was a teenager, which meant he trained at least four hours a day. Lately, due to the advent of mixed martial arts, the brothers, at the urging of their father had added boxing, Brazilian Capoeira, and Gracie Jiu-jitsu to their repertoire. That meant, even unarmed, the

93

McDaniels brothers were living breathing human weapons.

Stefan Vorster scoffed as he took a gulp from his glass and eyed the brothers with naked contempt.

"Oh really?" he smirked. "I bet I can take them, especially the darkie. Him I can beat with one hand tied behind my back."

Andre Van der Merwe, the seemingly levelheaded of the group looked at him as if he was nuts. On seeing this, Vorster laughed rather loudly, but no one other than his friends paid him any mind. This was, after all, a bar—albeit a high- class type, at least by Botswana standards.

CHAPTER 14

MEANWHILE, THE THREE BEAUTIFUL American tourists, Pamela, Jackie, and Misty, perhaps because of or in spite of the wine they'd been drinking, suddenly gathered the courage to go and speak to the brothers. They all stood up from the table where they were seated and walked to the counter where Sasha and Dumisani were parked. The brothers did not notice them right away because their backs were turned, as they took turns ribbing the bartender Bashi whenever he was on a brief pause in serving the patrons, who either came for a refill or to open a new tab.

The two brothers smelled their fragrance before they sensed their presence. Even though he had long ago spotted the women when they entered the facility earlier on, Bashi's eyes still lit up like a Christmas tree, since he was the first to spot them as they approached the counter.

"Hey, guys!" Misty said with a bright smile on her beautiful face.

Both brothers whirled on their stools at the same time and took in the sight before them. For a brief, fleeting moment, both Dumisani and Sasha wished they were better dressed, but they soon realized that their shaggy appearance and week-old stubble was really what attracted the girls and others in the room.

However, it was the American girls who had taken the initiative.

Sasha McDaniels, ever the ladies' man, was the first to shake the slender arm of the stunning brunette standing in front of him. She was wearing a short skirt that crawled a bit above her knees, and her shoulder-length hair was loose. She had on a pink blouse with spaghetti straps on her suntanned shoulders. The other two women, Pamela, also a brunette, and Jackie, a dirty blond, wore cut-off denim jeans and matching mocha-colored t-shirts that were purchased at a local gift shop immensely popular among the tourists. They were all tall, slender knockouts, beautiful in a different and exotic way – especially Misty.

"Oh yes, ladies, I'm Sasha McDaniels, and this is my brother Dumisani McDaniels," he said as he gestured at his brother who was seated next to him and smiled.

The ladies exchanged a quizzical look that he knew was coming and braced for what he sensed would be next. It never failed, and it always amused the brothers to no end.

"Brothers?" Misty asked, smiling suspiciously as she took a half-step back as if sizing up a Gucci handbag at an expensive store on Rodeo Drive in Beverly Hills.

Sasha and his brother were quick to notice that Misty had pronounced dimples on both cheeks whenever she smiled. Her teeth, just like that of the rest of her friends, were perfect.

"Yes," Sasha agreed. "As in blood brothers. Not even our mother can tell us apart."

The girls laughed. Either Sasha was pulling their legs, which was highly likely, or Dumisani, who up until now had yet to utter a single word, was adopted.

Or even more likely, the two were just really good friends.

"Tell them, Dumi," Sasha prodded as he playfully jabbed his brother in the ribs with his elbow.

"It's true," Dumisani agreed. He had been smiling at the girls nonetheless.

The three girls were now standing around the two brothers. The barstools were quite high, so even while seated, they were almost at eye level with the boys. They all smelled good, the two young men noticed, but said nothing and took in the near erotic fragrance.

"But seriously, you two are brothers?" Jacqueline, who preferred to be called 'Jackie,' asked too as she also took a step back, her hands on her hips, and sized them up the same way Misty had done earlier, as if the whole thing had been practiced.

"Yes," Sasha said.

"And why don't you tell us your names?" Dumisani impelled, and then quickly added, "Again, I'm Dumisani McDaniels and that's Sasha McDaniels." He echoed what his brother had already said with a playful wink and smile.

"Oh," Misty said, slightly embarrassed. "I'm Misty Abdul."

"And I'm Jackie Smith."

"Pamela Lavender, pleased to make your acquaintance, guys."

The brothers kept nodding and smiling at the girls as they revealed their names to them. And then in a practiced move, one that they had performed so many times, they reached into the pockets, took out their wallets, and withdrew their well-worn National Identity Cards, better known as '*O MANG*' (who are you, or in this case who you are) in Botswana. They methodically handed them to the girls, who stared at them in awe. They immediately put two and two together. It was most likely that Dumisani McDaniels was adopted, a truth which would have been entirely fascinating on its own, had it not been for the fact that they also shared the same birthday. This prompted many questions for the beautiful young women, but they resisted the urge. Anything more would have been prying and they knew it, so they dropped the matter for now.

The five then found a table near the veranda and ordered more drinks which the brothers insisted on paying for. Some thirty minutes later, the five of them at the round table facing the Thamalakane River were like long-lost friends reunited. The two brothers regaled them with their stories about the bush, growing up, and the self-deprecating humor to boot was more than the girls could handle as they laughed more than any of them could remember. Dumisani and Sasha were natural-born storytellers (particularly Sasha), and in Misty, Pamela, and Jackie they had an audience that was enthralled by raconteurs.

"And then what happened?" Misty asked eagerly as she clasped her hands together and placed them on the table in front of her, after taking a swig from her bottle of Castle Lager – glass be damned.

"Well, after making certain that the lion was dead," Sasha said and then deliberately wiped his mouth, a ploy to build the suspense. "Dad, Dumisani, myself, and a few others helped load him at the back of the truck."

"And boy, was that thing heavy," Dumisani, all inhibitions gone now as the combination of Percocet and beer worked in his blood, added with gusto.

"Yep," Sasha agreed. "And then we loaded the five hundred pounds plus, fully grown lion—dead, of course—on the truck bed, and the rest sat in the back with it."

"Was this an open or closed truck?" Pamela, who was seated at the other side of the table across from the boys asked, her glossy lips were slightly parted in what Sasha and Dumisani took to be bewilderment.

Jackie Smith was also spellbound, because all she could manage was a soft "Oh!" accompanied by a pair of wide eyes.

Sasha McDaniels, the consummate storyteller, continued, "Then the truck began moving, and then for some strange reason I'll probably never understand, Gomolemo, one of our ranch hands at the time, decided to sit on the lion's huge belly because it had taken up all the room at the back. And out of the dead lion's mouth came a soft roar. My goodness, you should have seen it, as God is my judge—how everyone except Dumi and I dove out of that speeding truck, thinking that the lion was still alive."

The girls stared at Sasha wide-eyed.

"Well, was the lion alive?" Jackie asked incredulously.

Dumisani fielded this one. "There was still some air left in its lungs apparently, so when Gomolemo sat on his belly, the air was let out as a slight roar, and that scared the hell out of the guys, prompting them to jump off like rats from a burning ship. It's funny now but it wasn't then."

The girls being college students themselves (they were all enrolled at the University of California, Los Angeles, UCLA, graduate program in International Studies) could tell that the twenty-something-year-old brothers were well-schooled.

"They thought the lion was still alive," Dumisani said again with a slight smile as he reflected on the memory before taking another sip from his glass.

Their audience gasped in horror, hands slightly covering their mouths as they imagined what in their mind's eye had to have been a horrific scene.

"Oh my God!" Jackie said, following a stunned silence, "Were they okay?"

"Miraculously, given that the truck was traveling at a little less than 35 kilometers per hour, save for a few bruises here and there, they were fine," Sasha said. He was suppressing a full-blown chuckle as he, like his brother, reflected on the memory.

Pamela Lavender, or 'Pam' as she preferred to be called, for the moment had to wonder if this was a tall tale and couldn't help but ask, "Guys, did this really happen?" There was a slight frown on her pretty face.

In somewhat of a comical gesture, Dumisani McDaniels smiled and raised his right hand.

"Yes, scout's honor."

"I'm talking about the lion," Pamela pressed on after taking yet another swig from her bottle. "Did the lion roar, or are you guys yanking our chains?"

Dumisani said, "Well Pam, its lungs were still filled with air when it died, so when Gomolemo sat on its belly, the residual air in its lungs came out as a slight roar through the mouth. I wish Dad had a camera handy at that very moment to record all that. I bet it would have been a hit with his employers, right, Sasha?"

Before Sasha could respond, Misty cut in, "His employers?"

"Yes," Sasha nodded. "National Geographic, among others, our parents do that nature stuff for them."

The three young women immediately stared at one another wide-eyed, their eyes flashing. The brothers also noticed this sudden change as well and wondered what had sparked that.

"What?" Dumisani asked, beating his usually loquacious brother to the punch. His glass was frozen halfway to his mouth.

Misty then said, almost in a whisper and in what sounded like total amazement, "You... You're not talking about Paul and Natalie McDaniels, now are you?"

The brothers smiled, finally understanding the ladies' bewilderment, and then nodded proudly. It was not uncommon for them to once in a while come across people who had seen their parents' work, especially the tourist types. This was never information they volunteered. They just let it play out, and it pleased them to no end when, as in this instance, the conversation led to that revelation.

"Yes, they're our parents," Dumisani said. The pride in his voice was evident.

Again, the girls looked at the brothers curiously, drawing their own conclusions, that being Dumisani McDaniels was adopted at some point in his life.

"Wow! Now that's cool," Pamela said, the first to recover from this new twist in the conversation. "We watched all their DVDs before we came here, kind'a like to familiarize ourselves with the country. We totally love their work—oh, and that award-winning piece about poaching and poachers was awesome."

"Thanks," Sasha smiled as he took another swig from his glass. "It's not that often we get to meet fans of our parents' work."

This, of course, was certainly untrue. They met fans of their parents' documentaries and even casual viewers of the *Discovery Channel* all the time. Their videos and later DVDs were sold at curio stores around town that catered mainly to tourists all the time.

"Can we meet them?" Jackie asked, her excitement barely in check.

Sasha said, "Sure, why not? You can join us for dinner tomorrow evening if you don't have any plans." His eyes were locked on hers for a couple of seconds longer before he added, "Mom and Dad are actually from California, did you guys know that?"

"Yeah, we heard," Jackie said. "I'm from California too. Which part are your folks from?"

"Southern California. Altadena, to be exact," Dumisani said, smiling. The exact city where the McDaniels originated was not common knowledge. The truth of the matter was that they had lived in Botswana for so long that people did not really care about the couple's origins anymore. To them, they were part of the 'Blue, Black, White,' a phrase that identified Botswana coined by local poet, playwright, and actor Donald Molosi.

The surprises, coincidences, or whatever one may want to call them kept coming, because Misty Abdul was once again wide-eyed.

"What?" It was Sasha McDaniels this time when he noticed the look on her face.

"Get out of here," Misty playfully slapped Dumisani, who happened to be closer to her, on the shoulder. "I'm from Altadena too."

"Really?" This time it was Dumisani who was wide-eyed.

"Yeah," she answered, her voice a bit higher. "Small world, isn't it? And Pam's from Newport Beach, and Jackie's from Burbank, all of them cities in Southern California not far from each other."

It was a good thing she added the last piece of information, because the brothers had absolutely no idea what she was talking about.

"Now Altadena," Dumisani said. "That's where that guy Gilbert Price is from, right, Misty?"

"Who?" Sasha asked, not wanting to be left out of this part of the conversation.

"That radical senator who is trying to run for President and has put himself on the map by insulting Mexicans and immigrants in general, calling them criminals that bring diseases and take away jobs from American-born citizens," Dumisani informed his brother.

"He's actually from Monrovia," Misty corrected him, and then quickly added, "Oh, that's a city east of Pasadena and Altadena."

"I see," Dumisani said softly and was about to expand on his answer when Misty interrupted him.

"You guys ever been to the US?" Misty asked. It became more apparent to the brothers that among the three girls, she was the classic chatterbox.

"Yes." It was Sasha this time. "But that was a long time ago and we were still kids back then, so, we don't remember much."

"We have an uncle back there, though. Sean Kane McDaniels," Dumisani added, smiling. He was beginning to like the beautiful, exotic-looking girl seating in front of him. Turning to his brother, he continued, "Sasha, remember how Daddy would never stop talking about him, and the fact that he's the only family he's got?"

Before Sasha could respond, at that very instant Stefan Vorster brushed by their table rather rudely, almost knocking it over, but succeeding in spilling a bit of the beer in a bottle on the table—almost in Jacqueline Smith's lap, who instinctively thrust backward in her chair. It was obvious that this maneuver was orchestrated on purpose.

CHAPTER 15

"HEY, EXCUSE ME!" Jackie fumed as she reflectively shifted her chair back.

The perpetrator did not so much as look in their direction as he headed to the long counter, let alone offer anything near an apology. Stefan knew he was being a total and complete ass, but he did not care. He, like the rest of his friends, were watching the McDaniels brothers interacting with the American girls, and with every drink consumed, their rage and jealousy grew.

The rest of the table watched in stunned silence, as the uncouth Afrikaner slammed both palms on the counter so loud that it briefly attracted the attention of the other patrons at the far end of the bar area.

And then loudly he said, "Hey, what does one have to do to get a drink around here?"

Bashi, who was wiping some glasses and expertly putting them in a tidy row in a cupboard above the cash register, quickly tossed the clean white towel he was using behind him.

"Coming right up sir," he said as he began filling one of the frosted glasses with lager. Vorster and his friends had opened a tab earlier in the day, so the bartender knew exactly which type of beer they preferred. There was a science in filling a glass with beer and not allowing it to froth at the top, and the young Motswana bartender was a pro.

"Yeah, yeah … I ain't got all fuckin' day, on with it." Stefan tapped an open palm on the counter again, causing quite a ruckus.

On seeing this, and never one to run from a fight, Sasha McDaniels felt he'd had enough. He quickly stood up and walked toward the counter and the offender.

"Hey, watch it, will you? There are women here," he said as he gestured at the table behind him.

With a drunken smirk, Stefan turned to glare at Sasha, Dumisani, and the girls. Only Sasha was standing. His brother and the girls were still seated at the varnished wood table.

"And just who the hell are you? My third-grade teacher?" the Afrikaner seethed.

Sasha took a step forward; there was a mirthless smile on his face. There were a few things Sasha McDaniels could tolerate, but racial prejudice, especially toward his adopted brother from birth, was not one of them, and he had seen it all growing up with a black sibling. It may not have been obvious to the American girls or anyone else who was watching this tense situation that could slowly escalate to a point where it might get physical, but Sasha knew why this man was acting this way. He was trying to get a rise out of the brothers, Dumisani especially, because he had seen the attention he was getting from the three beautiful women, two of them who happened to be white, and he did not like it one bit. Well, too bad for him, Sasha thought because if it was a fight this imbecile wanted, then the former National Karate Champion was more than ready to oblige him.

On seeing where this was heading, Jackie slowly stood up, walked up to Sasha, and gently pulled him back to the table.

"It's okay, babe," she said. "Let it go, don't sweat it."

Reluctantly, his eyes still on the other man and not for once straying away, Sasha took his seat. When Stefan turned back to the counter, his beer was already served in a frosted glass. Without even saying thanks, let alone acknowledging the bartender's presence, he took a large gulp of his larger. He then just as quickly slammed the glass on the counter, with some of the beer spilling on the sides.

Stefan wiped the corners of his mouth and in a loud voice said, "Is there any cold beer in this place?"

He then did something that not only astounded the two brothers and their female companions, but the rest of the patrons in the bar—except, of course, his friends. Even to this day, Dumisani and Sasha still shake their heads in bafflement over what happened next. Stefan Vorster actually took a few steps to the table where the McDaniels brothers were seated with their friends, dipped his forefinger inside Dumisani's glass, stirred the beer, stepped back, and then sucked his finger.

"Well, I suppose it's cold enough," he said.

Sasha's reaction was swift but calm. Clearly, this buffoon was looking for a fight, and someone needed to put him in his place. He looked at the astonished ladies and then at his brother, who also remained unruffled. Their eyes met, but in that brief moment the silent communication was deep as it was clear. The other McDaniels, the white one, was saying to his brother, the black one: "… *I got this Dumi, don't worry* …"

In a soft voice that was barely above a whisper, Sasha said, "Ladies, please excuse me." It was time to put this fellow in his place. He was obviously a spoiled little brat from birth who was used to getting away with anything.

The girls, sensing that something bad was about to go down, instinctively moved their chairs backward just as Sasha grabbed Dumisani's half-filled glass and flung the beer in Stefan Vorster's face. The beer caught him square in his open eyes, and it stung. He wiped his face with his shirt and charged at Sasha, who was already on his feet, but before there could be any altercation, two huge hotel staff who had unobtrusively drawn closer when they realized that a physical confrontation was inevitable intercepted his path. They had been alerted earlier on by the bartender, Bashi, when he sensed that with the way the Afrikaner was behaving, things were definitely going to get ugly.

One of the big bouncers turned to the other table where Stefan's friends were seated. They were paying rapt attention, and a couple of them, Chad Viljeon and Franz Potgeiter in particular, looked like they would join in, but the big fellow made a calming gesture with his palm, basically telling them that it would be a good idea for them to stay put. There was a look about him and the way he motioned that made the two understand immediately that perhaps it would be wise to do as they were instructed.

Sasha flashed a mirthless smile at Stefan Vorster as he was being dragged away, with difficulty at first, but he soon left willingly. They sat him down with the rest of his friends and stood watch over them, giving them time, and Stefan in particular, to calm down a notch. It occurred to Bashi the bartender, who had been watching the entire proceedings from behind his counter, that if it had been any other patron, he and his friends would have been asked to leave—not only that, but escorted out of the building and subsequently the premises with a clear warning that if they engaged in such tomfoolery again, they would be banned from ever setting foot on the property. Usually, one warning was enough, and for the most part the miscreants heeded this advice and stayed on their best behavior on their next visit and onward. However, Stefan and his friends were regulars, and their parents had some considerable pull in the village town.

"I suppose our time is up, Dumi," Sasha said.

His brother gritted his teeth as the rage finally surged through his veins like a tidal wave. Dumisani smiled to mask the delicious, icy chilliness that controlled his brain and the rush of wintry cold hatred that pervaded his body. He wanted to give no warning to anyone in this world, except of course his brother, as to how he felt at that very moment. Dumisani McDaniels wanted to hurt Stefan Vorster in a way he had never been hurt before.

The man had messed up big-time when he poked his finger in Dumisani's drink – how insulting was that? And how could one human being degrade another in such a manner? Especially in public, when his only crime was the color of his skin and because some pretty women were somewhat drawn to him? These were questions he knew he could not answer and, truthfully speaking, he did not need to. Dumisani McDaniels was not the one with a problem.

Pamela Smith said, "No need to hang around this joint. We're leaving too."

They all stood up, ready to go. The three girls realized that Dumisani, in spite of what had been done to him, was handling the entire fiasco with what they could only call 'saintly calm'. He was silent all along, keeping eye contact with his brother, who also returned the stare. It was obvious the two were planning something, considering that the uncouth Afrikaner's behavior, a challenge really could not go unanswered. The young man, Dumisani McDaniels, was fuming inside with a rage that pushed the limits of his discipline to the brink.

They all stood up, ready to go, and as they were filing out, Dumisani suddenly snapped his fingers as if he just remembered something.

"Excuse me, guys," he said. "I just need to use the toilet. I'll catch up with you guys in the parking lot."

Again, he gave his brother a knowing look, and Sasha nodded slightly to say he understood. None of the girls caught these subtle gestures. The brothers had seen Stefan and his two friends head to the can a few minutes earlier – it was on.

"In the parking lot, right?" Sasha said, even though his eyes said something else.

"Right," Dumisani agreed.

CHAPTER 16

THE MEN'S ROOM OF THE SEDIA RIVERSIDE HOTEL was spotless. It had several cubicles that housed the actual toilet seats, sparkling urinals, sinks, and a floor made of marble tiles, which were all shining and constantly cleaned by a cleaning crew that seemed devoted to their job. The room itself smelt fresh and clean.

It was here where Stefan Vorster had retreated with his two friends after Sasha had splashed the cold beer in his face.

Chad Viljeon said, "*Yerr* maan! Why would you let your feelings known in such a manner?"

"*Jaa* maan," Franz Potgeiter said. "You know that none of us can stand watching these *kaffirs* polluting our hangout regardless of the laws of this damn country, but you gotta be smart, man," he admonished his reckless friend.

He patted Stefan on the shoulder as the latter finished wiping his face with some paper towels before tossing them in a waste bin under the wash basins. He had been humiliated, no doubt, but he knew that his buddies were right. He had let his emotions get the best of him. However, one way or the other, Stefan Vorster was going to get even.

"Exactly," Franz agreed. "How are we going to justify backing you up when you pull a stupid stunt like that in public?"

"I couldn't help it, man," Stefan admitted. "I just can't stand these animals, especially when they start fucking white women – particularly that darkie. I don't care if he's got white parents and a white brother, he's still a goddamn *kaffir*!"

"Yeah, yeah," Chad said, trying to be the voice of reason. "But sticking your finger in his drink, man … I mean, what's up with that? And in public no less."

Stefan was known to do stupid things when drunk, and his friends thought they had seen it all, but this one took the freakin cake. Just as Stefan was opening his mouth to answer, the door to the restroom area burst open so suddenly and with such force that the three young Afrikaner men were taken by complete and total surprise, and more so when they saw who it was.

"Yeah, what was up with that, punk?" Dumisani McDaniels said as he entered with a frown on his face. He had been outside the door, and his somewhat dramatic entrance had them flummoxed.

He made straight for Stefan Vorster, the offender, who was directly in front of him, while he kept the other two, Chad Viljeon and Franz Potgeiter, in his peripheral vision. Andre Van de Merwe was at the far end of the room, so he was not an immediate threat. All this took at least half a second, enough time for the formidable McDaniels brother to gauge the situation and swiftly deliver a vicious front snap kick, which caught the still-surprised Stefan square on the chest and sent him flying to the other end of the room. When he landed on the floor, he slid on the smooth surface until the wall halted his momentum.

The speed, power, and precision with which he delivered this blow were so compelling that even his assailants gasped in astonishment. Right there and then, and without being told, the young Afrikaners knew their friend had picked the wrong man to mess with.

Dumisani was fully aware of what he was doing. In a street fight, there are no rules, and paradoxically that's the rule. Even for a skilled fighter like him, he knew that taking on three opponents at the same time, whose fighting capabilities were not known to him, was risky. Maybe two he could handle, so the idea was to take one opponent out of the equation—which was what he had in mind by focusing his first strike at Stefan, the main culprit—and subsequently neutralizing him if he could.

It is also believed and taught that the karate man never strikes the first blow, no matter how badly provoked. This is a creed that is preached time and again. However, in the real world where the line between living and dying can at times not be so clear, things are never that black and white. Dumisani McDaniels knew this, and in initiating the attack, he knew that all hell was about to break loose. And it did.

Whether it was by his own strength or the huge dose of adrenaline suddenly pumped into his bloodstream, Stefan Vorster was suddenly on his feet just as quickly as he had fallen to the floor, and charged at Dumisani with his upper body slightly stooped as if he was about to ram his head into Dumisani's belly. As he got closer, he began swinging wildly, first with his left and then his right fist, which either caught nothing but air or were easily parried away with one hand.

Initially, the other two friends, Chad and Franz, were too shocked and stunned to move. Their muscles were like ice as they remained rooted in one spot with their mouths still agape as they tried to reconcile the fact that this was actually happening right before their eyes. As for Andre Van de Merwe, he wanted no part of this confrontation, so he just stood at the other end of the toilet area, hands folded, and watched. He had warned the other three idiots not to get tangled up with the McDaniels brothers.

For a few seconds longer, Chad and Franz wondered whether it would be a good idea to intervene or not. The decision was made for them less than five seconds later after they realized that contrary to what they thought, Dumisani McDaniels was indeed a very skilled fighter, and their friend was taking a severe beating.

Twice Stefan Vorster got up, and he found himself initially on the seat of his pants, and the second found him sprawling on his back. Again, it was a front snap kick that floored him, followed by a spinning back kick to the face which put him out of commission for a while. On seeing this, Chad attacked with a flurry of punches, which Dumisani blocked, before he grabbed him by the arm and gave it a violent twist. This forced him to lean forward, and his opponent delivered a series of rabbit punches to the ribs. He let go of him, and as he staggered backward Dumisani executed a well-aimed side thrust kick, also known as the *yoko geri*, to the chest that sent him straggling into an open cubicle.

Chad fell back on the enamel tank. He hit it with such force that the tank cracked, and the lid fell to the floor with a loud clang. Immediately thereafter, water from the tank began pouring all over the place. Dumisani, after realizing that Chad had fallen and was not getting up any time soon, felt the third guy, Franz Potgieter, jump on his back. The water from the broken tank was now flowing freely and spread all over the floor, making it slippery.

With Franz still clinging to his back like a leech, Dumisani backpedaled as fast as he could and body-slammed him against the wall at the far end. He had to do that two or three times before he felt him weaken and finally slump to the floor. He was just about to finish him off with a kick to the side of his head when he felt a sharp, sickening blow square on his back that emptied the air out of his lungs.

It had been Chad Viljeon who had somewhat quickly recovered, grabbed the heavy lid of the enamel tank that had fallen to the floor, and then struck Dumisani with it, who was instantly weakened by the blow as he gritted his teeth, feeling the bile rise to his throat and the dizziness that came with it. He felt his knees wobble, and suddenly he was fighting to just stay on his feet.

Upon realizing this, his opponents seized the moment and rushed him. Following two quick punches to the stomach and face, Franz grabbed Dumisani by the front of his shirt and Chad grabbed his arms and pinned them behind his back. By this time, the fight was out of Dumisani McDaniels, and he was about to fall to his knees when Chad forced him back up on his feet. Stefan Vorster, now somewhat fully recovered, gleefully staggered toward the now-helpless Dumisani. There was a murderous glare in his eyes as his face took on a sinister look, made so by the blood that was trickling from the corners of his mouth.

He stood directly in front of Dumisani, who was still finding it hard to breathe, and growled, "Now, let's see what color you bleed, *kaffir*."

With that, he threw a right cross that connected just below Dumisani's right cheekbone. From the punch, Dumisani could tell that Stefan had had some kind of training, but that was too many beers and cigarettes ago. However, had it not been for Chad Viljeon

114

holding him, the blow would have spun him around before sending him to the floor.

"Shit!" Dumisani yelled in pain as he felt as if a grenade had exploded in his head.

CHAPTER 17

MEANWHILE, OUTSIDE IN THE PARKING LOT of the Sedia Riverside Hotel, Sasha McDaniels was busy chatting away with the three young American tourists. It was evident that the nasty incident that had occurred in the bar had been forgotten, at least by the women. Sasha was telling them of their plans to move to the United States, the country of their parents, in the not-too-distant future.

"Oh yes, there's a great chance that Dumisani may attend the Art Center College of Design in Pasadena," Sasha cooed with a broad smile.

Misty was impressed.

"How exciting, what will be his area of study?" she asked.

The girls, it turned out, had rented an off-road Toyota Hilux 4 X 4 from the local Avis, and Sasha was walking them to their truck.

"Journalism, with a minor in video production," Sasha said. However, he kept glancing over his shoulder at the entrance as he began to wonder what was taking his brother so long. He should have been back by now, he thought.

Misty again flashed that beautiful smile of hers as she used her forefingers on her left hand to move her long mane off her face, and said, "This is just fate, I tell you."

Her two friends, Jackie and Pamela, shared a knowing look and smiled. They had long since sensed that Misty most likely had the hots for Dumisani McDaniels and not his brother.

"Oh, I'll be coming too," Sasha, not wanting to feel left out, said with a wide grin.

"And what are you going to study?" Jackie asked. There was a hint of doubt in her voice, as if Sasha was not the academic type and that all he would be was a spare wheel or 'hanger-on.'

He hesitated a bit before saying, "Oh, well, I'll be looking into some business ventures." Sasha then quickly changed the subject by adding, "So it's set, right? We'll call you guys at the hotel?"

The girls nodded. They were shacked up at Riley's Hotel, which was a few miles east of where they were, and just like the Sedia Riverside Hotel was popular with tourists either on their way to the Okavango Swamps and its exotic lodges, or on their way back. The plan was that they would meet the following morning, and then he and his brother would pick them up in their Land Cruiser (which they planned on washing the moment they got home with the help of the ever-reliable Mr. Selepe), and take them to the forest area around Maun to show them more live game. The would even pitch a couple of tents and camp out in the open air with nothing but a real African night sky glaring at them, and then return to the McDaniels' ranch so the girls could meet their famous parents and join the entire family for dinner.

"I assure you, Dumi and I will be the perfect tour guides and gentlemen, and you don't have to pay us a thebe."

"A what?" Pamela frowned in slight confusion.

"A thebe," Sasha said and then immediately smiled and followed up with, "Oh, a penny to you, Pam, as in you won't pay us a penny and yet have twice as much fun as you would have had at one of those fancy lodges at the delta," he assured her with yet another smile.

"I see," Pamela smiled, finally understanding that Sasha was referring to the local currency.

"So, we'll see you guys later tonight," Sasha said. He was suddenly in a hurry as he quickly backtracked and practically ran to the hotel entrance. The girls just nodded enthusiastically as they anticipated the promised adventure. Sasha would later remember that moment for many years to come, and the look on the young American tourists' faces—full of life, beautiful and beaming, confident and yet innocent in their own right.

***

Inside the bathroom, the assault on Dumisani McDaniels continued unabated as the three men took turns punching him in the stomach, chest, ribs, and occasionally the face. By this time, Dumisani was putting up little or no resistance. The blow from the heavy toilet tank cover had weakened him to a point of just simply taking the punishment. Andre Van de Merwe had at one point tried to intervene on Dumisani's behalf but was roughly shoved to the far corner. It was by sheer devil's luck that up until now, no one had as of yet come into the lavatory.

"This will teach *kaffirs* like you to know their place and stay in it, *jy woer, kaffir?*" Stefan Vorster taunted as he delivered another right hook into Dumisani's stomach.

This one hurt like hell, because it caught him right on the solar plexus, emptying the air out of his lungs as he felt his knees wobble. Before he could fall, Chad and Franz held him fast.

At that moment, the bathroom door did open, and in walked Sasha McDaniels, who immediately froze in his tracks, for a moment not believing what he was seeing. The truth was that Sasha was not sure what to expect. Perhaps a little shoving, a few slaps, and that was to be the end of it. Definitely not the sight of his brother being beaten to a pulp.

The transformation on his face was instant and scary. On seeing this, the three assailants let go of Dumisani, who crumpled to his knees and then to the cold floor, where he lay still. Without taking his eyes off them and his brother, Sasha reached out with his left hand and locked the bathroom door. It was the type of heavy door that already had a locking mechanism built into it. The three took a few furtive steps back. They somehow sensed that this other McDaniels was a different animal altogether. As for Andre Van de Merwe, he stayed rooted in one spot and had hardly moved. Sasha immediately ruled him out. He had the unmistakable pleading *'I had nothing to do with this, please leave me out of it'* look on his face, and the other McDaniels brother understood it right away and was willing to accept the deal if he stayed neutral.

Sasha's lower lip trembled slightly as he said in a hoarse whisper, "My goodness! … Dumi! W-what have they done to you …"

He rushed to his brother and helped lean his back to the wall, and then looked again at the three who were now backed to the other end of the room.

"I'm going to kill you all," Sasha McDaniels said in a voice so intense that Stefan and his friends shuddered. It was not loud, nor was it soft. Sasha's voice had the proper tone to convey his tempered rage that was under control but ready to spill over like lava from a volcano. He approached the cowering men slowly, as if he was creeping up on some unsuspecting prey as his body swayed ever so slightly this way and that. The Afrikaners instinctively knew that *this* McDaniels was going to be a handful.

And indeed, he was, as a fight erupted the moment he charged at them without warning. It became immediately clear to Stefan and company that Sasha McDaniels' martial arts prowess was at an entirely superior level. Magnificent as Dumisani had been, Sasha was better. They made an attempt at self-defense, but all that was futile, even feeble. Sasha's specialty was breathtaking kicks, which he performed with such uncanny precision and grace that for a moment, even his three opponents gasped in amazement a split second before the kicks landed—blows that knocked them cold, vicious combinations of side thrust kicks, spinning back kicks delivered with such brute and yet controlled force that within seconds the fight, or whatever one may like to call it, was over as they lay on the floor twisting this way and that with limbs and fingers pointed at unnatural angles.

Right about this time, the fog was lifting from inside Dumisani's head, and his brother rushed over to help him to his feet. But Dumisani, not fully conscious, almost mistook Sasha to be one of his assailants and was about to attack.

"Whoa! … Easy, Dumi, it's me," Sasha said as he quickly grabbed him by the arms. "You alright, man?"

Dumisani did not answer, but instead laser-focused on his brother as he let him help him to his feet. There was blood trickling from the corner of his mouth, his left wrist was on fire, and his lower lip was puffed up like a shiny sausage. His left eye was also swollen to a point that it was almost shut.

"Yeah, man," he said at last. "I'm fine." Because of the blow to his back that had emptied his lungs of air, Dumisani was finding it difficult to put a sentence together.

Sasha was concerned. "You sure, man? Nothing broken?"

Dumisani touched his side and at the same time tried to rotate his left wrist and winced. "I think my ribs are bruised and my wrist is broken."

Sasha nodded and looked at the bodies still sprawled on the floor. Andre Van De Merwe was now seated in the far corner, eyes shut and hands over his head like a scared child trying to unsee what he just witnessed.

"Well, we'll have to have it taken care of. But in the meantime, let's get the hell out of here."

"Good idea," Dumisani agreed.

As they turned to leave, Sasha looked at Andre and said, "We're not going to hear about any of this, right?"

Andre simply nodded, in essence saying that he would have somewhat of a selective memory about what he saw and heard.

"Good," Sasha said.

They both left and exited the hotel through the kitchen, thanks to the bartender Bashi, as they were anxious not to be seen. Moments later, the brothers were in their Land Cruiser driving away and ready to face their father's wrath, which they knew, just as they were certain that the sun was going to rise the next day, was coming. They braced themselves all the way to the ranch.

CHAPTER 18

LATER THAT EVENING, the McDaniels were seated at the dinner table. The mood at the usually jovial table was anything but. Their father, Paul McDaniels, had spent the better part of the day straightening up the mess his boys had created at the hotel. They were lucky that charges of assault were not brought up on them. This, thanks in no small part to the fact that the McDaniels, in particular Paul and his wife Natalie, were good-standing people in the community, and the incident was at least for now swept under the rug.

The three Afrikaners had ended up at the local hospital after being carried out by stretcher from the bathroom of the Sedia Hotel, the brothers soon found out. The end result was not pretty—elbows had snapped, fingers were bent in directions they weren't supposed to go, and noses were flattened and bloodied. Dumisani had a severely sprained wrist, not broken as he had suspected, and a couple of bruised ribs he discovered after a visit to the family's private physician that Sasha had insisted on taking him to immediately after that brutal encounter at the hotel. He ended up with a sling on his right arm that he was to keep wearing for the next three weeks, which was why his mother, Natalie McDaniels, was dutifully cutting his steak for him. Sasha, on the other hand, was pretty much unblemished, with not so much as a bruise on him.

As the family sat at the dinner table, rumblings of thunder could be heard, which meant a storm of the blessed summer rain was coming at last. After filling his plate with rice, potatoes, vegetables, and steak, Paul McDaniels, who was seated at the head of the table as usual, looked at his two sons and shook his head in disappointment for at least the fifth time that evening. The boys instinctively looked at their plates as they braced themselves for the tongue lashing they knew was coming.

"I don't know how many times I have got to say this, boys – no fighting. Is it really that hard to walk away?" he asked rhetorically.

Dumisani shifted uneasily in his chair as his brother continued staring at his food. He then cleared his throat, and said, very much like an elementary school kid called to the principal's office, "Well, they started it, Dad."

And then his brother chimed in with, "Yeah, what were we supposed to do while that bigot poked his finger into my brother's drink? Come on, Dad, this is Botswana. We don't tolerate that kind of thing here – you know that."

"Be that as it may," Paul said. "Couldn't you have shown some class, walk away and be the bigger man?"

As he said this, Paul cut a piece of steak from his plate, used the knife to cover it with some steamed rice, dipped it into some gravy, and then hefted everything in his mouth.

"This is the new millennium, Dad," Dumisani countered. "The days of turning the other cheek are long gone."

"Right on, Dumi," Sasha said in mock triumph as he pumped his fist in the air for effect.

His brother could barely suppress a grin but stopped when both parents gave them a look that told them that this was serious. The couple, both of them in their mid-fifty's now, were aging gracefully. Their hair already had   strands of grey, and the lines on their faces amidst the permanent tan were getting deeper, but they still looked like their younger and beautiful selves.

"Okay, look what your resistance has led to," Paul said in a calming voice as if conceding defeat, at the same time making quotations marks in the air. "Two—no, three guys in the hospital with broken bones, not to mention the damage caused. Now, boys, I'm *not* saying not to defend yourselves when the situation permits, but this was downright thuggery."

The boys exchanged a quick glance, as if to say, *you go first.*

"What about my wrist, Dad?" Dumisani whined. "You're not saying anything about that, and yet it seems to me that you're in a way trying to justify those racists' actions."

His mother looked at her husband and nodded.

"You know he's got a point, darling," she said.

"Natalie, please, I'm the one trying to make a point here," Paul said. "Sean Kane, your uncle, used to tell me that the best offense is not to offend. I cannot condone our children engaging in fights, much less bar fights."

"But wasn't it your same brother who also said even that does not work sometimes?" Natalie McDaniels, very much playing the devil's advocate, said with a smirk on her face.

Paul sighed in resignation. He obviously was not getting his point through to his sons, especially with his wife being the typical mother hen protecting her brood.

"Well, I've said my piece," he capitulated. "Let's just go ahead and enjoy our dinner, even though I have to finish my talk with Jimmy Phillips first thing tomorrow about fixing this mess."

"Who?" Natalie asked.

"Jimmy Phillips, the owner of the hotel. We did an infomercial about him and his business a couple of years ago."

"Oh yeah, him," Natalie said after a mouthful of lettuce covered with Italian dressing. "And he has yet to pay the remainder of his bill."

On hearing this, Sasha opened his mouth to give one of his smartass remarks. However, his father noticed that, and his arm shot out to silence him.

"Not a word, Sasha. You're on thin ice as it is," he warned.

Instead of taking offense at what his father said, Sasha had a puzzled look on his face.

"You know, I've always wondered what that meant, '*on thin ice.*' How is ice thin?" Sasha asked, not in the least bit trying to be funny.

Paul McDaniels had to smile. Many times, he, just like Natalie, had to remind himself that even though his children were technically American by virtue of their parents, they were truly African. They had never lived in the United States, and even though they had in some ways adopted their parents' manner of speaking, their English was not in any way colloquial. They did not have the idioms and slang down like their parents, the type you can only pick up by living in a country.

"You know what? Never mind, but just know this: I did not teach you boys *Bujutsu*, *Gracie Jiu-Jutsu*, *Taekwondo*, and karate just so that you could go about hurting people."

The boys simply nodded as they continued eating in silence, and then as if to underline Paul McDaniels' point, there was a blinding flash of lightning that penetrated the curtains, followed by a deafening roar of thunder that caused the main generator that supplied the entire ranch with electricity to splutter. The lights dimmed for a few seconds before brightening up again. And then as if on cue, it began to rain hard.

The family looked at each other knowingly. Whenever that happened, the dimming of the lights, it meant that the generator was running out of fuel—diesel, in this case.

Sasha slowly stood up and said, "I will go fill it up. It's strange, though, because I could have sworn that Mr. Selepe took care of the problem and the generator had enough for three more …"

Instantaneously interrupting Sasha McDaniels in mid-sentence was the shattering of glass from a window close to the dinner table, followed by a Molotov cocktail that missed Natalie's head by a foot before it exploded into flames the moment it hit the wall. This immediately set the room ablaze, stunning everyone, before Paul, Sasha, and Dumisani reacted instinctively.

"Jesus Christ!" Paul shouted as he instantly reached for his wife's hand and forcefully dragged her to the floor. "Hit the floor, everyone …"

The brothers dove to the floor for cover. This was followed by numerous shouts outside, which meant that a group of unknown men were attacking the McDaniels residence.

"What's going on, Paul?" Natalie screamed.

As she said that, another Molotov cocktail crashed through yet another window, this time into the living room, which was adjacent to the dining room where the family was having dinner. Everyone was lying on the floor by now, and everyone was wide-eyed except Paul, who was wondering what the hell was going on.

"Dammit," Paul yelled. "We're under attack." As if that fact was not apparent to everyone around. "Everybody, follow me, and stay out of sight," he instructed as he began slithering on his belly like a snake and then doing the infantry crawl toward the master bedroom on the right, followed by his wife, Dumisani, and Sasha taking up the rear.

By this time, the fire was gaining strength. Once in the master bedroom, Paul, with the help of his two sons, pushed every available piece of heavy furniture they could lay their hands to, and used it to secure the door so that no one could easily break in. It became apparent why Paul was doing this as smoke from the other room began to seep from underneath the door, and other crevices, and into the bedroom. The documentary filmmaker was stalling so he could make contact with the local authorities and inform them of the peril they were in. They all began to cough as the smoke slowly thickened in the master bedroom. The smoke seemed to be affecting Natalie more than it did the others. With her hands covering her mouth and nose, and tears streaming down the soft skin of her cheeks, Natalie watched her husband as he frantically searched for something.

"What are you looking for, Paul?" she hissed.

"The walkie-talkie," he shouted. "I've got to call for help."

"But we've got to get out of here, Dad," Sasha said as he looked around, not for a communicating device, but for a way out.

"You're right, son," Paul agreed. "Hold on, Dumi, take care of Mom."

Without being reminded again, Dumisani grabbed a towel and used it to help his mother cover her face and mouth. As he did that, Paul slowly and carefully pushed the curtains aside, and his breath caught as he saw many more men running toward the house, and others to the servants' houses, two of which were already engulfed in flames. The men were all armed with, from what McDaniels could tell, the ubiquitous AK-47 assault rifles—the staple of liberation, violence, and mayhem not just in Africa, but the world over.

Among the brigands attacking the McDaniels residence was a medium–height, well-built man with muscular limbs. He was obviously their leader, Paul McDaniels could tell, by the way he was frantically gesticulating with both arms, one of which, unlike the rest of his men, held a pistol. He would at times fall back but barked orders nonstop. And from his tone and body language, it was obvious that he wanted his orders followed to the letter.

At first Paul couldn't tell who the brigand was until he turned his head and changed his face in profile. Again, and not for the first time that evening, his breath caught in his throat and the American felt literally sick to his stomach as he now realized the full impact of the danger his family was in. The man's hair was now white, but the scar that ran along the side of his face was still the most infallible point of recognition.

"Jesus Christ in heaven!" Paul McDaniels hissed under his breath as he recognized the leader. "Molo Sahili!"

He, Paul McDaniels, had helped orchestrate putting the master poacher behind bars. A sentence of which the poacher ended up serving 21 years, and now here he was to fulfill his long-promised and long-awaited retribution.

Paul looked around the large bedroom at his family. Dumisani was still making certain that his mother was breathing through the towel. There was a flower vase on the dressing table, which he had smashed and then used the water in it to wet the towel and cover his mother's face. Sasha on the other hand, after securing the door with some furniture, had finally found the walkie-talkie and was frantically trying to make it work.

"Quick," Paul said. He was suddenly gripped by a new sense of urgency and his voice reflected that. "We cannot stay here, we gotta move fast. It's Sahili and his gang. They're all over the place."

Dumisani looked up at his father in total bewilderment and said, "What are you talking about, Dad?"

Panting and almost choking from the smoke that was slowly but surely getting a grip on everyone, Paul, still looking for a way out said, "Molo Sahili, someone I helped put in jail for many years. Now he has come back for his revenge."

Dumisani was about to say something, but then he, like everyone else in the room, froze. What made them react that way was the unmistakable staccato chatter of gunfire that came in rapid succession—and to make matters worse, it seemed to originate at the back end of the property where the servant's quarters were located.

"Oh my God, Paul!" Natalie McDaniels exclaimed in horror as she grasped the meaning. "Nchadi and the kids, Mr. Selepe ..." There were now hot tears streaming down her cheeks.

"Not much we can do for them now. Come on, boys, help me."

Paul went on to smash the window of the master bedroom where the family had taken refuge. There was one problem, though, and it was major. All the windows of the McDaniels residence were fitted with burglar bars, and now it was clear that these were going to prevent them from escaping, or at least make the effort harder. They were trapped. At that very moment, there was a breach into the house, because they could now hear the voices of the marauders as they stormed into the house.

On hearing this, Paul, Sasha, and Dumisani took turns side-kicking the metal bars. When this proved to have little or no effect, the three men began kicking at the physical obstacle in unison. Just as the burglar bars started giving way, they could hear the invaders trying to force their way into the main bedroom by breaking the door down.

"Sahili!" they heard one of the intruders call out from the other side amid the chaos. "They're in here! Come quickly! I can hear them!"

After a while, a deep baritone voice could be heard.

"Good, don't let them get away. Tell the others to make sure that all avenues of escape are blocked, and we will have them trapped like mice."

On hearing this, the men redoubled their efforts, and then at last the bars gave way. They were immediately hit by a blast of much-needed fresh air, but with it was the smell of smoke that came from the servant's compound. The downpour, which they'd hardly noticed amidst the chaos and in spite of its ferocity, was now reduced to a drizzle, and just as Dumisani rushed to his mother to help her get through the breached window, as she would be the first out, someone on the other side of the door unleashed a steady volley of machine gun fire which splintered the door. A few of the bullets struck Natalie McDaniels in the chest and stomach. The impact of the projectiles was such that she spun around for a moment before she fell to the floor, dead.

Dumisani froze in horror, his eyes trying to unsee what they just saw as he watched Natalie McDaniels, the only woman he knew to be his mother, crumple to the floor without a sound. There was already blood trickling from the corners of her mouth, which meant at least a couple of bullets had pierced her lungs.

"Mom!" Dumisani screamed.

"Natalie!" her husband also screamed as he rushed toward her.

Like his brother, Sasha also froze, and as such was a step slower behind his father, a move that probably saved his life. Because right at that moment, another volley of bullets struck through the already-splintered door hitting Paul McDaniels in the chest and face. In the process, he took the brunt of the bullets that would have surely hit his son. As he fell to the floor, Paul faced his sons. His face was grotesque, almost half of it gone and his jaw was loose.

However, somehow, he managed to say, "G-get out of here, boys."

Sasha was the first to turn and bolt for the window, but his brother Dumisani froze with horror. He had just witnessed his mother, the only woman who had loved him unconditionally, the one woman who never wavered in her love for him, his ultimate protector when they were kids growing up who was constantly picked on by others because he was an 'oddball,' die in his arms. Now, he saw a mortally wounded man, a man he knew as his true father even though he was white, his face now grotesque as death claimed him fade before his very eyes, not to mention that he had also taken the barrage of bullets that would have killed him.

This was more than he could handle. Everything else, the sound of gunfire, the shouting of the marauders faded in the background as he stared dumbfounded at the dying man. What was life worth to him now that the two most important people in it, excluding Sasha, were so violently and unexpectedly taken away from him in such a brutal manner? At that moment, Dumisani McDaniels wanted nothing more than to join them.

Upon realizing this, Sasha grabbed him by the arm, snapping him out of his reverie and sorrow, reminding him that he still had a brother worth living for.

"Come on, Dumi!" Sasha hissed.

As the door finally gave way, the two brothers looked at one another and quickly made for the window. The bars were loose now, and with that they were able to dive through and land on the soft soil that was their mother's garden. And then at that moment, again as if on cue, it started to rain more.

As Dumisani began crawling away, ignoring the pain from his wrist, he noticed that his brother was not beside him. He turned to see Sasha crouched under the seal of the broken window.

"What in the hell are you waiting for?" he hissed. "Come on, let's go." The bitterness in Dumisani's voice was unmistakable, but the grief of losing their parents one after the other and right in front of their eyes had yet to register.

At that moment, one of the brigands came to the open window, AK-47 in hand, and spotted Dumisani among the vegetables. He took aim in one swift and obviously practiced move and was just about to open fire when from underneath the window seal, Sasha grabbed the weapon, tore it out of his hands, and just as swiftly reversed the move by jabbing the butt end of the machine gun into the man's chest. When the move caused the man to bend forward, Sasha grabbed him by the head and threw him out the window. The attacker landed on his back with a thud, and before he could get up, Sasha, assault rifle now held in both hands, fired a full automatic clip from less than three feet. The impact of the bullets shredded the bandit in two.

After quickly disengaging the banana-shaped magazine and turning it around, then reinserting it back into the assault rifle, Sasha rushed over to his brother's side and immediately took cover. He was breathing hard.

"Are you okay?" he asked his brother.

"Yes," Dumisani said. Like Sasha, he too was breathing hard.

Hot tears were streaming from their eyes as the anger of their parents' slaying mounted with every minute.

"I'm gonna kill these bastards, Dumi, I really am," Sasha hissed as he bit his lower lip to stop himself from screaming out loud.

They both crouched on one knee as they hid among the plants, which in this case happened to be fully grown maize stalks. It had been raining sporadically and it started to rain again. The brothers again cursed the lack of cell phone connection in this area, because hot as their rage was, deep down the brothers knew that they were faced with an overwhelming force of well-armed and bloodthirsty killers, and their chances of surviving this encounter were almost none, but they were going to fight with whatever means at their disposal. As more and more of the assailants crowded the bedroom window, obviously searching for them, Sasha lifted his weapon and fired away.

To account for the fact that the automatic weapon jerked upward upon squeezing the trigger, Sasha aimed a little lower, and when the rounds spewed from the automatic rifle, three bodies were hit and fell backward. The rest scattered the moment they realized that there was an active shooter they now had to deal with. They had made the unforgivable mistake of standing too close to one another when they were looking for the brothers.

There was then a brief pause as the marauders began to regroup, and the brothers pondered their escape. Right now it was about staying alive by surviving the attack, even though on numerous occasions the brothers had to wonder why this was happening. Robbery was obviously not the motive, because before he succumbed to a hail of bullets, their father had warned them that Sahili had come for his revenge after he had helped put him in jail. But the question remained, though – who really was this Sahili? Certainly, over the years growing up, Sasha and Dumisani had heard bits and pieces about the poacher that Paul McDaniels had made an award-winning documentary about, but was their father's crime, in Sahili's eyes, so bad that he had to come blazing as he did? That was the question.

CHAPTER 19

Molo Sahili And The Raiding Party

THE ATTACK ON ELEPHANTS and the wanton plundering of its ivory in and of itself offends any decent human being around the globe. However, the poacher Molo Sahili took his exploits even further. Ruthless, efficient, and slippery, he was responsible for the killing of many elephants and the men assigned to protect these beautiful creatures, to an extent that his name had become synonymous with terror in all of Africa south of the Sahara.

So, when news hit the airwaves about the capture of the notorious poacher and a few of his surviving cohorts, the country could talk of nothing else. He was escorted, under heavy guard, first to the military base in Francistown, transported by helicopter, and from there to the maximum security prison in Gaborone, where he awaited trial. Since this was to be a high-profile case, the trial was scheduled to be held at the high court in Lobatse.

Before the trial, and indeed during Sahili's arraignment, the prosecutors and all those in their team were awed by the legal team the poacher was able to put together. They were the best that money could buy, which spoke volumes about the kind of syndicate that backed him. He was not, as many people believed, a common outlaw who lived with animals. He was much more than that and on the strength of this, Sahili was charged with poaching and the murder of the tracker Sam Xaraga. He was saved from the gallows by a technicality.

Having gained independence from the English in 1966, Botswana is a nation with a highly active and efficient capital punishment. It was said that you could easily get away with murder in Botswana, but if by some unlucky chance you were tried, convicted, and sentenced to death, exhausted your appeals including a 'Hail Mary' (clemency from the president), you would definitely hang. And as of that moment in time, 1988, twelve people had already been executed by the state since independence.

The Sahili defense knew this, and they did all they could to mitigate the damage that had been put forth by Lieutenant Motang and his men. The way the defense counsel saw it, Paul McDaniels was the weak link from which they could create reasonable doubt. You break him, the defense believed, you break the entire state's case – formidable as it was.

When McDaniels took the stand, the prosecutor John Balebetse walked him through the events of the day that led to the point where he encountered John Ntemwa. The courtroom in Lobatse was packed that morning since the case had taken up interest not seen since the infamous trial a few years earlier of one Clement Gofhamodimo, a young Motswana man who was tried, convicted, and executed for the 1978 murder of a Swiss tourist named Beat Rauchenstein. Even though his body was never found, the circumstantial evidence was damning, and that's what sent him to the gallows.

The moment Balebetse was through with his direct examination, it was time for 'The Magician,' 'The Legal Gymnast' Drake Moribame to mount his cross-examination of the star witness with the hope of knocking him off his game, and finding a crack in the state's case that he could exploit and bring the entire 'house of cards' down, as he called it. Without any pleasantries usually afforded defendants, Drake Moribame went on the attack from the opening bell.

"So!" Moribame said as he gleefully rubbed his hands together. "We've already established that you were at the scene on the day in question, allegedly filming my client and his men, is that correct?" he asked, pointing at the defense table.

Sahili was seated among a team of lawyers from the prestigious firm. His transformation was remarkable. The neatly trimmed hair and the light blue Brooks Brothers suit made him look like the CEO of some Fortune 500 company instead of the bandit that he was

"Yes, sir," McDaniels answered confidently.

In contrast, he was dressed down compared to the poacher. He wore a faded pair of jeans, a white t-shirt, and on top of it a long-sleeved safari shirt. It had been a trying week and a half for the American. He had to make sure that his tracker, Sam Xaraga had been taken care of by making and paying for all his funeral expenses, and tracking down known relatives, which in itself proved to be a challenge because the San people, especially those not inclined to the modern way of living, were primarily nomadic people. But he was able to track them down anyway and Xaraga was given a wonderful though emotional sendoff. What was left now was to grant him the justice he so richly deserved, and Paul McDaniels was here to make certain that it was.

"Good," Drake Moribame said, jolting McDaniels into the here and now. "And where was the deceased at this moment?" the lawyer deliberately did not use his name so as not to humanize him.

"He was behind me, as always."

"And then can you tell the court what happened?"

"I heard a slight commotion behind me. At first, I thought it was Sam moving closer to whisper something, but as it turned out that wasn't the case. It was, as I later found out, Mr. Ntemwa sneaking up toward me after he had killed my tracker."

Moribame pounced at this.

"Oho, you actually saw him with your back turned to what was happening, right?"

Typical lawyer, McDaniels thought, splitting hairs. It's obvious it was no one other than the scum he's defending who murdered Sam.

Aloud, he retorted, "If you say so."

"And how do we know that it was not you that killed him and made it look like it was one of my client's men?"

Now this was silly, and if the whole thing was not serious, the American would have laughed outright at the absurdity of this question. On the other hand, it showed the desperation of the defense counsel.

Instead Paul said, matter-of-factly, "Okay, let me put it this way, sir, since I was there and you were not. Mr. Ntemwa tried to creep up on me after he slit my friend's throat to do the same to me, but unfortunately for him, he got more than he bargained for. He's lucky I did not kill him when I had the chance."

There was a slight murmur among the audience and some nods in agreement by some who were familiar with Paul McDaniels' prowess in the martial arts, the ultimate form of unarmed combat. This clearly was not what the high-priced lawyer from a prestigious firm wanted to hear, so he decided to switch gears. His plan to paint McDaniels as a possible murderer had backfired.

The lawyer then said, "So it was not my client, Molo Sahili, who murdered your tracker, or as you conveniently put it, your friend, right?"

That subtle jab could not go unanswered, so McDaniels decided to counter with one of his own by saying, "I think that has already been established, sir."

There were a few chuckles here and there that could be heard, and again Moribame bit his lower lip in frustration. His scheme to rattle the American was certainly hitting a brick wall at every turn.

"Please answer yes or …"

"Yes," McDaniels said quickly, cutting the lawyer off before he could finish his sentence.

Again, there was some chuckling, which caused the judge to reach for his gavel, but as he was about to call the court to order, normalcy was restored all on its own.

"That said," Drake Moribame said in a voice devoid of frustration, though the American was getting under his skin, "My client cannot be charged with common purpose as the state is doing, am I right?"

"Objection!" the prosecutor John Balebetse thundered as he practically sprang to his feet. He was tired of all this nitpicking. "The learned counsel for the defense is making a statement in matters way beyond the witness's expertise."

"Sustained," Judge Kavindama agreed. "Ask a question relevant to what the defendant knows about the day in question."

Drake Moribame smiled and nodded before saying, "Okay, I'll rephrase. Mr. McDaniels, you did not hear or see my client Molo Sahili give or imply a kill order on your tracker, now did you?"

"No, and his name was Sam Xaraga, not tracker"

"Fine, whatever, but he was *your* tracker nonetheless, right?"

Before McDaniels could answer, the prosecutor cut in again. This time he did not bother to stand up.

"Objection, Your Worship. Argumentative," he said.

The judge, the Honorable Kabelo Richard Kavindama, one of the few judges who looked regal in his post-Colonial wig, agreed.

"Move on, counselor," he ordered.

Attorney Drake Moribame paused before spreading his arms momentarily and letting them fall to the side as if to say, *okay fine,* and the judge noticed.

"No need for the theatrics, counselor."

"Sorry, Your Worship." He then looked around and then went on to try to bend McDaniels' testimony over the next two hours into the tiny box of reasonable doubt, but he had met more than his match in the American, who proved to be a rock. In the end, he was forced to accept defeat. "No further questions, Your Worship."

Sahili's team was eventually able to prove that John Ntemwa acted on his own. The fact that the prosecution was unable to prove that the poacher was himself a murderer who had trained men to kill any enemy they came across, therefore giving common purpose, could not be proven beyond a reasonable doubt, and Sahili escaped being charged with murder—whereas John Ntemwa was, and was subsequently hanged a few years later.

That was how Sahili ended up getting his 22-year sentence without parole to be served at the maximum security prison in Gaborone. And while serving his long sentence, the convicted man proved just how resourceful a leader he was. First of all, he came with an outsized reputation that preceded even him and earned him the type of respect among fellow convicts that every inmate craves. Through contacts from the outside, and since he was adept at the art of smuggling, Sahili became a one-man cottage industry in prison.

It became a known fact that if you wanted anything from chewing gum, cigarettes (the currency and lifeblood of prison life), and toilet paper to gourmet food including cooked steak for special occasions, a bottle of brandy, or anything within reason, Molo Sahili was the man to see, even for illicit contraband such as high-value drugs like cocaine, speed, and marijuana. He ended up churning such a huge profit that in time, he had almost the entire prison guard on his payroll. These were men he paid well to look the other way, and pretty much run the prison the way he wanted without word of his activities reaching the wrong people in power.

He soon had minions working for him, 'errand boys' and servants who wanted to get as close to him as possible so that they could be afforded the privileges only he, Sahili, had in the palm of his hand. These were mostly young men who up until meeting Sahili had absolutely no purpose in life and no direction. To them, the master poacher was a god.

Since he was serving a long sentence, many of his boys were released sooner, but even on the outside they still maintained contact with their mentor. There were also instances where some would deliberately commit some crime and let themselves be arrested, or violate the terms of their parole or probation, and find themselves back where they felt they belonged. In the end, Sahili had established a network of well-disciplined and well-trained criminals that stretched far and wide.

All this had a purpose. After his arrest and subsequent conviction, his Far East benefactors dropped him like a hot potato. He was no use to them now that he was in prison, and to make matters worse, his arrest had brought them unwanted attention, and the documentary by the American assured Interpol also began paying close attention to the syndicate. The twenty-two-year sentence did not help, either. Sahili would be an old man by the time of his release and of no use to anyone.

Along with all this, the brigand Molo Sahili blamed one man – Paul McDaniels. As far as he was concerned, the American was going to pay. This was made worse by the fact that a year into his sentence, the McDaniels documentary '*The Elephant And His Enemy*' premiered to rave reviews the world over, and Sahili's notoriety was assured.

Sahili ended up serving nineteen years. He had aged considerably during his time behind bars, judging by the complete whiteness of his hair. He was old but not broken. The fire in his heart, the thirst for revenge, and the resolve to make Paul McDaniels pay for what he supposedly did to him did not diminish even after all these years. If anything, his steadfastness had only grown stronger.

Thus upon his release from prison, nineteen years later, a totally forgotten man with minor arthritis in both hands, Sahili was back in his home country of Angola, since he was summarily deported upon release and declared an undesirable. He was able to revive, or rather reenergize, his network comprised of the eager young men he had met in prison. It took a year and a half of training at least thirty of these young men in the skill of fighting first with weapons like the pervasive AK-47 assault rifles, as well as hand-to-hand combat, and most importantly, the art of poaching. Their base of operation was the Caprivi Strip just northwest of the border between Botswana and Angola. Here they could remain hidden for months on end, conducting their training in utmost secrecy with no one even realizing that they were there.

Almost twenty years of incarceration can be a nightmare for any sane man, and Molo Sahili was no exception. While on the inside, the world changed in leaps and bounds, and in this electronic age the changes were exponential. Sahili got to find out as well that the elephant population in Botswana had multiplied tenfold, and with an international embargo in place banning the trade of ivory worldwide, especially the selling of illegal ivory, its value quadrupled on the illegal market. Ivory now traded at $3000 a kilo. There was also a new enterprise to look into that interested the poacher quite a bit and was worth exploring – human trafficking.

There was, however, one obstacle that needed to be dealt with and taken out of play immediately, and that immovable impediment was Paul Luke McDaniels. He had, through his network of spies, come to learn a lot about the man in the year he had been released from prison. And most of that information had also come from 'Google.' McDaniels had done well for himself since the last time they met.

The American had become well-known thanks to his documentaries, especially one in which an infamous poacher had been captured red-handed—and not only that, but the entire takedown had been caught live on film with nothing staged for the cameras, except of course the subsequent interviews given by the young lieutenant Fredrick 'Freddy' Motang, who had since risen rapidly through the ranks and had become a one-star general; a Brigadier General of The Botswana Defense Force.

It took another year and a half, but Molo Sahili, through protracted negotiations which included many encrypted emails (he had learned fast) and rare face-to-face meetings, the poacher had established a network of clients in Dubai, Hong Kong, mainland China, Japan, and the United States. These were businessmen involved in the elite and dark trades of ivory and young girls. However, before the first shipment could even be negotiated, Paul McDaniels and anyone else in his way would have to be eliminated. With the American, though, this war had become personal.

***

Sahili found a place in the thick forest of the Caprivi Strip just on the other side of the Botswana border. It was well hidden even from the sky in case there was any sort of aerial surveillance, of which there turned out to be none, since really by now Molo Sahili was for all intents and purposes a forgotten man—a nonentity, as far as the powers that be were concerned. That was why he was able to move his base of operations as close to the border as possible without attracting unwanted attention. However, if there was one thing the poacher had learned during his years behind bars, it was never to underestimate the power of the state, or the military for that matter.

Even the best laid and well-thought-out plans could go haywire. All it took was one unforeseen loose end like treachery and betrayal from one of his men, as had happened with Patrick Lefatshe. Over long periods of solitude in his jail cell, and the bits and pieces of information that had been fed to him, Sahili had been able to figure out that Patrick Lefatshe, the man who had been way down the totem pole in his organization, had been the traitor, and from the information he had given to the authorities, without being touched or having the information beaten out of him, law enforcement had been able to blow the whole thing wide open.

Many nights he had dreamt of subjecting the turncoat to a slow and painful death, but Patrick had died of AIDS a few years after Sahili's incarceration and thus was denied retribution, a fact that deeply saddened the poacher, for he had wanted an example made of the deserter. In any case, he had to accept the hard, cold fact and move on.

That was why this time, he kept things as close to the chest as possible. Information, especially the overly sensitive type, was compartmentalized and even then, it was on a need-to-know basis and his men did not need to know everything at once until the last possible minute. For instance, when their training that was to last six months began, the twenty-four men under his command knew that their target was a ranch near the village town of Maun. The who and the why was not communicated. The men also knew that after that undertaking, they'd begin their selective hunting of elephants for their tusks. Specific places where the animals would be found, at say the Chobe National Park and the Moremi Game Reserve, were unknown to them. That included the plan to kidnap comely young maidens, methodically hook them on heroin, and then sell them to an elite clientele across the world that specialized in human trafficking and prostitution.

However, even as much as he wanted to cloak everything in secrecy, Sahili had to trust someone – at least to a certain extent. His partners in crime, men like John Ntemwa, people he had trusted with his life, were gone. Indeed, Ntemwa had been convicted and sentenced to death by hanging for the murder of Sam

Xaraga, and the execution had been carried out three years later after all his appeals ran out and clemency from the president had been denied flat.

Then in came Advent Monyatsiwa, a young man he met behind bars. Why Advent ended up in prison was in itself a very bizarre and twisted story. Born and raised in the capital city of Gaborone, Advent came from a straight-laced, well-to-do family. He attended good private schools as a youngster, and much later graduated with a Bachelor of Commerce (B.Com) from the University of Botswana.

There was also one thing Advent loved, and that was the martial arts, a discipline he was introduced to while growing up. As he grew older and grew into the art, he was soon ranked among the best, sometimes even mentioned among such names as Sizwe Ryan Biko, the all-Africa Karate Champion and Tidwell 'Teddy' Modise, the one-time National Champion who had since fallen off the grid and as far as everyone knew and tuned into that world, did not compete anymore.

One thing Advent was known for was his grace and extraordinary flexibility. He could perform front and sideways splits and left and right leg suspensions over his head for long periods of time. A feat many a martial artist can only dream of. Standing almost six feet tall, slender, extremely good-looking, and very likeable, Advent Monyatsiwa had the world at his feet—or so it seemed.

Things started going wrong for the young man upon graduation. It started innocently enough. Armed with his undergraduate degree in commerce, he quickly got a job as a teller with a bank from South Africa that had recently opened several branches in Botswana in all the comfortable business locations in the country, including the towns Lobatse, Francistown, and Selibe-

Phikwe, before they became cities, with their main branch in the capital, Gaborone.

Being an ardent martial artist, Advent worked out like a fiend. He jogged five miles early morning before and after work and trained equally hard at the local *dojo*. And thanks to his daily meditation, he had an abundance of energy and an alert brain that none of his coworkers or supervisors could match. While most people his age relatively new to the working world went to bars, and some engaged in recreation drugs, his mind was not dulled by such proclivities. Knowing that banking was indeed a particularly good career, he steadily improved by reaching and teaching himself anything that had to do with banking.

As a result, Advent's rise within the institution was meteoric. Primarily, promotions within banks are slow. Moving from, say, the waste department to teller and then foreign exchange, for example, could be slow and arduous, sometimes taking a minimum of seven years. To become a branch manager, one had to climb the greasy little rungs that may take up to fifteen or even twenty years in a best-case scenario. Backbiting and jealousy are the norm in an industry that pays just enough to barely keep one's head above water and away from true starvation until that lucky individual reaches a managerial post where the real money was. Because as a bank manager, you got to share in the profits the branch made.

Advent's trajectory surprised even his immediate supervisors, who immediately felt threatened by this young man's prowess. He moved from being a teller to waste department assistant supervisor, and finally full-fledged supervisor, in eight months, still a record at that particular bank to this day, and then with the institution suddenly expanding and opening new branches across the country, it was almost a foregone conclusion that Advent Monyatsiwa was to head one of the new branches that were set to open in Jwaneng, Mahalapye, and Orapa. With the first two already earmarked for operation in the next few months, Advent was in line to head the branch in the diamond mining town of Orapa in the northeast part of the country, which had the potential of being a very highly lucrative branch.

It was right about this time that the bottom fell off. Banks were using paperwork to balance their tills until a new system with computers was introduced. The program was called '*Genesys.*' It was supposed to be revolutionary and user-friendly, eliminating the laborious work associated with paperwork. The computer system assigned to the tellers was supposed to get rid of that problem. Customers were supposed to deposit or make withdrawals and other transactions that the tellers took in, and then at the end of the day, the computer did its magic and balanced the drawers by simply pressing a button. The teller would then sort out the cash, checks, and slips, and send them to the bank vault called the 'Treasury.'

Many times, new systems that are supposed to make life easier can at times complicate it. Because *Genesys* had only been performed in a testing environment, so to speak, there were still kinks and bugs to eliminate, and Advent Monyatsiwa became its first victim. On the third day of using the system, his cash drawer was short close to three thousand Pula. A large amount, considering that his salary was P975 per month. His immediate supervisor, a South African white named Carl Du Plessis, who not only felt threatened by this young upstart but had ambitions of his own, saw his opportunity to pounce.

What was more, Du Plessis, just like Stefan Vorster, was born in a country where it was the law to hate Black people. He intended to not only get Advent fired on suspicion of stealing cash from the drawer which led to his shortage, but destroy him in such a way that he would never be employed by any financial institution in the country, or even neighboring states. It did not matter that the real error was discovered a few weeks later and many others started experiencing shortages in the tens of thousands. If anything, Advent's case was the least compelling compared to the others that arose, but the damage was done. What was worse, instead of the bank, and Du Plessis in particular, admitting their mistake, they covered it up and Advent's reputation remained tarnished. The jury was out – Advent was a common thief, plain and simple.

Somehow, through some former colleagues at the bank who did not regard him as toxic, Advent got wind of what had happened, how the error had been found, and by what means Du Plessis fought to keep it hidden. And that was when he swore revenge, with the target for that retribution being the banker and his former supervisor, Carl Du Plessis. To drown his frustration at this moment of unemployment, which truth be told was not of his own making—and being young and broke, the worst thing that could happen to someone in Botswana—he took to drinking a lot.

It was during one of these drunken moments, alone and lonely because his friends and girlfriend had deserted him, that he had what alcoholics refer to as a 'moment of clarity.' He wanted to hurt Carl Du Plessis. That is why one afternoon, not too long afterward, found him semi-hidden and disguised in front of the Capitol Bank building branch on Haskins Road in downtown Francistown, waiting for Du Plessis and discretely following him home on his motorcycle.

He knew that the banker was a bachelor and lived alone, but when he got there, what was he going to do? Maybe rough him up a bit? He was not sure, but a nice little beating for the man who had succeeded in derailing what was once a promising career would go a very long way in granting Advent some measure of satisfaction. Beyond that, he had no idea what the end game would be, but for now the young man was not thinking that far ahead.

Things went wrong for Advent, however—very wrong, in fact. On finally stalking Carl Du Plessis to his residence, which happened to be on the outskirts of the city, east of downtown proper in a brand-new suburb of well-to-do residents, Advent staked out the home of the unsuspecting banker until dark. When Du Plessis stepped out of his house via the kitchen door to empty his trash bin, Advent was on him like a hungry cat on an unwary mouse. He was armed with nothing but his hands and feet, which considering his vast training were deemed lethal weapons.

The first blow was a well-implemented front snap kick to the belly, which bent the victim forward, and a few other well-placed kicks were met with little or no resistance at all. These blows could be explained away and even mitigated, as the subsequent trial would prove. However, the *coup de grace,* which was the stamping of the man's head several times when he was already lying helplessly on the ground was inexcusable. Du Plessis ended up with a broken jaw and a hairline fracture to the skull. The injury to the brain was minimal, but it was enough to disqualify the South African from the rigorous work of the banking industry.

Advent would have gotten away with the crime, except that unfortunately for him there was an eyewitness to the assault who caught the whole thing on film by recording the incident on her phone before calling the police and an ambulance. Even though the footage was grainy and taken from a distance, as she happened to have been at her kitchen sink when she saw the whole thing, it was nonetheless damning, because it was clear what was going on and who was performing the deed. After Du Plessis was down for the count, Advent had taken off his balaclava to take in some air, and in doing so his face was caught by the young woman's phone camera, albeit for a brief second, but during that moment his identity was confirmed without a doubt. He was swiftly arrested soon thereafter.

It was at his trial at the magistrate's court, also on Haskins Road in downtown Francistown and close to the City Council Offices, where everything was brought out into the open by the defense to somewhat explain Advent's actions. His employment with the bank, the rapid rise, one promotion after another, the introduction of *Genesys* and the disaster that followed as a result. Most unflattering of all to the prosecution's case was when a brave former colleague blew the whistle on the fact that the difference in Advent's cash drawer that had gotten him fired was indeed the bank's error, which was later covered up by the victim due to his personal animosity toward Mr. Monyatsiwa, the young lady, Lillian Setlalekgosi, who was still employed by the bank, revealed.

The defense, of course, seized on this as a mitigating factor for their client's behavior to explain that with no employment, which was caused by the plaintiff, Advent had become temporarily insane. The main culprit, as far as the defense counsel was concerned, was now seated at the prosecution's table, head shaved and bandaged, his jaw wired and tilted in such a way that nobody in the court, including the judge, would miss the extent to which he had been physically abused and the mental trauma that came with it. The South African, Carl Du Plessis, was afforded the same tender loving care shown to a rape victim or a battered spouse, and the prosecution was determined to get its pound of flesh from the rapist – Advent Monyatsiwa.

In the end, Advent was found guilty on all charges—assault, grievous bodily harm, and attempted manslaughter.

"There were a number of avenues you could have aired your views, young man, instead of taking the law into your hands," the Judge, The Honorable Lamech Mamuze, admonished while pronouncing the sentence. "There was a union you could have appealed to and other possibilities to explore. Yes, Mr. Carl Du Plessis acted irresponsibly and with malice when instead of revealing that a mistake had been made, and if addressed would have most certainly vindicated you and opened the great possibility of rehiring with the bank's deepest and most sincere apologies, I assume. You instead, Mr. Monyatsiwa, decided to lie in wait for the perfect opportunity to attack Mr. Du Plessis. Whether or not your intention was to scare him as you claim and maybe rough him up a bit, the fact is you carefully planned this assault, which means it was premeditated. You laid in wait, and then tried to slip away without being noticed and none would be the wiser, which tells me that your intentions were clear from the onset. Considering the fact that you're a trained mixed martial arts fighter, there could be but one outcome, and a man of your capabilities should have known better."

Advent and his two lawyers winced. This was not good at all, it meant that the judge was going to come down hard on this one, and they were correct in that assumption.

Following a brief pause as Judge Mamuze consulted the paperwork in front of him, he sentenced Advent Monyatsiwa to fifteen years to be served at the maximum security prison in Gaborone. Sentence to begin immediately. There was a collective gasp in the courtroom that instant. The punishment had been incredibly harsh, and some people, including some legal analysts, were quick to point out that it was that way because the victim in this case was white and to some small extent, he was a man of eminence in the financial institution.

That was how Advent Monyatsiwa got to meet the man who would become his benefactor, Sahili, since the notorious poacher was also serving his sentence at the same prison in Gaborone. It was here that Advent became a bitter man, furious at society for having robbed him of the best years of his life. Once again, just like it had been with his very first employment with the bank, Advent felt he had been unfairly punished. The flames of rage in his heart were further fanned by Sahili, and thus society was going to pay.

It had been relatively easy for Advent to embrace a life of crime, even while in prison, and pledge his undying loyalty to Sahili, the man who would be his mentor, and he the poacher's most trusted adjutant in a way John Ntemwa could have not even hoped. The young man's loyalty remained resolute even when he was released a few years earlier than his boss, and he helped run his criminal enterprise on the outside and bring its level of sophistication into the electronic age.

So, a few years after Sahili's release as a prohibited immigrant in Botswana, Advent was informed of a target that needed to be eliminated before their criminal organization could be fully operational. The young man did not ask 'why,' but only 'when' the mission would be carried out.

CHAPTER 20

Present Day

Meanwhile, the flames from the McDaniels' Ranch attracted the attention of off-duty Police Officer Herbert 'Junior' Pilane, known to everyone by his moniker since he shared his name with his father, who was a retired law man well known for his utmost dedication to his chosen career. It remained to be seen if the younger Pilane would turn out to be anywhere near the warrior his father had been. It just so happened that his parents' farm was located some seven miles south of the McDaniels' Ranch. Like everyone in the exotic village town, he was familiar with the McDaniels family. In fact, he had been at the police precinct that very afternoon when reports came that there had been a fight at the Sedia Hotel, and that the two unusual brothers had been involved.

Like a few of his contemporaries, Junior had silently applauded the brothers' actions, and as far as he knew so did his immediate supervisor, Sub Inspector Cornelius 'Think Tank' Baruti. The victims in this case—Viljeon, Vorster, and Potgeiter—were known troublemakers and almost always got away with their transgressions, and it was time someone put them in their place. There had been reports of public drunkenness, assaults, verbal abuse, and a handful of rapes that had been reported mainly perpetrated on locals. However, when it was time to initiate an arrest, files got mysteriously lost, and witnesses suddenly developed amnesia, changed their statements, or simply refused to testify in court, open or otherwise. So, in time the three young men ran riot in Maun without fearing the consequences. In their minds they were untouchable, and it was hard to argue with that fact.

This, of course, was until the McDaniels boys did their thing. Sasha and Dumisani had no way of knowing, but they had become instant heroes at the local police station for inadvertently getting rid of a vexing problem. Now when Junior Pilane saw the flames from a distance, he grew alarmed. Something was definitely amiss. What prompted the young constable to hit the brakes of his Toyota Hilux was when he heard a crackling sound that to the untrained ear sounded like firecrackers, going off in rapid succession.

As they were Americans, Junior Pilane knew that the McDaniels held a firework display at their ranch every Fourth of July to celebrate their nation's independence, and the spectacle was known to draw people far and wide to watch this incredible event. There was a problem, though, and Junior was very quick to realize that. It was mid-March, which meant something else, something sinister, was going on. Whatever it was, it was not good, which led him to only one conclusion – the McDaniels ranch was under attack from men with heavy firepower.

With that in mind, Junior turned off the lights in his mini truck and pulled over to the side of the dirt road before it intersected with the identical road that led to the entrance of the McDaniels ranch. The moment he stepped out of his truck, he immediately smelled the smoke. Not a good sign at all, he thought to himself.

Herbert Junior Pilane had joined the police force two years earlier as a constable. He joined at that rank, the lowest in the force, because he had not fared well in his Junior Certificate National Examinations. That meant promotion in the near future was going to be extremely hard to come by, and Herbert Pilane was an extremely ambitious young man. By all accounts, he was a very dedicated young officer. Always first at the station and last out. He volunteered for every assignment in front of him and then some, and his bosses loved him. There had been some rumblings lately that a promotion to sergeant was a possibility.

When rumors like that started floating around, that only meant he had to double his efforts, seize the initiative when the time came, and be on the lookout for any opportunity that would catapult him to promotion. The fire he saw at the McDaniels ranch and the smoke he smelled even from close to half a mile away, compounded by what he believed to be gunfire, was in fact a possible initiative he may have to seize. Besides, the McDaniels were pillars of the community, international celebrities who had cast his nation in the limelight countless times. Checking out to see they were okay could hardly hurt his aspirations. Indeed, if there was trouble, and he was the first to respond, and doing that on his own could propel him.

To minimize his profile, the young constable crouched on one knee, whipped out his police-issued mobile phone that also doubled as a two-way radio and did not encounter the same issues as a cell phone needing a cell phone tower to connect calls would, something that was very difficult to do when on the McDaniels ranch. And as luck would have it, a cell phone tower was scheduled to be erected close to the McDaniels ranch the following month. His plan was to report his suspicions to the police station he'd just left.

Even though they're trained in all aspects of combat, policemen in Botswana do not carry firearms, much less low-ranking constables, unless of course in special circumstances. It is only the elite unit within the police force known as the Special Support Group (SSG) who carry firearms at all times and are called in situations where the bad guys are armed and likely to fight back.

Junior's instincts told him that this was probably a situation that warranted SSG intervention. With a racing heart, he debated with himself whether to make the call or not. It took a lot to mobilize the unit. Junior would have to call his immediate supervisor, who in turn would go up the chain of command until all was ready to go was in play. Given that it was late at night, there would be a few angry people if it turned out that the call was for naught, and in the process he would torpedo his promotion.

If, on the other hand, he suspected foul play and did not report it and then it was later found out that he was in a position to do something about it but did not, was a situation or scenario he could not even begin to contemplate, let alone imagine – that's how bad it was.

"To hell with it," Junior Pilane said to himself. He was following the old axiom: it was better to be safe than sorry. He pressed the speed dial button on his phone.

When the night duty officer answered, Junior immediately identified himself and hissed, "Get me Inspector Keagile on the double. I have reason to believe that the McDaniels ranch is under attack."

This got the night duty police officer's full and undivided attention. The McDaniels name was huge in

Maun. In spite of that, it took almost five full minutes before the young Pilane was finally patched through to the captain, and in as calm a voice as he could muster, he explained in glowing detail what he saw, heard, and suspected. He embellished a little at times because he was not certain about what exactly was happening.

The captain listened patiently. Gunfire, especially the continuous type, was not something you heard about all the time in that part of the country; that is if Constable Herbert Pilane's report was to be believed. And the captain, John Mosimanegape Keagile, a twenty-two-year veteran of the force, had no reason to suppose otherwise.

Following a lengthy silence after Junior was done talking, Captain Keagile said, "Pilane, I want you to listen carefully."

"Yes, sir."

"This could be an extremely dangerous situation, and I want you to stay out of sight and away from the ranch until help arrives. Mute your phone but keep it close. Am I understood, young man?"

"Yes, sir!"

The captain ended the call, and Junior was left alone in the dark to ponder his position. Captain Keagile had estimated that it would take another thirty to forty minutes before an armed response could be orchestrated. That was an eternity as far as the young constable was concerned, and for all he knew by the time the SSG was mobilized and dispatched, it would be too late. He decided to act unilaterally, in essence disregarding a direct order to stay put. Herbert Junior Pilane was following another tried and true cliché this time: It's better to ask for forgiveness than for permission.

***

"To hell with it," Junior spat as he looked around again. It was dark and he could still hear the gunfire, though now a bit sporadic.

With a thumping heart, he looked at the back of the driver's seat. He had no weapon, not even a knife. There was a lug wrench. It was no police revolver special or Glock 19 machine pistol, but it was better than nothing if that meant creeping up on an unsuspecting criminal. He made certain that the truck was well hidden before he silently trudged along the gravelly dirt road that lead to the McDaniels ranch.

As he silently plodded along the dirt road, the four-pronged lug wrench in hand, constantly looking around to make sure that there was no immediate threat, Junior spotted a truck parked in the bushes beside the road. Upon seeing it, he hit the ground on his belly. His heart was now pumping wildly as the adrenaline surged through his veins. He remained that way for a while as he fought to get his breathing under control, his head raised a few inches above the ground like a Mamba getting ready to strike.

There was someone in the car. He could tell because of a red orb that kept glowing on and off, which meant someone was smoking a cigarette in the dark cabin of the truck. This meant two things—the person was a lookout and also part of the raiding party, and was also awaiting their return. The truck was their getaway car apparently, and Junior thought if he could somehow disable the truck and the driver, that would buy time for the SSG's Strike Force to arrive before they escaped.

His mind made up, Junior crouched as he tiptoed toward the truck. He tapped the window on the driver's side, still crouched, and as the driver opened the door, the words "What the hell?" froze on his lips as Junior struck him with the lug wrench on the side of the head—not hard enough to crack his skull, but enough to knock him out as he fell back in the car like a log. Junior did not bother to check for a pulse as he reached for his handcuffs in his back pocket and used them to cuff the man to the steering wheel before he looked around the cab and on the floor and found the one thing he hoped he would locate, which was an AK-47 machine gun which had been spread on the victim's lap just moments ago. Junior Pilane was armed now as he quickly and silently trotted to the McDaniels ranch.

CHAPTER 21

"SPREAD OUT AND FIND THEM!" Sahili screamed.

The two brothers, Dumisani and Sasha, heard the voice of authority issue a command from inside the bedroom as his voice carried through the broken window. This was punctuated by the rambling of thunder. The brothers had been too preoccupied with staying out of the line of fire to realize that it was about to rain again at any moment.

"Find them!" the voice came again.

This time, from their hiding place among Natalie's vegetable garden, the brothers looked up to see a tall, sinewy man standing to the right side of the broken window. Even in the darkness they could tell that his hair was completely white, and that by the way he was barking orders and gesticulating frantically with both hands, the man was their leader and most definitely the enemy Dumisani and Sasha had been warned about.

"That has got to be Sahili," Dumisani murmured in his brother's ear.

"Yeah," Sasha agreed between gritted teeth.

The tears were still flowing as the brothers finally placed a face to the force of their rage. Sasha slid the other gun he had taken from the second man he killed and handed it to his brother.

As Dumisani looked around, wondering which direction would be the best to take in case their present position became too hot to defend, he said, "I won't be able to use this, Sasha," he gestured at the AK-47.

Breathing hard, Sasha said, "It's easy, just like the guns we use when we go hunting. Aim and shoot. Now, let's spread out."

Dumisani wondered about his injured wrist, and was about to say something about it but decided to not give it any more thought as Sasha showed him how to switch the assault rifle from automatic to single-fire. And then, as Sasha had suggested, they spread among the plants in Natalie's garden, mainly the maize stalks, which gave them ample cover. They watched quietly as the brigands leaped from the window one at a time, some of them from both sides of the house, weapons ready as they cautiously spread out in the garden, searching for their quarry.

Both Dumisani and Sasha watched as the men, close to twelve of them, silently approached. Their hearts were beating wildly. The man they really wanted was their leader—taking him out, they knew, was like crushing the head of the Mamba. But for some reason, Sahili seemed to be hanging back, ready to sacrifice a few men if need be. When the intruders were about fifteen feet away, Sasha opened fire. He squeezed the trigger, not pull, but squeeze and hit his man center of mass. He did not aim for the head, since he knew that head shots, though highly effective, could also be elusive.

Dumisani, in spite of his sprained wrist, followed suit, spraying his aim from left to right while Sasha went from right to left. In less than five seconds, six men fell to the ground while others, who had not been hit, upon realizing that they had walked straight into an ambush, dove to the ground, and rolled this way and

163

that. In less time than it took to think, the assailants realized that the McDaniels boys were not the sitting ducks they hoped they'd be.

The sound of return fire from the brothers attracted more men who were concentrated on the other end of the house. They had just finished laying waste to the McDaniels' servants and their families, among them the maid Nchadi, her husband, and their two toddling children. Even the long-time ranch hand, the ever-reliable Mr. Steven Selepe, had received a bullet in the forehead. It was clear that these men were on a mission of making sure that in the end, there would be no living witnesses to their crimes.

On seeing more men reinforce their flanks, Sasha gestured at his brother to spread out even further and said, "Engage to full auto, Dumi, and spray at anything that moves in our direction."

Dumisani and Sasha McDaniels were hunters in their spare time and over the years they had become quite adept at the art. This meant they usually hit what they aimed at. In spite of the seemingly overwhelming numbers against them, they were soon able to trim the number of the attackers to a somewhat manageable size. It all came down to ammunition. So, what they would do was switch their weapons to full automatic when they saw their enemies advancing and for the most part standing close to one another, revealing the fact that they were poorly trained or were once again underestimating the brothers. Not that Dumisani and Sasha were well-trained insurgents or anything close to that, but at least they knew not to stay close to one another in a gunfight. In doing so, you were setting yourselves up to be picked off like fish in a barrel.

After bringing a few down, the brothers would quickly and silently crawl or even roll to a different vantage point, switch to single fire, and continue their onslaught. After a while, it became apparent that their ammunition was running low and their target, Molo Sahili, was still out of sight, hidden somewhere they supposed amidst the debris that had once been their parents' bedroom. With this realization in mind, Sasha had an idea.

"Dumi," he hissed in a voice just above a whisper.

"Yeah?"

"Follow me," Sasha said.

Without another word, Dumisani, just like his brother, infantry crawled to the northern end of the large kitchen garden as fast and as silently as they could. Ever since they were toddling kids, Sasha was always the leader and his brother the follower, and it had nothing to do with race or a feeling of inferiority on Dumisani McDaniels' part. Dumisani trusted his brother's instincts, and Sasha was one of those rare people who had them in spades. That was the thing with intuition, Dumisani had come to realize. Some people were born with it, and some were not. Dumisani was gifted with the same, but not at the level of his brother's; Sasha was at an almost supernatural intensity.

However, what they did not realize was that at least two of Sahili's men had anticipated this maneuver long before and were perched in a tree lying in wait, from where they would pick the brothers apart with their high-powered sniper rifles.

Sasha was the first to emerge from the end of the garden amid the maize stalks, and his brother appeared a few meters to his left moments later. And just as the two snipers were about to fire their kill shots, they were hit from behind by a gunman they had absolutely no idea had them in his sights from the get-go and was waiting for the perfect opportunity, apparently it had, because he grunted with satisfaction as he watched the two men fall lifelessly to the ground like ripe fruit.

The brothers looked up in astonishment and out of the bushes, brandishing an assault rifle similar to one they had been carrying was someone they had never seen before. He was a clean-cut young man, unlike the thugs they had just encountered. Even from where he was, they could see the police badge he was flashing for them to see. The man was obviously a friend.

Forgoing any formalities, he said to them, "Quick, this way, follow me."

The brothers, their clothes and faces caked with mud, got up silently, and still crouched at the waist to reduce their profile and not make themselves easy targets, threw caution to the wind and followed the young stranger, not even entertaining the fact that this could be another one of the wily Sahili's elaborate traps.

"Who are you?" Dumisani asked the moment they caught up with him and were running eastward through the savanna that made up most of the McDaniels' ranch, heading toward the well.

"I am Junior Pilane, a constable with the Botswana Police."

The brothers exchanged a quick glance, and both said at the same time, "The police?"

"Yes," Junior said. "Off duty. I was on my way to my parents' farm when I saw the flames from the main road, not to worry," he continued. "I've called it in, and help should be arriving any minute now."

This was more than comforting to hear, because for all they knew, Sahili and his men were hot on their heels. On the other hand, Dumisani thought he had seen the young man before, which made him confident in believing that he was who he said he was.

"Just know that the bastards murdered our parents, and we think everyone else on the ranch," Dumisani lamented.

On hearing this, Junior Pilane stopped and said incredulously, "What?"

Even in the dark, the brothers could see the shock in his eyes.

"Yes," Sasha said as he fought back tears.

"I'm so sorry, guys, I wish I had the means to stop it," Junior said, panting. He then turned to run again, and the brothers followed, easily keeping up with him because running was something that they did all the time as part of their rigorous training routine.

"I know where their leader and the rest of them will be heading, and we will be waiting for them there. This time he'll be in for the surprise of his life," Pilane said.

It was at that moment when they heard the most beautiful sound of approaching helicopters, which they immediately pegged to be those of the vaunted Special Support Group of the police force. This was before they saw two of them coming from the north and flying low as they made for the McDaniels ranch.

CHAPTER 22

IT DID NOT TAKE LONG before they reached an opening among the bushes and came across a hidden Toyota Hilux truck in the savannas near the dirt road that lead to the McDaniels ranch, where it intersected with the main one that ran north to south. North is where it headed to Maun, and south to the neighboring farms. The truck, a four-wheel bakkie, as it was known in these parts of the country, was well hidden in the bushes beside the intersection. The three men with Junior Pilane in the lead approached it with caution, and as silently as humanly possible.

Sasha and Dumisani were a few steps behind the constable, still wondering what all this meant. Junior then raised his fist, signaling the brothers to stop, a signal they immediately understood and did as instructed and looked around. The young constable then spread his fingers. The brothers understood the gesture to mean that they should fall to the ground by taking cover, and spread out. This they did as they hid among the shrubs and watched Junior slowly approach the bakkie, gun raised, and then with his other hand open the passenger door of the truck. The interior light revealed a man handcuffed to the steering wheel with his head slumped on it.

It dawned on the two that the driver had been incapacitated, most likely by Junior. They understood at once that this was the getaway vehicle that belonged to the marauders. And they also realized that they could be returning at any moment. Junior beckoned after realizing that there was no immediate threat, and the brothers appeared from unexpected hideouts on either side of the truck. The young constable was visibly impressed. These two were no ordinary civilians, which meant that the stories he had heard about them were true.

"Listen up," he hissed the moment the brothers were close by. "I manhandled this guy earlier on when I realized that your home was under attack, so chances are we will be having company very soon. Do you understand?"

"Yes, sir!" Sasha and Dumisani answered at the same time.

"I have already disabled this car, so it's not going anywhere. What we're going to do is wait right here, and set a trap for whoever comes. We can't just assume that all of them will be apprehended. My gut tells me that a few will escape or already have – chances are it will be their leader and a few of his cohorts."

The brothers agreed. During their mad dash through the bushes they had heard sporadic gunfire the moment they heard the helicopters land on their parents' property, but now the gunfire had since long ago ceased. So, they did as instructed. With Junior Pilane in the lead, they lay flat on their bellies among the long grass a few feet from the bakkie, and with thumping hearts, they waited.

It did not take long before they heard the sound of several footsteps in the dark of at least two men running mightily toward the hidden truck. Whoever it was, was secure in the knowledge that the bakkie was safe and that they would make a clean getaway.

"Wait until they're all in the car," Pilane instructed in a loud whisper. "Scratch that," he said, changing his mind. "Wait until they're almost at the truck. They will be distracted by the unconscious driver, and that's when we'll make our move, and not a moment sooner. Am I understood?"

The brothers simply nodded, indicating that they did indeed understand. On the other hand, Junior Pilane was impressed and in a way pleased with himself. As a constable, he took orders all day and every day. It was nice for a change to be issuing them finally, albeit to civilians. The McDaniels brothers began controlling their breathing to calm their racing hearts and not be overwhelmed by excitement or even an unhealthy dose of fear, which they knew could be detrimental.

The tears were long gone, but they knew they would be back as soon as the grief of losing their beloved parents in a matter of minutes hit and hit hard. Right now, it was about retribution, the pleasure of putting a bullet between the eyes of the rogues who had murdered their parents in cold blood. And just as that thought crossed their minds, two men broke out of the savannas and ran toward the bakkie to what, they assumed, was freedom. Even in the dark they could tell that one was older and the other a bit younger.

Molo Sahili! The brothers knew at once, and it took great strength to stop themselves from opening fire the moment they made the connection.

"Thapelo!" they head Sahili shout just loud enough to be heard. "Start the engine." He was clearly out of breath. The years in prison, it appeared, had taken their toll. No longer was he the fit young man who could

170

keep a steady pace ahead of even some of his best runners.

When the man called Thapelo did not respond, he increased his pace and quickly yanked the driver's side door angrily as he carelessly tossed his weapon, an automatic handgun it would later turn out to be, on the truck bed. Thapelo's head was slumped on the steering wheel and it looked like he was asleep. Sahili cussed under his breath. This was unbelievable, and the driver would need to be taught a painful lesson. He was about to shake the driver when suddenly he thought of something and called out to his companion, standing a few feet away and looking around to make sure everything was okay.

"Advent," he called out to the younger man. "You make sure …"

However, the rest of his words froze on his lips.

"Stay right where you are, Sahili!" Junior Pilane's voice cut through the darkness like a sharp blade.

The poacher froze as he looked around, trying to discern from which direction the menacing command came. The younger man who had accompanied him also froze dead in his tracks and was about to turn around and skedaddle, but the sound of several clicks from what seemed like a couple of other automatic rifles reminded him that that would not be a good idea at all.

"That goes for you too, young blood. You think of making for the forest, and I'll pump you full of holes, you understand?"

He did, because just like his boss, he knew that the rigadoon was up as he slowly raised his hands above his head, his weapon also long since discarded. And then just as suddenly, the McDaniels brothers stepped out from their hiding places, their weapons aimed at the two fugitives. Sahili, his hands still up in the

171

universal gesture of surrender, took a furtive peek at his driver, who supposedly had been waiting for their return upon causing havoc at the McDaniels ranch. Pilane could only guess what the poacher was thinking and gladly filled in the blanks for him.

"Don't worry about him, you sack of goat shit. He's not going anywhere, least of all drive you to freedom." The taunt in Pilane's voice was unmistakable and so was the pride, and he had every reason to be – he had collared a big one that was surely going to fast-track him to sergeant. This was the kind of arrest every law enforcement officer dreamed about.

Sahili and his accomplice stared at the constable and then at the two brothers, who were slowly approaching them, guns aimed at their chests. For the veteran poacher, it was a sense of *déjà vu* as he recalled a similar incident that happened over twenty years ago.

"B-but how?" Sahili managed to blurt out before he could stop himself. This raid had been planned to the last possible detail, taking into account every possibility, like avoiding capture – *how* had he been so badly outflanked?

"Rule number one," Pilane said, still keeping his eyes on the two men, his finger on the trigger and ready to squeeze a few rounds if Sahili and his companion were stupid enough to make any sudden moves. "Well, rule number one is that you do not, and I repeat *do not* leave your getaway vehicle out in the open and easy to find, because that's exactly what happened."

As he approached the two men, Sasha and his brother were suddenly facing the opposite direction, making counterclockwise moves, scouring the surrounding bushes to make certain that no more of Sahili's men would be coming. Sahili, on the other hand, was still racking his brains wondering again how a plan that had taken twenty-one years of scheming and dreaming could have gone so badly array. Was there yet another traitor like that bastard Patrick Lefatshe in his midst? He was forced to wonder.

He had gotten away with murder the last time, basically on a technicality if truth be told, for it had been John Ntemwa who had faced the gallows. This time, he knew, he would have no such luck – not with the blood of two renowned documentary filmmakers on his hands. There was no escaping the hangman's noose this time. His life as he knew it was gone.

***

The plan to ambush the McDaniels residence was supposed to have been simple and straightforward. Paul McDaniels and his reputation of being a savvy and tenacious documentary filmmaker preceded even him, and for Sahili to implement his grand plan of exporting stolen ivory and human trafficking, the McDaniels and in particular Paul would have to be taken out. His base of operation, the Caprivi Strip, was to be his launching pad where he would orchestrate his attack first on the McDaniels and then later on the elephant population of the country. That was the plan at least and his capture had, as far as he could tell from his present predicament, laid waste to all those intentions.

After sending his spies, among them his trusted lieutenant Advent Monyatsiwa, he was able to determine that the McDaniels residence, in fact a ranch, was on the outskirts of the village town. It was about twenty miles away from the nearest Police Station. Even better, he was able to determine later, was that cell phone signals were spotty at best, but for the most part nonexistent because a cell tower had yet to be built even though one was in the works. This meant that the police would be the only threat to impeding his attack, and by the time the law had any inkling about what was going on, he and his men would be long gone and a major thorn on Sahili's side would cease to be a problem forever.

Further surveillance of the McDaniels ranch was to prove that the documentary filmmaker did not have any kind of security at all, not even guard dogs. To seek help, they would have to make a phone call via their landline. An attempt that would be rendered moot if the wire was cut a few minutes before the actual assault.

With all this intelligence at his disposal, Sahili picked a time and day to launch his attack on the McDaniels ranch. He was also very much aware, and so were his men, that Paul McDaniels and his two sons, Sasha and Dumisani, were exponents of the martial arts. As a result, his men were under strict orders to shoot them on sight, and under no circumstances try to engage them in hand-to-hand combat. Everyone, except perhaps Advent, was given that order, and only as a last resort, because Advent's job was to watch Sahili's back at all times. His main objective, if there ever was one so crucial, was to take a bullet for his boss if need be. This, however, was one decree Advent was not certain he would carry out if the time came, because just like his boss, he was into self-preservation.

For days on end, Sahili's men kept an eye on the McDaniels. There were fifteen men in all assigned to this mission. Molo Sahili, since he was a prohibited immigrant, or P.I. as it was sometimes known, kept out of sight while his men conducted the reconnaissance.

They watched the McDaniels brothers enter the Sedia Riverside Hotel, even while they interacted with the beautiful women whom they made to be American tourists.

They heard about the altercation with the Afrikaners. The Sahili spies did not get to witness the actual fight, for fear of giving themselves away, since it happened in the men's room. They did, however, witness the Afrikaners carried out in stretchers and rushed to the hospital in an ambulance, and by the time the police arrived to interview onlookers, the brothers had simply vanished. All this was repeated to Sahili in real time via cell phones. Their leader was at the moment cooped up at a safe house in the village, ready to pounce when the moment came.

The assault was planned for that very evening. Rain clouds had been gathering since late that morning, and the master poacher welcomed this respite, because that would give them perfect cover when it came time to execute their raid. By this time, though, Sahili had studied the McDaniels routine to a point that he could almost recite it in his sleep.

The servants started preparing dinner at around 6:30 pm and served it promptly at 7:30pm, at which time the entire family would be seated at the dining room table. That was when they would be absolutely vulnerable. When that happened, his men were to slowly move into position, like morning fog, hours before the actual attack was planned. They had been arriving in twos and threes all day, so as not to arouse suspicion, and positioning themselves around the McDaniels ranch at strategic locations to stay hidden in the bushes, where they remained until they got word from their leader via short-range walkie-talkies that it was time to attack.

The fact that they did not have any dogs on the ranch told Sahili where Paul McDaniels' thinking was as far as the safety of his family and workers were concerned. Besides not having dogs, the man did not even have any kind of alarm system to protect the main house. Not that these, dogs, and an alarm system, would have stopped a motivated intruder like himself, but at least it would have slowed them down a bit. A delay, no matter how slight, could mean the difference between life and death in situations like this.

Besides, Sahili thought sardonically, didn't he warn this man many years ago that he would one day come for his revenge? He'd made it known to the American that he was a foreigner who was poking his nose in affairs that did not concern him. Lastly, and this took the cake, McDaniels had released that film to the world that documented Sahili and his men arranging transportation of the tusks they had taken from the elephants and rhinos they killed, and their capture, all caught on film. By so doing, didn't the American know that he had, with that act alone, created an enemy who would keep coming until one of them was dead?

Paul McDaniels, Sahili decided, had clearly underestimated his foe. Never mind the fact that his sworn enemy had been locked up for almost two decades at the infamous maximum security prison in Gaborone. The fact that he had not been executed, like Ntemwa, and really as he should have been had the prosecution been able to point to his guilt without a shadow of doubt, meant that that colossal mistake the Botswana government had made was about to be paid back in a big and bloody way.

CHAPTER 23

SAHILI HAD LONG DECIDED that the best time to attack was when the McDaniels were at the dinner table. That way their guard would be down, and an all-out attack of such a magnitude would be the last thing on their minds. At the dining room table, McDaniels and his sons would be far from their firearms. He knew that they kept their hunting rifles in a special closet in the living room that was always locked when not in use, and the fact that his sons were excellent marksmen. They hunted big game like kudu, antelope, and occasionally gemsbok when it was open hunting season.

To add to his advantage, one of the McDaniels sons, the black one, Dumisani, had his arm in a sling thanks to an altercation that had happened earlier on at the Sedia Riverside Hotel. Advent had been among the men Sahili had sent to spy on the McDaniels brothers the moment they picked their scent at the hotel, and had mentioned that the fight had been over some American girls who happened to be tourists over details he deemed unnecessary, except for the fact that the black McDaniels was hurt and most importantly would not be able to handle a firearm effectively on the chance that he could get to one during the raid.

Their assault was supposed to work like a charm. Sahili had divided his men into three groups of five, with a few men in reserve and another waiting with the getaway vehicle. The leader of each group had a walkie-talkie on which he could communicate with the other attack team. They then waited, and the moment their leader yelled the command "Go!" two groups rushed to the house from diagonally opposite sides, one man in each armed with a Molotov cocktail, one of which was thrown through the dining room window, and the other through the living room window, causing complete chaos in the process as intended.

The third group was to rush to the back of the main house where the servants, their families, and a few of the ranch hands, including the ever dependable Mr. Steven Selepe, lived, with orders to kill them all and leave no one alive. Everyone, including and especially the McDaniels, were to be killed – that was Sahili's order, and one that could not be contravened no matter what.

It is always believed that the less complicated the plan, the most straightforward it is, the better. Rushing the McDaniels home without further hurdles by just sheer number and most effective of all, the element of surprise, was more than enough as far as Sahili was concerned. Attack the home, overpower the occupants, riddle them with bullets was all it would take, and be gone before anyone could do anything about it. However, even the simplest, well-laid plans can go haywire in a way that can leave the perpetrator flabbergasted. Perhaps someone should have reminded the veteran poacher of that.

No matter how carefully laid a plan of attack may be, there's always the unknown, the unseen, the unscheduled, like the intervention of a young police constable who just happened to be on his way to see his parents at their farm a few miles south of the McDaniels ranch. In operations such as these, this phenomenon is known as the '*X-Factor*', and Sahili and his men were to get a healthy dose of it.

Thanks to a booming economy prompted by the discovery of an AIDS vaccine and crude oil by a local medical scientist, Dr. Solomon Zimu, whose proceeds increased the gross domestic product (GDP) by over 300% and counting, which began during Sahili's incarceration, the police force and many institutions like it were well funded and equipped. Their training and technological expertise had increased exponentially as well, which meant the force had, among many other new things, a quick reaction team that had access to battle-ready and tested helicopters.

So when Junior Pilane notified his captain about possible trouble at the McDaniels ranch, the latter being celebrities in their own right who had given a lot back to their adopted country and community, the birds filled with members of the Special Support Group in full combat gear, were already on their way by the time Sasha and Dumisani were holding their own in their mother's garden.

After putting down a few of Sahili's men and then later assisted by the young constable, who appeared from nowhere, they wondered where he was leading them until they arrived at the open-canopied Toyota Hilux bakkie, which as Pilane soon explained was the brigand's getaway vehicle, and after securing their position they laid in wait for whoever would show up. As of yet, Pilane had not reported his current position or that he was with the McDaniels boys who happened to be safe and sound. He was milking his advantage for all the glory he could get at the moment.

Meanwhile, at the McDaniels home and the surrounding ranch, Sahili and his men were scouring the area looking for the McDaniels brothers. When one of his men asked why they were exerting so much time in doing so when in truth the main objective of killing Paul McDaniels was realized, and in the process risking being seen or worse still captured when they should have left, Sahili's answer was, "When you find a snake with its babies, you kill it, because if you don't, one day those baby snakes will grow to be big snakes, which in turn will bite you."

It was while they were trying to do just that when the entire place lit up from above as the two low-flying helicopters closed in, one from the north and the other from the south, their high-powered search beams pointed at the mayhem below. Some of Sahili's men, out of sheer panic, one would imagine, tried to fire at the helicopters, but the rounds from their automatic rifles did not even make a dent in the armored exterior of the American-made Sikorsky-UH-60 Black Hawk helicopters.

To make matters worse for Sahili and his men, the unit deployed, the vaunted SSG, were trained for such situations. The birds circled around the burning homes, whose fire was beginning to subside thanks in large part to the rain that had been pouring intermittently.

"*Put down your weapons*!" a voice from a megaphone announced from one of the choppers, and just to make certain that their message was understood, they repeated it in Setswana. That way none of the malcontents could say they were not warned if they got hurt or killed. That was on the small chance this ended in a courtroom. The men froze as they looked up and around, and the loud voice from the circling chopper continued, "*There is nowhere to run, you're all surrounded. Comply now or be shot to smithereens, this is your last warning*!" The voice and its intended threat carried over the rotor wash.

The men looked up again, and sure enough saw a man dressed in jungle fatigue gear at each of the door guns of the chopper, aiming the deadly duo gun at them and itching to fire. Both men had helmets on with lip mikes attached, which meant they could clearly hear the kill order if it was given.

All this time, Molo Sahili and his sidekick, Advent Monyatsiwa, were hidden in the kitchen area of the McDaniels home. The rest of his men, besides Advent for now, meant nothing to him. They were just cannon fodder as far as he was concerned. For an equivalent of fifty dollars U.S. per head, he could in a month or two recruit a fresh conscript of at least twenty, train them better this time, and go after the McDaniels boys.

"Fire at the helicopters. Bring them down, and don't let them catch any of you alive!" Sahili screamed at his men.

He mentally kicked himself for not bringing his grenade launcher, even though in all fairness it would have been like trying to cover a rabbit hole with a bulldozer for a mission like this. Now he was thinking he would have used a grenade to blow up the McDaniels while they were having dinner and be done with it. A job that would have required two people at the most and be gone, and none would be the wiser. But no, he had wanted to look into Paul McDaniels' eyes before firing a bullet in between them, or riddle his face so he had a closed casket if one of his men got to him first. In his mind, vengeance must always be absolute, and vengeance must be profound.

Nevertheless, Sahili had to wonder how the police responded so quickly when he himself was certain that all communication to the outside world, much less the police, had been cut off. Surely Thapelo, his man at the rendezvous point who awaited their return, should have warned them. The poacher had to admit that just like them, Thapelo must have been taken by total surprise. The helicopters had flown in silently, lights off, and only announced their presence the moment they arrived at their target – them.

It was time to make his escape. The instant his men started firing at the helicopters, he gestured at Advent to follow him. Using the confusion to their advantage, they crawled through the kitchen, then the living room, all of which were still blazing from the fire, and before long they were outside and out of range from the helicopter searchlights. *Good*, he thought, his men were keeping them busy. The SSG men were beginning to rope down to the ground, picking their targets with remarkable accuracy that before long, and just as the last SSG man, all of whom were clad in state-of-the-art body armor, hit the ground, the surviving Sahili men had since laid their weapons on the ground and raised their hands high above their heads in surrender. Fighting these elite warriors was suicide, and just like their leader, these men were very much into self-preservation.

*** *

The short battle of his men against the SSG was a welcome reprieve for Sahili and Advent, because by the time his men capitulated, he and Advent had made it to the surrounding forest and raced toward where they expected to find Thapelo waiting. For a man already in his early 60s, Sahili was quite fit and nimble, even in the dark, and it took everything his much younger and trusted accomplice had to keep up. And when they finally arrived at the rendezvous point where the getaway vehicle was supposedly waiting for their return, the two men were dealt the biggest surprise of their lives.

CHAPTER 24

"STAY RIGHT WHERE YOU ARE, SAHILI, or I'll blow your head off!" Pilane warned again. "You even look at me sideways and you're dead, is that understood?"

Sahili, his hands still up in the air, nodded. He was chiding himself for getting rid of his weapon when he carelessly tossed it at the back of the truck. Even in the dark he could still see the chrome snub-nosed .357, and glanced longingly at it. He must have made some subtle subliminal move toward it, because suddenly the dirt at his feet was riddled with bullets from an automatic rifle.

"I know what you're thinking," the young constable said. "Make another move and the next bullet will be in your kneecap, and believe me, old geezer, it's going to hurt real bad. So please try me, because for once I would love to hear you scream with pain, you murdering swine," he spat.

When he was certain that the threat was well understood, he pulled out his cell phone. At this particular place, a little over half a mile from the McDaniels ranch, coverage was spotty, which meant it was hit or miss, but the special police mobile phones had a strong signal that could ping cell phone towers much further away, the nearest which was in the middle of the village town. This meant Junior Pilane would have no trouble reaching his colleagues. Without taking his eyes from the two captives who still had their hands up in the air, he made the most important call of his career – the call that would most likely give him that big promotion he had dreamed of.

Apparently his colleagues were still scouring the surrounding bushes, looking for any remnants of the Sahili gang, when they got the startling call from the low-ranking officer, who had been off duty of all things. Whoever he spoke to promised to be at the scene as quickly as humanly possible, and that more men were on their way from the main precinct in Maun.

All this time, Sahili's cohort, the young Advent Monyatsiwa, hands still in the air, had been eyeing the two brothers constantly. First Sasha and then Dumisani, and back to Sasha again. The brothers were well known to him, especially Sasha McDaniels, who had been active in the martial arts tournament circles for quite some time.

Sasha could read a challenge in the other man's eyes in spite of his hopeless situation. He knew why, and the other half of the McDaniels brothers was more than willing to oblige him. What was more, he needed an outlet for the anger and grief that was slowly seeping its way from his into his veins and into his soul. This bastard had more than a hand in his parents' death. As the two sized one another like cobras ready to strike, increasingly members of the SSG and other squad members from the main police station kept arriving like a pack of hungry hyenas to a kill.

As more and more vehicles arrived and the two helicopters hovered above, the ambush scene was suddenly lit up. It would not be long, one of the policemen at the scene thought, before the media and in particular the lone TV station of the village town got wind of this. It would all be riding on the bravery of the young constable Junior Pilane, who disregarded orders to stay put until help arrived and decided to go at it alone, in the process saving the brothers' lives, not to mention impeding the escape of a notorious criminal.

Meanwhile, the stare-down between Advent and the brothers, especially with Sasha, continued. Even as Advent was being handcuffed behind his back, the mad-dogging continued.

"What?" Sasha said as he took a step toward him.

"I remember you," Advent said with a bit of a sneer. "Three years ago, at the tournament in Gaborone at the Grand Palm Hotel. We faced off in the semifinal. I beat you fair and square and the referees gave you the win because you are white, nothing more. We both know that I was the better fighter."

Now, this was funny to a point that Sasha had to chuckle in spite of the circumstances. It clicked in Sasha's mind why the young bandit and murderer looked familiar, but that was beside the point, because either the man had a terrible case of amnesia or he was in some sick, twisted way trying to goad Sasha into a fight. And why not? Sasha thought the man's life as he knew it was over, so why not have a little fun while he had a chance, right? It was true though, Sasha recalled, the two did face off in the semifinals of the National Karate Championship. A title that was eventually won by one Tidwell 'Teddy' Modise.

But then again, to even suggest that Advent had beaten him in that semifinal match, and for him to indicate that a victory for Sasha had been manufactured simply because of the color of his skin, was just plain ludicrous. The fight actually had to be stopped midway because it was a three-point tournament. Sasha McDaniels had scored six unanswered points before the three-minute bout elapsed, which made him the clear winner, basically by a technical knockout. This after neutralizing Advent Monyatsiwa's greatest strength – his spectacular kicks were arguably better some would say, plus he was a far more versatile fighter than his opponent, who happened to be very one-dimensional. This meant you take away his strength, you got him where you wanted. He did also recall a rumor that Advent was an ex-convict who had served a little over seven years in prison for some crime Sasha could not readily recall.

By the time the other officers and members of the elite unit arrived at the scene, Sahili was immediately secured and handcuffed behind his back, just like his prodigy and the remnants of his gang who had been captured and not killed. They were placed in the back of two police trucks fitted with mesh wire where the windows were supposed to be, and were getting ready to be transported to the main jail in Maun, where they would be booked.

Constable Herbert 'Junior' Pilane was getting his fair share of pats on the back for a job well done. Even his immediate supervisor, Sub Inspector Cornelius 'Think Tank' Baruti, also present at the scene, offered his hearty congratulations. He did advise the young man that even though what he did went above and beyond gutsy, it would serve him well going forward not to make it a habit to disregard a direct order. That said, the sub inspector was going to highly recommend to the captain that he be promoted to sergeant after all this was done. The future looked bright for the young man.

Meanwhile, an interesting scenario was brewing between Sasha McDaniels and the captive, whom he estimated to be about ten years older or slightly younger but still in superb shape. The name slowly came to him: Advent Monyatsiwa, who just like him and his brother was a very capable martial artist. It now occurred to both brothers that after that tournament, Advent fell off the grid and was not seen again. Now they knew why.

Pilane was given the honors of formally charging and arresting Advent after the rest had been packed in the two trucks with their boss. He said, "You're under arrest for the murder of Paul and Natalie McDaniels, and a whole lot of other people we have yet to identify at the ranch."

At the mention of their parents' names, Sasha and Dumisani had to be restrained from lunging at the cocky and seemingly uncaring outlaw who showed not even an iota of remorse at what he had done, or at the very least had been part of in a big way. It became apparent that everything was under control as far as the remnants of the Sahili gang were concerned, because members of the SSG began arriving at the scene on state-of-the-art dune buggies that could travel on any terrain. Again, thanks in main part to a police force that like many institutions the nation over had all the funding they needed.

The vehicles and the dune buggies were soon parked in a circular formation at the arresting site that was lit up like a Hollywood movie set, with Advent Monyatsiwa, hands handcuffed behind his back, seated in the middle like an elusive animal that had finally been captured.

Yes, this had been Constable Herbert Junior Pilane's collar, his arrest, and he had no doubt caught a big one in Molo Sahili. A man who had obviously not learned from his almost twenty-year incarceration, and had come back for some misguided and twisted revenge over a man who was just doing his job back in the day, over twenty-two years earlier, by documenting his capture on film. Paul McDaniels had not provided the intelligence that had led to Sahili and his fellow brigand's hideout, nor had he planned and executed the operation that had finally led to his capture. All that had been done by then-lieutenant Frederick Motang, now a brigadier general.

Paul McDaniels and his trusted guide and tracker, Sam Xaraga, who by the way had been killed in the takedown by one of Sahili's henchmen, had been present to show the world that Botswana cared about her wildlife, especially its elephants and rhinos, which were on the brink of extinction on the entire continent, and that the government would do everything in its vast power to protect these precious animals.

Sahili was lucky the first time around in that he had escaped the death penalty, but instead got what under the circumstances was a paltry twenty-two-year sentence. What many of these law enforcement men were thinking that night was that Sahili, if he was smart, which given his background he certainly was, had some money stashed away in some bank accounts no government could reach. After his release, he should have gotten his money, dirty as it was, cut his losses, and retired to some remote corner of the world. He should have fallen to his knees and thanked the God he did not believe in, and retired in peace in case someone in his not-so-distant past discovered another charge that had no statute of limitations, like murder, linked it to him with irrefutable proof, and came looking for him. The psycho just didn't get it.

Instead, he had corrupted younger men like this Advent Monyatsiwa, once a promising lad with a bright future ahead of him, they found out, because in their vehicles they had mobile computers attached to the dashboard that could link up with local satellites, and bring up his background information in real-time.

Botswana was fast becoming a first-world nation, thanks in no small part to the Zimu Space Program that had launched three satellites into space, known also as the Zimu Satellites, so they could pull up his entire file and life history. Sure enough, the once young man had received a raw deal in his sentencing for attacking the white man who had been his boss to a point of almost cracking his skull wide open, but mitigating circumstances were enough to suggest that the fifteen-year sentence he got as a result was a bit on the punitively unforgiving side.

That sentence did not rehabilitate him, in spite of the fact that he was let out after serving almost half the sentence for good behavior. Instead it had turned him into a maniacal criminal, angry at society at large and ready to exact vengeance on anyone unlucky to cross his path, like the McDaniels couple and their servants. How many more victims lay in his wake? There were two more right there with him, and instead of cowering, hanging his head in shame, he remained as defiant as ever, even daring the white brother to a challenge. Nothing was exchanged verbally, but the men were astute enough to see it in his eyes. That was when one of the officers came up with an idea—and the others, mischievous and eager for a treat, decided to back him up.

"So, you say Sasha McDaniels did not beat you at a tournament two years ago? Is that what you are saying?" the impish Sergeant Steven Moepi said, smiling. He was a known prankster at the precinct, and every one of his colleagues and subordinates, including Junior Pilane, loved him.

Advent, who was seated on the ground, his hands shackled behind his back as he waited to be loaded into one of the trucks to soon be transported to the station in Maun, suddenly perked up.

"Oh yes, I beat this white boy fair and square. He won only because the referee kept getting in my way."

Moepi smiled. *This is good, this is good,* he thought to himself. After all, he could always step in if things got out of control.

"What do you say, Sasha? Are you going to let that insult go unanswered?" he smiled at the young man. Please say yes. For once I would like to see someone kick that annoying smirk off this piece of shit's face.

Sasha could feel his cheeks burn as the anger seeped through his body and his face flushed, but not to a point that it could be noticed in the dark. However, if this was headed where he thought it was, he knew that anger would be a big detriment. He would need a clear mind.

"This lying murderer is having a wet dream," Sasha said. "Why don't you uncuff him, and let's settle this once and for all?"

Sasha McDaniels was never one to start a fight, but he was not someone who ran from one, either.

Noticing the change on his brother's face, Dumisani, his right hand back in a sling again after being checked on by the police medic, decided to step in and thrust his left arm forward across his brother's belly to stop him before things really spun out of control.

"Come on, Sasha, this piece of crap is not worth it. Can't you see what he's trying to do?" said Dumisani.

"This piece of human refuse, Dumi, had more than a hand in murdering our parents. This may be the only chance we may have to exact a bit of personal revenge for both of us. Come on, Dumi, let me teach this son of a bitch a lesson."

His brother nodded and stepped back, letting Sasha go ahead and accept the challenge. The police officers who were gathered around were now watching these developments with peaked interest, and as word got around, more men came forward, even those who were behind the steering wheels of the pickup trucks that were about to transport the prisoners to the station, though some SSG men stayed put and aimed their weapons at the surrounding bushes just in case this had been another one of the clever ruses by the poacher to distract them from an ambush of some sort.

Some of the men were not too pleased about this proposed gladiator-like fight. The most prudent thing would have been to load up and leave as quickly as possible. Out here they were in the open and thus vulnerable, in spite of the fact that they were heavily armed and the helicopters above kept watch on things. All these elite law enforcers were well versed in the doctrine of ambush, a tactic that was very effective in guerilla warfare.

You see, ambushes were set up in one of three ways. The first, and the most common, was to lie in wait and spring the trap on the unsuspecting quarry. The way was to lure the target in. Act like you need help, and then when the target steps in to offer assistance, you have them right where you want them. The third and final way is to distract the target. Get them focused on one thing, and then hit them from somewhere else. At the moment this is what the SSG men were most worried about. This Advent fellow could be distracting them by offering to fight the McDaniels boy, so they had to remain alert. For all they knew there could be more of Sahili's men hiding, men that they and the birds above had missed who were ready to pounce. Nothing could be put past the crafty rustler.

In any case, many of the cops who had been arriving at the scene in droves and were not part of the SSG caught wind of what was brewing. Word was spreading that there could be a no-holds-barred fight between two well-trained martial artists, and in spite of themselves, the cops were eager to see this one go down. Before long, someone had the brilliant idea of taking wagers. For some reason, Advent Monyatsiwa was a 2-to-1 odds on favorite, these from some of the constables who had accompanied the initial attack by the SSG and had seen him in action before he vanished into the night with Sahili. Someone should have briefed them more about Sasha McDaniels.

Suddenly, there was loud and long maniacal laughter that came from the back of the police van that was fitted with mesh wire where the windows were supposed to be. It was from the bound and handcuffed Sahili. Apparently he had heard everything, and was watching these developments with amused interest.

Then just as suddenly, before anyone could ask what was tickling him, Sahili peeked through the mesh wire said, quite seriously in fact, "My boy Advent will tear that white boy apart to a point that you will be forced to shoot him the moment he does, and then make up a story thereafter, some crap that he caught a bullet while resisting arrest."

"Is that right?" the only ranking officer thus far, Stephen Moepi retorted with a smile of his own. He had been secretly collecting the wagers and was currently holding the purse strings.

His question was meant for Sasha McDaniels, who had since surrendered his weapon to one of the constables and was already stretching his limbs, ready for a no-holds-barred fight.

It was Sahili who answered, "Yes, I know for a fact. My boy is the best there is. In fact, he'll beat up that white boy so bad that his bastard brother will join in." The sound of his voice echoing in the interior of the police truck sounded as if he was speaking into an empty drum.

The man was truly a hardened criminal and murderer, the arresting officers thought. Here he was, arrested again after society showed him mercy the last time by not sending him to the gallows like he so richly deserved. Now they had multiple murders they could tie him to, and yet here he was, acting like he was in charge. Even for the two brothers, just hearing his voice caused their blood to boil.

When all was ready, and the prisoners secure and ready to be transported, Sergeant Moepi went over to where Advent had been forced to sit with his hands still cuffed behind his back and grabbed him by the elbow, forcing him to his feet. He then took a key out of his pocket and with it uncuffed him. And just like Sasha, Advent began stretching his limbs, showing off his trademark flexibility by first performing forward and then sideways splits, leg suspensions, twisting his neck this way and that, and finally, like a prizefighter began bouncing on the balls of his feet. He was ready.

The police vehicles and the dune buggies moved a little closer, and the circle became tighter with all their lights turned on. As both men entered the makeshift arena, Advent again impressed the onlookers with his flexibility. He raised first his right leg straight like a pole above his head and kept it there for close to thirty seconds, but to the spectators seemed like ten minutes, and then did the same with his left leg. Some men began hollering, and the bellowing rose to a fever pitch when Sasha McDaniels did the same before he shadow-boxed for a while to loosen his arms.

As Sasha stepped forward to face his opponent, Dumisani pulled him to the side and whispered in his ear, "Remember, Sasha, you're facing a guy who has nothing to lose. His next stop after you're through with him is the big house, where he probably will be facing the death penalty, and that makes him a very dangerous adversary. Brother, do not, and I repeat, *do not* underestimate him."

Sasha got what his brother was saying. This man had crossed them in ways no one ever could have, which means his emotions could get in the way of thinking clearly. What Sasha McDaniels had in mind, as more men gathered around, hollering and catcalling, more than eager to watch this cockfight, especially those who had weighed in their bets, was to hurt Advent Monyatsiwa bad. Should he kill him? Surely as an exponent of the martial arts, there were moves he could perform in a split second that could send him to his maker.

"Don't worry, Dumi," Sasha said. "I got this. The son of a bitch killed our parents or at least had a hand in doing so. I got this." He patted his brother on the back several times as he headed to what had become a makeshift arena ceremoniously lit with headlights from the circularly parked vehicles.

What the cops were doing was illegal, of course. The most prudent course of action would have been to load up the surviving captives, including Sahili, as they had done, and head to the police station and book them, but these men were not above bending the rules a bit and have some fun at the expense of these bandits who had attacked and almost wiped out an entire family, including their workers—innocent people, for that matter—and they wouldn't mind watching one of them take a beating. Of course, they would step in if at any moment they felt the McDaniels kid, whom they all heard was a very capable fighter, was on the receiving end of the beating they hoped would rain on Advent.

The two young men faced off at last, their torsos bare, flushed, and broad as one might expect from young men who took their physical training very seriously. It soon became clear that both fighters were 'kickers' due to their incredible flexibility and spectacular display of aerial roundhouse kicks, spinning jump kicks, and back kicks – in fact, everything in their vast arsenal was on full display with none getting the upper hand in the initial seconds. Every clash of bodies was met by a cheer from the onlookers who were keeping a close eye and ready to end it if they felt that the McDaniels kid was fading.

Almost a minute into the fight, which in reality is a lifetime, Sasha decided to adjust his style of fighting. He realized that front snap and spin kicks were ineffective against a fighter of Advent's capabilities and skill level, as the fellow was just too good. So far he had been able to counter everything Sasha had thrown at him, and at some point was backing him with his own barrage of front kicks, which were delivered with uncanny speed and precision, so much such that Dumisani almost joined in, but was stopped by a quick gesture from his brother telling him to back off and that he got this.

Sasha decided to resort to Thai boxing, a technique very common in mixed martial arts and Gracie Jiujutsu style. This was after he discerned that Advent Monyatsiwa, good as he was, and the guy was pretty good, was a one-dimensional fighter – he relied mainly on his kicks. If Sasha could take out that aspect of his fight, he would have him beat.

After thwarting a few of Advent's attacks, which were a front kick again, followed by a roundhouse kick—he was becoming the aggressor now, as he sensed that Sasha was waning a bit—Sasha countered by assuming the *Kibadashi* or 'horse riding stance' where the legs are spread wide, shoulder length, and squatted a little with his torso straight and solid, waiting for the next attack. It did not take long, and Advent did exactly what Sasha expected him to do.

He delivered another of the roundhouse kicks that had become trademark. Sasha pivoted on his left foot counterclockwise, which meant he was almost facing sideways when Advent's kick came, and stuck his elbow out, while the rest of his arm was curved toward his left hip. Monyatsiwa had been aiming for his kidneys, but instead the inside of his foot struck Sasha's elbow, one of the hardest parts of the body. The pain was horrific as it shot through his right leg like dye in water, rendering it totally useless, because now he could hardly put any weight on it as he staggered and hopped backward, cussing himself for falling so easily for the trap the white boy had laid for him.

Sasha knew exactly what his opponent was going to do next in less time than it took for most people to think, so this time he pivoted on his right foot as Advent, charged now with mad, red fury, attacked yet again. Perhaps it was because of the adrenaline that was still pumping through his bloodstream that he was not aware the wily Sasha McDaniels had baited him into yet another trap, which was very similar to the first because this time it was Advent's inside left foot that was met by the other hard elbow – now both legs, Advent's primary weapons, were useless.

From then on it was a field day for the other half of the McDaniels brothers as he beat Advent to jelly. He did not throw his punches and kicks in flurries but in timed, slow-motion sequences that carried the full weight of his power and grief. Even as Advent fell to the ground on his back, barely putting up a fight, Sasha went on his knees, Advent's belly now in between his legs, and pounded at his face. Now, because the brothers, whenever they performed their daily pushups, six hundred of them, at clips of fifty, they did them with their fists and fingers, so their hands were hard as granite. Thus each blow split Advent's face so that by the time Sergeant Moepi stepped in to put an end to this beat-down by pulling a screaming and weeping Sasha McDaniels away, Advent Monyatsiwa's face was no longer recognizable. It was grotesquely disfigured and one bloody mess.

CHAPTER 25

THE HOME THAT SASHA AND DUMISANI McDaniels grew up in was in shambles. The only house the brothers knew was burned almost to the ground, and the fact that it was thatched made matters worse. The roof had caved in, and according to the firemen still at the scene who had been dispatched, the damage could have been worse had it not been for the rain, the blessed rain that had poured in at intervals. Miraculously, the side that had been their parents' bedroom was still very much intact.

And this was where the brothers had rushed to the moment they were taken back to the scene by the remaining policemen, while the rest transported Sahili, a badly injured Advent Monyatsiwa, and the rest of the captives, under heavy escort, to the local police station with one of the police helicopters following above. Again, they did not put it past the crafty Sahili to have a contingency plan for a rescue attempt on their way to jail. They need not have fretted about that. The notorious poacher's organization was scattered to the four winds and in shambles. With the head decapitated, there was no way they could regroup and continue with their campaign of poaching, smuggling, and later human trafficking. The Sahili gang was put to rest at last. Add to that, even a few diehards had been scared off by the incredible firepower that had been brought to bear by the police and their vaunted elite unit, the Special Support Group.

The man should have left Paul McDaniels alone. The documentary filmmaker and his family posed no threat to the plans he had in place rather than reporting them, if and when he was caught, like what had happened twenty two years earlier. Yes, the American was world-famous, which in itself was dangerous. Taking out a man of that stature posed its own risks in that it would have brought unnecessary heat on an organization they were trying to bring to fruition. Advent had argued against attacking the McDaniels as passionately and as respectfully as he dared, but the poacher could not be swayed. Why this man Molo Sahili held such a vendetta against a man who had captured him on film over two decades earlier was beyond anyone's understanding, including his prodigy's.

Advent Monyatsiwa, his most loyal and to an extent '*Yes Man,*' had questioned his master's plan and purpose from the beginning. Paul McDaniels was just one man, and it would take more than that to bring down a syndicate as they had planned. Now here he was at the back of a police truck, being transported to a cold hell he had vowed to himself that he would die before returning to. To make matters worse, his jaw where several of that McDaniels' punches and a couple of kicks had landed, throbbed like nothing he had ever felt before in his life. That and every part of Advent Monyatsiwa's body ached; he even suspected that two of his ribs were either badly bruised or broken. And what's worse was that there was nothing he could do about it, because his hands and feet were shackled. *That white boy can sure pack a punch, can't he*? he thought wryly to himself.

As if reading his thoughts, one of the constables seated at the back of the truck to keep a close eye on the prisoners said, "That white boy got you good, didn't he?" He flashed a toothy, mischievous grin.

Advent did not answer, but instead looked outside at the coming dawn through the mesh wire and watched the trees as they sped past. He was finished, and he knew it.

***

Five days later, the two brothers stood forlornly by their parents' gravesite. Mourners had come from far and wide, even a representative from the Office Of The President was present to deputize the man himself. The service was held in a huge tent that had been pitched in front of the now-dilapidated home.

The brothers sat side by side in what could be called their 'Sunday's Best', dark suits with identical neckties. Their faces were grim as they gazed vacantly at the caskets that held their parents. It was inconceivable to them that this was it. They would never see their loving mom and dad ever again. Even as the preacher, Father Colin Lesley, an old family friend, gave the eulogy, people would come up to them and offer their heartfelt condolences, which were accepted with a subtle nod. It was well known that their parents were killed for what they truly believed in—the conservation of the nation's wildlife and the beautiful documentation of creatures in their environment. The McDaniels, Father Lesley said as he concluded his eulogy, were indeed a soft target if there ever was one.

Noticeably absent that day was Sean Kane McDaniels, their uncle. A onetime fighter now crusader, he was on one of his missions and no one knew where exactly. Their maternal grandparents had even made the journey from Mesa, Arizona, where they had retired to. Not present were Paul McDaniels' parents who had since died a long time ago, and other relatives were unknown to the brothers, so the only true closest relative was their absent uncle.

As the service went on, both brothers' minds drifted back to that dreadful night after Sahili, Advent, and the surviving marauders were booked and jailed. Sasha and Dumisani were led back to the ranch under heavy police escort. By the time they arrived, there were two fire trucks parked at the front and back of the decrepit home putting out what little fire was left.

Even though they did not feel like it, they forced themselves to enter their parents' bedroom where they knew the bodies still lay, since the local coroner had yet to arrive and were informed that he was on his way after being told that it was now safe to travel to the McDaniels ranch. The firemen and the police and now detectives who had been flown in from Francistown, let them be and instead waited for them before the bodies could be removed. The charred, bullet-riddled door to their parents' bedroom was still closed as the bothers stayed rooted in one spot, at least three feet from it, silently bracing themselves for the horror that they both knew awaited them on the other side.

When at last Sasha pushed the door open, the brothers stood frozen for what seemed like a full minute. The once clean, immaculate, and neatly kept humongous room that had been their parents' master bedroom, and sanctuary, looked like it had been hit by a bomb. Everything was upside down and strewn all over the place. Natalie McDaniels' priceless ornaments and other artifacts were smashed all over the burnt carpet. However, what made the brothers' breath catch was the smear of blood that led to the other end of the upturned king-sized bed.

The smear of blood, as it turned out, belonged to their father Paul McDaniels. Somehow, with superhuman strength and in spite of his mortal wounds, the dying man had while on his belly dragged his already-dead wife away from the flames that would have incinerated her body, and placed it where the fire would not reach her. He then crawled to a drawer where he kept his belongings, and with one final push it seemed, grabbed a large manila envelope and evidently clasped it to his chest for his sons to find, which they did when they turned his blood-soaked and partly burnt body over.

The thick manila envelope contained very important documents it turned out. Paul and Natalie McDaniels were responsible in life as they were now in death, the boys would soon find out. Both parents had each a life insurance policy that amounted to two and a half million dollars, which if spent with care, could sustain the brothers for the rest of their lives. The policy holder was a company based in Omaha, Nebraska. Also within the manila envelope was a deed to the ranch, which was in both Dumisani and Sasha's names, a checking account at a Barclays Bank branch in Maun with close to seventy-five thousand dollars, a key to a safety deposit box that had a bundle of notes in U.S. currency that amounted to $25,000, and something that made their breath catch once again. Two U.S. passports, one for Sasha and the other for Dumisani.

Apparently, and this came as somewhat of a surprise to the brothers, Paul McDaniels had contacted the U.S. State Department after the boys were born, who in turn referred him to the Immigration and Naturalization Services (INS), later to be renamed The

Department of Homeland Security (DHS) and registered his sons as foreign-born American citizens. There had been a problem at first with Dumisani's situation, because his mother had died at childbirth and had not given him up for adoption, but somehow the McDaniels couple had overcome that slight obstacle, and Dumisani McDaniels, just like his brother Sasha, was a bona fide United States of America citizen with a passport, social security number, and all the benefits and rights that came with being a citizen of that nation.

The brothers had to wonder. Botswana does not allow dual citizenship, but somehow Paul McDaniels was able to get some kind of exception for them. This part of their lives had been kept from them, but even though their father had never anticipated his demise so early in life, let alone at the hands of the notorious poacher, he and his wife had planned for every contingency. Perhaps it was the nature of their jobs because they dealt with wildlife, but Paul had also made a provision in his will that should both parents lose their lives before the boys reached the age of 18, which was the legal age of adulthood in the United States at least, then his brother Sean Kane McDaniels was to assume parental custody of the boys. This part of the will, though, was rendered moot, because by this time the brothers were past the age of 21, which was recognized as adulthood in Botswana.

With all this in place, the brothers understood that to mean that their parents, and their father in particular, wanted them to begin a new life in the United States. After all, Dumisani had already been accepted at the Pasadena Art Center College of Design to study film, and Sasha was supposed to tag along with him, even though he was still undecided as far as his education was concerned and perhaps traveling to the United

States would broaden his outlook, open his eyes to new possibilities.

It took a while before they boarded that flight to Los Angeles—eight months, to be exact. During that time, they rebuilt their home and leased the ranch out to a wealthy local couple, the wife of who had been good friends with their mother, who also promised to keep Natalie McDaniels' garden alive. Molo Sahili was tried, convicted, and sentenced to life in prison without the possibility of parole. Advent Monyatsiwa for his part received a twenty-five-year sentence, the rest of his accomplices received sentences ranging from ten to fifteen years, and with that, the Sahili gang was broken up forever. For now, at least, the elephants of Botswana were safe.

BOOK THREE

CHAPTER 26

THE UNITED STATES OF AMERICA.

WHEN THE HUGE JUMBO JET began its descent toward the world-renowned Los Angeles International Airport, better known as LAX, Dumisani and Sasha were from their pothole window able to admire the magnificent view below. The high-rise buildings that made up downtown Los Angeles, the twisting network of freeways with cars lined up like ants, the vast metropolitan area of the greater Los Angeles area that stretched far and wide and in all directions, was enough to tell the brothers that this was not Maun or the Okavango Delta where they grew up – this was a new world they were entering, a gateway to a brand new life.

Since they were recognized as American citizens at the port of entry, they cleared immigration without any hiccups or batting an eye, even though they did draw a bit of staring from a few of the immigration officers who stamped their passports when they noticed the same birthday, place of birth, and last name. In less than an hour after clearing customs, they were on an airport shuttle that took them to what would be their new home, the city of Altadena. An unincorporated area approximately 14 miles east of downtown Los Angeles.

The brothers admired the view from the shuttle as it negotiated its way along the 110 freeway all the way to where it ended at Arroyo Parkway, which in turn took them through the magical city of Pasadena, and then on to Lake Avenue, a busy street that ran north to south. Since it was late July and mid-summer, the surrounding was breathtaking on this late Saturday afternoon. The brothers looked around and then at each other, and silently communicated their thoughts. The money from their parents' life insurance was tucked away in a trust account right here in Pasadena, after it had been moved from the bank in Omaha, Nebraska. It was more than enough money to start a new life, any life. The future looked bright and they both smiled at one another, one of only a few times they had done so since their parents' murder.

The neighborhood began to change somewhat as the shuttle drove up Lake Avenue toward the magnificent Foothill Mountains. It then made a left turn onto a small street named Sacramento that was lined with single-family homes, duplexes, and mini apartment buildings. Before reaching their destination, the brothers had noticed numerous placards at almost every other turn—campaign placards, it turned out—most of which read, '*Gilbert 'Gil' Price For President*' or '*Vote 4 Gil In November*', '*A Priceless American Beacon*' one campaign placard screamed. There were also similar messages on billboards, and windows both residential and commercial.

It occurred to Dumisani, the more studious of the two and the reader, that this was an election year, and that one of the Republicans vying for the White House was a far right-leaning candidate from nearby Monrovia named Gilbert Price. The man was so alt-right with radical views like advocating for more prisons, the kind that were built for profit more than rehabilitating the convicts, comprehensive immigration reform that called for foreigners to carry identity cards that recognized them as such to weed out illegals and deport them, and his signature policy – a border wall between the United States and Mexico to stop the flow of illegal immigrants into the country. His ideas were dangerous, but even more disturbing was that his rhetoric, which was getting him on the news reels, was starting to resonate with possible voters. Especially the lobbyists who could deliver the three states that could tilt an election: Florida, New York, and the crown jewel of them all – California.

The voice of the driver brought him out of his brief reverie.

"This is it, gentlemen," he smiled. "822 East Sacramento Street, Altadena, California." He rolled out the last word. "Again, welcome to the United States," he added with yet another smile before he stepped out to help them get their luggage from the back of the shuttle van.

Sasha then said, "Thank you, sir. How much do we owe you?"

"Oh, that will be $84.00 for the two of you," the ever-smiling driver said as he placed the last bag on the ground by the brothers' feet.

There was also a silver metal case that housed Dumisani's film camera equipment that he was already holding. It almost never left his sight, because it contained his most prized possession: a high-definition Canon XL-H1 camera. Modern day cameras had become smaller and more compact as the years went by, and some film students and professionals could achieve the same effect with their smartphones as they would with a traditional camera, but for some reason

Dumisani never saw the need to upgrade and preferred the bulky camera instead. If he were to get another camera, he told himself, that camera would be the 'RED,' a very costly piece of equipment that he could afford, but for now his beloved camera would do.

After the shuttle left, the brothers looked around, taking in the new surroundings. It was late afternoon, and everything looked and felt different. They were in a brand new world with no one but each other to depend on, at least for now. For a moment both brothers felt pangs of nostalgia, thinking of the home they left behind but that passed quickly as their eyes settled on a shingle hanging by the driveway that read **"Two-Bedroom Apt. For Rent"** and the address at the bottom. All arrangements had been made prior to their journey, and they were expected by the property manager.

Sasha looked around again before he faced his brother, and they smiled once again. It felt to them as though they were turning a new leaf.

"Well, here we are, Dumi."

The premises had eight apartments in all. The units were all on the top floor with single-car garages at the bottom. The front apartment had the word 'MANAGER' stenciled on the door. They got their bags and rolled them along as they walked to the manager's front door. Dumisani rang the doorbell, and a few seconds later an attractive thirty-something-year-old white woman, Julia Armstrong, opened the door. She was wearing a long summer dress, and her chestnut brown hair was pulled back in a neat ponytail without a strand of hair out of place. There was a quizzical look on her face as she tried to figure out who these two strangers with luggage at her doorstep were.

"Yes?" she said. "How can I help you two gentlemen?" She asked as she looked first at Dumisani and then at his brother.

Sasha took a small step forward, smiled, and said, "Hi, we're looking for Ms. Julia Armstrong."

"I'm Julia Armstrong."

She was a bit taken aback by the young man's accent, even though she shouldn't have been. This, after all, was Southern California, one of the most diverse places in the union. The two young men were definitely foreign; she could tell by the way they dressed and carried themselves. She probably would have guessed that in spite of the drawl that she could not place.

Both brothers stretched their hands out for a handshake.

"Pleased to meet you, Ms. Armstrong. I'm Sasha McDaniels and this is my brother Dumisani, or Dumi if you prefer. We've talked over the phone and via email."

Julia's face suddenly lit up and broke into a beautiful smile upon realizing who she was dealing with.

"Oh yes," she said. "The gentlemen from Botswana. Pleased to meet you in person finally, welcome to the U.S."

When it was time to make a move to the new world, as the brothers often referred to it, they had through some helpful liaison at the American Embassy assisted them in finding a place to live in Altadena, their preferred destination, some two months before they were set to depart. The lease had been agreed upon and signed, and payment for the first and last month had been made all through the embassy in Gaborone. What was left was for the brothers to show up, just as they now had.

"Thank you," Dumisani said.

Julia Armstrong's lips started to form a smile but then just as quickly that puzzled look returned to her face. Dumisani and Sasha had to fight to suppress the laughter that was building up inside their lungs. They had seen that look so many times and knew what was coming.

"E-excuse me, did you say you're brothers?"

"Yes," Sasha and Dumisani said as one.

Not one to be nosy, even though she had a thousand and one personal questions, Julia Armstrong stepped aside to let the young men inside her comfortable-looking apartment.

"Well, come on in, gentlemen. I wasn't expecting you until tomorrow, but that's okay."

A few minutes later, the two brothers were seated in the immaculately furnished and decorated living room on a couch facing their soon-to-be landlord. The glass coffee table was between them, and on it were two glasses of grape juice and a tray of assorted cookies she had served earlier on. She had her reading glasses on as she went over the necessary lease paperwork with them. She then handed them copies of the lease agreement and a hardcopy version of the original receipt she had sent to them for the first and last month's rent during their email correspondence.

Julia then said, "And these are copies of your lease. The first and last month's rent has already been taken care of, thank you very much, and these are the keys to your apartment. I took the liberty of getting extra copies, two for each of you. I'll take you to your apartment as soon as you're done signing the lease. It's furnished according to your specifications. What's left is for you to fill up the fridge."

Always the more polite of the two, Dumisani smiled and said, "Thank you very much, Mrs. Armstrong."

"Call me Julia, and that goes for you too, Sasha."

There were smiles all around as business had been concluded much to the satisfaction of all parties involved.

"Thank you very much, Julia," Dumisani said. "Speaking of filling up the fridge, where is the nearest supermarket?"

"Oh, it's just walking distance from here. I'll show you where it is in just a moment. I'll also give you a list of all the local fast foods that do deliveries."

The brothers stared at each other in astonishment.

"You can actually have someone deliver fast food to your house?" Sasha asked.

"Absolutely!"

Julia was about to give them an '*Are you kidding me*?' look, but had to remind herself that her newest tenants were fresh from a developing country where such things had yet to be the norm.

"Wow, how convenient," Sasha smiled. He was beginning to love the United States.

Julia said, "All your utilities are up and running, except your landline, cable, and Wi-Fi, which I was told will be working within 24 hours."

The woman was truly efficient, and the brothers thanked her for it.

CHAPTER 27

THEIR TWO-BEDROOM APARTMENT was located at the very end of the eight-unit building, and just like the rest had a single-car garage at the bottom. Inside the garage was a brand-new washer and dryer, as promised by their landlord. The kitchen was spacious enough for a round dining table complete with four matching chairs. As with the rest of the apartment (something the brothers kept referring to as a 'flat'), it was well furnished, including the two bedrooms whose doors faced each other, and clean with a faint smell of paint.

They took their time unpacking and hanging their clothes in their respective walk-in closets. In the living room, which overlooked the driveway, Sasha and Dumisani began placing the family pictures that had miraculously survived the fire. The corners of the frames for some of the pictures were charred. It was a very poignant moment. The brothers had to consciously force their gaze away from the various pictures of their parents to that of their enigmatic uncle, the Reverend Sean Kane McDaniels.

Dumisani was the first to break the uneasy silence that hung in the air like a dirge.

"I wonder how we're going to get hold of him."

"Yes," Sasha said. "I mentioned in the letter that we will be moving to the U.S. and even gave him this address. Hopefully, the letter reached him."

The brothers once again stared at one another for a while, silently communicating their thoughts. It was amazing how much the brothers could converse without words. Their uncle had not attended their parents' funeral. Granted, he was in some remote village in the middle of some jungle in Borneo carrying on his missionary work, and thus could not be reached, or so the story went. However, they had expected to see him during the eight months that followed, but it was not to be. Their connection to him was a long, heartfelt letter postmarked from Tibet, a month after the funeral, expressing his condolences of course and promising to reach out to them 'as soon as humanly possible – God willing.' Both Sasha and Dumisani wondered if that would ever happen. For now, Uncle Sean Kane McDaniels remained just that – an enigma.

"Yes, I hope so too," Dumisani said after a long pause. He had been in deep thought just like his brother, and just as suddenly another thought hit him. "How about those girls, Misty, Jackie, and Pam?" he asked excitedly as he snapped his fingers.

It seemed like light years away from that one afternoon when they met the young, attractive tourists at the Sedia Riverside Hotel in Maun. Obviously, the brothers' lives had changed drastically that very evening when they were supposed to have taken the girls out, and subsequent events led them to forget about them until now.

Sasha said, "I tried Facebook. Man, I wish I knew more details of at least one of them, like their address and phone number here in the United States. Do you know how many people share the exact names and exact same city as them? Thousands, but I'll keep searching." Apparently, he had not forgotten about the girls, which was typical of him

"Well, maybe we'll get lucky and run into one of them, or it was never meant to be," Dumisani said as he glanced at his watch. "I think we should go to that supermarket close by that Miss Julia told us about before it gets too late, and see a bit of the neighborhood."

They had agreed not to sleep the moment they arrived at their new home so as to avoid jet lag, which they knew was bound to happen because of the long flight, including a stopover in Zurich, a total of twenty-eight hours.

"What are we going to use, cash or travelers' checks?" Sasha wanted to know.

"Travelers' checks I suppose," Dumisani said.

He reached for his shiny camera case next to the coffee table, opened it, and took out the black outsize film camera, the Canon HD XL-H1 High Definition camcorder that used mini digital video cassettes and MMC cards. Though big, the camera was surprisingly light and compact for its size. Dumisani turned it on, checked the charge on the battery, and soon found out that everything was in order.

"What do you need that for?" Sasha asked as soon as he realized that his brother was planning on bringing the camera along.

"Remember, Sasha, I'm going to study TV production and journalism, and one of my first assignments is that I film my surroundings and the very first sights I come across. Since we decided that walking to the supermarket is a great way of familiarizing ourselves with our new neighborhood, I thought, why not?"

"I see," Sasha nodded even though he honestly did not.

***

Walking up Lake Avenue in Altadena, the view, especially on a late afternoon, is spectacular even to those born and bred in this beautiful all-American city. For foreigners like the two brothers in a strange land, it was simply breathtaking. The road stretched up toward the foothills of Mount Wilson and cut through an exclusive neighborhood. In the immediate vicinity of the palm-tree-lined street, like almost any other in this city, were 'Mom and Pop' businesses like hair salons, coffee shops, a gas station, and an automotive brake shop.

It had rained the day before, quite unusual in Southern California as they were in the middle of summer (early August), and because of that the infamous Los Angeles smog was gone, giving them a picturesque view of the mountains ahead of them like something out of a postcard taken of a valley and hills of a Swiss Alps village. It was stunning.

Dumisani filmed all this with his enormous camera that rested on his shoulder and even provided a short narrative as he did this, or each time he felt the need arise. He could always fix it later. For now it was knowing where to put it. At times he would ask his brother to walk ahead of him and filmed him as he took in the sights. Two country boys from the hinterlands of the Okavango Swamps, what some people would call the boonies, suddenly thrust into the metropolitan area of an all-American city. Surprisingly, at least to the brothers, the street seemed deserted.

At that time, the brothers had no idea that unlike the Los Angeles area or even neighboring Pasadena for that matter, Altadena was a very safe and quiet city.

They did though get some stares from a few pedestrians they encountered, mainly because of Dumisani's filming. Though not at all unusual in Southern California, and even especially in Altadena, people liked watching films being made even by a lone cameraman with no crew. One thing the brothers were not was self-conscious, in spite of the fact that they were still new to the land. This could be attributed to the fact that Karate made them assured to a point that they believed in themselves and their abilities.

As they walked passed Elliot Junior High School and approached Jones Supermarket, the closest to them since it was within walking distance as Julia had promised, Sasha stopped abruptly and looked at the business properties across the main road, which meant he was facing west. There was a vacant building with a 'FOR LEASE' sign. By the looks of things, it seemed the building had been empty for a while, because some of its windows were broken and others boarded up completely. Weeds had taken over what once used to be the parking lot. Sasha McDaniels saw beyond that. They said this was the land of opportunity, and he saw opportunity in that abandoned building.

"What?" Dumisani asked. His camera was still running as he followed his brother's gaze. The sun was already setting and the buildings across the street cast a long shadow.

"Wouldn't it be nice to open a *dojo* out here?"

Dumisani caught his brother in full frame as he said this. It was perfect, natural, no acting, unrehearsed, something he knew was going to impress his professors at the Pasadena Art Center. He was capturing the true images and live shots of a young African, a white African at that, in his most honest moment in a peculiar land that was to be his new home

10,000 miles removed from where he was born and raised – a stranger in a strange land.

"Yes," Dumisani agreed as he continued filming. "We've always talked about it. Wouldn't that be something?"

The siblings smiled at the thought as they turned a corner into a small street that led to Jones Supermarket, with Dumisani happily filming his documentary. Across the street from the store was a silver SUV with tinted windows. Even if Sasha and Dumisani had seen them, they would have never guessed that the three occupants, all of them young white men in their mid-twenties to early thirties, were up to something. Indeed, something spectacular was about to happen.

CHAPTER 28

THE THREE WHITE MEN—Charles 'Charlie' Evans, Reggie McNeal, and Erick Russell—were tense. The car had been stolen the day before in Fresno and the windows were tinted, but with this particular score that was most likely to end up with a dead body, meaning a murder rap for the three of them, they were not going to take any chances. To further conceal their features, they were all wearing dark Ray-Ban sunglasses. Charlie Evans and Reggie McNeal were seated in front, while the geeky-looking Erick was in the back tinkering with a laptop.

The man behind the wheel, Charlie, said, "They should be here any moment."

He looked at the man seated next to him, the ex-marine Reggie McNeal, who nodded but otherwise said nothing. There was a high-powered sniper rifle with a scope fitted with a silencer resting on his lap.

"You only got one shot at this," Charlie reminded him. There was a nervous ring in his voice.

"I never miss," Reggie said softly but confidently.

The two other men did not doubt that for a second. Reggie McNeal, a veteran of the second Iraqi war, had seen a lot of combat during his three tours in the sandbox and was among the top two snipers in the unit, but his career with the Marines had been cut short thanks to a dishonorable discharge for insubordination. There were also rumors of a cocaine habit that had gotten out of hand.

"Showtime," Erick said from the backseat without looking up. He was still tapping the keys on his laptop.

At that moment, a white windowless van, except on the driver and passenger side that was headed northbound on Lake Avenue, turned right on the small street and passed the parked SUV before turning left into Jones' Supermarket parking lot. Erick was tracking all this via live streaming on his laptop. He had hacked into the store's security mainframe. That way he was in control of the security cameras that were set to stop recording the moment everything happened. The actual footage was being fed live into an external flash drive that was attached to his laptop to review later, to make sure that everything went perfectly.

***

Genuine Bank is headquartered in the financial district of downtown Pasadena, in an area where Colorado Boulevard and Lake Avenue intersect. With numerous branches spread across the San Gabriel Valley, southern, central, and northern California, its growth had been significantly rapid that in time it became a threat to more established institutions like Bank Of America, Wells Fargo, and Union Bank.

The secret to their success, and indeed their guiding principle, was treating the customer as king. They take pride in face-to-face interaction with the consumer. This simple philosophy is the reason businesses large and small were attracted to them. With chain stores like Jones's, they sent their specially built armored cars that could blend in with other vehicles to collect the previous days' cash and check payments.

These Genuine Bank armored vans were fitted with bulletproof windows and reinforced panels with armor plates that were also bulletproof, and could resist explosives like grenades and land mines. The vans were manned by two drivers from a fully vetted security company. No one but the head honcho of the bank knew the routes and pickups of the armored vans, whose job it was to pick up the previous day's takes from the different business establishments, mainly supermarkets and independently owned businesses, and then deliver the proceeds to the bank's vault in downtown Pasadena. They were also responsible for filling up the in-store Automated Teller Machines (ATMs), which they owned.

There were at least six such vehicles tasked with this job in the San Gabriel Valley, and on average they hauled at least $2.5 million in cold, hard cash. The take was much larger on Mondays because there were no pickups scheduled on weekends, and the ATMs needed to be fed with fresh $20 bills. One of the two security guards of this particular van that pulled into the Jones parking lot happened to be Martin Anderson, a retiree in his late 60s who had taken this job because after working airport security for over forty years, he just could not deal with the superannuated life.

This job was easy for Martin. All he had to do was drive the van and when they made their stops, keep it secure while his partner, a bright, young, conscientious black man named Dedrick Bellamy whom he had grown to adore like a son, went either to pick up the cash, or drop it off – each time with his sidearm drawn, locked and ready. Both men were excellent marksmen. The back of the van was dark and contained bags filled with coins and others stacked with bills. All this, in addition to what Dedrick was picking up, was going to bring the total to $3 million according to their last count. After which they would be feeding the ATMs that needed more cash.

The van parked almost parallel to the store. Martin pulled out a clip file that was resting between the driver and passenger seats, put on his reading glasses instead of the company-issued sunglasses, licked the tip of his forefinger, and paged through the papers until he got to the one he was looking for.

"Says we're picking up $188,452.10 from this location," he said after taking another closer look to make sure that the figures were correct. He then replaced his specs with the sunglasses.

Dedrick simply nodded and said, "Yep." He was, just like Martin, wearing a similar pair of company-issued sunglasses. They were so dark that they could see each other's reflections in them.

With his hand on his holster, he looked around the parking lot from inside the armored van, and then at the store entrance before he punched an electronic code on a keypad on the side of the door where the manufacturer's lock would normally be. There was a hissing sound, and the heavy door slid open. Dedrick made one last swoop of his surroundings before stepping out of the van, hand still on his holster, and walked quickly to the double-door electric glass entrance before he disappeared inside the vast supermarket.

Martin watched his partner, whom he noticed like before was still looking around before he disappeared inside the building. Based on prior experience, he knew it would be another ten to fifteen minutes before he reappeared. He had been jonesing badly for a smoke. He reached into his front pocket, took out a pack of Marlboro Red cigarettes, and fished one out.

With the cigarette dangling from the corner of his mouth, Martin looked around and punched a combination on the keypad on his side. He was violating strict company policy by opening his door even a crack, which he did once in a while to let the smoke out through the breach, because the windows did not open as an added security precaution. The guards were under strict orders to *never* open the doors under any circumstances while waiting on a pickup, or any place else for that matter, until they were at their secure facility which happened to be in an underground parking lot at the bank's main office. However, whenever the nicotine craving came calling, it was hard to resist. It would not be the gradual death this habit caused that would end his life, but something more instant and deadly.

He cracked the door about ten inches, fired up, and was soon puffing as quickly as he could and immediately felt the relaxation set in with every puff. Martin Anderson was about to take another drag from his cigarette, when suddenly the interior of the van was clouded briefly with a pink mist of flesh, blood, bone, and brain matter, which exploded from the other side of his head causing his body to pitch violently to the side, almost landing on the passenger seat.

His body was still twitching when the driver's side door was yanked wide open, and Reggie shoved the body to the side like a sack of potatoes, jumped in behind the wheel, and drove away. He did not floor it as one might expect out of sheer panic and anxiety to get the hell out of Dodge. Instead he casually drove out of the parking lot, and even waited for a car to pass by before he turned right and then left onto Lake Avenue. A few minutes later, the silver SUV, this time with two passengers, soon followed, making a clean getaway with over $3 million in cold, hard cash.

Right around that time, unaware that a daring heist had just taken place, Dumisani and Sasha walked out of the supermarket. Sasha was carrying two plastic bags filled with groceries, and Dumisani was right behind him with his camera filming. He already had a working title for this project, and it was growing on him. He was required to hand in the edited and polished version on the first day of school, "*The Brothers' First Day In America*". He had mentioned the title to Sasha, and he laughed and said it was a bit 'blatantly inauthentic and cheesy,' but Dumisani just laughed off his brother's suggestion. He was always his own worst critic. Besides, titles always changed, and he could still come up with another one after watching the entire video recording.

Nowadays, particularly among students, people used miniature camcorders and even smartphones to film their projects, which was why Dumisani got more than a few curious stares as he followed his brother with the outsize camera. He made certain to keep Sasha, and only Sasha in frame while inside the store. It was only when they were at the entrance that he made the angle wider, catching the entire parking lot in the background with his brother as the sole subject.

When they were leaving the premises of Jones's Supermarket, his brother turned, grocery bags in hand, looked straight into the lens, smiled, and said, "Next time get a smaller camera, Dumi. I hate the attention."

They both laughed because nothing was further from the truth. Sasha McDaniels loved the spotlight, the attention. While his brother was a bit more reserved, the kind of person who felt most comfortable behind the camera and not in front of it. However, what they did not know was that at that moment, Dumisani McDaniels had unwittingly caught the entire heist on film. It would be a while before they became aware of that, and that knowledge was accompanied by a rude awakening.

***

Dedrick Bellamy, Glock 19 in one hand, the other holding a case that contained last night's take, watched the two brothers and had to suppress a smile. The two were foreigners, no doubt. It was evident from their accents and the way they carried themselves— probably tourists, judging by the ridiculously large camera the other was holding as he filmed his companion, whom he followed around like a puppy. He noticed though that the cameraman was careful not to film the other patrons, himself included, without their permission. Apparently they were smart enough to know that was a cardinal sin in the film industry.

He waited until they disappeared through the double glass doors, nodded at the manager, someone he had come to know very well over the past two years working this job, and walked quickly, as he always did, back to the van. When Dedrick stepped out of the store and into the parking lot, it took just one look from left and then right to realize that the armored van was gone. His heart gave a painful lurch. Right there and then Dedrick knew that something terrible had happened without being told. He also knew that Martin Anderson, if he were to be found, was a dead man.

"What the hell?" Dedrick managed to gasp before he turned and quickly rushed back into the store.

Larry Adams, the supermarket manager, was in his glass cubicle at the front corner of the store overlooking the numerous cash registers, going over some paperwork when he looked up and saw the Genuine Bank security man, Dedrick Bellamy, practically running toward him. He had never seen the young black man so agitated; usually Dedrick was a cool customer. This was made worse by the fact that he was still holding his Glock in plain sight.

Standing up from his chair as he removed his reading glasses, the manager asked, "Hey, Dedrick, what's wrong? Did you forget something?" His eyes were suddenly focused on the unholstered weapon.

The armored van security man practically yelled, startling nearby customers waiting in line at the cash registers who were within hearing range.

"Call 911, Larry, we've been robbed!"

"Robbed? What do you mean robbed?" Larry Adams, equally perplexed by the news, bellowed in absolute surprise. This was not supposed to happen, not with a Genuine Bank Armored Van. The vehicle was supposed to be foolproof.

"Martin and the van are gone."

"Jesus Christ!" was all Larry could say as he rushed for the office phone. He thought of sounding the store alarm but thought better of it. Such a thing would cause a stampede.

CHAPTER 29

THE GENUINE BANK HEIST, as it became known, had been a perfect robbery. A broad daylight swoop that left no fingerprints, no eyewitnesses, or any other forensic evidence. The perpetrators just up and vanished with no trace. The armored van was found at a vacant lot three miles west of Altadena in a small, affluent city called La Canada. They left it running, and after several hours, someone took note and called the police.

They found the body of Martin Anderson crumpled on the floor of the passenger side of the van. Part of his head was missing, and a good portion of both it and brain matter was spread all over the place, which meant he had been hit by a high-powered bullet from an equally powerful gun at close range. It was a bloody mess, too grotesque even to look at, but a forensics team immediately went to work. Since the doors could not be opened from outside, the police and detectives had to wait for a member of the bank to arrive, deactivate the alarm, and unlock the door to let them in.

It immediately became apparent that they were dealing with sophisticated criminals who had foiled a tried-and-tested security system. What's worse was that they had left little or nothing in as far as physical evidence was concerned. Even the bullet that had killed Martin Anderson was the frangible kind, the type that broke into little fragments the moment it made impact with maximum damage. The killing was cold-blooded as it was senseless.

Ad nauseam, 90% of the time at least, armored car heists were inside jobs according to the Federal Bureau of Investigation, and the investigators had to take a hard look at Dedrick Bellamy and the victim. Had Martin Anderson been a part of it and then was double-crossed once the criminals got what they wanted? And here began the investigation. What baffled the experts was that for the most part, such heists almost never ended up with someone getting killed. Naturally, and as was to be expected, Dedrick Bellamy was questioned at length by the detectives and the FBI who had been brought in by the local police, who happened to be the Altadena Sheriffs, for their expertise, and it did not take long for them to find out that the young man was just as perplexed as they were. Still, the investigators were mystified as to how the criminals had been able to pull it off.

It wasn't until the lead detective, Ricardo Chavez, asked Dedrick to recount their normal daily routine in painstaking detail that he somewhat was able to piece together bits and pieces of how this daring heist had been carried out. After thoroughly backgrounding Martin Anderson, it was found out that the dead man, just like his partner, had nothing to do with the theft. During Dedrick's narrative of their day-to-day activities, he realized that it was probably Martin's smoking habit that had caused a breach in the armored van's security that the thieves were able to exploit.

Detective Chavez was able to find out that whenever he could, Martin would crack the door open just wide enough to let the smoke from his cigarette escape from the resulting crevice. This was of course against company policy and thus strictly forbidden, given the cargo. At any stop, while Dedrick or sometimes Martin himself were doing a pickup, one of them stayed with the vehicle at all times and while waiting, the doors were to remain shut and locked at all times and were not to be opened under any circumstances. Martin had clearly violated company policy, and that had cost him his life.

The robbers had probably known that about Martin Anderson. Most likely, they had been following the armored van over a period of time, and in doing so probably discovered that chink in the armor that Genuine Bank had elaborately set in place. There had not been much to go on in as far as physical evidence, because the thieves had made sure of that.

So the most logical conclusion they could reach, and this they agreed to a man, was that the robbers had followed the armored van to Jones's Supermarket, then waited for Martin Anderson to crack his door open and start puffing away – something they had come to expect. And once that happened, they silently drove by and with a high-powered Rifle of some kind, most likely fitted with a silencer, fired at the unsuspecting security guard through the crevice.

With this in mind, the authorities realized that they were dealing with a group of cunning, ruthless, and dangerous criminals with some sort of training, most likely military. They were also technically savvy; they would soon find out. Aside from not having any physical evidence, other than the dead body of the elderly security guard Martin Anderson and the abandoned armored van free of its precious cargo, no fingerprints, Detective Ricardo Chavez and his men were dismayed to discover that none of the store's surveillance cameras had captured anything.

This was unheard of—astounding, really. It was obvious that the criminals had hacked into the supermarket's computer mainframe, and then disabled the cameras about ten minutes before the actual takedown. They began working again exactly 26 minutes after the suspects were long gone. Even worse, the hackers had left no trace the authorities could follow. It was as if they were never there.

"This crew, whoever they are, is good," Detective Chavez had said to his female partner, Chelsea Mclintock.

"I agree," the beautiful brunette said with grudging admiration.

With this in mind, they cast their net even wider. Everyone was questioned—the store manager, Larry Adams, his entire staff, including the janitors, were put through the wringer. No one was beyond suspicion, even employees at the bank were questioned, some as many as two or three times. However, it did not take long for the detectives to realize that this had not been an inside job as they had at first suspected.

This had been a well-planned and well-executed heist. The criminals had planned this to the last possible detail, leaving no stone unturned, leaving nothing to chance. They had executed the deed in a timely and swift manner and then up and vanished like a puff of smoke. And as the investigation ground to a halt with no suspect, or suspects in sight for that matter, and with the crucial first 48 hours coming and gone, they had no choice but to seek the public's help by involving the media. That meant asking if anyone saw anything unusual that fateful afternoon to come forward, no matter how inconsequential they thought their information was, after all, the detective knew that it was from the seemingly incongruous upon which a pattern would begin to evolve, and a well-planned heist began to crumble.

From experience, the veteran detective knew that no plan was totally foolproof. Someone must have seen or heard something, even though they may have not known it at the time. Criminals make mistakes, and it's a small crack in their carefully laid plans that would bring their whole house of cards down. Detective Chavez was looking for that small crack. It had to be there somewhere, and that was why he needed the public's help by involving the media. Genuine Bank even sweetened the pot by offering a $100,000 reward for any information leading to the arrest and conviction of the person or persons involved in the robbery of the armored van, and the subsequent murder of one Martin Lyle Anderson, a beloved father, husband, grandfather, and friend to many.

CHAPTER 30

GILBERT "GILL' PRICE'S RISE in the political arena was nothing short of meteoric. A Monrovia California resident, and from 'old money,' his grandfather started first by owning a radio station in 1952. That number soon grew to over a dozen and soon added television stations, and with that, the business kept growing and evolving as it passed from one generation to the next.

During this time, the Price family business had incorporated high-end real estate, a trucking company with a fleet of 35, several brokerage firms, and numerous Taco Bell and McDonald's franchises. The Price corporation, and many like it, did take a major hit financially during the 2008 real estate meltdown and was forced to sell off a number of its major real estate properties under market value, but managed to survive.

It was at this time that Gil Price decided to run for public office. He ran first for mayor in his home city of Monrovia, which he won easily but served only one term because his eyes were on a much bigger prize— an unfilled US Senate seat that was vacated after the original senator, who was in his early 70s, was forced to step down when it was discovered that the politician was carrying out an extramarital affair with a junior staffer young enough to be his granddaughter.

With so much at stake, and what with a presidential election coming up in three years, it was crucial for the Republicans to maintain their slim majority in the Senate, so he was given a choice by the party's brass: finish out the remainder of his term (he had a little over a year left) and declare that he would not be seeking reelection, or face the public spectacle and humiliation of having his sins exposed to the world. The choice was easy.

After a tough slog with a young opponent like him, a firebrand from the opposing party, Gilbert Price was able to capture the Senate seat. A hardcore conservative, he ran on issues that resonated with many like him who were skeptical of expressing their views in public, especially in a state like California, which had over the years since Ronald Reagan was governor evolved to hardcore liberal leanings.

Gil Price believed, first and foremost, in strong national security and tighter border control to curb the flow of illegal immigration into the country from Mexico and South and Central America. Thus, illegal immigration and since it targeted a very vulnerable group of people who could not fight back became his strongest talking point. He advocated for the building of for-profit private prisons in which to house illegal immigrants, and a wall on the Mexico border, which he said that country was going to pay for. On these points alone, Gil Price's star shot up rapidly because no one could talk of anything else. He stirred a pot of controversy that got him free publicity on right-leaning media outlets like Fox News, for instance, and others like it, including the regular news. His rhetoric was so inflammatory and divisive that he generated a type of free publicity never seen before.

"The majority of these illegals become freeloaders, putting a strain on our local economies and the country as a whole. Many of them are criminals, rapists, and drug dealers, which is why I call for the building of more prisons to show that the days of the American free ride are over, it will be a new dawn, a new America, and by that I mean AMERICA FIRST!" he would say at his campaign stops, and the phrase '*America First*' suddenly caught on and became his campaign's slogan. It was simple, catchy, and very effective.

It did not matter that none of what he said was true, because in politics and campaign lore, the truth was almost always the first casualty. What mattered was that all his rhetoric was enough to resonate with his base and the traditional red states. To them, he was a patriot who would bring about greatness for America, which according to them had been fading for quite some time. Gil Price was the outsider who would change Washington, drain the swamp so to speak by bringing back true American values. He went on to talk about the sanctity of marriage, and by that he meant marriage between a man and woman. He advocated for less government intervention when it came to such things as healthcare, Medicare, and stricter measures when it came to social programs like welfare. Gil Price preached about self-reliance and promised that if elected, he would bring about an America where such values would be made possible.

Price went on to make the case for America on the international stage. He called for American companies that manufactured goods in foreign countries to return, promising all sorts of tax breaks and other incentives that would entice them back. That, he said, would reopen the long-abandoned factories and recreate many of the jobs that were lost in the American heartland. He even touted a universal income of $1000,00 every month for every American earning less than $150,000 per year. This, mind you, had been a bold idea by an opponent from the opposing party, who had since dropped out of the race during the primaries but had been popular among voters from both parties. Ever the opportunist, Gil Price ran with the concept and made it his own.

He also promised to invest more of his time and energy into education, to curb the influx of skilled foreign workers in such fields as medicine, software development, and inventions. According to Price, America was a land that had invented most of the things that made life comfortable: the airplane, the computer, the internet, electricity, the automobile, and so on; so in his mind, he said time and again, there was no reason why the United States, a great nation and the most powerful in the world, let alone the wealthiest, should be importing foreign workers – he was going to make America great again.

However, like any other politician, he knew that campaigns, especially presidential campaigns, are very expensive. A candidate can have the best ideas, policies, and other such qualities, but if he did not have the money to run a successful campaign, he was dead and buried. Gil Price needed serious backers for his campaign. Granted, he came from a wealthy family, but in this new age where television advertising had to run around the clock in states that were regarded as 'battlegrounds' and not only advertising on TV, radio, on social media platforms such as Facebook, Twitter, Instagram, and other such mediums, a candidate needed a war chest of at least $400 million.

That was not enough, though. To ensure a clear path to the White House, in effect victory, Gil Price also needed to hire a bulldog of a campaign manager. That person would not come cheap, and there was only one such man. That man was Justin Miller, a San

Diego native originally from North Carolina who had in the past successfully managed two presidential campaigns. No one in the history of the republic had managed three successful bids for the White House, and that fact alone would be enough to lure the campaign strategist out of retirement. It was a record that, if successful, would be almost impossible to break and thus etch him into the history books.

For this undertaking, Miller demanded a fee of $2 million, which included a non-refundable retainer of $1 million and an additional $2 million bonus if Gil Price's campaign was successful. Money which at the moment he did not have and was still seeking ways in which to get it. This was where the younger Price, Gill's brother Declan, got involved. With an initial fee of $1 million, the campaign was able to reel in the big fish, and the first thing he did was conduct an unofficial poll among potential voters. The candidate polled well.

The next thing Miller did was hire two private investigators he trusted implicitly and had used before to conduct a thorough background check not only on his client, but the entire family. This firm consisted of former FBI field operatives, which meant they were really good at digging up hidden skeletons in somebody's past. Skeletons that an opponent may manipulate at the most inopportune moment and derail a well-run campaign at its momentum.

Gill Price passed the preliminary background check and a few more that came afterward, but that of his only sibling was worrisome. Raised by two parents who were devoted to one another, Gil and Declan lacked for nothing, of course. They attended the best private schools they could get into. They were taught to strive to be the best at everything they did, never back away from competition—embrace it, was the family dictum. That and never start a fight, but never run from one either. Strive for utmost success and once attained, never apologize for it either.

***

Declan Price wanted his older brother to become the next president of the United States of America more than he wanted anything in his entire life, and that was saying a lot. With his brother rising to be the most powerful man in the world, there was absolutely no limit to what individual heights he could reach. The possibilities were endless, so the idea that Declan Price's intentions stemmed from brotherly love was ludicrous. The younger Price was in it for himself, with his brother as president the sky was the limit as far as personal wealth and power in his own right.

However, Price was the type of family member who had issues in his past that, if unearthed by an overzealous reporter looking to break the biggest story since Watergate, could upend a well-organized campaign. There was the case of a young coed at an exclusive private high school he and his brother attended, who had overdosed on heroin supplied by Declan that the family, with its money and power, and not to mention powerful political connections at the state and government level had the entire matter swept under the rug. Money changed hands, favors were called upon, reporters were bribed or threatened, and in the end the whole matter was made to go away. But Declan Price's past was still a potential powder keg that could explode any moment.

That's why when Gil Price began throwing hints about a potential political career, and when speculation became reality, he began to purposely distance himself from his younger brother. It was something his then-political advisor who had handled his mayoral run called 'branding.' Gil Price, he intoned, was a brand name, or at least had to be built into one—and a brand name, just like the Coca-Cola name brand, could not be associated with anything toxic.

Declan understood all this, which was why he did not mind at first being frozen out, in essence the odd man out as the Price political machine went full throttle. He watched as his only sibling rode the political ladder first as mayor of his hometown Monrovia, and leapfrogged to the United States Senate and then gained national recognition with his hardline immigration rhetoric and the 'America First' mantra.

It was when Gil Price announced his intention of running for the highest office in the land, that his younger brother decided to discreetly jump on his political bandwagon. When he heard that his brother had formed a presidential exploratory committee to determine whether running for president and, most importantly, winning the race was a possibility, he secretly and through an offshore account sent a check for $125,000. The contribution took a hit on his personal finances, because at age 38 (Gil Price was 41) he had all but exhausted his trust fund which had been established by his parents when the siblings were still teenagers.

Now, once he heard that Gil Price polled well against possible rivals and that his campaign could finally be taken seriously, he decided to involve himself in the race by coming up with the money to secure the services of Justin Miller, the only man who could almost guarantee his brother's victory for the highest office in the land, and he knew where he could get the $2 million to meet the political strategist's hefty fee. He would donate it anonymously until such time

241

as he was ready to inform his brother that it was he who had made the contribution, and the source of that money would be the Genuine Bank van.

CHAPTER 31

LATER THAT EVENING, Sasha and Dumisani were preparing dinner, something their mother taught them. Learning how to cook, reminding them that one day they'll be on their own, they got to know the bare essentials of life. They were dividing their time between the kitchen and the living room, the forty-foot plasma television playing the news. Sasha, who was not paying particular attention to it since he was rearranging the couches and the glass coffee table, suddenly froze. Something the beautiful female news anchor said had gotten his full attention.

She was reporting live from the scene, apparently, because in the background there were flashing lights from at least five police vehicles, a fire engine, an ambulance, and what looked like a county coroner van. The flashes from the police cars were very clear now that it was nightfall in a parking lot that looked very familiar to Sasha McDaniels.

The words '*Genuine Bank Armored Car Heist*' were emblazoned at the bottom of the screen. Sasha unconsciously leaned closer as he sat on a couch facing the plasma TV set that was mounted on a table mount meant specifically for it, and then suddenly a green bar stretched from one end of the screen to the other after

Sasha reached for the remote and increased the volume.

"Authorities say this was a real brazen robbery carried out in broad daylight. What's worse is that there were no eyewitnesses, no DNA, at least not just yet, or any other physical evidence to lead them to the criminals thus far, and the police are currently appealing to the public to offer any clues ..."

At that moment, the camera panned sideways and focused on supposedly the exact spot where the Genuine Bank Armored van was possibly hijacked. If the viewers were expecting to see blood, a body maybe with part of its head missing, or any such gory details, they were disappointed because there was nothing to see. And then at that moment, as the Field Reporter was about to say more, she suddenly pressed her left hand to a tiny device that was inside her ear, like she was listening to an incoming message of some sort. There was an uncharacteristic silence on the part of the reporter as she nodded in silent agreement.

She turned her focus to the camera and said, "I apologize about that, folks, but I'm just getting some breaking news from our main studio that the police in La Canada just found the hijacked armored van in an empty parking lot, and we're sad to report that the driver, 62-year-old Martin Anderson, a father of three and a grandfather of five, was found dead in the vehicle. It is reported that over $2.5 million that was collected from business establishments around the San Gabriel Valley is missing. This, according to the authorities, is the biggest and most brazen heist in the history of ..."

"Dumi ... Dumi!" Sasha called out excitedly to his brother, who had just finished dicing up the tomatoes he was going to use to prepare beef stew, which he was good at making and they both loved.

"What?" Dumisani said from the middle of the kitchen as he used a knife to scrape the sliced tomatoes from a miniature cutting board and into a skillet already on the stove with the diced onions frying in the olive oil. It was time to add the tomatoes because the onions were already brown, meaning that they were ready for the tomatoes to be added. The aroma was great, and it reminded them of the kitchen back home.

"Come here quickly," Sasha said excitedly as he pointed at the plasma TV "You're not going to believe this, man."

"What is it, man?" Dumisani wanted to know as he stuck his head through the opening in the wall between the living room and the kitchen, slightly irritated. He could never put it past his brother to make a big deal out of nothing.

"Look," Sasha said again, still pointing at the high-definition screen somewhat triumphantly.

"Yes, I know we have got a nice TV, Sasha. What is it?" Dumisani said in a voice laced with sarcasm.

"Look at that, smartass."

"It's an anchor reporting the news, so what?"

"Dumi, when are you going to learn to pay attention, man? That's at the place where we were earlier today, the supermarket, can't you see?"

This piece of information suddenly got Dumisani McDaniels' full attention as he squinted at the screen to get a better look. His eyes narrowed at first, and then opened wide. This was unbelievable, he thought. They were just there.

He asked, "What happened?"

Sasha said, almost excitedly, as if he couldn't believe it himself, "Someone hijacked an armored car full of cash, about $2.5 million, and took off without a trace. As a matter of fact, they just found the van. The money is gone, of course, but the driver was murdered."

"My goodness, when did this happen?"

"They say around 4:45pm today."

Dumisani reflectively consulted the chronometer on his hand before looking up to face his brother as his eyes lit up

"That's around the time when we were there, Sasha," Dumisani said almost in a whisper. He went on to ask, "Are you certain it was today?"

"Yeah, man," Sasha said, smiling like an eight-year-old opening his Christmas gifts. "Isn't that amazing?"

Dumisani said, "Yes, but I did not see an armored truck, did you?"

Having dealt with the police in the recent murder of their parents, and knowing cops are pretty much the same all over the world, Dumisani was wondering if they and everyone else who was there that day and around the time of the crime would be called in as potential witnesses and asked about what they saw and heard. After all, they would be easy to find, especially in this day and age where surveillance cameras were just as commonplace as cell phones were. And his brother did not seem to realize that the last thing they could afford was to be dealing with the police.

"Exactly the point," Sasha said, still smiling. "Apparently this armored car is different from the ones we're used to. This one is a van, like the panel vans we have back home, except it's totally reinforced from the inside out. The doors are even programmed to open and lock only by the guards inside the vehicle. They didn't go into detail, of course, but seems to me that the system is foolproof. It turns out that the guards' job is to pick up last night's takes from all the big businesses that make their deposits at this one particular bank, and fill up their in-store ATMS."

"So they were doing a pickup at the same supermarket we were at, around the time we were there?"

"That's what I've been trying to tell you, man," Sasha said somewhat triumphantly.

"Christ!" was all Dumisani could say as he went back into the kitchen to finish cooking dinner, shaking his head slowly. He did not know why, but this did not feel good at all.

Even as he entered the kitchen, Dumisani McDaniels still could not shake the foreboding that this Genuine Bank Armored car hijacking, as it was now known in the media, was somehow going to drag him and his brother into an abyss he did not care to imagine. This whole issue was wrought with danger. He did not know why, but somehow they were headed to it like one of those moments where you see that a car crash is inevitable, but you can do nothing about it except hold on tight, shut your eyes, brace for impact, and then hope and pray that the moment passes as quickly and as painless as possible.

"Please Lord," he muttered under his breath. "Let it not be so."

"What was that, Dumi?" his brother called from the living room, still glued to the TV. He was now flipping through the channels, and there were, to his utter delight, quite a few to choose from because they had all the premium channels. It was part of their rental agreement.

"Oh, nothing, man," Dumisani lied. He did not see the need to burden his brother with his thoughts.

"I'm still trying to locate at least one of the girls. I may have tracked down Misty Abdul, but I can't be one hundred percent sure. We'll see," Sasha said.

"Thank God for Facebook, yeah?"

"Indeed, brother, indeed," Sasha replied as he finally settled on a movie on a streaming channel (they all were now, apparently) he had just only recently heard about called *Hulu*.

CHAPTER 32

FOUR DAYS LATER, THE THREE MEN—Charlie Evans, Reggie McNeal, and Erick Russell—met again at a safe house in South Pasadena as planned. The robbery had gone perfectly, and if there was any lingering guilt over the killing of the driver, Martin Anderson, all three men did a great job of not showing it. Even though not said, just mentioning the victim's name would have been seen as weakness. The driver was nothing but a casualty of war as far as they were concerned, a piece of trash that could be picked up and tossed into the garbage and forgotten about.

What was also not said, but known by all three men, was that they were now all tied to a murder. Any slip, intentional or otherwise, meant that they would all go down for it. Their mysterious employer, Declan Lowell Price, had also reminded them of that, which meant that none of them would have any motivation to run to the authorities in the unlikely event that any one of the three found religion now or at a future date, because murder had no statute of limitations.

After Martin Anderson was ambushed and killed, and the van hijacked, Reggie McNeal, the shooter who also happened to be an army trained sniper, assumed the wheel and drove the armored van to a predetermined location, which happened to be an abandoned parking lot in nearby La Canada that was located off of Foothill Boulevard, underneath the 210 Freeway overpass with Charlie and Erick following close behind in their white SUV. Erick was driving the SUV and did not right away drive to the rendezvous point where the armored van would be stripped of its precious cargo and dumped, but instead took a prearranged route that had been thoroughly mapped out and even rehearsed with a couple of dry runs.

So upon leaving Jones's Supermarket parking lot, the armored van, this time with a totally different person behind the wheel, turned left on Lake, with the SUV close behind at first, and made another right on Orange Grove Avenue, and took yet another surface street before the SUV peeled off and then met at the agreed upon place in La Canada. At times they would double back and then resume the short jaunt.

The freeway was not even entertained. This was done to make certain that there was no one else following them. The chance of that happening was remote in the extreme, but one does not successfully hijack a state-of-the-art secure armored truck with no known vulnerabilities by being careless, or leaving anything to chance. You checked and rechecked your flanks, leaving no stone unturned, which was what the trio were good at.

Even before they arrived at the agreed-upon site, the SUV took the lead and scoped the area and the immediate surroundings to make certain there were no surprises in store for them. All this time, while driving the armored van, Reggie McNeal was not worried about being seen, for one the windows were tinted, and the van because of its make and color blended in nicely with others, which made it difficult for possible eyewitnesses to positively identify it. In a way, Genuine Bank's efforts to camouflage the true intent of the vehicle and what it carried, in this case, had worked against them.

When the commandeered armored van finally stopped at the designated area, it took the three men less than ten minutes to transfer all the loot, and in some instances money cases into the silver SUV. The body of Martin Anderson was ignored with affected unconcern. The engine was left running and that's how it was found some three hours later.

Reggie and his confederates, following instructions already in place, and still taking the necessary precautions then headed to the safe house in South Pasadena. The house was a condominium on Richards Street in the exclusive neighborhood off Fair Oaks Avenue. As per plan, they were to leave the cash there in the well-furnished three-bedroom house, which happened to be one of the many properties owned by the Price family, and go their separate ways, and then return after three days to review the surveillance videos to make sure that everything had been purged, and the cyber break-in would not be traced back to the burglar, Erick Russell. These were the strict instructions from the boss.

This, however, was something Erick could have done with his eyes closed. Again, instructions from 'the boss' were that Erick Russell, because of his ability, his expertise really, to hack into any computer and not leave a trace was very crucial to his long time plans. And as such his life, at least for the moment, was extremely vital, which is why the two other men, Reggie McNeal and Charlie Evans, were to keep an eye on the young hacker. Their lives were expendable, but not his.

That was why they were back that evening at the safe house to review the footage. They arrived at different times, with McNeal arriving last. His mind was in turmoil. Not for the killing, since they had been paid well for the job—$33,000 each. It had been $15,000 for taking the job and another $15,000 for completing it successfully without a hitch. It went so well that 'the boss' threw in an extra $3,000 as a bonus for a job well done. It was important to keep these men happy, at least for now. McNeal did not know how much the cargo was worth. In fact, none of them did until they heard about the actual amount on the news.

He should have kept driving; he had said to himself. Kept going and disappear to some corner of the universe where he could not be found. After all, for a man like him, anything close to $3 million was more than enough for him to vanish. In the end, though, he realized that it was a fleeting thought. The people he was dealing with were not to be trifled with. They operated at a level not even he could comprehend, and they had shown that they were connected in places he could not even imagine. Take the heist, for instance. They had to have known someone, or had a level of penetration inside the Genuine Bank Corporation that gave them the information to know where the armored van would be at what time and with how much. No, he realized, they would find him, and they would kill him before he even had a chance to spend the money.

In the end, he had to be content with what he had. After all, 'the boss' had hinted that if he stuck with him and played his cards right, this could be the beginning of a life of wealth that not even he could have dreamed of. *Well*, he thought, *we will have to see about that*.

The living room was the only area in the house that was sparsely furnished as one would expect in a home that was barely inhabited. There were just the bare bone necessities—a wooden floor, a set of couches, a coffee table—but it was in the dining room area where they were gathered, seated around a large mahogany table in the middle of the room. On it were three state-of-the-art laptops running. Erick had just finished setting and firing them up when Reggie entered the house. Each one of the men had a key, so when he unlocked and entered the living room, the two other men Erick, and Charlie, barely looked up from the three laptops lined up next to each other.

Without so much as a 'good evening gentlemen,' something that would normally be expected since the three men had dropped off the stolen cash three nights ago and then split in different directions, Reggie quietly headed to the kitchen, opened the freezer, took out a chilled bottle of vodka, and fixed himself a drink by diluting the liquor with orange juice. He did not bother to ask the other two if they wanted one, because there were already two glasses with what looked like bourbon on the dining room table.

Erick Russell, the computer geek and cyber pirate, was already duly engrossed and captivated by the three screens in front of him. Everyone was silent as Reggie McNeal walked slowly to where they were, sipping from his glass, and stood a few feet from the two seated men, towering over them from behind. And when all three screens from the laptops were on, it then occurred to McNeal that they were looking at the footage from the surveillance camera of first Jones's Supermarket, then the Elliot School right next door, and finally the business across the street from the supermarket.

It was apparent that the three men, and whoever was pulling their strings, 'the boss' in this case, were not leaving anything to chance. They may have pulled off what one astute reporter called, '*The perfect crime, pulled off by brazen and sophisticated criminals who were able to circumvent a true and tested state–of-the-art security system,*' but they knew better. There could be a loose end somewhere, and if it was there, they would have to find it before the cops did. As far as they were concerned, there was no such thing as a perfect crime. There could have been something that had been overlooked, and they were reviewing the footage Erick was able to store in a flash drive he was going to get rid of later, to make certain that nothing that could bring down the whole house of cards had been missed.

"Is that all the relevant footage?" Reggie McNeal asked, breaking the silence.

Without turning to look at him, Erick Russell said, "Yes. I hacked into only those that matter."

"And were you able to wipe them clean without anyone knowing you were even there?" McNeal wanted to know.

Erick did not know if he should laugh or get angry. He hated it when people like Reggie asked such facetious questions—he sure as hell never asked the sniper if he was sure people he killed were dead—so he would appreciate it if these people who knew nothing about what he did would leave him alone. Instead, he nodded yes as these thoughts flashed through his mind.

Erick had gotten in trouble with the law and was looking at hard time in a federal prison thanks to his hacking escapades, had it not been for Declan Price's intervention. The two knew one another from high school, but in a peripheral way. Their paths crossed later in life after Declan heard that Erick had been arrested for hacking into a local bank and transferring a couple of million to a numbered account in the Cayman Islands. The part that impressed 'the boss' Declan Price was that Erick had been caught not because he had been clumsy in his exploits and left a trail that could be tracked back to him, but because the theft was done on a dare with a couple of fellow hacker

254

friends who wanted to see how good he was. Then one drunken night at a local bar, Erick foolishly bragged to the wrong person about his plunder.

When Declan heard about what had happened, he convinced his brother, who at the time was contemplating a run for the open California State Senate seat, that the young hacker was someone who may someday prove useful, so using whatever influence and favor he could garner, the charges were mysteriously dropped. When that happened, Gil Price warned his brother that that was the last favor he was going to give. He was running for something higher and did not want to know what his brother was up to, in other words, Declan would be on the outside looking in. The heist, as it turned out, was his way back into his brother's campaign's good graces, because with the spoils, he was going to entice the storied campaign strategist Justin Miller.

So, when Declan Price needed help with his Genuine Bank Armored car heist project, all he did was call in the marker he had with Erick Russell, who naturally was anxious to show his gratitude.

Thus, right now when Reggie McNeal asked again if he was able to wipe the store's mainframe and that of the school and other relevant places, his answer was, "Yes, Charlie, for the twelfth hundredth time there is no way this can be traced back to us, or even know that I was there at all. They'll probably blame it on some malfunction or something, I don't know."

"Every angle?" McNeal insisted anxiously.

"Yes," the young hacker sighed. This was getting boring, but he understood where the assassin was coming from. There could not be any loose ends or else they were doomed, and that was putting it mildly.

"Okay, good," McNeal said. "Let's go over them again, starting with the one on the street."

He pulled out a chair, turned it backward, and sat behind the two men. Erick worked his magic as his fingers danced on the keyboard. For a computer genius, Erick Russell did not fit the typical stereotype of the computer nerd, geek, or whatever they may be called. He was clean-cut, well dressed, with a handsome face that did not need the required spectacles so prevalent among people of his kind.

Soon they were looking at footage from a security camera at a store across the street on Lake Avenue, facing Jones's Supermarket and let it play. They saw themselves turn right onto the small street, Calaveras, and then pull over to the side and wait. Exactly twenty-two minutes later, the Genuine Bank armored van arrived at the scene, and the men tensed as if all this were happening in real time. Shortly thereafter, the van disappeared from view when it made a left turn into the supermarket's parking lot.

Erick Russell could have easily fast-forwarded through the mundane stuff, and focused on the actual takedown, but American prisons are replete with wise men who thought that overlooking the seemingly uninteresting material, the inconsequential, was nothing but a waste of time. They were going to have to sit through the entire footage at hand, even if it took all night – too much was riding on this to take the risk.

They did catch a glimpse of the McDaniels brothers, and not out of negligence or overlooking. They were simply out of focus, like everyone else who was of no consequence. The moment they were satisfied that they had gone over every single frame, they switched to the main camera, or the 'money cam' as they called it, which was the store's footage that had been erased and was now in Erick's possession.

The view shifted to the middle laptop after the first was paused, with plans to review it yet again just to make certain that nothing was missed. Again, in this business, particularly with this job, they could never be too careful. Even if it meant studying every single frame to a point of redundancy, so be it. The instructions from 'the boss' could not have been any clearer.

The trio, Charlie, Erick, and Reggie, now leaned toward the screen even closer. This was the crux of the operation. Yes, the supermarket's security mainframe had been hacked by the best of the best in the dark cyberworld who now owned the footage, and the crime could not be traced back to them—Erick Russell had assured them of that, and based on past experiences, a single assurance was enough to appease them about this phase of the operation.

They watched the security guard, Dedrick Bellamy, leave the van after looking around, clearly surveying the area for any possible threat like he had been trained, walk to the entrance of the supermarket, and vanish shortly thereafter. After what seemed like an eternity, the driver's side door cracked open, followed soon thereafter by a puff of smoke. It was riveting for the three men watching, as if this was a great suspense movie unfolding right before their eyes.

It was clear to the audience that the driver, Martin Anderson, who they had come to know pretty well, or as well as anyone could really, had been dying for a smoke. They had obviously been studying his movements and knew that his vice was the crack they needed in this seemingly impregnable vehicle.

They watched as he quickly puffed away as he waited for his partner, knowing what was coming next. It had also occurred to Reggie McNeal and his accomplices that of all the places, this was the one pick-up where the Genuine Bank security employees felt the safest. That was why Dedrick Bellamy went in

257

alone to pick up the money. Someone should have reminded them of the axiom that the most dangerous place in the world is where you felt the safest.

Soon thereafter, the silver SUV came into frame as it drove slowly to the parked van, just like any other in the parking lot. It barely paused as it drew level with the driver's window, and they would have missed it entirely had they not been expecting it—a slight puff of smoke from the SUV's open passenger window as the heavy bullet was discharged from the sniper rifle, which killed Martin Anderson instantly. Almost immediately, Reggie McNeal jumped out of the moving car, yanked the driver's side door of the van open, hopped in, and then seconds later it pulled away and followed the SUV out of frame.

McNeal almost chuckled when he saw a discombobulated Dedrick Bellamy as he came out, realized that the van was gone after looking around, and when he finally believed his eyes, rushed back into the store at almost full sprint. The screen had just switched to another scene when suddenly McNeal thought he saw something that he should not have missed. Even though the forefront of his mind was focused on what he, Charlie, and Erick were watching, he was fully aware of the surroundings, what the other men were *not* watching.

Nevertheless, he almost missed it. Particularly because the subjects, in this case, had at first been obscured by the flummoxed Dedrick Bellamy and were a bit out of focus because of the shadow cast by the overhead roof. It did not register in the former Marine's mind until the picture on the screen changed to showing the van now on Calaveras Street, and about to make a left on Lake Avenue.

Perhaps it was a relic of his experience in his two tours in the Iraqi war, and him being one of the best snipers in his company regiment, where incredible eyesight and instinct were a prerequisite. Instinct was something you were born with, or you were out of luck, because this was a virtue that could not be taught. That was why he trusted his impulses more now than ever before, because it had saved his life on more than several occasions.

"Freeze, Erick," he said. "What was that?"

"What?" Erick asked as he turned to face McNeal for one of the few times that evening, because there was some sense of urgency in the former Marine's voice.

"Go back and run it in slo-mo."

Erick hit a few keys, and the scene switched back to the point where the van was leaving, but this time in super slow motion, and then when it got to the point where he wanted, he immediately stabbed his index finger at the top right-hand side of the screen and said simply, "There!"

The computer nerd immediately froze the screen, used some sophisticated software to enhance the image even further, and then pressed 'PLAY' again. On the screen, which was now as clear as daylight, oblivious that one of the greatest and most brazen armored car heists was going on, were Dumisani and Sasha McDaniels.

Right there, in living color, they watched Sasha McDaniels facing his brother, who was pointing a camera at him, filming as if they were shooting some kind of documentary. From where Dumisani was standing, his camera was pointing directly at the Genuine Bank Armored van which was waiting for the security guard Dedrick to return, which also meant that he'd caught everything on tape! Reggie McNeal felt the blood drain from his face. Suddenly, he felt very sick as sweat stung his armpits.

The two morons, whoever they were, had unwittingly caught the entire take-down on camera. If this ended up in the hands of even a brain-dead prosecutor struggling with the elementary civics of the law, this would be explosive. It would be courtroom gold. They would have to track those two down and get that incriminating evidence before they even knew they had it, McNeal thought.

The former Marine was horrified as he again felt his stomach lurch. The sickening sensation rose from the pit of his stomach and up to his face, and suddenly the room was hot like a sauna. It began to spin, and for a moment Reggie McNeal thought he was going to faint.

"Please tell me that is not a camcorder that guy is holding, and that he did not just unknowingly film the robbery and subsequent getaway. Please tell me that?" he said to no one in particular. His voice was hoarse, but that was not all, the other two men as they realized the full import of what he was saying unfold before their very eyes, sensed fear in the other man's voice, an emotion the assassin had never openly expressed since they'd known him.

They had planned this heist and mapped it to the last possible detail for the past year and a half, taking into account every single possibility, learning everything about the drivers including Martin Anderson's penchant for breaking the one company rule that got him killed, to practicing evasive maneuvers and tactics by planning a quick 'ditch' of the vehicle in case of a car chase from law enforcement with an elaborate diversion. To crown it all, they even took it an unprecedented step further.

In this electronic age, where everyone had a cell phone that could record live images, the thieves with the help of the super cyber geek and hacker had even taken the extraordinary step of blacking out the Wi-Fi connection of the store and surrounding areas for a period of thirty-five minutes. Just enough time to carry out the assault on the armored vehicle and its driver, and be gone before anyone knew what was going on. They had, as far as they were concerned, left nothing to chance.

However, in any undertaking, there is almost always something that will pop up. It is the rarest of operations that go off without a single hitch. Even with the best-laid plans, there's always the unforeseen, the unexpected. What some may call the 'x Factor', like the sudden appearance of two young men using, of all things, an outdated and yet effective high-definition camera (Erick Russell was able to determine its make and model, and the fact that it used mini digital recording tapes or flash drives) unwittingly filming the crime in its entirety.

Such was life. She had an ugly and at times brutal way of taking the unexpected, unforeseen, and unimaginable, like the live recording of a sensational crime, and turning it into a frightening reality.

"Oh my God in heaven!" was all Charles 'Charlie' Evans could say. Inwardly, he said to himself, *We're doomed. No question about it.*

Everyone suddenly felt sick. For all they knew, that tape was in the hands of the police, and they could be on their way. As that frightening thought flashed through their minds, they unconsciously looked at the door as if expecting armed men clad in black Ninja outfits to break it down at any moment. They all knew what the stakes were—federal prison was no joke, not only because you served at least 85% of your bid, if you were lucky, as they would have to be in this case, but they all faced a murder charge unless somehow the two unknowns on their screen could be neutralized.

Silenced permanently before whatever they caught on tape saw the light of day. Again, Reggie McNeal felt sick to a point of wanting to throw up.

And not only that, the contents on that flash drive or mini digital cassette tape, whatever, had far more reaching consequences than any of the men in the room could have known, at least at the moment. Whatever was caught by that camera would most certainly derail a campaign whose ultimate destination was residency at 1600 Pennsylvania Avenue – in other words, the White House.

"Jesus Christ in heaven," the former Marine muttered softly for the second time. "Please tell me this did not just happen. Christ! Tell me that my eyes were deceiving me." It was one of those moments where he was like a child who thought just by wishing or willing something, whatever it was, it would simply go away, vanish, like it never happened.

However, Reggie knew that to get out from under this and perhaps even get ahead of this potential catastrophe, a saner head would have to prevail. The last thing they could afford to do right now was panic. He immediately whipped out his burner from his pocket and dialed a number from memory, which was only to be used in situations such as this.

When his party answered with a gruff, "Hello?" the former Marine sniper did not even bother to identify himself.

"Aeries," he said, using the other party's code name. "We have a very serious problem and need to speak in person NOW!"

His party had never heard McNeal so agitated.

CHAPTER 33

THE ALTADENA TOWN AND COUNTRY CLUB is a private exclusive member equity club. The private club is nestled in the foothills of the San Gabriel Mountains encompassing several verdant acres of tennis courts, gardens, swimming pools, and a fitness center. The club is also an elegant venue for social gatherings, offering several ballrooms and full service catering for both members and in some certain special circumstances, members of the public. The club, though exclusive, serves many of the local communities, including Altadena, Sierra Madre, Arcadia, La Canada, and San Marino.

It was also at this country club and in one of their private rooms, which looked more like a five star hotel suite that was constantly swept for listening devices, where Declan Price preferred to conduct his top secret meetings. Before leaving the Safe House, Reggie McNeal had Erick run the footage again and asked him to freeze the frame at the point where it clearly showed the faces of the two young men, one white the other black. They looked to be college students. There was also something about them that the former marine could not readily put a finger on, he did not know what it was, but it was there.

They appeared fit, but of course that was to be expected of people their age. There was, however, something about them, a walk, a carefree attitude seldom seen. In any case, after he had Erick lift their pictures from the surveillance footage and run it through a facial recognition software using the DMV, but they got no hit at all, which was strange but certainly not the end. The next step was using the database of the Department of Homeland Security. However, this was where Erick Russell drew the line. After what happened the last time with that Bank a couple of years earlier, he was not willing to tempt fate again.

Sure, he could go in and out of the Department of Homeland Security's supercomputer without his intrusion being detected, but he just was not comfortable going that route. When McNeal insisted that he just go ahead and do it, assuring him that they were Teflon, backed by powerful people, but as of yet could not tell them who they were, the young hacker simply shut down.

Reggie thought of levelling threats at the cyber pirate, telling him that he was already in too deep and that backing away from this assignment would make no difference, but decided that that would be counterproductive. Instead, he asked Erick to send the pictures on a highly encrypted file to an email he provided. It occurred to him that the Senator might just have the necessary clearance to have someone at DHS match the pictures through a back channel so that there would be no official record of the inquiry.

That was why the following night Reggie McNeal was at the Altadena Country Club to meet with his employer, Declan Price. His two accomplices Charlie and Erick remained hunkered down at the Safe House for now until further instructions. Through yet some back channel, and this time via the Altadena Sheriff's Department, the primary investigators of the Genuine Bank Armored Van heist, they were able to find out that there were no leads whatsoever in as far as apprehending the suspects, and it did not look promising at all. It was just a matter of time before the FBI stepped in, so far they were keeping their distance even though for all intents and purposes this was a federal crime. From what Declan was able to gather, the feds had given them 48 hours to crack the whole thing wide open and time was running out.

Armed with this knowledge, Reggie McNeal knew that they had to act quickly. With the full might of the federal government and a limitless budget, you throw a bunch of hungry, young, bright, and motivated special agents at a case, and they will hammer and keep hammering at the cracks, piece everything together until they put the whole thing together, which meant it would be a matter of time before the Feds knew that there was someone out there who had the incriminating evidence literally in the palm of their hands, and they could not allow things to get that far. This thing needed to be killed before it even started evolving into a life of its own.

These were the thoughts going through Reggie McNeal's mind as he eased his Sedan, a 1996 Toyota Camry, into the premises of the exclusive country club. The silver SUV had been taken to a chop shop in Los Angeles, where it had been dismantled piece by piece and sold off. In the end it was like it never even existed. Essentially, further purging everything and anything connected with the Genuine Bank heist. This was done of course in case someone noticed the SUV in and around the time the armored van got hijacked.

A few minutes later, Reggie McNeal was led to the private room where Declan Price and two men he did not know were waiting. The room was large and nicely decorated and furnished with a well-stocked fridge. It reminded McNeal of one of those luxury suites they call a 'Box' at one of those football stadiums or at NBA basketball games.

There was a shiny conference mahogany table in the middle of the room, and Declan was seated at the other men flanked by the two strangers McNeal had never met. They were standing erect as they followed the newcomer with their eyes the moment he entered the room. They looked like enforcers more than anything else.

Without saying a word, Reggie McNeal paused and out of his pocket grabbed a mobile phone and pressed a few buttons. The device was equipped with an anti-eavesdropping measures to frustrate anyone who might try to listen in on their conversation. The room had been swept twenty minutes earlier. McNeal knew that, and the other men in the room knew that he knew but said nothing. In fact Declan Price was glad that his men were taking security measures seriously. He had preached that from Day One that *'You could never be too careful, especially when discussing things not meant for other people's ears.'*

Once satisfied that the room was bug free and secure, McNeal took a seat at the opposite end of the conference table. Price, foregoing the normal greetings and all the unnecessary chitchat, got right to the point.

"So you said someone might have witnessed the heist and worst of all have it on tape?"

Even though his face did not show it, Price had been horrified by the news that two random strangers may have unwittingly filmed the entire robbery homicide.

In fact the man had gone totally ballistic. This was the one thing that could bring the entire operation crumbling. An undertaking that had taken two years of careful planning, lots of money, bribes, and sometimes threats. Not only that, its failure and subsequent discovery could have far reaching repercussions the least of which was stiff jail sentences, and not just for him, but his brother who currently had sights on being the most powerful man in the world.

If word got out that the Campaign Manager, who had already begun crafting his message, had been paid with money from illicit gains, in effect 'blood money', the dirtiest of all, and even if Gil Price had plausible deniability, but just the mere mention of something like this would be enough to touch of a scandal never seen or heard of in the history of American politics. Declan Price just knew that it could not even be allowed to get that far, even a whiff of an outrage of this magnitude could not even be borne, let alone imagined or suspected.

Despair and anger seized him in equal turns. Declan 's anger was worsened by the fact that he could not turn it loose on anyone. Reggie McNeal and his men had carried out their duties with aplomb. The possible recording of the crime was a curveball that came from nowhere, not even left field, and had been least expected let alone imagined.

It took a while, but when he finally cooled down and came to his senses, he began thinking of a way out of this possible catastrophe. When the solution, or at least part of it began forming in his forever scheming mind, he smiled. "Of course!" he said to himself as he snapped his fingers, and went on to work the phones and his contacts the next morning before his meeting with McNeal.

Using a backdoor channel at the Department of Homeland Security, better known as DHS, Declan Price, now armed with an image of the two young men who had probably filmed the murder/robbery, the young assistant he was able to cajole by playing the Gil Price card told him to sit tight for at least a couple of hours so she could see what she could come up with.

After the September 11 terrorist attacks in 2001, then President George W. Bush signed into law the PATRIOT ACT, a backronym that stands for *Uniting and Strengthening America by Providing Appropriate Tools to Intercept and Obstruct Terrorism*. The law, among other things, compelled law enforcement agencies, the military, the intelligence community, in fact, 'the who' alphabet soup to share information that would safeguard the country, and do away with the professional jealousy and competition that was prevalent in these communities, and encourage a spirit of mutual cooperation.

The Immigration and Naturalization Service (INS) had been dissolved in 2003 and became the United States Citizenship and Immigration Services (USCIS), under the auspices of the DHS, and part of the DHS was collecting data on any person documented or not on United States soil. Thus when the lady at the Department of Homeland Security office told Declan that she would get back to him within the hour or so, that meant she was going to try and match the screen grabs that he gave her with the vast resources at her disposal. It was illegal of course but that did not matter, Price had promised her the moon and the stars to come with it later.

The hour and half it took turned out to be the longest in Declan Price's life and for good reason. This could *not* go wrong. They had to find that recording before it saw the light of day and possibly take it and the two boys who made it out of play. Thus when the lady called back, Price answered his mobile phone before it could ring for a second time. He listened for a while without taking any notes, since he prided himself with being gifted with a photographic memory, but he did ask her to send him the information via encrypted email.

"Thank you very much Sandra," he said. And just as he was about to click off he added quickly, "I'll have you on my Christmas list."

***

"So," Declan Price said as he rubbed his hands together with what to Erick McNeal seemed like ill-concealed glee, "Someone may have witnessed this, and worse still have it on tape?"

"Yeah," Reggie McNeal said as he threw an uncomfortable glance at the two hulking men standing like statues behind his boss.

There was something on the other man's face that Reggie could detect that made him feel even more uncomfortable, the Senator's younger brother seemed to be taking the whole thing lightly, he had the look of an opponent in a game of chess who knows that you have fallen into his trap.

"Don't worry about them," Price scoffed as he read McNeal's concerns. He then pointed at the two men standing behind him and said, "They're professionally deaf and mute, but I trust them with my life."

McNeal nodded as if to say, *okay whatever, it's your show boss, but can we get to the real issue of the matter please?!* Aloud he said, "We gotta act quickly Sir, any idea how we go about doing that?"

Price nodded again with ill-concealed delight, snapped his fingers, stretched out his right arm to the side and without turning, opened his palm at one of the men behind him, who immediately turned, reached for

269

a folder on a small table, Reggie had not yet noticed until now, and handed it to his boss.

"I was able to find out who those two are," Price said, enjoying the look of total surprise on the other man's face. "The two are brothers actually, stepbrothers to be exact. Foreigners, or shall I say foreign born because they're in fact American citizens. They arrived in the country three days ago. Their names are Sasha and Dumisani McDaniels, they were born and raised in Botswana, their parents, Paul and Natalie McDaniels, were renown documentary filmmakers and nature conservationists both of whom were murdered by poachers who were subsequently tried, convicted, and sent to the gallows, at least their leader, one Molo Sahili, currently on death row was scheduled to be executed in a couple of months but a stay has been granted pending one final appeal from the president, a hail Mary really since one had never been granted in a capital case. It was after that trial, in which the brothers were stellar witnesses for the state, when they decided to implement their rights as American citizens and relocated to this country." He paused for dramatic effect, but mainly to see of Reggie McNeal was trekking the story – he was spellbound.

"Go on," McNeal egged on as he leaned forward in his chair.

His mouth was slightly agape as he wondered how Price could have come up with so much, so quickly, and in so little time. But on second thought, he knew he shouldn't have been surprised. This of course was the electronic age, and he had realized long ago that the man he worked for had far reaching tentacles of power not even he could imagine, however this was breathtaking, the seeming ease with which this man could get so much information with so little to go on.

Again McNeal patted himself on the back for being on the side of Angels.

"They have come to this country," Price continued, "To begin a new life, meaning that they have yet to know their way around, which should make them easy picking," he smiled at the last jab. "It says in that report that they have an estranged uncle, Sean Kane McDaniels, former SEAL with the United States Navy's Special Warfare in Coronado California, who has since vanished to some third world hell hole, where it's believed he is a missionary of some sort. They should be easy to find and deal with, permanently, we cannot afford to have any loose ends."

There was a self-satisfied smirk on Reggie McNeal's face as he came to the same conclusion as his boss. The two brothers were easy prey, and they did not know it.

The former marine and sniper knew what to do without being told, because he said, "I'll get on it right away Sir." A thought suddenly occurred to him. "Since this seems like a neck down job really, shouldn't we use our contacts at the Sheriff's department? Perhaps scare them into giving it up?"

Declan looked at him as though he was insane as he slowly shook his head.

"No, you realize that if we involve them there's a chance that they'll know what we're up to and that will invite more unwanted questions, right?"

McNeal winced at his apparent lack of foresight and said, "Damn, sorry boss, didn't think of that."

Price waved his arm as if swatting away a fly to indicate that it was no big deal really and said, "Put them under light surveillance for a day or two and then pounce. Find out what they know first, who they've told, and then shut them up – permanently."

He did not have to spell it out, but in plain language he was telling Reggie McNeal to kill the brothers and make certain that their bodies are not found, something he had done before on numerous occasions at the Senator's younger brother's behest, who then slid the folder across the huge shiny mahogany desk at him.

"That has all the information you will need I summarized about the two freaks, and anything else that you might need to know about them."

It was a dismissal. McNeal grabbed the folder, stood up straight and out of sheer habit almost flashed a salute, but instead tucked the folder under his right arm and turned to leave. He was just about to reach for the doorknob when Declan Price's voice froze him dead on his tracks.

"Miguel and Hector will be coming with you to make sure that the job is done right." He gestured at the two men who, even up to now had not even cleared their throats, let alone speak.

"Come again?!" Reggie was surprised by this. On matters like this one he preferred to work alone, or with people he himself picked, men he could control.

"This is a very important undertaking McNeal."

"And you think I can't handle it?" the ex-marine wanted to know, his professional pride was prickled.

"Like I said Reggie, we cannot afford to take any chances."

"But these are just two jungle boys boss, they probably never even seen a traffic light in their lives until now," he whined.

"I get that McNeal, but this is a job that needs to be done quickly and quietly."

McNeal nodded and for the first time got a good look at the two men who had not moved, but still stood erect. He noticed for the first time that their hair was close cropped, suggesting that they had, just like him, a military background probably Special Forces training. He scanned the men from head to toe. The man named Miguel looked Hispanic and his skin was darker with a pockmarked face that seemed not to smile. The other, Hector, was white.

They both had a certain lean athletic quality about them. Broad shoulders, thin waist, developed legs, all three parts in perfect balance. McNeal had worked with guys like these two before, and his thoughts immediately went back to his experience in the army and the Iraq war. Special Forces type were a strange bunch and sometimes frowned on those who did not have their training, or were not part of their fraternity. He wondered how this was going to pan out. There was however one thing that McNeal noticed about the two men, Hector and Miguel, because it was something he had seen in himself, and it was the eyes, fierce eyes, imposing eyes - the eyes of a killer.

They then agreed to meet later that evening to plan and begin surveillance on the two brothers. For a man like Declan Price, who prided himself on not missing anything, there was however one glaring omission in his backgrounding of the McDaniels brothers, and it was huge. An unforgivable error that was totally inexcusable, and that being the brothers, Sasha and Dumisani McDaniels, were in fact exponents of an art as old as time itself. The art of the unarmed, the empty hand – the martial arts. In other words, the two unusual brothers were living breathing weapons.

CHAPTER 34

STARTING A NEW LIFE IN A NEW PLACE, much less one over ten thousand miles away from the old one can be daunting for any person. For two boys born and bred on a ranch in an African countryside, and then suddenly finding themselves in the most developed industrialized, urbanized nation in the world can be an absolute nightmare, and that's putting it mildly.

It was not necessarily the high rise buildings and the freeways, the brothers had been to Johannesburg, Cape Town, Pretoria, and other such cities in South Africa. The culture shock was the one thing Sasha and Dumisani had a hard time adjusting to, and they both knew that it was going to take them some time to adjust to that fact. Southern California is known as the 'melting pot' of the United States of America because of the many nationalities that settle there. However, the siblings, especially Dumisani, were shell shocked by the overwhelming number of Asians they saw and encountered. It then occurred to them that it made sense because Southeast Asia was across the Pacific Ocean.

There was then the relearning of things that were opposite from what they were used to. For instance, cars drove on the right hand side of the road as opposed to the left. And because of that they got lost at least twice when catching the bus since they were waiting on the 'wrong side' of the street. Then there were the little things like food, particularly the burgers, fries, and coke that were known as the American food. The brothers found that, and especially the much hyped 'Big Mac' to be mediocre at best. As for the colloquial stuff, they knew that with time would get it down, like referring to a 'toilet' as 'bathroom' and an eraser as a 'rubber', which in the US meant a condom.

One thing though that Sasha could not seem to easily adjust to was their circadian rhythm. Their biological clocks were still on Botswana time, or more accurately, Southern African period. That meant they stayed up late and into the wee hours of the morning, slept in, and woke up late. Julia, their landlord, had explained to them that she had a tenant also from Africa a few years earlier, who had experienced the same thing and that sooner or later their bodies would adapt.

All this was normal of course, and the siblings knew that with time they would adapt just as their landlady had told them. The downside though was that their bodies were beginning to feel the effects. For people who trained every single day, except Sundays, to be thrown into a compulsory state of idleness took a bit of getting used to. That first week was spent trying to find a Dojo that could measure up to their skill level. There was one in Altadena not too far from them, and a couple in nearby Pasadena, unfortunately, none of them measured up.

In fact there was a disturbing trend that soon became apparent to the McDaniels brothers. Many of the dojos were too commercialized in a manner of speaking, and that is to say the *Senseis* of these particular schools were mainly businessmen. The more bodies inside the studio, the better, because that meant more revenue. The brothers were also appalled at the grading system applied at these dojos.

Normally, and as tradition dictated, a beginner, which in this case is a White Belt progressed to the next stage, which is Yellow Belt, then Orange, Green, Blue, Purple, and then three stages of the Brown Belt before earning a Black Belt, or *Shodan* – a process that with utmost dedication took at least three years. At these institutions that they came across, Sasha and Dumisani found out that the instructors, in a sense business owners, added 'sub belts' in their grading system so as to keep the students, particularly paying practitioners, much longer at earning their Black Belts than was necessary.

Seeing all this was when Sasha McDaniels's resolve to open his studio grow stronger. He was going to work with troubled kids, he decided, and from the little he could tell since his arrival in the United States, they were a dime a dozen in this country. He was planning, with his brother's help, to head in a different direction. Sasha was going to find a space, turn it into a state of the art dojo, complete with ultramodern equipment, a game room with pinball machines, X-Boxes, Foosball, and the like. The rule would be that no one would enter the game room until they completed their training for the day and homework. He would have a fulltime staff who would see to that, and all this would be paid out of his own pocket.

The more Sasha thought about it, the more the idea began to grow in his mind. He was certain it would work. While Dumisani was at school, he'd be putting his plan into action and see it to fruition. When he went to bed that night, he did so with a smile on his face. Sasha McDaniels had found his true purpose in life – his calling. He was going to help troubled kids in the neighborhood and beyond.

The next morning he and his brother decided to 'shock' their bodies back into the shape it was accustomed to. It had been two weeks since they did a formal workout, and they were beginning to feel the effects. Bodies that are kept at an optimum level of fitness like those of Olympians, as was the case with the brothers, need to be engaged in exercise at all times. When that does not happen, the body reacts by getting tired quickly, feels a little sick, sluggish, and dull with a tightness behind the eyes.

Another bout of inactivity, and the subject starts to experience minor flu like symptoms like body aches and lightheadedness, which then leads to the body being susceptible to infections and or injuries. This was the stage at which the brothers were. There was only one cure for it and that was exercise, which is exactly what they did that morning.

They began with a clip of fifty pushups to get the blood flowing, stretching and even more stretching, and when they felt loose enough, took a jog up Lake Avenue toward the mountains. This was a stretch of about two and a half miles, and was a grind because they were running uphill. Lake Avenue ends right at the foothills of the San Gabriel Mountains with its peak being Mount Wilson, on which are the aerial towers that service most of the local television and radio stations. From here, there was an entrance of what used to be the Cobb Estate, which was, aside from being a tourist attraction (primarily the local type), a very popular hiking area.

Inside the former estate are numerous hiking trails, one of which leads to a popular mini waterfall. It was on this trail that the two brothers, Dumisani and Sasha McDaniels, decided to expand on their workout. With Sasha waiting at the waterfall, close to half a mile away, stopwatch in hand, Dumisani began his sprint run.

He leapt over a rotting log and immediately ducked beneath a branch arching down from his right. It would have been easier to drop and roll, but the maneuver would have cost him time. In his experience, almost three quarters of a second.

Dumisani entered a clearing and increased his speed. Both brothers were excellent sprinters, although Dumisani was the faster of the two. He took the steepest line up the dirt slope, staying low to minimize his profile. Not that he was expecting danger or an attack from anyone hiding in the foliage on either side of him, but ever since their deadly encounter with the poachers back home, the brothers had incorporated anticipating sudden surprise attacks into their training regimen.

His thighs were on fire, but his legs and heart were handling the workload with an ease which surprised even him. Dumisani knew why and up until now he had kept that knowledge a secret even from his brother. The one a day 10mg of Oxycodone had become two and the dosage was now at three a day. He had also discovered that when he chewed the bitter tasting pill their effect was immediate, which increased his blood's ability to carry oxygen to his muscles. That was the reason why he was performing at optimum level and feeling euphoric at the same time.

Sasha suddenly sprang from his hiding place, which had been a clump of bushes beside the winding path and intercepted his brother as if he were some unexpected intruder. Dumisani's reaction was swift. He took two steps and the moment his right leg touched the ground, he used his leg as pivot and performed a graceful overhead somersault over his brother's crouched form, and landed on both feet then quickly turned to face him. The move had been so sudden, and so unexpected that Sasha was momentarily stunned before he quickly recovered, and immediately went on the offensive by executing two front snap kicks which were easily parried.

The brothers continued their light sparring, holding back what primarily would have been devastating blows. It went on for another five minutes before they both paused almost at the same time, and went on to catch their breath. Always one not to accept that he had been bested, Sasha said, "Your speed was rather optimum today Dumi."

"What are you trying to say? That I'm not good enough?" Dumisani fumed in spite of himself, at the same time wondering if his brother knew he had taken some stimulants.

"I said no such thing," Sasha said as he raised his hands, something both brothers did occasionally to expand the lungs as they took in more of the much needed oxygen.

"What then?"

"Nothing, it's just that I thought your speed was rather unusual that's all."

"So?"

"So nothing, I thought you'd take it as a compliment," Sasha said as he wiped his sweaty brow with the back of his hand.

His face and arms were a slight patch of red, something that happened whenever he was involved in a rigorous workout.

"I see," Dumisani said as he realized that his secret was safe for now, even though he knew that sooner or later he would have to tell the most important person in his life that he may be having a serious problem.

"Great workout, nonetheless," Sasha said as he looked around the bushy surrounding that in a way reminded them of the vegetation at the ranch back home.

"Kind of reminds me of home," Dumisani declared, as if he were reading his brother's thoughts.

"Sure does," Sasha agreed as he readjusted the belt pouch on his waist. It was facing backwards during the initial stages of their exercise session, Dumisani had not noticed it up until now.

"Why bring that along?" he asked as he pointed at the fanny pack.

"Well, we don't have our California IDs yet. So in here I have our passports, cash and my emergency credit card."

Dumisani nodded but said nothing. It was time to head back home, and soon they were trudging along one of the numerous hiking trails that would lead them back to the entrance of what used to be the Cobb Estate, and then to Lake Avenue where they planned to take a slow jog back to their apartment.

***

When the brothers got home, they took a shower in their respective rooms, both had a bathroom and shower. Dumisani was the first to finish, and as he dried himself and wrapped a towel around his waist, he heard the landline in the living room start ringing. He quickly reached for the slippers underneath his bed and put them on, his muscular torso still bare, along with remnants of the shower running down his body like tiny rivulets.

He wondered who could be calling their home at 9:31 in the morning. He just hoped it was not one of those people trying to sell them some knickknack over the phone. They had had more than enough of those pushy telemarketers already.

"Hello?" he said into the receiver with what could be perceived as a frustrated sigh, he was not going to be nice today.

A female voice on the other end that sounded vaguely familiar suddenly got his heart pumping fast. *It can't be*, he thought to himself. *No way*!

"Hi, this is Misty Abdul. Dumisani? Is that you?"

Dumisani McDaniels froze as he could hear the smile in her voice. It was one of the tourist girls they met at the Sedia Riverside Motel in Maun, the one he liked with the long dark hair whose parents were from Iran, and was born in the U.S. the very pretty one with luminous bedroom eyes.

"M-Misty?" he stammered, not for one second believing his ears. "Misty Abdul?"

"Yes Dumi," she chuckled. "It's me."

"My goodness Misty, h-how did you get this number? How did you find us?"

He still could not believe this was happening. Adding to the fact that he and Sasha had just engaged in a rigorous workout that got his blood flowing again, plus a nice hot shower, he was practically euphoric.

"Your brother friended me on Facebook and then I looked through his profile to make sure it was the right Sasha McDaniels and boom there it was, your home number," she said.

Dumisani gripped the cordless receiver even harder as he sat down. His knees were suddenly weak.

"Wow," he managed to say. "Thank God for social media, because we never got the chance to hook up as planned back in Botswana."

There was an uncomfortable silence from both of them because they knew what was coming next.

"Yes Dumi," Misty said. There was a tinge of sadness in her voice. "My deepest condolences to you and your brother, we heard about the raid. The girls and I were distraught – we still are as a matter of fact."

"Thanks Misty," was all he could say as he felt the familiar lump start to expand in his throat.

This was followed again by another round of uncomfortable silence. The wound, one that would never completely heal was open and bleeding again, and the beautiful woman at the other end of the line sensed it. It was time, she thought, to steer the conversation to somewhere else nicer.

"Hey, I would like to swing by if you guys don't mind," she said in a voice so chirpy that she sounded like an excited high school girl, who just got the news that she made the high school cheerleading squad.

"Of course, are you kidding me?"

It was going to be great to see someone he knew albeit briefly other than his brother, and in a foreign land no less. It was amazing, Dumisani thought, how life worked out sometimes.

"Great, give me your address and I'll see you in less than an hour."

It made sense because now he recalled that she lived in nearby Pasadena.

"Can't wait." He had a broad grin on his very handsome face.

"You boys hungry?" she wanted to know. "I can pick up something on the way."

They had more than enough food to whip up something real quick, and chances were she was going to pick up some fast food, something they had temporarily sworn off, but then what the hell? A very beautiful girl, a knockout actually, was about to light up their home so why care?

"That will be very sweet of you Misty."

"Thanks Dumi," she said. "See you soon."

"Can't wait," he repeated and really meant it as he hung up the phone with the big grin still plastered on his face.

As he turned around, he realized that his brother, just like him, had a large towel wrapped around his waist and had been standing at the entrance of the hallway that led to the living room and had been eavesdropping on the one sided conversation.

"What was that all about?" Sasha asked with raised eyebrows.

"You're not going to believe this man," Dumisani said excitedly.

"What happened?"

"That chick, Misty Abdul called man," Dumisani answered with a wide smile on his face.

His brother smiled and said, "Misty? The tourist?"

"Yes indeed."

Suddenly Sasha's brow twisted as he thought of something and said, "How did she …"

"God bless Facebook Sasha," Dumisani interrupted. "She saw your friend request, apparently your little ploy worked. I gave her our address by the way, and she'll be heading out here in less than an hour."

Apparently forgetting that he had just stepped out of the shower and that his torso was bare, Sasha unconsciously glanced at the wristwatch that was not there.

"That means soon Dumi," Sasha said. "Let's get the place ready man." He then looked at his brother, a sly grin started to play on his face as he asked, "Do you know if she's bringing any of her friends?"

"She didn't mention that and I didn't think to ask, I was just too excited to hear her voice. Amazing isn't it?"

"Yeah," Sasha agreed as he turned to head to his room to put on some clothes.

"I guess we'll find out from her about the others," Dumisani said. He was still supercharged and visibly excited at seeing the beautiful woman again. She had been a fading memory thanks to the life changing events that had happened to them over the past few months since they last saw them at that bar in Maun in what seemed like another lifetime ago.

They were soon dressed, both them in fresh sweatpants and matching tops, discarding the ones they wore earlier. Sasha's was grey and had the fanny pack strapped around his waist, while Dumisani had a blue pair of Nike sweaters, a white t shirt and an unzipped matching top. The living room and the house in general did not need any cleaning, but they found it necessary to move the longer of the two couches to the opposite side from where it had been, and moved the plasma TV to the side where the window was.

All throughout, in anticipation of Misty's arrival, for all intents and purposes their very first guest, Sasha had a sly grin spread all over his face the entire time. Dumisani could not help but notice as he studied his brother's face for a moment, and knew exactly what he was thinking.

"What?" Dumisani said. "You think you're going to get her in bed?"

Sasha's smile widened even more as he said, "The reason why I was asking if she's coming with of her friends is because I was thinking more for you."

"What are you talking about?" Dumisani frowned, he knew exactly where this was going.

Sasha gave another one of his goofy smiles that never ceased to get under his brother's skin, and said, "Misty is mine." As if it was a forgone conclusion.

Dumisani scoffed and said, "I don't think so Sasha, you may have found her, but she's got the hots for me, I sensed that back home – you'll see."

"You're crazy man," Sasha said. "It's me she wants," he continued. "I knew it then and I know it now."

He was still grinning. Some people, particularly the ladies found it irresistible, and he knew it. To his brother, especially during moments such as these, it was downright annoying.

"That's beside the point Sasha and you know it. Why you got to have all the girls man?"

Sasha stopped smiling, and suddenly there was tension brewing between the two young men. It was obvious that Dumisani had sparked a painful memory best left unsaid.

"I can't believe you're still dwelling in the past man," Sasha said softly.

"It still hurts Sasha, you knew Tshidi and I had a good thing going, but no you had to step in and confuse her."

The girl in question, Motshidisi Mosidila, was a beautiful woman the brothers had met two and a half years earlier, well more accurately, Dumisani had met, when Paul McDaniels travelled with his sons to the capital city Gaborone, to interview possible anchors for a wildlife show Paul and Natalie were planning to launch for an international audience, which meant she was a real knockout as all other prospects who had come to audition were.

Determined to use local talent and not outsource to neighboring South Africa, where he knew there were more than enough candidates, Paul placed an AD in all the major newspapers calling for auditions of local young women who could be possible anchors for the new series he and his wife were planning.

The response was overwhelming. Paul rented a conference room at the Avani Gaborone Resort and Casino to conduct auditions. On seeing the young ladies lined up to be called one at a time, for a one on one camera tryout, in front of Paul McDaniels and a couple of assistants McDaniels knew he had a long day ahead of him, because picking the best was not going to be easy. It seemed as if the prettiest ladies the nation had to offer were all lined up for this once in a lifetime opportunity. It was among these many hopefuls that Dumisani spotted the lovely Motshidisi Maureen Mosidila.

Things got off to a real good start between the two of them until later that day between call backs, as they were at a table having lunch when, as Sasha was walking by, Dumisani introduced his lunch date, the knockout of a woman Motshidisi, to his brother. After the tried and tested routine of showing their '*O Mangs*' to prove that they were indeed brothers, Dumisani, thinking that the deal was closed, insisted that Sasha join them at the table.

A colossal mistake it turned out, because all of a sudden the lady, Motshidisi, or Tshidi, as she preferred to be called, could not keep her eyes off the other McDaniels. The fact that he was white and could speak Setswana fluently and in the local vernacular no less, though not quite rare nor common either, was quite a novelty and a turn on. Not to mention that, just like his brother, he was also very handsome was just the icing on the cake, and the poor girl was instantly swept off her feet not by Dumisani, but his brother.

"I couldn't help that she had the hots for me Dumi," Sasha said, snapping his brother out of his brief reverie down memory lane.

"You shouldn't have encouraged her man." There was an edge to Dumisani's voice as he felt a long ago suppressed anger fighting to break free.

Sasha on the other hand did not think the whole thing was a big deal. If the girl Tshidi, or whatever the hell her name was, liked him while his brother was trying to put the moves on her, and she was not even subtle about it, then she was not worth the trouble of chasing, let alone be with. As far as Sasha was concerned, and with some justification, these were the kind of women who leave a string of broken hearts in their wake.

So taking the whole thing lightly as this thought crossed his mind, Sasha said, "Did I tell you that she was a great kisser too?"

"That's not funny man!" Dumisani's nostrils were suddenly flaring.

"Man one time we kissed for two hours straight, and her voice over the phone was damn near erotic."

That pushed Dumisani over the edge as he felt the rage that had been steadily building suddenly explode like a volcano. Again that was the thing with Sasha McDaniels, he could be very annoying like that. The two had fought a lot like regular siblings do when they were much younger.

"I said stop it man!"

"Oh what?" Sasha smiled.

Without warning, Dumisani shoved his brother, who after stumbling a few steps, as this was unexpected, answered with a savage but playfully hard thrust of his own. However, the two soon realized that they had since outgrown this behavior because they soon starred at one another for a while as the tension subsided, and then burst out laughing. They were both being silly and they knew it. The brothers laughed until their eyes filled with tears. After a brief hug, they finished dressing, and straightened out the kitchen and living room in anticipation of Misty's visit. At one point Dumisani was about to ask his brother why he was still carrying his fanny pack, which he had since moved to the small of his back by rotating its belt, but then thought better of it and decided to let it go.

CHAPTER 35

Since there really wasn't much to straighten out because by and large the brothers were neat and orderly by nature, a virtue they were taught from childhood, they were done in almost no time. They tried to look casual and hip in their brand name sweatpants and matching tops made by Nike, and looked good in them, nonetheless.

By all accounts, Misty Abdul was going to be their very first visitor, and the brothers were a bit nervous. They both liked the girl, there was no denying that. Now who she was going to pick if at all her mind was in that direction was a little more than a coin toss. Both brothers were extremely handsome, athletic built, and well spoken. The only difference was that one was black and the other was white.

Even though he did not say it, and in all likelihood never would, Sasha McDaniels thought he had an edge over his brother because of the two, he was the extrovert, the life of the party in a manner of speaking, and a foreign accent to boot. Dumisani on the other hand was more reserved, the kid who attracted women via his ears, which was to say he was the kind of man who listened patiently to a woman when she spoke, instead of waiting to talk like his brother. Women, he had long since observed, were attracted to men who listened to them. This was where he thought he had an edge over his brother, but it was going to be interesting, he reflected with a slight smile, as they waited for their guest.

The doorbell finally chimed and both brothers, even though it had been expected, almost jumped in anticipation.

"That must be her," Dumisani, in spite of himself, jumped to his feet in excitement like a ten year old about to be given free rein in a candy store.

Sasha, who was seated closer to the door also sprang to his feet a split second later than his brother, and said quickly, "I'll get it Dumi."

"Okay."

His brother then rushed to his room where he opened his dresser, and lifted his neatly folded clothes and retrieved a bottle of pills from its secret stash. Dumisani had hoped not to need a dosage of the powerful pain pills, Oxycodone, which also happened to be a narcotic, to ease his nervousness he no doubt knew was going to be intensified by Misty's presence, and then without thinking pocketed a few of them for later, just in case.

Plus the pain in the wrist from the injury he suffered in the fight with the Afrikaners was flaring up, and he needed to numb it for now. At least that's the excuse he kept telling himself. He was hooked, and it was getting worse with every day that passed. And the fact that he was keeping that part of his life from his brother, meant he was now on a train that kept gaining speed with no place to jump off.

He quickly threw two pills in his mouth, ground them to dust with his molars, and washed the powder down with some water from a bottle on top of the dresser meant specifically for that purpose. He did not have to wait long before bam! The familiar feeling of euphoria hit the moment the powder in his intestines worked itself into his bloodstream, and then hit his cerebral cortex. It felt good as he closed his eyes for a few seconds and took it in. He remembered hearing someone, he did not remember exactly whom, but it was back home who said, '*If something you ingest feels really good, it's probably not good for you*'. However, like any other narcotic of its kind, Oxycodone throws logic out the window, and for now he was ready to meet the woman of his dreams.

Meanwhile, in the living room, Sasha strode to the door in great anticipation with a million dollar smile, one that he was boyishly proud of, splashed on his face. When he opened the door three fierce looking men with close cropped hair and well-formed limbs were at the doorstep, one of them immediately pointed a 9mm Uzi Sub Machine Gun fitted with a thick black silencer *pointed at his face*! Sasha's smile instantly turned into a confused frown.

He did not like the dead look in their eyes. The cold stare in their eyes that he had seen before, the like that he had seen in killers like Molo Sahili.

Quickly recovering from his initial shock, Sasha involuntarily took a half step and said, "What the hell is this?"

Even though his heart was pounding to a point that he thought the interlopers might hear it, his voice was even, calm which caused the three men to hesitate. This was not what they expected. In their minds, the brothers were supposed to wilt at the sight of such firepower as a silenced Uzi. On the other hand, it tasked Sasha McDaniels's entire manliness not to take another few steps back.

With such people, he had long since learned, you never yielded an inch if you could, you had to show them that you were not scared even if you were, because they could not tell the difference, Sasha knew, so long as he had his breathing under control, they could not sense it. Besides, the McDaniels boys had in the not too distant past starred down much ferocious men, men with faces of lions – Molo Sahili and his brigands.

One of the men, Hector St. John, his eyes not even for a split second wavering from Sasha, said calmly, "Hands in the air Mr. McDaniels and slowly take two steps back."

Jesus Christ, they know who I am, Sasha thought with a sinking heart as he slowly did as he was told. This certainly could not have been some bizarre mistake. These men were after them, and they had not been in the United States for more than two weeks. At first, he had a fleeting thought that maybe the previous tenant had been a criminal of some sort, and had crossed some very dangerous people and here they were to exact retribution over God knows what, but unfortunately for them their quarry was long gone, but that was certainly not the case apparently because the man waving that damn Uzi in his face had called him by name.

Another thought occurred to him as he slowly, still with his hands in the air, backed into the living room. Could this be Sahili's doing? Did his tentacles reach this far? Impossible! But still he had to wonder. It just couldn't be. Sahili was a brigand, a poacher, basically a common criminal. A tad above the rest admittedly, ruthless and cunning, but not sophisticated enough to pull off something like this and so soon. So no, it couldn't have been him, the ultimate McDaniels nemesis calling the shots from a death row prison in Gaborone over ten thousand miles away.

"What do you want?" Sasha asked with a calmness in his voice that again surprised the intruders.

They did not answer him, instead they were looking around as if they were searching for someone or something. Sasha wondered what they were up to as he furtively glanced to his left and then to his right, wondering if his brother was aware of what was going on. At that moment, the three men spread around the living room. One of them, Miguel Bustamante also pulled out a silenced Glock and pointed it at Sasha. With his free hand he tried to shove him backward, but the latter stood his ground, his arms still raised.

Miguel gave a mirthless smile and said, "Tough guy, huh?"

"Pretty much," Sasha retorted, as he wrecked his brain to buy time, perhaps for Dumisani to figure out what was going on, hide then maybe escape through the second story window and go get help. But even as he thought it, he knew it was not going to happen, his brother was just as clueless as he was, and he would come budging into the room any second and the intruders will have them right where they want them.

"What the hell do you guys want? And don't tell me you're cops, and whoever you're looking for does not live here anymore, we …" and right at that moment he caught himself, he had no idea who these people were and if they knew anything about his brother. "I just moved in," he said and immediately winced, he was being unnecessarily garrulous.

The other two interlopers kept looking around the living room, making Sasha wonder again what it was exactly these men were seeking, this while the fierce looking Hispanic man Miguel Bustamante still had his Uzi pointed at him.

"Where's the other guy?"

"What?! … Who are you talking about?" Sasha asked, playing dumb and at the same time fighting to keep his voice even. He was terrified, no doubt, these guys had brought some serious firepower to just be looking for someone, and the fact that they had not even bothered to hide their faces gave him cause for concern. It meant they were out to hurt them.

"Hey, hey, we ain't got time for games. Where's the other guy? The guy with the camcorder?" Hector St. John suddenly snapped as he turned from looking around and pointed that damn gun at Sasha too.

Now Sasha McDaniels was really frightened. It was *them* they were after. But why?

To his astonishment and utter dismay, he heard himself blurt out, "My brother … Dumi?"

"Yeah, yeah," McNeal said a bit irritated. "Where is he and where's the damn tape? I'm not gonna ask you again," he said as he took a step closer at Sasha, who was now totally confused, pointing the silenced weapon.

What tape were they talking about? Sasha wondered again.

"What tape are you taking about?" the young man wanted to know, giving voice to his thoughts.

"Like he said," Miguel Bustamante prodded. "Don't make him ask you again, now for the last time, where's the camcorder your brother was using and all the tapes that go with it?" He was obviously getting irritated by all this stalling by Sasha as he slowly placed his finger on the trigger, ready now to kneecap Sasha McDaniels if need be.

Obviously attracted by the commotion, Dumisani burst into the living room in a rush. He had been lying on his bed, waiting for the Oxycodone to get a good grip on him when he heard the hubbub. At first, he thought it had been the TV or that the drug he had taken was making him hear things that weren't there.

"Hey, what in the hell is going on here?" Wide eyed, Dumisani was beyond flabbergasted at what he saw. His brother, hands in the air and three strangers pointing guns at them, and in their living room no less! Two of the guns were instantly pointed at him.

"Dammit Dumi," Sasha hissed. "I thought you'd get the hint and …"

"Shut up!" the other man, who had been doing all the frantic searching around the living room, Hector St. John, snapped.

St. John continued pointing the Uzi at a shocked Dumisani, but a bit more menacingly and the young man who, like his brother, instinctively threw his arms in the air, he had also seen enough movies to know what to do. He tried to keep his hands from shaking as immediately a thought ran through his mind and he was most certain his brother's as well – *not again please God*!

"The camcorder with the tapes, hand them over – now!" St. John ordered.

"Why?" Dumisani asked, still totally perplexed not at the moment making the connection.

"I said *now*!" St. John hissed.

Dumisani and Sasha realized that criminals, just like cops, and it didn't matter what nationality they were, liked to ask the questions, not answer them.

The camera in question was in a silver metallic casing at the corner of the living room in plain sight, which was probably why the intruders had missed it. The case was on the side of the room where the plasma TV was sitting on its stand. It had been there after their first ever trip to the neighborhood supermarket, and Dumisani had not touched it since, let alone review what he had recorded. He was in fact planning to do that the next afternoon.

The plan was to review the footage and then edit it all before classes started, which was still about three and a half weeks away. Dumisani felt he had time to procrastinate a little. Editing was a long, arduous, but ultimately rewarding undertaking. Plus, he told himself, he still needed to settle down.

Dumisani and Sasha made brief eye contact. The two knew each other intimately, and in that brief moment they communicated a lot. These men were here to kill them after they got what they wanted that was certain. There was no way they were going to leave living witnesses to tell their story. The brothers had been through this before.

"It's over there," Dumisani said calmly as he pointed to the opposite corner of the room where the camera actually was.

He was standing almost at the entrance of the living room, where it adjoined the tiny hallway that led to the kitchen, the main bathroom shower, and the two bedrooms. So when the three men instinctively turned their heads to look at what he had been pointing at, as he knew they would, as did Sasha, they were distracted for a fraction of a second. It was all the brothers needed.

Dumisani McDaniels leaned backwards, twisted his body to the right and performed an acrobatic somersault move before landing with what could only be described as grace, in the kitchen, and disappeared from sight. This was followed by a volley of bullets from St. John's suppressed Uzi, as he fired at where Dumisani had been standing just a few seconds earlier. The air was filled with a haze of plaster dust. Sasha was horrified, thinking his brother was hit.

"Dumi!!!" he screamed.

It was a cry of horror, desperation, anger, and might. It was the heightened *Kia*, the martial arts war cry that for a split second froze the other two gunmen, time enough to give Sasha McDaniels the time to kick the weapons out of first McNeal, and then Bustamante.

The rapid snap kick on the underside of Reggie McNeal's wrist sent a paralyzing jolt of pain that shot up the entire length of his arm, instantly numbing it as the silenced Uzi clanged harmlessly to the floor.

And just as Bustamante was raising his weapon to fire at Sasha, the latter's foot landed on the floor in front of him, and then used it to pivot his body into performing a lightening quick spin back kick that caught Bustamante on the elbow, making him whirl and fire wide, and as he staggered backwards, his Uzi also falling to the floor, Sasha hopped forward from the floor with both feet and as he landed on him, executed two straight punches to his chest and face, dropping him like a sack full of salt.

Then without even looking, reacting on pure instinct and adrenaline, his leg shot out in a powerful mule kick that caught the advancing Reggie McNeal on the upper left side of his belly right where the ribcage was. The blow sent McNeal flying across the room with a pair of cracked ribs. The pain was excruciating as he fought to breath, and at that moment McNeal realized that he had never in his life been hit so hard.

He lay on the floor dazed, face up, not able to breath and could only watch helplessly as Sasha McDaniels quickly, methodically, but altogether very thoroughly dismantle Miguel Bustamante, himself no shrinking violet, like he was not even there. Who were these McDaniels brothers? He wondered for the first time since they were sent on this mission. They had been expecting to find two docile kids, who would pee down their pants legs at the first sight of a real gun pointed at them, and not just any gun, an Uzi fitted with a Silencer – *not* two cornered Wolverines. The boss had missed a very important fact about these two unusual brothers, they were well versed in the art of unarmed combat.

Meanwhile in the kitchen, as Hector St. John went after Dumisani, leading with his weapon stretched out in both arms, his quarry, after springing to his feet, immediately pressed his back to the kitchen wall by the door and kicked the Uzi out Hector's hands. When his attacker staggered backwards, Dumisani feigned like he was going left and then immediately swung to his right, quickly arched his right foot, catching his opponent above the heels, and swept his legs from under him. Hector St. John hit the back of his head hard on the floor and barely stayed conscious as he felt the bile rise to his throat.

Through sheer will power and desperation, Hector turned on his stomach and crawled back where he had come, the living room, searching for his weapon. And before his fingers touched the silenced Uzi, Dumisani was on him like a hungry cat on a fleeing mouse. It started first with a kick to the belly, which basically incapacitated him, giving Dumisani the time to pin his arms with his arms with his knees, and unleashed two powerful straight punches to the face, splitting his lips and dislodging a couple of teeth.

"Who the hell are you guys, and what do you want with us?" Dumisani McDaniels roared the moment he felt his opponent weakening from the blows.

"Fuck you!" St. John said as he immediately pursed his lips and got ready to spew a gob of blood filled spittle at Dumisani's face, but the latter immediately realized what he was about to do, and folded his fingers at the top knuckles and immediately delivered a lighting quick strike at his throat, making Hector St. John chock, cough, and gag on his own spittle.

"I'd be more careful with my choice of words if I were you," Dumisani retorted.

He punched him repeatedly on the face again. He did not throw his blows in flurries, but like the expert he was, it was in timed, slow motion sequences that carried the full weight of his strong and ripped body.

Dumisani was about to deliver yet another blow, his hand cocked midway when there was suddenly an ear splitting scream at the open doorway, and the sound of a paper bag full of something and filled paper cups falling to the floor.

They all looked up to see who it was causing this raucous, and the sight froze the McDaniels brothers. There, standing at the living room doorway, hands covering her mouth, eyes wide as saucers in genuine terror, was a stunningly beautiful brunette with enchanting brown luminous bedroom eyes. The woman standing like a divine nymph goddess was none other than Misty Abdul. The breakfast she had promised to get for the boys was now scattered at her feet.

Dumisani, his hands still grabbing at the collar of Hector St. John, was the first to recover somewhat.

"Misty?!" he gasped in utter shock. With what was happening to them at the moment, he had totally forgotten her impending arrival, and quickly realized the danger she had inadvertently walked willingly into.

"Oh my God Dumi," she said in a shaky voice. "Sasha? W-what's going on?" she stammered.

"Get out of here Misty!" Sasha yelled as he struggled to subdue the two men.

Maybe because she was in shock, stunned at what she was witnessing but Misty hesitated, and remained rooted at the same sport. In seeing this, and acting with incredible quickness, Miguel Bustamante suddenly broke free from Sasha's grip, grabbed one of the silenced Uzis that was lying on the floor rushed to where Misty was standing, and practically ripped her blouse as he stood behind her, arm hooked around her chest area so that he had good control over her, and pointed the gun to her head.

"The camcorder and all the tapes that go with it NOW, or I'll blow this bitch's brains all over the floor while you watch, and still give me what I demand. What's it gonna be?" Miguel Bustamante smiled ruefully. He had them where he wanted and not only that, but had the ultimate bargaining chip – Misty Abdul's life.

Damn!

Dumisani quickly stepped away from his man, hands spread to his side, and Sasha did the same.

"Okay, easy man. Let her go, she has absolutely nothing to do with this," said Dumisani.

The other two men, Reggie and Hector were slow in getting up. They had been on the receiving end of a terrific beat down, and their battered, bruised, contorted faces said it all.

Sasha, panting, then said to his brother, "Dumi … give them whatever it is they want man."

"Yes, and they'll let us be, right Sasha?!" Dumisani scoffed in spite of their situation.

"Just do it Dumi," Sasha hissed between clenched teeth, his eyes still fixated on Bustamante

"Are you okay Misty?" Dumisani asked, as he wrecked his brain to find a way out of this quandary.

"H-having a time of my life I guess sweetie, what's …"

"Shut up!" Bustamante shouted.

They were at a stalemate, and the brothers had to think fast if they had even a prayer of getting out of this one alive and saving Misty in the process.

CHAPTER 36

THE MOMENT THE ORDER WAS GIVEN to find the McDaniels boys, get the video recording, learn what they knew and most importantly who they told, they were to eliminate them. The three hired goons Reggie McNeal, Miguel Bustamante, and Hector St. John immediately went to work. First order of business was finding out where the brothers lived. With Erick Russell's help, they were able to determine from the surveillance camera footage from the businesses that caught their image that they had walked to the Jones Supermarket establishment, which meant they most likely lived within a two square mile radius.

With a little more prodding from the cyber pirate, they were able to find and lock down their address. And like the professionals they were, they did not rush into executing their plan. The trio waited, studied the mood and rhythm of the neighborhood before they made their move, they learned who the other tenants were in the McDaniels's apartment building, where they worked, what times they were home, and other such information they could use to their advantage.

One of the men, Miguel Bustamante, even posed as a local cable man complete with a cap and uniform and pretended to check the cable lines and box in the apartment premises. This was so he could determine who was home at what time and when. Since this was supposed to be a 'snatch and grab' job, it was very important that there be no witnesses to what they were about to do. This would have to be done right because they were to do this job in broad daylight, which meant they were to hit the McDaniels brothers at a time when there were few or no tenants in the nine other apartments.

It did not take them long to find out that since the brothers had barely arrived in the country, they had no ties to the community, no friends they could locate or people they visited. The brothers did not work, even though they found out that the black one, Dumisani, was set to enroll at the Pasadena Arts Center to study Television Production and Journalism, but that was a few weeks away. It also made sense to Bustamante and company, once they were in possession of all the intelligence on the brothers, why he had been filming with that damn camera on the day of the robbery.

10 am, Miguel Bustamante realized, was the best time to raid the brothers. By that time, same for the manager, Julia Armstrong, those not at work pretty much kept indoors. Julia, they found out, pretty much worked all afternoon monitoring her online business, even better was that the two other tenants, an old retired couple pretty much did the same.

The plan was to knock at the brothers' door, subdue them and then take them to a secret location, which in this case was a soundproof warehouse in the City Of Industry, approximately 15 miles southeast of Altadena, bleed them of all they knew, kill them quietly, and then at dead of night dispose the bodies off the coast of Long Beach by wrapping them in chicken wire mesh attached to weights that would keep them at the bottom of the ocean, never to be seen or heard from ever again. And most importantly, the most crucial witnesses to the Genuine Bank Armored Car Heist, and the damning evidence in their possession will have disappeared and none would be the wiser.

Everything was already prepared and set in motion. The van in which the gagged and bound brothers were to be transported in was prepped and ready, and so was the soundproof warehouse, the thirty foot fishing boat already fueled, ready, and docked at the marina in Long Beach.

The van, just to be on the safe side, was going to be destroyed after the job was completed. Once More, they were not going to leave anything to chance. However, the indefensible, inexcusable, and deplorable mistake these supposed professionals made was to grossly underestimate their targets whom they regarded as 'soft', naïve, and from some African backwater who probably never saw a freeway, let alone a skyscraper, in their lives.

When Bustamante realized, albeit too late, at the ease with which the brothers man handled them, he had been forced to wonder and he was certain his fellow goons were of the same mind frame – who the hell were these McDaniels brothers? That they were well versed in the martial arts was a no brainer, but what type of martial arts he had no idea.

In the modern era, the martial arts had evolved and its participants, just like the art itself had developed. There was a worldwide phenomenon called the 'Mixed Martial Arts', which had taken the world by storm. However what these two unusual brothers possessed was something even he, with his Special Forces training, had never seen. It was something beyond the physical limits, something that had reached a spiritual insight.

How else could he explain the ease with which three armed men, two of them with Special Forces training could be dismantled with such ease? He, just like Reggie McNeal, had to wonder how the people who had sent them on this mission that was supposed to have been a cakewalk, could miss such a very important aspect about the two brothers? Because had they known about the brothers fighting capabilities, Bustamante was certain that they would have planned things differently.

For one, they would have brought more men. Certainly, the downside of that would be the greater possibility of someone seeing them. A number of people coming to an apartment building, no matter how you try to disguise it, was bound to attract unwanted attention. The kind that may prompt some busy body to pick up the phone and call the local Sheriff or the police, which then could certainly complicate matters.

Secondly, they would have had to come up with a plan to separate the brothers somehow. He was not sure how they would have accomplished that, but Bustamante was certain they would have thought of something. Separate the brothers and then hit them with overwhelming force, especially the white one named Sasha. There was no denying the fact that the two brothers possessed fighting skills that were superb – out of this world even.

However, even among the best of the best, there were just those who were head and shoulders above the rest, and the McDaniels boys were that rare breed. In other words the difference between participating in the Olympics and winning the gold. And that Sasha McDaniels, Bustamante learned, was something else. My God! He was in a class all by himself, scarier was the fact that the other brother, the black McDaniels was not too far off. One could even argue that he was slightly better depending on the opponent. It was only the sudden and unexpected appearance of the girl

Misty, or whatever her name was that made the difference, and had tipped the scale in their favor.

Now Miguel Bustamante had full control of the situation. The muzzle of the silenced Uzi was pressed on the side of the side of the beautiful woman's head, and the brothers knew that any mishap and Misty's head would explode right in front of them, a sight none of them couldn't even begin to imagine, let alone see it unfold.

"Now, for the last time hand over the camera and all its contents – NOW!" Bustamante, now in complete control, said in a very menacing tone. And the fact that he had just had his ass handed to him by the two brothers, Sasha in particular, made him all the more agitated and eager for some payback.

And as a show of his determination, he used his free hand to squeeze the back of Misty's neck with so much force that she gasped, as her eyes bugged out in suffocating pain.

On seeing this, Dumisani raised his arms in supplication and said, "Okay, okay, easy man. I'm getting it right now."

Without waiting for an answer or approval, he walked over to the other end of the living room where the camera case was, picked it up and raised it for Bustamante and company to see.

"Good," Bustamante said as he relaxed his grip on the beautiful woman. "Now, slide it over to me, nice and slow."

"And you'll let her go?"

"After we confirm that it has the material we're looking for," Miguel said. His eyes were focused now on the silver case, like a miser eyeing a bar of pure gold.

Dumisani was about to stoop to the floor so that he could slide the case over to Bustamante who then did an astonishing and totally unexpected thing. Without warning, he raised his weapon and struck Misty at the back of her head, who shrieked, before instantly crumpling to the floor like an overcooked noodle.

The reaction from Dumisani McDaniels was impulsive as it was instantaneous, perhaps that is why it worked perfectly.

"You bastard!" he screamed. It was the wildest, deepest anguish of the soul. Much similar to the instinctive reaction of a lioness protecting its cub, a lion safeguarding its pride.

At the same time, Dumisani scooped the case from the floor and flung it at Bustamante, which struck him in the face. The move was so sudden and so unexpected that when it hit him in the face, he reflexively squeezed the trigger and the volley of bullets hit the plasma TV and part of the wall, causing the plaster to fly all over. There was a brief scream of pain and the sound of bullets thumping into flesh, as some of them sliced through Hector St. John as he was slowly getting up.

When the others turned to look at him, St. John's body was sprawled on the floor, his eyes sightlessly staring at the ceiling, as blood began pooling around him. The death had been instant.

When Miguel Bustamante's arm went up, Dumisani ducked low, grabbed his arm and twisted it so hard that he was forced to drop the Uzi. With Bustamante's arm still in his grip, he twisted again until the inside of his elbow was up, and the Dumisani went down on one knee and brought the arm hard on his head.

The resulting sound was sickening as Miguel's elbow broke like a two by four snapping under considerable weight. He howled in pain as he fell to the floor, and rolled this way and that with his arm stretched in an unnatural angel. And there in lay the brothers chance to escape. They knew that by fleeing, they'd force the attackers to give chase, and thus draw them away from the unconscious woman.

Dumisani grabbed the case, just as Reggie McNeal was reaching for the fallen weapon, and Sasha somehow had the presence of mind to stoop to the floor and grab Misty's smartphone which had clattered to the floor with the brown paper bag of food she had brought with her, and the two were soon out the door and descending the steps three at a time. Not long after that they were sprinting like a pair of gazelles down the driveway before making a left on Sacramento Street, and ran for their lives.

In spite of the dizziness that engulfed them and the beating the endured at the hands of the brothers, Reggie and Bustamante were soon on their feet, their weapons rechambered as they headed out the door to go after the McDaniels brothers with the badly injured Bustamante in tow, his injured hand dangling on his side as he winced in pain.

"What about the girl?" Miguel Bustamante wanted to know as he whirled around and gestured at the unconscious figure sprawled on the floor.

Without even turning, Reggie said, "To hell with her, let's go."

As far as they were concerned, the woman, did not know who they were and what the stakes were. With the vast resources at their disposal, they figured they could have her neutralized later if necessary.

The surviving hitmen had a much more important objective, and that was to get that damn camera and the incriminating evidence it contained by all and any means necessary. The two goons had no way of knowing this, but the success or failure of a Presidential Campaign depended on the capturing of that camera. They also had to for their own sake, because their boss expected that of them, he was a man who did not tolerate failure from his subordinates, and was known to deal with it in the harshest way possible. Failure, he believed, set a bad precedence.

With this in mind, McNeal hissed, "We can't let them get away."

Being the great sprinters they were, the brothers were now almost at the intersection of Sacramento Street and Marengo Avenue, which was a little over one thousand feet from the driveway. There were very few people out and about, and the two young men, one white the other black, got more than a few strange looks as they blew down the street as if running for their lives, which they basically were.

As they made a left on Marengo at full trot, Sasha looked over his shoulder and was in time to see the two assailants, one of them holding his elbow, running toward a grey van with no windows, and he knew they would be coming after them. Sasha McDaniels had to think fast. The two were strangers in a strange land. Other than Misty Abdul they knew no one, and two determined, and not to mention, now angry killers armed with deadly Uzis were after them.

Ahead was the main street that separated that part of Altadena from Pasadena, and at the corner house on the left of the junction of Marengo and Woodbury street was a property with five bungalows, and right at that moment the electric main gate was opening, the brothers observed, and a silver 1985 Cadillac de Ville was backing onto Marengo, with an elderly lady who looked to be in her late 60's behind the wheel.

Perfect! Sasha thought as he increased his pace, leaving his brother as he raced now at full speed toward the car.

Dumisani was about to wonder what Sasha was up to, when to his astonishment, he saw him sprint ahead of him, and when he got to the vehicle, immediately yanked the driver's side of the door open, unbuckled the shocked old lady's seatbelt and gently but firmly yanked her out of her car. The old woman was too stunned to resist as all this unfolded in less than ten seconds.

* * *

Born and raised in nearby Pasadena, Virginia Perry had lived her entire 71 years in the San Gabriel Valley, and at least fifty of those in Altadena. She still recalled with much fondness when lots of the city was filled with Orange Tree Orchards, and milk was delivered door to door from a cart pulled by two horses. Mrs. Perry had watched the city boom with many investors buying real estate by the bundle, some far seeing entrepreneur had predicted that one day in the future, land and real estate in Altadena was going to shoot sky high – that person was dead on accurate.

Virginia was glad that at the time she and her late husband Ron Perry had saved up, and bought a property with six bungalows, five of which were instantly occupied by long time reliable tenants, and she and her husband, up until his passing five years earlier had lived in relative comfort on the rental proceeds they got every month from the tenants.

This morning, like every other of the week, she was on her way to meet with her cronies, and other retirees, for a game of bridge and catch up the gossip like they had been doing for the past thirty five years. The group that had started off with fifteen members was now down to six. The number had dwindled because some of the members had either moved to retirement homes, died, or simply lost interest.

It had started off as an all-white group, not by design, because Altadena was by all accounts and just like Pasadena at the time, an all-white city. As the demographics of the city changed, so did the racial makeup of the group. Also not planned to be that way, the bridge club had representatives from all races. There were a few black women, Hispanic, Asian, and a Native American in the Bridge Club.

Virginia was for some reason feeling jovial that morning as she backed out of her property's driveway. This was a feeling she had become accustomed to whenever it was time to meet with her friends, and play bridge. As the mint, clean, and well-kept 1985 Cadillac de Ville finally backed out of the electronic gate, she saw a young white man racing toward her side of the door.

It wasn't until the door was wrenched open that the older woman was startled. The young man was panting with what seemed like fear, as he unlatched her seatbelt, gently tugged at her arm and unceremoniously dragged her out of her car.

Then to her utter astonishment, the young man said, "Ma'am, normally I wouldn't do something like this."

The first thing Virginia noticed, other that the fact that she was being car jacked in broad daylight, was the fact that the fit and handsome young man had a strange accent.

At first she was thunderstruck, but managed to say, "W-what?! How dare you young man?"

"There are men coming after us Ma'am and they're trying to kill us, why? I have no idea," Sasha said, he was still panting but had since long gotten control of his breathing. "So we're forced to borrow your car.

We'll bring it back and if they're any damages incurred we will be happy to shoulder the cost."

At that moment, Mrs. Perry looked over Sasha's shoulder and saw another young man, this one black also dressed in matching sweatpants and top. He was also huffing wildly, standing on the sidewalk a few paces away, his head swerving around, he just like the young man carjacking her looked clearly troubled.

"Are you out of your mind?"

Sasha felt like they could debate this point later, right now it was about survival, his life and that of his brother was at stake. With that in mind he gently pushed the older woman to the side, looked inside the vehicle like he was looking for something, and when he noticed her handbag on the floor by the passenger's side seat, he took it and then hooked it, just as gently on Mrs. Perry's shoulder, and then beaconed at Dumisani, who seemed a bit hesitant at first but followed suit as if to say, '*Okay, what the hell, right? We're in enough trouble as it is, what difference will carjacking do?*'

"Come on Dumi," Sasha yelled as he gestured frantically at his brother. "Let's go!"

His brother wavered again, but only for a brief moment before he rushed to the driver's side of the car, upon realizing his mistake, he cussed beneath his breath and changed course and rushed to the other side. Having grown up in a culture where cars drove on the left hand side of the road, he had forgotten that simple fact that in the United States everything was opposite. Sasha was already behind the wheel, revving the engine as a stunned Mrs. Perry looked on. Moments later, the beautiful car, the cornerstone of the American automobile industry, roared off toward Woodbury Avenue, and turned left before it disappeared around the corner.

Virginia   stood in the middle of the road flabbergasted. She had heard of carjackings, read about them and even seen news bulletins about that, but that was in another world far from her. Thus, she never thought in a thousand years this could have happened to her, let alone in her beloved Altadena, considered to be one of the safest cities in the world. However, the old woman had a nagging feeling at the back of her mind, this particular carjacking did not fit the bill of a regular car theft.

It seemed to her that the young man with a strange accent was genuinely scared for his life, running away from something or someone hell bent on killing him and his black friend. What was it he had said? *There are men coming after us Ma'am and they're trying to kill us, why? I have no idea ...* that was unusual from a car thief. Perhaps there was some truth to what the strange young man had said. With that in mind, Mrs. Virginia Perry knew what she had to do, and had to do it quickly.

She was fumbling with her handbag, digging into it to pull out her cellphone, when she heard the screeching of tires on the asphalt coming from the north side of Marengo Avenue, and she looked up to see a grey windowless van speeding toward her. She was just in time to scuttle away from the tarmac, and onto the sidewalk as quickly as her quacking bones would allow, and in the process almost drop her phone.

The van skidded to a halt and the tinted glass window on the passenger side of the van slid down, and a man pocked his head out. She was just in time to see something that looked like the menacing muzzle of a gun disappear on the inside of the door, which made the old woman shudder in fright. Virginia Perry did not immediately like the look in the other man's eye.

"Excuse me lady," the man said gruffly – no manners at all, Virginia was quick to notice. "Which way did those boys run to? One is white and the other is black?" even though the man was asking, his question was phrased like a statement.

"I … I …" Virginia stammered.

Without wasting time, Reggie McNeal immediately lifted the Uzi that was on his lap, and pointed it at the terrified woman. Too much was at stake to waste time with niceties.

"Perhaps this will jog your memory, no?!"

With every second that passed, the McDaniels brothers were getting away, and with them the precious information that could sink them.

Virginia had never in her life had a gun pointed at her, and this scared her more than anything she had ever encountered.

Before she could stop herself, Virginia heard herself say, "They went that way." She did not want to help these men, whoever they were, but then again the young men had taken her car. And thus she pointed at the corner where she had last seen her beloved Cadillac vanish, and again to her horror, she babbled inanely, "They t-took my car, it's a silver 1986 Cadillac de Ville. Please tell them to bring it back to me when you find them."

Virginia also wanted to add that she was going to call the Sheriff, but some instinct, some acute sixth sense she'd acquired over her long life told her that freely volunteering that kind of information to these people would probably get her killed right there and then, so she decided to keep her mouth shut. The old woman was conflicted, she had revealed enough as it is, and in spite of herself, Virginia Perry felt the need to protect the young men somehow, which was why she was kicking herself for revealing the make and model of her stolen car to these men.

Virginia had seen evil in her life, the eyes were after all the windows of the soul. There was a vast difference between the eyes of that young man with the strange accent, and the one who had just pointed that ominous gun at her. That man was pure evil if there ever was such a thing.

She reached into her purse again after the van sped off, presumably in pursuit of the young men who had taken her car, and reached for her phone, which she had unconsciously dropped back into her bag when she heard the van approaching. Like many people her age, Virginia had become quiet adept at using this modern and yet very convenient device. Like many law abiding Altadena residents, she had the Sheriff's number on speed dial. She even knew the captain of that precinct. The captain was in fact a tall, beautiful black woman named Daphne McMillan, and had been credited with keeping the all American city one of the safest in the nation.

Virginia Perry pressed the speed dial, and was immediately connected to a live person and she reported all she knew. A few minutes later, a black and white Altadena Sheriff's car arrived with its blue and whites flashing. They were in the vicinity and had responded to the radio call. A 'BOLO' or 'Be On The Look Out' in law enforcement parlance was then quickly issued for a Silver Grey 1986 Cadillac de Ville. The occupants were described as two young men, athletically built, one white the other black in their mid-20's, and possibly being pursued by men in a grew windowless van, possibly a Dodge Ram or Chevy, and the pursuers were considered armed and dangerous.

The quarry were not armed as far as the victim could tell, but should be treated as possibly hostile. The chase was on, and soon the cities of Pasadena and Altadena was buzzing as never before, because this would soon involve car chases and gunfire.

CHAPTER 37

IN THE MIDST OF A DARK PAINFUL HAZE, Misty Abdul thought she had a voice calling at her as if it were echoing at the end of a long foggy tunnel. She tried to focus, but the pain on the back right side of her head was dull and persistent.

"Hey young lady, can you hear me?" the voice came again, insistent, followed by the snapping of fingers. "Young lady … young lady?" the voice continued.

She forced her eyes open, and as her blurry vision came into focus, she saw a middle aged white man looking at her curiously. He had blond shaggy hair, most likely a throwback from his hippie days, was turning grey and more so on the sides of his head. The man had piercing blue eyes that somehow reflected incredible kindness. Though she had never seen the face before, it somehow looked familiar.

As her vision became even more centered, Misty realized that she was lying on the floor. It was then that things began clicking together in her mind. She had come to see Dumisani and Sasha, had brought them breakfast even, and then there were scary men with guns.

As she was coming around, her vision getting clearer with every second, she noticed the black shirt the man was wearing, and something that made her whole body shudder – a white clerical collar.

"Oh God," she said groggily. "This is it, I'm dead and you're administering the last rites, a-aren't you Father?"

The stranger looked at her and smiled. There was something about that smile, that look that again looked familiar, especially with the dimples on the cheek that she had seen on someone, yes, Sasha McDaniels.

"No young lady," the stranger said, still smiling. "I'm Sean Kane McDaniels, what happened here, and where are my nephews?"

There was a trace of alarm in his voice as he glanced around the living room at the chaos. The furniture, specifically the coffee table, the bookshelf, the plasma TV and other items like the picture frames were upside down, and strewn all over the floor. It looked as if the place had been hit by a bomb. Most discontenting though, was what looked like fresh bullet holes on the walls of the living room. And most ominous of all, the dead body of Hector St. John.

Misty slowly sat up on the floor, holding the back of her head in obvious pain, and then looked at the man of God in surprise. The fog in her mind was clearing fast.

"Your nephews?" she asked with a twisted brow.

"Yes, Sasha and Dumisani, where are they?"

"I had just come over Father and then … then there were these men with guns," Misty said. She was obviously trying to piece her thoughts together in her mind in chronological and sensible order. She thought she was probably slightly concussed because the desire to sleep was suddenly overpowering her, but she knew the worst thing she could do was give in to it.

"Guns?" Sean Kane McDaniels brow twisted with unease. "Who were these men young lady?"

"I really don't know Father, and the name is Melissa Abdul, or Misty if you prefer."

"Okay Misty, and it's Sean Kane, or Sean if you prefer," he mimicked with a mirthless smile. "What did these men want?"

She shut her eyes tight as another wave of pain washed over her, and then in between gritted teeth blurted, "How the hell should I know!"

Misty immediately regretted her answer the moment she noticed again the clergy collar around the older man's neck, and instantly covered her mouth with her hand.

"Oh, I'm sorry Father."

Again Sean Kane McDaniels grinned, he had heard it all and more before.

"It's okay Misty," he smiled reassuringly at the beautiful young woman.

She had killer looks, McDaniels observed. Looks that could tempt even the most chaste of men, and wondered how she fit in all this chaos he had stumbled into. He looked around again and shook his head in disbelief.

"Evidently, my boys are in grave danger. Tell me everything you know, starting with this." He spread out his hand, and in it were spent shells from what he knew was a 9mm Uzi Semi-Automatic. McDaniels had gathered them while Misty was still out cold.

"Okay," Misty nodded, even though in all honesty, she knew less than nothing. She had not heard from the brothers until that chance encounter with Sasha on Facebook, and then she walked in on something she would have never anticipated even in her worst nightmare.

"Good," Sean Kane McDaniels said as he gently helped the young woman to her feet. "But we need to get out of here. Is there a way of getting hold of them? Do you have their cellphone number or some way of communicating with them? I get the feeling they're on the run and need my help more than they ever had in their lives."

At the same time he had to wonder what his nephews had gotten themselves involved in, to have men come bursting into their apartment, and in broad daylight no less, with the clear intention of killing them. It just did not make any sense. The boys were in the country for less than a week, not enough time to make these types of enemies, or was he missing something? He had to find them. Even more worrisome to the former SEAL was the dead body that was lying sprawled on the living room floor in a pool of blood.

Misty searched her pockets looking for her phone, but she came up empty. She looked around and everywhere, no phone.

"Mr. McDaniels," Misty said, still looking around and padding her pockets one more time. "I can't find my phone, and I could have sworn that I had it with me when I came here."

She was almost certain about that. Could the goons have taken it with them? She wondered. Before she could give voice to her thoughts, they started to hear the distant wail of police sirens coming closer and closer. Sean Kane McDaniels, the former navy SEAL , a Special Forces ace, and later undefeated three time Karate champion of the world before he found the Lord, did not like the sound of it.

The man of God made a quick decision, "I think it's time we get out of here Misty and *now*!"

"Shouldn't we wait until they get here Father McDaniels?" Misty asked, visibly perplexed at this suggestion.

"Normally Misty, that would be the right thing to do, but something tells me I got to get to them before the cops do. Trust me, my way is quicker and my boys could be in grave danger for all I know. Come on let's go."

He practically dragged her with him, and Misty could not help but sigh and roll her eyes in befuddlement. Things were definitely upside down. She came this morning, extremely excited at reuniting with the two adorable young men she and her friends had met at the other side of the globe. Now they were in her part of the world, in her home city no less – how cool was that? She had wondered aloud. In fact such unbelievable coincidences never happened.

Misty Abdul had expected the reunion to be a memorable occasion, to see two young men, one of who she had fallen in love with. She had not expected to stumble onto a scene that involved men with guns. What were the McDaniels brothers embroiled in? It was hard to imagine those two sweet and charming lads to be in on something at a level that required the reception she was forced to witness.

"The day just keeps getting better and better," Misty said hardly concealing the cynicism in her voice as she rolled her eyes again.

She followed the reverend down the steps to the driveway, he kept looking around as the sounds of the sirens grew louder. He motioned at the beautiful young woman to follow him behind the apartment building, this so no one could see them. Moments later, they were walking quickly on Sacramento Street toward Sean Kane McDaniels's vehicle after he advised Misty to leave her Jeep right where she had parked it, with the assurance that he would come get it later himself.

The Reverend Sean Kane McDaniels knew the peril he was putting himself into, as a man of the cloth, the right thing to do would have been to wait for the authorities and tell them everything that he and Misty knew, and then let them handle it from there. Fleeing the crime scene and with him a potentially crucial witness was something that could land him in legal problems that could have far reaching repercussions, not just from the law's point of view, but the church, this was something that could get him reprimanded, or worse defrocked.

However, something, some instinct that came about as a result of his military training, and the martial arts indoctrination, told him to handle this one on his own. The people who had come after his nephews had shown a kind of reckless abandon that told him that these were people who were not going to stop until they achieved their objective, which was to kill his nephews, he Reverend Sean Kane McDaniels would have to find them before they did and figure a way out of this. The brothers were in a strange country, far away from the familiar surroundings they were accustomed to, and that meant that the people who were after them would find them with ease. McDaniels knew that the only way to save them was to find them before the bad guys did, and the beautiful young woman he had just met, Misty Abdul, was the key.

CHAPTER 38

SASHA HAD A DIFFICULT TIME handling the stolen car. It was, like almost all modern American made cars, an automatic transmission. However, after making a left turn on Woodbury Avenue (named after the Woodbury brothers who founded the city of Altadena), he made quick right on New York Drive. On more than several occasions, he almost crushed into oncoming traffic and soliciting a blare of horns from angry motorists punctuated by obscene gestures more French than American, or English.

"Easy man," a more than tense Dumisani said. "This is America man, remember to stay on the right lane."

"I'm trying Dumi," said an equally tense Sasha as he constantly glanced at the rear end mirror. "This will take some getting used to." He then veered back into the right lane.

Having driven on the left hand side of the road all his life, and then suddenly having to keep on the right, especially knowing that determined killers were in hot pursuit was almost more than he could handle, and the size of the vehicle made the task particularly daunting. Even the gadgets on the console were on the wrong side, in that every once in a while whenever he tried to turn the blinker to indicate that he was turning left or right, he ended up turning on the wipers instead. However, with every yard covered, and every mile gained, Sasha was getting the hang of it.

He then made a right turn onto Hill Avenue, which ran north to south, and pulled over to the side of the street at a section that was entirely covered by shades of overhanging branches from the palm trees lined up on the side of the road, something that was prevalent on the streets of Southern California.

The brothers paused for a while in silence, each of them wondering how their lives could have been turned upside down and in a blink of an eye. They had come to this country to begin their American dream, but now that dream had turned into a nightmare. How could that be? They wondered with pounding hearts as they looked this way and that, each car that passed regarded with suspicion as their paranoia hit highs not even they could have imagined.

"Stay alert man," Dumisani said to his brother.

"Don't I know?!" Sasha snapped.

Like his brother, he was also breathing hard. Not from fatigue but from fear, very much like the fear he felt when Sahili and his brigands attacked their home. It was a feeling of *déjà vu* that was almost impossible to envisage.

There was a sudden frown on Dumisani's face as he came to a frightening realization. "How about Misty man? What are we going to do about that Sasha?"

For an answer, his brother reached into his pocket and pulled out a smartphone Dumisani had never seen before.

"This is her's," Sasha showed it to his brother. "I picked it from the floor before we left, not sure why, but I figured it could come in handy."

Dumisani said, "Good, now how do we get hold of her and find out if she's okay if we have the one thing that she could use to communicate with us?"

Sasha winced as he and his brother looked around for the umpteenth time, but did not answer. Had he miscalculated by taking the beautiful woman's phone? He pushed the thought out of his mind and focused on the issue at hand – their survival. All was quiet except for the squawking of the red crowned Pasadena Parrots. Urban legend has it that the exotic flock began with birds that escaped a burning pet store, or we released from the Butch Gardens when it closed. In reality, some escaped their confines, and some were released from the pet trade. Then the highly social birds got busy. If there ever was a misnomer about the Pasadena Parrots and how they came about this was it.

"You think we lost them?" Sasha asked.

"I think so," Dumisani said, far from certain of course, but hope as the say runs eternal.

Again they fell into a long uncomfortable silence, and then Sasha voiced the one question that had been on their minds.

"Dumi, what the hell is going on? Who are these guys and what do they want from us?"

Dumisani replied by saying, "You guess is as good as mine Sasha, I mean they seemed to know everything about us and some. How can that be? How's that even possible? I mean, we just got here no way wo could have made enemies that quick right?"

Sasha had to ponder over this strange incongruity.

"Yes," he answered softly and in deep thought. "They even referred to us by name, this is after I thought it was the classical example of mistaken identity, you know, like they were looking for someone who lived at the place before us? No?"

"Yes," Dumisani agreed. "Considering the fact that we just moved into the place and we don't know anyone except Miss Armstrong, our apartment manager, I would say that would have been the most logical conclusion."

"So how man? And isn't it amazing that they wanted your video camera so badly that they were willing to kill for it in broad daylight? What have we unknowingly gotten ourselves into Dumi?"

For an answer Dumisani said, "I think we have got to report this to the police Sasha, and I mean right away."

His brother nodded and then said, "Good idea Dumi, but where's the damn police station?" There was an iciness in his voice that Dumisani detected.

"Look, this is not getting any easier for both of us now, is it? But we have got to find a way out of this man … it's our fat in the fire here."

Sasha nodded slowly and said, "But first things first, we dump this car like right now. Hopefully, the owner will find it soon with the help of the cops. To tell you the truth Dumi, I feel bad for jacking the car from that poor old lady, and will definitely find her and apologize to her some day when all this is over."

All of a sudden, a thought came to Dumisani, it had been in the recess of his subconscious mind, struggling to break free, but suddenly it came to the surface so clear and so loud that it blocked out his brother's voice. Sasha was talking but suddenly he could not hear him.

"What do you think Dumi?" Sasha asked.

His brother was gazing forward through the windshield in deep thought as if focused on something on the tarmac ahead.

Sasha noticed and looked closer at his brother and snapped his fingers at him as if rousing him from a hypnotic trance.

"Hey … Dumi". He snapped his fingers again to break him out of his reverie.

Dumisani turned slowly and looked at his brother, and said with a quiet intensity that Sasha had only seen when he was pondering over something very significant.

"Sasha," Dumisani said, as he narrowed his eyes to focus more on what he was thinking. "Do you remember the news?"

"What news?"

Dumisani suddenly shifted his gaze from the street ahead, and faced his brother so he could look him in the eye. He always did this, Sasha knew, when he was about to say or ask something very important.

"The news about that hijacked armored van Sasha."

"Yes," Sasha nodded as he wondered where Dumisani was going with this.

"I had my camera with me when we went to that supermarket that day Sasha? Remember? And as you know, part of my first assignment was to film my new surroundings. What if, and that's a big *what if,* but then again what if these people who came after us saw me using my camera and thought that maybe, just maybe, I might be in possession of some incriminating evidence?"

For an answer, Sasha chuckled, not giving what his brother said much thought – typical.

"Come on man Dumi," Sasha said. "There could be …"

"Just humor me Sasha. We were there, according to the news, when this thing went down, right?" Dumisani paused for a moment to make certain that his brother was tracking what he was saying before he continued. "And I was filming you and also catching the surrounding in my frame, then and check this out, what if I unknowingly caught something and they did not like whatever it was I inadvertently filmed, and by that I mean the actual robbery?"

A jolt of electricity shot through Sasha McDaniels's entire body as he suddenly realized what his brother was suggesting. His eyes popped wide in bewilderment.

"Dumisani," he said in a quiet and yet ominous tone. "What if you caught the entire heist on tape and not know it."

"Exactly!" for one of the few times of in his life he wished he was wrong, but considering what they had just gone through, and the way those thugs came bursting in their apartment demanding the camera told him that there was no other logical explanation.

Dumisani had not even looked at a single frame of the footage he had shot on that now momentous day. In fact the hard drive was still in the camera, which was still in its casing, now at his feet. Like any modern camera, including the professional type, it had a miniature viewfinder on which he could instantly replay the footage.

"Okay," Dumisani said with a heavy sigh. "Let's see what we got."

He bent down to retrieve the silver case that was at his feet so he could get to his camera. As he did that, a bullet cracked through the quiet early afternoon air, shattered the back window of the Cadillac, missing Dumisani by less than a foot, before it went through the windshield, leaving a hole that immediately spider webbed the right side of it, before it went out.

"Son of a bitch!" Sasha yelled. "They found us!"

They instinctively looked back through what was left of the rear window, and saw a dark grey cargo van closing in on them, with Reggie McNeal, his upper torso sticking out from the passenger side, brandishing a high power sniper rifle fitted with a silencer and bringing it up to bare, so that he could fire again. This after he chambered another round after firing the first. All the men in the van, from what Dumisani and Sasha could see, were wearing balaclavas for understandable reasons, they were out in the open now and it would serve them no purpose if some keen, or even half dead observer to see their faces, especially in this day in age where everyone carried a phone with filming and picture capturing capabilities.

"Go man, go!!!" Dumisani screamed at his brother.

Fortunately, the car was still running when Sasha had pulled over earlier to figure out what in heaven's name was going on. So all he did was floor the accelerator of the powerful eight cylinder vehicle as the tires screeched, and the Cadillac pulled forward at incredible speed that in no time it was pulling away from the pursuing van. The bullets were coming no less, but somehow Sasha was able to evade them. He instinctively turned at sharp corners at a moment's notice and the smell of rubber soon permeated the interior of that car, but the brothers hardly noticed – it was all about getting away from their deadly chasers.

In the midst of the chaos, Dumisani yelled, "Do we even know where we're going Sasha?"

"I don't know man, I don't know!" Sasha yelled back as he knitted his brow and gripped the steering wheel tight, at the same time keeping one eye on the road and the other on the rearview mirror, praying with every sharp turn that he had lost the van, but like a bad memory, the men where dogged pursuers. "I just want to get away from these bastards."

They were now heading south on Hill Avenue, a busy street to begin with, that oncoming cars began pulling to the side when they saw the Cadillac coming at them at top speed. They were reaching speeds of up to 65 miles/hr. on a street whose posted limit was 35 miles/hr. Some drivers who were obviously unaware that a hot pursuit was in progress, flashed their lights and blared their horns in anger at the lunatic who should have known better than to drive so recklessly in a residential neighborhood of all places.

The grey Dodge Ram van was still behind them, and when it was closer, Reggie would then, as discreetly as possible, lean out of the window and fire. It was obvious what he was trying to do, and Sasha in spite of the situation at hand was amazingly keeping his cool as he would throw a quick glance at the rearview mirror, and violently swerve the Cadillac to the left, and then just as quickly to the right. The former Marine sniper was aiming for the tires to try and immobilize the vehicle, and Sasha McDaniels, who had also quickly gotten a hang of the classic American automobile, realized that and was thus far doing an excellent job, for even he knew that a moving target was the hardest to hit even for the best marksman in the world.

Some shocked pedestrians who saw what was going on, quickly whipped out their phones, and dialed 911 just as Sasha made a death defying swerve that would have resulted in a head on collision with a huge produce truck, and in so doing side swiped a parked car, causing sparks to fly as metal scrapped on metal.

With all this going on, and the frantic calls made, it did not take long for the air to be filled with the familiar sound of police sirens as multiple black and whites, having got the call from the dispatcher, raced to the scene. The chasing goons heard this too and

329

immediately pulled back before eventually peeling off, turned around and raced in the opposite direction. Normally, they would have had a police scanner at the ready, but this was supposed to have been a simple 'snatch and grab' job, not one that involved car chases, risk of exposure, and all the other things that could complicate an already complicated mission.

This gave Sasha the chance to gain on them and then turn into an obscure alley off of Holliston Avenue, a street also in Pasadena that ran parallel to Hill Street. The alley dead ended at a small wooden fence almost ten feet tall, and Sasha had the presence of mind to turn that car immediately around and face the direction he came and wait. He was ready to make a mad dash again if he saw something even remotely similar to a grey van make a turn into the alley. With thumping hearts, the brothers waited. Several police cars sped past, and to their relief none of them even slowed down to take a quick peek in the alley, let alone glance in their direction.

The alley was a dead end, and they knew that if the goons found them here, they'd be trapped and this time there would be no mistake. After they saw what the brothers were capable of, there was no way in hell they would come any closer – they would shred them to pieces with those deadly Uzis and thereafter grab what they came for. The two brothers would not let that happen. They had to keep moving before this place became too hot. As they waited to see if there would be any more police cars passing by before they made a break for it, steamy white smoke began to bellow from underneath the hood. This certainly was not good.

"We will need to ditch this car," Sasha said, stating the obvious, but it helped in breaking the uncomfortable silence.

"Good idea," Dumisani agreed. "The car has most likely been reported stolen by the owner even though we just borrowed it." Following a brief pause he added, "Just promise me we will do right by that poor woman once this is over right?"

Sasha, deep in thought and still looking around simply agreed by nodding slowly. Returning the car after paying for the obvious damages and some was the least of their problems right now.

They waited again, and again nothing happened. All was quiet, even the sirens had long faded in the distance, even the Helicopter they had seen but had no idea was part of the police seemed to have vanished.

"Think we lost them for real this time?" Dumisani asked hopefully.

"I sure hope so," Sasha said. "I would think they took off the moment they saw the police."

"Okay, good. What do we do now Sasha?"

"First is to get away from this car as far away as possible and wait until it's dark," Sasha answered.

They both knew the quandary and danger they were in. What was worse there was a dead man in their apartment, they could claim he was killed by mistake by one of the man, but who would believe them? And for all they knew the cops could be at their apartment questioning Misty, that was the best scenario. The worst was that the goons could go back and get Misty, interrogate her, or could be in the process of doing so, and then kill her, and being the very attractive woman that she was, the brothers, especially Dumisani, could not put it past them to take advantage of the situation and taking turns raping her, before putting a bullet in her head. He fought hard to push the terrible thoughts out of his mind and figure ways to get out of this one alive.

Dumisani then said, "Shouldn't we be talking about how we should at least report this to the authorities? After all, we have done nothing wrong, and if my camcorder caught what we think it did maybe it will help us, no?"

It was obvious that the brothers had a differing opinion going forward. What they also did not know was that unlike back home, it was easy as dialing *911* to get the police's attention and explain their predicament. They had a lot to learn in their fatherland, and that being things worked much easier in a developed country as opposed to where they came from.

Sasha thought about this for a moment as he scratched his chin, and then after a while he came to a decision and said, "I think you're right Dumi, but before we do that, we need to wait because we will need the cover of darkness. We're being hunted and only God knows who else is out there, and we need to find the nearest Police Station, bear in mind the people after us could be watching that too, so we have to be very careful."

"You're right," his brother nodded in agreement.

The two then abandoned the vehicle in the alley in which they had taken refuge, for now it was about survival. What was worse is that they were not familiar with this part of town at all. In fact, and unbeknownst to both young men, was that they had been going around in circles in their desperate attempt to evade their deadly pursuers.

After commandeering the old woman's vehicle, Sasha had made a left on Woodbury Drive and a quick right on Lake Avenue, then another left on Washington Boulevard less than a mile going south, which took them to Hill Avenue where they made a right turn, and onto other numerous small streets that eventually led them to the small dead end alley off of Holliston Street.

Luckily, since they had ditched the vehicle in a relatively quiet neighborhood, there was not much activity on Holliston Street as they walked up the road in search of a place where they could lay low for a while until dark, and at the same time get a chance to review the footage on Dumisani's camera, so as to find out exactly what had caused these men with guns to come after them. What was on that tape that these men wanted so bad to a point of wanting to kill them? Because there was no doubting their intention – they were hell bent on eliminating the McDaniels brothers.

The case held new meaning now because Dumisani was clutching it as if their lives depended on it as it very well did. The brothers though were careful not to draw any unnecessary attention to themselves as they made their way up the quiet street, which like many others like it, was flanked by very tall palm trees very synonymous with Southern California. The street led them to where it intersected with Washington Boulevard. They kept glancing this way and that, even though they tried very hard not to be too obvious about the fact that they were two frightened boys fresh from Africa.

The brothers were silent for a while as they kept a close eye at every occasional vehicle that drove by, ready to break for the nearest backyard or the many rose bushes they passed. There was however a major concern they had yet to voice, and that being the wellbeing of Misty Abdul. They had succeeded in luring the attackers away from her. The brothers were aware that she had been knocked unconscious, but they did not think her state was precarious to a point of life threatening, or at least they hoped not. They imagined that the police must have shown up by now and were questioning her. Their fate, the McDaniels brothers knew, rested on what she told them.

Once again, Sasha felt for Misty's phone in his right pocket, willing it to ring. What worried him now was that the charge on the state of the art smartphone was running low, and was going to die at any moment and it was going to be the devil's luck to find a place or the chance to recharge it. Just one more thing to worry about since they had no charger, Sasha thought. They had left their apartment in such haste that they did not have their phones either.

The only redeeming fact, if it could be called such, was that Sasha still had his fanny pack clipped around his waist, for some reason he had not yet taken it off when they returned from their morning workout. In it were their passports, in case they needed to show some sort of identification in situations where ID was needed, while they waited for their California IDs, some cash, a few Traveler's Checks, and a credit card. It wasn't much money, but enough to lay low for a while as they figured things out. Returning to their apartment was certainly out of the question.

There were a few 'Mom and Pop' stores, a dry cleaner, and restaurants at the intersection of Washington Boulevard and Hill Street. This area was mainly in the middle of the two streets, Hill and Holliston that ran parallel to one another. There was a restaurant whose terrace faced an alley and on it where a few chairs and tables where customers could relax and enjoy their food, while not having to be forced to deal with the forever running traffic as this was a very busy intersection. This was where Sasha and Dumisani decided to while away time until dark, at which time they planned to make their first move.

CHARTER 39

THE PEACE AND QUIET of the once serene '*Foothill Gardens*', the apartment building of Sasha and Dumisani McDaniels was suddenly a thing of the past, as one Police car after another, with its blue and white flashing of the vaunted Altadena Sheriff Department, descended on the scene like a wake of hungry vultures on the dusty plains of the Serengeti. The apartment of the McDaniels brothers, suddenly at large, had become a crime scene.

Several neighbors had heard the deadly commotion coming from the young men's apartment, the shouting, the screaming, and the occasional '*pop pop*' sound from the suppressed Uzi's was at first attributed to a television whose volume was turned to capacity. However, when they saw first Sasha and then Dumisani running for what seemed their lives, they knew something was amiss.

"And how do you know they were running for their lives?" the first responding officer, a beautiful young Caucasian rookie named Jamie Douglas had asked the retired tenant, Donald Vincennes, who had heard the ruckus, seen the brothers flee, and was the first to call the Sheriffs.

"Oh yes," the old neighbor said excitedly. "Them boys was running like hell, then we see these men in hot pursuit, they was waving guns at them, cussing, and that's when Maggie and I shut out blinds and called you guys as soon as we could."

The young officer frowned and said, "Maggie?"

"Yeah," Mr. Vincennes answered. "Maggie, my wife." Apparently Maggie was cowering somewhere inside her house since she was nowhere in sight.

A little later, after being let into the brothers' apartment by the landlady, the place was swarming with deputies extremely careful not to interfere with what had now become a crime scene. The body of Hector St. John lay on the floor at the other end of the living room by the smashed Plasma TV, near the large window that overlooked the driveway. The blood from the two bullet wounds had gathered and congealed under his torso and head. He had fallen on his back so he was facing the ceiling, and his eyes were wide open, starring sightlessly at the ceiling. By now, as the CSU technician was taking pictures from different angles, rigor mortis was already setting in.

The two detectives, Daniel 'Danny Boy' Frazier who was in his mid-fifties with thick greying hair and Ricardo 'Rick' Chavez who was at least twenty years younger than his partner, were the last to arrive and were focused mainly on the cadaver in the McDaniels's living room. This had now become a murder investigation.

After clearing the room the moment after the CSU technician had finished taking the pictures, they reached into the inside pockets of their suits for their disposable rubber gloves and put them on. The younger of the two, Chavez, since he still had a pair of better knees than his partner, was about to squat and take a closer look at the body, when the young deputy, Jamie Douglas burst into the room, no knock, no 'excuse me'. She obviously had something extremely important to say since she had her miniature notebook open, on the other hand was her cellphone. She had just finished talking to someone apparently.

Both men looked up at her, before Detective Danny Boy Frazier said, "Okay shoot deputy Douglas, it's Douglas right?"

"Yes," she said quickly, before she added, "His name is Hector St. John, a bounty hunter who happens to be an ex-cop, and before that he served two tours in Iraq before being dishonorably discharged."

The two men looked at one other before Chavez asked, "Which precinct?" this was getting weirder by the minute, the detectives thought.

"LAPD, Rampart Division before joining the army, was discharged in 2002. Some say he was involved in the Rampart Scandal."

The two men exchanged a knowing look. The Los Angeles Police Department's Rampart Division scandal involved widespread corruption in the Community Resources Against Street Hoodlums, otherwise known as CRASH, an anti-gang unit of LAPD in the late 1990's. More than 70 police officers either assigned to, or associated with the Rampart CRASH unit were implicated in some form of misconduct, making it one of the most widespread cases of police corruption in U.S. history, responsible for a long list of offenses including unprovoked shootings, unprovoked beatings, planting of false evidence, stealing and dealing narcotics, bank robbery, perjury and the covering up of evidence of these activities.

So when the junior deputy Jamie Douglas revealed that the dead man had been a member of the Los Angeles Police Department at some point, who had been implicated in the Rampart's scandal no less and also dismissed as a result, the two detectives just knew somewhat that this was not going to be an ordinary case. It had the makings of far reaching consequences to which extent the two men did not even want to speculate.

"Thank you," Detective 'Danny Boy' Frazier said simply, but in a tone that seemed to suggest that her work was done for now, if she had nothing more to add.

Catching the drift, the young female deputy smiled uneasily, before she left room and headed outside to join her colleagues in securing the perimeter on the outside of the brothers' apartment. Neighbors from up and down the street were trickling in, in twos and threes as the news spread in the relatively quiet neighborhood, and watched from as close as the cordoned off area as they could get. Many of them, including the landlady, Julia Armstrong were wondering what it was the new tenants were involved in to attract such a ruckus. Julia shook her head in astonishment. It just seemed inconceivable to her that two sweet young men she had just rented the apartment to, and new to the country could be involved in something even remotely heinous.

Back in the house, Detective Daniel Frazier looked at the sprawled body and then at his partner and said, "What do you make of this Rick? An ex-cop, and now bounty hunter murdered?"

Ricardo Chavez just simply nodded softly and said, "Bizarre to say the least."

"What were these boys involved in?" his partner wanted to know.

"Hard to tell because according to the apartment manager, these two arrived a few days ago from Botswana if you can believe that, never been to the U.S. before, except when they were toddlers, which of

338

course doesn't count, and that should make them easy to find."

Chavez again shook his head in confusion as he looked at the body again, and around at the once neatly arranged living room, now in complete disarray as if it had been hit by a hurricane.

This had to have been one hell of a take down, Chavez thought, but aloud he said, "This just keeps getting weirder and weirder, what are we missing here? Could it be a simple case of misidentification, in that they were after the previous tenant?"

"Not a chance," the man they called 'Danny Boy' Frazier shook his head. "The last tenant was a disabled man on social security who lived here for over twenty five years before he croaked about two months ago."

Chavez nodded then studied the bullet holes on the walls and said, "Someone wants them dead, that's for sure."

'Danny Boy' added by saying, "Who and why is the million dollar question at the moment."

Frazier was about to say something more, but then again and just like before, the two men were interrupted, this time it was a male, clean cut, young white deputy with broad shoulders, and a barrel of a chest, made even bigger by the Kevlar vest underneath his khaki short sleeved shirt. The nametag on his upper right above his pocket read 'Dickens'.

"Detectives," the young deputy, Brian Dickens said as he quickly entered the room, while careful to watch where he stepped because any misstep, literally, would be potentially contaminating the crime scene. And just like his counterpart earlier, he had something equally important to say. The young deputy looked to be in his early 20's and was the typical rookie, eager to impress and make his first meaningful collar, especially on a potential murder investigation, and this bizarre murder scene looked very much like one that would do it for him.

"Yes Deputy Dickens?" Ricardo 'Ricky' Chavez prompted when it seemed as if the young deputy was caught in some internal monologue.

Dickens swallowed hard, embarrassed that he was caught up in delusions of grandeur while there was an investigation to concentrate on, and consulted the miniature notebook in his hand, similar to that Jaimie Douglas had. By the look of it, these small notepads were standard department issued.

"Another report just came in that says two young men fitting the description of the tenants of this apartment, were seen carjacking a vehicle from an old woman not too far from here, a Mrs. Virginia Perry. She's at the precinct as we speak, and there's been a car chase apparently. Pasadena PD are on it, with a few of ours," he announced.

"What on earth is going on?" 'Danny Boy' Frazier wondered aloud.

Rick Chavez then said to the young Deputy, "Has an APB been put up with a clear description of the brothers and the car, and added to it that they could be armed and extremely dangerous?"

The deputy nodded, "That's already been done Sir."

APB stood for 'All Points Bulletin', an emergency call the law enforcement put up to all others and sometimes to the community at large when seeking help in ferreting out fugitives fleeing from the law.

Chavez looked at his partner and said something they already knew, "To get to the truth, we need to find these boys. We need to get that APB out to the public including business owners in the vicinity."

"Isn't that a bit much, involving businesses and the public?" Detective Frazier asked his partner as they both straightened up after stooping at the dead body on the floor for a while, and getting ready to collect the spent shells, and all other evidence they would need in case all this ended up in a courtroom.

"I don't think so," Chavez said confidently. "The sooner we get these brothers the sooner we will get to the bottom of this."

Frazier sighed and said, "I'll have to update the captain about this, even though she can be a bit squeamish when it comes to APB's involving the public, but I say we go in hard and heavy with the whole cavalry, basically put word out that the two are suspects in a murder investigation involving an ex policer, leave out the part that he was a bounty hunter, that should speed things up."

Rick Chavez, the junior of the two, with obviously less field experience than his partner in such matters, did not quite see things the same way.

"We don't know that for certain Frazier," he protested. "That kind of alert will get every trigger happy uniform the temptation to shoot on sight, and then where will that leave us?"

"You got a better idea?" Sometimes Frazier could be rough around the edges, a bare knuckles street fighter who would do almost everything to realize his objective.

"Yes, I say we get word out that they're wanted for questioning. The young men were obviously attacked and there's a lot we don't know," Chavez said as he spread his arms around the room to point out the obvious. "This could have been a clear case of self-defense and they're on the run for their lives as we speak, with the attackers in pursuit."

Detective 'Danny Boy' Frazier had to consider this for a moment, as he walked to the window, and scratched his chin thoughtfully.

"Dickens!" he called out to the young deputy, who appeared as if he had been waiting just outside the door.

"Yes sir?"

"Get word out on the street, on social media, to all our snitches, and bail bondsman to be on the lookout for these two. Give a full description as to who they are, and send pictures as well. Let it be known that the two are wanted for questioning. Make it known that contact should be made to us upon immediate sighting, and not to try and apprehend the suspects themselves. They're strangers in this country, so that should make it easier for us to find them."

"Yes sir, anything else?"

"No." It was a dismissal.

And just as quickly, Deputy Dickens was gone just as fast as he came, Frazier turned to his partner with a look that said, '*Happy now*?'

At that moment there was another knock at the door, this time it was two county men clad it white from the Los Angeles County Morgue, carrying a stretcher, ready to bag the body and transport it. The two detectives stepped into the kitchen area where they could speak in private.

Detective 'Danny Boy' Frazier said, "Bear in mind Chavez, whoever did this killed an ex-cop, someone who used to be one of us, and if it's these boys, we gonna have to come down hard on them. There's enough crime as it is, more than we can handle, and now we got to import murderers?"

Like before, Ricky Chavez shook his head in disagreement. This was not how detectives worked and Frazier of all people, his partner thought, should know better. He was already convinced of the brothers' guilt before they had even reviewed a fraction of the evidence.

"There you go again Frazier," Chaves said, giving voice to his thoughts, "We don't know for certain if it's them, and we won't know that until we talk to them."

Frazier nodded, there was a smirk on his face as he said, "That is if we get them alive."

His colleague, Detective Ricky Chavez had to wonder what his partner meant by that. Were the brothers already marked for death even though there were still many unanswered questions? The young detective did not like any of this. His partner was not behaving like he normally did. Something told him that he would have to somehow reach the brothers before his partner did.

CHAPTER 40

ALTHOUGH SHE WAS A PASADENEAN, born and raised, Misty Abdul's parents both of them medical doctors, they had, once they reached their 50's, bought a nice four bedroom house in nearby Arcadia. Named after the city in Greece, this mainly upper middle class city shares its border east of Pasadena and located 13 miles northeast of downtown Los Angeles, in the San Gabriel Valley and the base of the San Gabriel Mountains.

It is the site of the Santa Anita Racetrack, and home to the Los Angeles Arboretum and Botanic Gardens. Following Misty's directions, Reverend Sean Kane McDaniels drove his Nissan Altima down Lake Avenue until they got on the 210 East on ramp. They each wrecked their brains wondering what happened to Sasha and Dumisani.

As they made their way to Misty's parents' home, who conveniently were out of town on an extended vacation, the two peppered one another with questions. Misty then recalled that at one point during their original encounter back in Botswana, the brothers did indeed mention, albeit briefly, a somewhat reclusive uncle, a onetime World Karate Champion, (three times) who had given his life to The Lord after he retired from competitive sports, and was constantly travelling the world preaching the gospel, help build

344

schools, dig wells, and feed the destitute at remote corners of the world.

As these thoughts began stringing together in Misty's mind, she recalled reading somewhere that the good reverend had not attended his brother and sister in law's funeral in Botswana, after they were killed by marauding poachers during a home invasion. It was then the reverend's turn for the round of questioning after the Altima was on the 210 east freeway. What was Misty doing at his nephews' apartment? How did she know them? Who were these men who she had walked in on as they held the brothers at gun point? Any idea where they could have gone? Misty warned that her smartphone, if indeed one of the brothers had taken it, was running low on the charge since she had planned to recharge it when she got to their apartment. Her phone, they knew, could be key.

By the time they made their exit at Baldwin Avenue, and turned right, in effect heading south, McDaniels realized that the beautiful young woman, Misty Abdul, was just in the dark as he was. Quintessentially, they were back to square one. However what was of paramount importance right now was tracking down and finding his nephews before anyone else did, in particular the bad guys.

Misty had suggested her parents' home for the simple reason that they were out of town for a few weeks. The Abduls lived in a quiet neighborhood away from Altadena and the chaos, and thought this would be the ideal place at which they could figure out what to do next. The reverend agreed. He was a bit concerned though what the neighbors, who knew the owners were not home, would think if they saw the beautiful young woman enter the house with a middle aged man old enough to be her father in the middle of the afternoon, but quickly pushed the thought out of his mind. Sean Kane McDaniels had more important things to worry about than some busy body, every neighborhood in the world, from the worst slums to the most exclusive communities had one.

The living room was cozy and well furnished, with artifacts and decorations that immediately gave the impression that Misty Abdul's parents had done very well for themselves during the course of their illustrious medical career, and were well travelled. She then directed the older man to sit on one of the expensive leather couches, while she practically ran to the family landline and snatched the receiver from its cradle and instantly dialed her cellphone number. For all his travels to the remote villages of the world, Reverend Sean Kane McDaniels did not possess a phone, something that was very rare in this day and age. On the other hand, Misty's heart was beating at a rate she could only guess was 110 miles/hr.

The call went straight to voicemail – just as she had feared it would.

"I think the phone is off," she said to Sean Kane with a frightened look on her face.

"Are we even certain that they have it Misty?" The reverend wanted to know.

Misty had to ponder over this one, and at the same time the look on her face justified the fact that her imagination was running amok, all of them with worst case scenario endings.

She said, "There's only one way to find out, I'd …"

At that moment they were interrupted by an emergency bulletin on the television set, which Misty had turned on when they entered the living room. What the news anchor was saying made her sick to the stomach that her knees began to wobble.

"The two suspects are considered armed and dangerous, so if you have any information regarding the two, please contact the nearest precinct or dial 911. The two men, Dumisani McDaniels and Sasha McDaniels are sought in connection with the death of one Hector St. John, an ex-cop with the Los Angeles Police Department. Once again, the suspects are considered armed and dangerous …"

"That's a damn lie!" Misty screamed as she almost threw the icepack she had been using to massage the bump at the back of her head, where one of the goons had hit her with the butt of his gun, at the expensive plasma TV. "I was there," she continued. "It was Dumisani and Sasha who were running for their lives, it was they who were being attacked."

Maintaining his cool, but just as frightened as Misty while not showing it, Sean Kane McDaniels said, "I have got to find them."

He had not realized, up until now, that he had sprung to his feet with amazing speed, grace, and agility for someone his age that Misty gasped, and quickly got control of herself. Only the shocking news about his nephews would have initiated such a reaction from the reverend.

McDaniels looked at the screen again, the anchor woman was still talking, but he could hardly hear her. The faces of his nephews were displayed in the background, which meant that every law enforcement officer, trained men with guns, were on high alert and looking for them. This was all too much to handle, it's like his nephews had been charged, tried, and convicted without due process whatsoever. These boys had barely arrived in the country and already they were being branded killers who had to be put down at all costs. Something was wrong with this picture, could there be someone, some force out there trying very hard to deflect what really happened and turn his boys into patsies?

What troubled Sean Kane really was his black nephew Dumisani, lately cops had been shooting black people practically on sight. No, he was not going to let that happen. It was bad enough that his nephews had lost their parents in a brutal way, and had come to start a new life in a country where dreams supposedly come true, and he would be damned if someone was fighting to take that away from them. As a former Special Forces trained veteran, this McDaniels knew a thing or two about disinformation, and this had the makings of such a scenario.

He began thinking, not like a man who had given his life to the Lord, but as a trained operative on the field, and he could come up with one possible scenario. His nephews, whether they were aware or not, possessed information or knew something that if brought to light would implicate some very powerful person or persons, and the first thing to do was discredit the brothers in case they ever tried going public with what they knew.

The next move would be to eliminate the brothers the moment they had them in their sights. The beautiful young woman Misty had mentioned that the men were after Dumisani's casing that had his camera, she said she heard them demanding for it while one of them held a gun to her head, before knocking her unconscious.

It was obvious that the case they were after was of great significance, and most likely the brothers had taken off with it, and the high speed chase talked about on the news meant that the thugs had not gotten what they were after. Whatever it was, he thought again was of great importance to them. That much was obvious by the way they invaded his nephews' apartment in broad daylight. It would have been an easy matter for them really, of waiting until Dumisani and Sasha left their apartment for them to break in and steal the casing. Why had they not done that? Reverend McDaniels wondered again.

Sean Kane did not need to be told that right now, the odds against the brothers were insurmountable. They were in a foreign country and in a neighborhood they barely knew, it would not take the men who were after them long to find them, torture them to learn what they knew and most importantly, who they had told and thereafter eliminate them. It was also almost a foregone conclusion that after the brothers were silenced for good, the beautiful young woman, Misty Abdul, would be next. He had to act quickly and now.

As McDaniels ran these scenarios in his mind, he knew that he would have no choice but to use his contacts from the old days, a life he thought was long behind him. But now he knew that the past was a dogged pursuer, sooner or later it catches up with you. He also realized that reestablishing his old acquaintances might take time, but he would not worry about that, it was all about finding his nephews.

"I'm coming with you," Misty said, snapping him out of his reverie and in a voice that suggested that the matter was not up for debate or discussion.

"I don't think that would be a good idea Misty," McDaniels said. "This could be extremely dangerous, and I really think you should stay in case they make contact with you."

The lovely young woman, as if she had not heard a single word McDaniels said, reached for her purse which she had placed on a small table next to the side of the main couch, and said, "We will debate that in the car Father McDaniels."

349

"I mean it Misty, you are *not* going. These are dangerous people we're dealing with, and I can't afford to worry about you and my nephews at the same time."

"Do you know my phone number Father McDaniels?"

Damn! He thought, but aloud he said, "What does that have to do with anything?"

"Sooner of later you're going to need it to get hold of them, right?"

"Yes," he admitted, not liking where this was going.

"Well, I guess I'm coming then."

At that moment, and from her tone, the man of God decided that there would be no point arguing with her, which in truth would be another problem piled on the many he had to deal with, so he reluctantly nodded and they were soon out the door headed to his slightly beat up but clean beige 2002 Nissan Altima. However, he needed to set some ground rules.

"You have got to promise me something though Misty," he said.

"I'm listening," she said as she shouldered her bag.

"You do whatever I say, and when I say and no arguing, are we clear?"

She nodded.

Great, Sean Kane McDaniels thought, one more thing to worry about.

CHAPTER 41

JERRY'S BILLIARDS IS LOCATED at the corner of Lake Avenue and Washington Boulevard at the east central neighborhood of northern Pasadena. For a place as large as it is, with at least ten pool tables, it is very intimate with lighting that even during the day, appears as if its night. It is touted as a 'Family Place' but in reality it is hardly a place where one would take their family, mainly because of the atmosphere and the type of crowd the establishment attracts. On Friday and Saturday nights, the place is always packed, because in addition to serving alcohol and food hot from the grill, there are usually pool and dart tournaments taking place, two events that can inevitably create a somewhat ruckus and rowdy atmosphere.

It was nighttime when the two brothers, Dumisani and Sasha McDaniels stood from across the street at the northern side of Washington Boulevard, and watched the place. While doing this, they were careful to lurk in the shadows of the side trees and do as little as possible to attract attention to themselves. Knowing that there were people, the bad guys in particular, searching high and low for them, and possibly law enforcement, the brothers had tried to disguise their look a bit.

Using the bit of cash Sasha had in his fanny pack, money that was meant to be used for emergency purposes, but certainly not the kind of emergency where they would be fugitives running from the law, the brothers had purchased a couple of backpacks at a Rite Aid Store a few blocks away at the corner of Hill and Washington, one of which hid the camera after discarding its metal casing, a pair of loose fitting sweatpants and tops that blended easily with the crowd, two baseball caps, and dark sunglasses, and then threw away the clothes they had been wearing that morning. Most importantly, Sasha had the presence of mind to purchase a cheap portable phone charging unit for Misty's phone, especially when he realized that her smartphone was running out of juice.

Since the billiard place was less than three blocks west from where they'd been hiding, and plotting their next move, Sasha and Dumisani agreed that Jerry's Billiards was the closest establishment to a bar, and bars or taverns were the likely places for free information as people in these places almost always talked freely, the brothers then decided that they would take a chance with this place and risk exposure, but it was important to find out what the word on the street was regarding them.

However, instead of just walking into the place, the two young men decided to watch it from a distance, understand its vibes, the type of clientele it attracted, and most importantly if there were other people beside them who would be observing the place just like them on the chance that they showed up. The brothers had been doing that for the past two hours until they were certain that there was nothing out of the ordinary happening at the place, and thus deemed it safe to make their move.

"I would think all seems okay from what I can tell," Dumisani told his brother.

"Yes," Sasha agreed, his eyes still fixed at the back and front entrance of the establishment. The main entrance was on the busy street of Lake Avenue, and the back, which was used more than the front they realized, faced the parking lot that was also shared by other business places like a hair salon, check cashing joint, a few take away restaurants including one that sold Mexican food, and a few clothing shops. "However, I think only one of us should go in while the other stood guard," Sasha went on to suggest.

Having grown up together and basically inseparable since birth, the brothers had long since noticed that the fact that one was white and the other black, always made them stand out. People, even casual observers almost always paid them close attention whenever they were together. They saw that too only earlier that day, when they were having a late lunch at a small family owned coffee and sandwich shop they also used as a hiding place after ditching the Cadillac and changing clothes. Them seen together would be an infallible point of recognition by their pursuers.

Dumisani nodded and said, "If so then either one of us should use the back entrance."

They had now moved to the bus stop across the street, after stepping out of the shadows, where Lake Avenue and Washington Boulevard intersected. They were on high alert now as they crossed the busy street after the traffic light turned green with the caricature of a man walking in green indicated that it was time for the pedestrians to cross. They kept as mush distance from one another as they did this, with Sasha walking in front, and Dumisani about ten feet behind him. To any observer, the brothers looked like any other of the

353

millions of pedestrians crossing the street of any major city around the world.

As they got closer, they noticed that the business place next to Jerry's Billiards was a Taekwondo Martial Arts studio, closed at that hour, the salon was in fact a 'Nail Salon' and a few others, which explained why there were many other cars in the parking lot beside those that belonged to the Jerry's Billiards clientele. The area where the backdoor was located was dark like the rest of the parking lot, with sporadic lighting here and there, something that suited the McDaniels brothers just fine.

When they got to the back entry, Sasha said to his brother, "Try to remain invisible Dumi, and be on the lookout while am inside." A precaution he need not have voiced because that went without saying, their lives were being threatened by men who risked doing so even in broad daylight when the probability of being seen and reported was highest, and if they could risk that what was a semi dark parking lot to them?

"No need to remind me about that Sasha, I know!" There was some starch to Dumisani's voice, like he hated being lectured to by his brother on things that were obvious even for a child to see.

Sasha nodded and gave a mirthless smile as if to say 'sorry man' before he disappeared through the door, and Dumisani retreated in the dark shadows as he kept an eye on things. The place was not as buzzing as Sasha expected it would be, and that made him wince a bit. A quick glance around and he could tell that the room was larger than he had expected, with about ten pool tables lined in two rows of five, and most of them were empty.

The customers, he noticed was mostly Hispanic, a few who actually looked up from their tables the moment the young but fit looking white man walked in. Sasha tried to make himself look as if it was business as usual, like he was a regular at the place, but he fooled no one. Anyone could tell from a mile away that he was a stranger in a strange land. His body language betrayed all that he had been trying to avoid and some.

Sasha then headed to the counter with high barstools that were empty at the moment, and sat on one of them. The bartender was also a young Hispanic man with a clean shave, shifty eyes, and a thin moustache that made his face resemble that of the actor John Leguizamo. And strangely enough, the nametag on his t-shirt read 'Juan', which is John in Spanish. With business seemingly slow, he was working on a crossword puzzle but immediately snapped to attention after noticing the young patron.

"What can I get you *senor*?"

"A Heineken for now Juan," Sasha said with a forced smile. He did not intend on getting smashed or even finish his drink, because he knew that a young white man alone in a pool bar without a drink screamed surveillance.

Juan said, "Coming right up, wanna open a tab?"

"Haven't decided yet but I'll let you know."

"No problem pal," Juan said as he turned to get one of the icy cold beers the place was famous for.

Juan also noticed that his new patron spoke with a strong accent he could not place and was slightly taken aback by it. Such a thing, particularly in this part of town was a bit unusual. There was also something vaguely familiar about the stranger he could not readily put a finger on, but was right there under the surface, in the recesses of his subconscious mind, fighting to break free. He pushed the thought from his mind, as he concentrated on the task at hand.

He popped open a bottle of Heineken and put a napkin under it, after placing it in front of Sasha, who nodded his thanks and continued to stare into space. As Juan turned to head back to the glasses he had been wiping earlier, he suddenly remembered why the young white man looked familiar, and caught himself just in time before snapping his fingers as the realization occurred to him.

He went into the tiny office away from the counter and register, but because of the glass partitioning on one side, the occupant could still keep a hawk's eye view of the counter and the register, and most of the floor of the pool hall. Add to that, there were several monitors that received and displayed the feedback from a number of surveillance cameras fixed at strategic corners of the establishment, inside and outside.

There was also a huge desk inside the tiny office that took up most of the space, filing cabinets, and a fax machine, which is where Juan was right now standing and studying a 'WANTED' flyer that had arrived a few hours earlier from the police. Based on past experience, he knew that such a circular had been sent to public places like Jerry's Billiards where people hung out, and would have likely seen the two young men who were wanted by the authorities. One of the two young men wanted, according to the flyer, matched almost exactly the young white man with a strange accent now seated at his counter. Jerry looked again from the fax and through the one way glass at Sasha, and then again at the flyer – there could be no doubt. It was him.

According to the information on the circular, the two young men, Dumisani McDaniels and Sasha McDaniels, *what the hell*? Juan had wondered earlier when he noticed that the two shared the same last name, were wanted for 'questioning' (a euphemism for arrest as far as Juan was concerned) in connection to a homicide that involved a former LAPD officer. They were considered armed and dangerous, something that did not quite jive with what Juan saw with his own eyes.

He folded the flyer and placed it in his back pocket, as he wondered how he was going to handle this. Juan was not going to turn him in. The Salvador native, and now a proud Green Card holder was from the streets, which meant he adhered to a certain type of code. He was not a *saplon*, a *chivato*, a *snitch*. If anything he was going to do the direct opposite. Juan was going to warn the young man to get the hell out of dodge and that time soon.

Sasha, as far as he could tell, had either mastered the art of hiding in plain sight, or was a moron of the highest order he had ever come across in his entire life. Usually, people who kill cops, if the information on the flyer was to be believed, hide deep and then flee as far away as possible with the likely destination being a country that has no extradition treaty with the United States of America. By the time he got back to the counter to talk to Sasha, the latter was taking a sip from his bottle and seemingly getting ready to split.

"How much do I owe you?" Sasha asked when he saw Juan appear from the back.

He had picked up on the fact that the bartender had been following him with his eyes ever since he got there, and was doing a poor job of being discreet about it. Did he know something? Sasha had to wonder.

"Let's just say it's on the house," Juan Morales said, as he made quick eye contact and then around the room as if what he was saying was not meant for others to hear.

Sasha was taken aback by this. There was such a thing as free lunch after all, but free booze at a pool bar no less? Never, unless the bartender knew something and was trying to keep him at ease until the calvary arrived, either the cops or the bad guys. Could that be it? Sasha McDaniels wondered.

"Really?!" Sasha said, trying to hide his surprise, but mainly his sudden suspicion of the man.

"Yeah, really," Juan Morales gave a weak smile, but his mind seemed elsewhere and the former National Champion's antenna was suddenly up.

"Why this generosity?" The guy didn't even know him from Eve for Christ sake.

"Let's just say I felt like it," was the somewhat vague answer.

Juan then looked around and then leaned as close to Sasha from behind the long marble counter as he could, then said, "I think you should get out of here like right now man."

Sasha felt the sudden stab of cold fear in his chest but managed to suppress it. He needed to know what this man knew.

"What on earth are you talking about?" Sasha faked ignorance, his heart was pounding wildly, even though he had a pretty good guess as to what was going on. Word was out, and him and his brother were in mortal danger, he just wanted to know how much Juan Morales knew and to what extent.

For an answer, Juan reached into his back pocket, and pulled out the '*WANTED FOR QUESTIONING*' flyer, thanks to the electronic age, it was amazing how quick such information spread. He then straightened it out, and then without arousing suspicion showed it to the stunned youngster from Botswana.

"This came in about two hours ago," Juan said.

Now was time to throw caution to the wind and come clean and tell this bartender why he was here, so he said, "Actually man, I want to know how to get to the nearest police station so that I can explain the situation, you see there's been a big misunderstanding, some guys came to our …"

He immediately stopped in mid-sentence when he saw the look on Juan Morales's face. It was the look of genuine horror and concern.

"That's assuming you get to the precinct," Juan said rather ominously.

This time it was Sasha McDaniels who was confused. "And what's that supposed to mean?" he asked in a fierce whisper, the Heineken was long forgotten.

"Jesus Christ! What? Are you stupid man?"

"Okay, enlighten me," Sasha McDaniels leaned closer. "What the hell am I missing?"

It now seemed as if this little exchange at the bar counter began attracting the attention of other patrons, in particular a group of tough looking Hispanics at a pool table, about three tables away. There were at least five of them with gang and prison tattoos that covered their arms and necks.

Juan looked around again, and then in a fierce but forceful whisper said, "It says here," he pointed at the flyer now lying on the counter in front of Sasha. "That you and this other dude in the picture are wanted for murder of an off duty cop." He stabbed the flyer again with his index finger to add more emphasis to what he was saying.

Sasha was horrified. Even he, a foreigner, fresh from the boat in a manner of speaking, knew that this was one country in which you could never kill a cop, no matter your reasons or how justified you may be. You can never kill a cop and live to tell the story, active or not. Even in self-defense, as was in Sasha and Dumisani's case, clean cop or dirty cop, none of that mattered, they were going to come down on you like the plague for killing one of their brethren. Sasha McDaniels now knew the world of danger he and his brother were in. It was not only the bad guys after them, the McDaniels brothers had the full might of the law to contend with. And the law was going to respond with self-righteous savagery.

It was not a matter of thwarting the goons who were on their trail. Now it was a matter of survival, and after Juan Morales's sobering revelation, the brothers were left with only one option, and that was to get the hell out of the country as soon as possible. Maybe, Sasha thought, once out of the country and if they could somehow make it back to Botswana unscathed, they could then find a way to clear their names, something they would do with the full backing of the Botswana government, who would learn the truth from the brothers themselves and get it known through proper diplomatic channels.

"What?!" was all the horrified Sasha could utter.

What Juan Morales said next only made matters worse.

"This means a cop sees either one of you, they have the motivation to shoot you on sight." The words hit like a mortar shell at the pit of his stomach.

Sasha sighed. The young man had to will himself to take several deep breaths to bring his blood pressure down, and think things through. The worst thing he could do was let fear dictate his next moves – limited as they were.

"That can't be," he said in a low voice and as if he was trying to convince himself. "We did not intentionally kill anybody. If anything *we* are the victims, ambushed at gunpoint in our own flat."

Juan looked at him strangely, twisted his brow and said, "Your own what?"

"Flat." Then added quickly, "Apartment." Sometimes Sasha had to constantly remind himself that some things and names were different in this part of the world.

"Oho," Juan said as he nodded with comprehension then added by saying, "But man, I suggest you get out of town as soon as possible with T.J. being the first destination I'd be thinking of if I were you."

Sasha narrowed his eyes and asked, "What is a T.J.?"

"Tijuana."

"And what's Tijuana?" Sasha wanted to know, sincerely bewildered at what this bartender and supposed new friend was talking about.

Juan Morales rolled his eyes in disbelief and a look that said he was dealing with a moron of the highest order, for this certainly was a new one. He thought, even working as a bartender he seen it all, but this one took the cake.

"Now I'm beginning to believe that you had nothing to do with all these things they're saying about you, are you kidding me?"

"Oh really?" there was a trace of sarcasm in Sasha's voice.

"Anyone who does not know or heard about Tijuana cannot possibly be a criminal, let alone a cop killer," Juan replied sincerely and not trying to be funny. He then said, "Anyway, T.J. is a city in Mexico just across the border, keep heading south past San Diego and to the border, and once you get there, cross the bridge and you'll be fine."

Juan then looked around again, and leaned closer to tell him more. Apparently, their little powwow seemed to have drawn the attention some of the customers, three in particular he could tell, who had since stopped playing and were leaning of their pool sticks as if trying to listen in on every word exchanged between the two in spite of the din floating around the huge room. That was the downside of working in a bar, Juan thought, particularly one not frequented by women, you had way too many nosy people hanging around. A long conversation between the bartender and a customer not seen before because the clientele pretty much knew one another, was sure to draw attention.

Juan Morales was genuinely drawn to this young and yet completely naïve and clueless stranger, and wanted to help him as much as he could without snagging himself into some 'aiding and abetting' beef the authorities may try to pin on him, but even then, he thought, he could just plead ignorance and then keep his mouth shut. He had known killers his whole life, and was once a member of a street gang while growing up in East Los Angeles, though mainly as a 'lookout', and had been in trouble before. This young man with strange accent was certainly no killer, even though by looking at him he was no pushover either. It was possible he had been suckered into something he had absolutely nothing to do with.

Deciding to go all out, Juan Morales tore out a page from a notebook he took from underneath the marble counter, and sketched a rough map complete with possible routes to take him to the San Diego border, and what to do when he got there, which was to cross the bridge like any other gringo on his way to have a good time in the border town, like visiting one of the brothels were young Central American girls were waiting to provide pleasure for a few American dollars.

"Okay now get out of here man," he said as he pushed the paper with the sketch on it at Sasha.

"Thanks Juan," Sasha said as he quickly folded the paper and placed it in his front pocket. "One day when this is over I'll come looking for you to thank you properly," he said as he got up to leave.

Sasha would have shaken the man's hand but as it was, he had taken up too much of his time, plus even he knew that by talking to the man, he would have possibly put him in danger and in the bad guys' eyes, and even the police, he would be guilty by association.

After Sasha turned to leave, he was briefly distracted by two new customers, and man and woman, perhaps the only one as far as he could tell, who wanted to book a table and buy a pitcher of beer, so he did not notice the three rough looking Hispanic men with tattoos, who had been paying close attention to him and the bartender, exit via the backdoor, the same Sasha had used to enter the establishment.

CHAPTER 42

ALL THREE MEN, Dino Gonzales, Pedro Jimenez, and Ernesto Rodriguez were big bald, muscular, and in their early 30's. The thick tattoos on their arms and necks told their story – ex cons who also happened to be gang members. They all wore baggy khaki pants and white t-shirts which defined their barrel chests even further.

It had been Dino Gonzales, who had noticed Sasha enter the room just as he was about to bend over the pool table, and smack the white ball into the hole. He had even paid closer attention when Sasha took off his sunglasses to speak to the bartender, Juan. Besides, who wore sunglasses at night unless he was up to no good?

He finished slotting the ball into its hole, and then without being too evident, he looked at Sasha McDaniels again, and then gently nudged Ernesto in the ribs to get his attention.

"Ernesto," he said. "Doesn't that gringo look familiar?"

Ernesto threw a quick glance at the counter and then back at the pool table. Apparently he was more inclined at winning the game than looking at other people, they had bet money all around and that was what was at stake.

"No *homs*," he said before taking a sip at his beer bottle. "8 Ball, let's reck 'em up boys, $100 down this time suckers!" Ernesto Rodriguez had been on a winning streak lately and was determined to keep it going.

At first, the other two men were more interested in starting another game, but Dino was insistent, until he finally got them to see what he was seeing. Sasha was busy talking to Juan, and every now and then would throw a furtive glance around the room, but at no one in particular. The young white Motswana had never been a fugitive from justice in his life, much less in a foreign country, so for a bungling first time renegade, his body language told the whole story.

"He sure looks like one of those dudes on the six o'clock news *homs*," Pedro confirmed after studying Sasha for a while without being too obvious.

Dino then said, "Do you think there could be a reward involved for turning in a white boy running away from the police *ese*?"

This went against the grain of the streets they were raised in, and Ernesto Rodriguez was the first to point that out as the other two high fived each other, already thinking of the possible reward money and not even mentioning the favor they would garner from the cops when they turned this young man in. If he was here, then the other could not be far away, they thought.

"Come on guys, knock it off. We've got a game to play, besides, you could be wrong about this guy, and since when did we become a bunch of *chivatos*? I say we leave this one alone *homs*," Ernesto implored.

However, the prospect of gaining favor with the local police and being on their good side, began to grow on the other two and they did not seem to be listening to their friend. They were now, in spite of themselves, looking at Sasha and Juan with impunity.

"There's only one way to find out," Pedro said.

The moment Juan finished serving the new customers, Dino and Pedro were at the counter looking at him wide eyed like kids opening presents at Christmas.

"Tell me that's the guy on the news Juan," Pedro said excitedly.

Juan Morales played dumb. "What?"

"Yeah dude," Dino quipped. "That's one of the guys 'Five O' is after isn't he?"

Juan then tried to deflect, which in itself was like saying '*yes guys that's him indeed*' but instead said, "You guys had too much to drink, why don't you go back to your game?"

The fact that Juan Morales did not outright deny that the young white man was indeed who they thought he was, got their blood boiling with excitement. They were now convinced that it was certainly one of the two the cops were after. This was unbelievable, the whole world was looking for these two and like a gift from Heaven, here was one of them literally in their sights.

"Come on man," Pedro said. "A clean cut white guy comes in an untrendy place in this neighborhood all by his oneself, hardly touches his drink, and then leaves in a jiffy … you know he got to be running from something," he added with a goofy drunken smile.

"Yeah, I knew something was not right," Dino added, very pleased with himself. "There's no way that guy was not one of the dudes the cops are after."

"You guys are way off base. Should I get you another pitcher? On the house of course," Juan practically pleaded.

Dino and Pedro exchanged a quick glance, now they were absolutely certain that they were on solid ground. The three friends had been coming to this joint for the past three years, and not once during that time had Juan Morales offered them a drink *on the house*, not even on credit – never!

"No man, we just wanna find out if it's him, but now we know it is, and am sure there's some sort of reward for turning his ass in," Pedro said, again his eyes gleaming at the thought of what lay ahead.

Juan just smiled and raised his hands as if in surrender. While speaking to Sasha McDaniels, he had noticed the man's knuckles on his hands. Juan Morales also refereed low end mixed martial arts tournaments for extra money, mostly underground stuff conducted in abandoned buildings, underground parking garages of tenants who chose to lend a blind eye to such human 'cockfighting', and knew the hands of a brawler when he saw them, and that young white man was certainly one.

Reading Juan's silence and evasiveness as confirmation, the two ran out through the back door to go after Sasha McDaniels. Pedro Jimenez was on his cellphone as he followed his friend, and from the brief one sided conversation Juan was able to catch, he knew that the other man was talking to the cops, or at the very least a 911 Operator, who no doubt would be warning him to stay put, and in as nice and as professional way as possible to not do anything stupid until the police arrived. However, Juan knew exactly how this one was going to go down.

"Dumbasses," he said to himself as he picked a clean white rag, turned and began wiping some clean glasses, and arrange them in a neat line in a designated cupboard above the cash register.

***

Dumisani McDaniels gave his brother a head start of about ten paces before he emerged from his hiding place in the bushy flowers beside the back entrance of the billiard hall. He looked around a few more times, before he quickened his pace and caught up with him. They were in the back parking lot of the mini mall, walking eastward toward a small dark street called 'Sinaloa' that ran north to south, and therefore ran parallel with the major Lake Avenue.

"Well?" Dumisani asked his brother the moment he caught up with him and handed him his backpack.

"Bad, as in very bad Dumi," was the gloomy response from his brother.

Dumisani could suddenly feel his bowels turn to water. *When does this end?*

"Bad?" Dumisani asked in a hoarse whisper. "What do you mean bad?" he asked again, as he grabbed his brother by the sleeve of his shirt so he could turn to face him.

"They have us on a *wanted* flyer Dumi, we're wanted for murder," Sasha said as if even he could not believe it.

It had been a home invasion for Christ sake! They were in their flat, *oh yes sorry Juan, apartmen*t, minding their own damn business like millions of people around the world in their homes do, when these men with guns barged in, demanding something that was not theirs to begin with, and even ready to kill them for it. Wasn't there a law in their constitution that allowed them to defend themselves and their home with force if they had to? They had done just that and now they were being blamed for it? Absurd did not even begin to describe this, someone had distorted the facts in their favor and now they were being hunted.

The two brothers had gone over all this exhaustively that afternoon while on the run, and agreed wholeheartedly that if there ever was a case of self-defense and justifiable homicide, then this was it. Now, if they were wanted for murder, the most heinous crime in the book, it meant that they were up against an enemy who had the power to tilt any irrefutable facts in their favor. Juan Morales's revelation earlier on confirmed that.

"That's madness Sasha!" was all Dumisani could think of saying.

They were in big trouble, there was no question about it, as they paused for a second to let the gravity of the situation sink in. They were conveniently hidden at the darkest corner of the parking lot, wondering what to do next.

Dumisani broke the uncomfortable silence by saying, "Did you at least find out where the nearest police station is, so at least we can explain ourselves?"

His brother opened his mouth to say something when suddenly a voice interrupted him, and for a moment this froze them. They turned to face two strangers standing side by side, even in the semi darkness they could see the tattoos on their beefy arms, which were folded on their massive chests, and on their necks. It was apparent that the two pumped iron every chance they got. However, it was the self-assured smirk on their faces that told the brothers that these two Hispanic nimrods were trouble walking on two feet.

The bigger of the two, Pedro Jimenez, stepped forward and said, "We thought we'd save you the trouble and turn you in ourselves."

Sasha and Dumisani were too stunned to speak as the two approached menacingly. Sasha on the other hand thought the two looked vaguely familiar. He then just as quickly remembered that he had caught a glimpse of them when he was in the pool bar, talking to Juan.

The bastards must have eavesdropped on our conversation while I was speaking to the bartender, Sasha thought, as he mentally kicked himself for not being a little more discreet in his interaction with Juan. Damn!

Pedro, mistaking the look of surprise on the brothers' face for fear smiled more threateningly and said, "See, my buddy and I got a couple of felonies between us, so turning you two bozos in will make us look real good to the cops."

The smaller of the two, Dino, not to be undone by his friend decided to add his two cents and said, "Don't forget our parole officers Pedro."

There was a gap on the upper set of his toothy grin. It looked so annoying that Dumisani felt like he wanted to slap that silly grin off his face.

"Oh yeah, that too," Pedro agreed, very pleased with himself.

The brothers looked at one another and then at the two interlopers, these had to be the most talkative and stupid would be muggers they had ever come across. Just one other minor nuisance they had to deal with. When does this foolishness end? Dumisani and Sasha asked themselves in unison.

Sasha, not surprisingly, was the first to speak, "Eh fellas, stay out of this."

Damn foreigners! Dino thought, the moment he heard Sasha speak. I bet the black sidekick is foreign too.

"Look," Dumisani said, like his brother he had had just about enough of this claptrap. "You guys have had too much to drink, so why don't you go on back and mind your own damn business?"

I was right, he's foreign too, Dino thought gleefully. *This is going to be real easy.* Aloud, he declared, "Jeez Luiz Pedro! It's definitely them."

He then went on to mimic Dumisani and Sasha's accent, "Look you guys have had too much to drink …" It was an atrocious impression because it was a mockery.

Sasha felt the anger rising from the basin of his stomach, he had given these idiots more than enough time to rethink their situation and head back, and if he was to hear any more of their crap, someone was going to get hurt, and it certainly was not going to be him or his brother. If these bozos kept pushing … he decided to give it one last try.

"Hey!" he said, raising his voice just a tad. "I don't know what you guys think you're up to, but now is certainly not the time. My brother and I have had a pretty rough day. Come on Dumi, let's get the hell out of here."

He then tagged at Dumisani's sleeve, and the brothers turned to leave to find a place where they could plan their next course of action. On seeing this, Pedro and Dino, offended that the two would even have the audacity to turn their backs on them picked up their pace until they overtook the brothers. They were now right in their faces, and they were seething.

"Not so fast *pendejos*," Pedro said. "You're staying right here with us until Five O gets here. See we already put in the call." He reached into his pocket, fished out his phone, and waved it in Sasha and Dumisani faces to underline his threat.

"We can do this the easy way, or we can do it the hard way," Dino added. Again he was flashing that self-assured idiotic grin that Dumisani had quickly grown to detest.

As they stepped closer, invading the two brothers' space, it took every ounce of Dumisani McDaniels' training to restrain himself from slapping that silly grin off his face. Instead the brothers shared that familiar look – one that said, *oh it's on now!*

And just to piss them off even more, Dumisani said, in as calm and yet mocking voice he could muster, "How about we do it the hard way?"

It is said that the Karate man never strikes the first blow, akin to the cliche nice guys finish last. However, for those who have stared death in the face, the brutality of life will tell you that such rules don't apply on the streets. Thus, when the blow came, it came without warning, a lighting quick front snap kick executed by Dumisani to the solar plexus of the hoodlum Dino Gonzales, who doubled over before falling forward, which meant it had been a masterly strike. It came without further warning. On his way to the pavement, Dino's nape was exposed and on to that, the third degree black belt delivered the *coup de grace*, which was an elbow strike.

With this blow, Dumisani held back at the last possible second and therefore did not hit him as hard as he could have, otherwise the goon would have suffered a raptured spine that would have instantly turned him into a vegetable, paralyzed from the neck down for life. Instead, it was lights out for Dino Gonzales before his unconscious body hit the pavement, face first, arms on his side and heavy like a sack of corn. Moments later, a pool of urine gathered under his unconscious body as his bladder involuntarily released.

The other hood, Pedro Jimenez's eyes and mouth were still wide open with astonishment at witnessing the swiftness of Dumisani's attack, when Sasha curled his fingers at the knuckles and struck him on the Adam's apple with equal velocity that his victim did not see until it was done. And like his brother, he too had pulled back a little. However the pain was horrific, like nothing he had felt in his entire life and for a moment Pedro Jimenez thought he was going to die.

As he staggered backwards, both hands clutching his throat, Jimenez knew instantly that these two were professional fighters or at the very least were trained at the highest level. He realized too late that he and his friend had kissed a cobra, as he opened and closed his mouth like a flopping fish on the ground. And before he could regain his balance, Sasha stepped forward with his right foot, used it as pivot, and from it leaped in the air, his body half twisting and sent a flying spin back kick that saw the heel of his foot hit the right side of Pedro's head. However, just like the knuckle strike, the power of the kick was controlled but performed with only what could be called grace. And just like his friend, he fell to the ground and was out cold long before he landed partly on Dino's unconscious body, but mostly on the hard pavement.

And just like that, it was over in no time. The brothers looked around, searching the semi darkness to see if there were witnesses to this quick, brutal, and yet efficient beat down. When they were satisfied that there were none, they nonchalantly shouldered their backpacks, which they had since lain on the ground inside a flowerpot that had been built around a pole that was supposed to illuminate that part of the parking lot, and casually walked to Sinaloa street which ran parallel with Lake Avenue, and soon vanished in the dark.

CHAPTER 43

JERRY'S BILLIARD'S WAS ALREADY BUZZING with activity as the clientele increased, when a battered and bruised Dino Gonzales and Pedro Jimenez staggered into the pool bar, like a couple of giants walking on mosquito limbs. Their faces were bruised from the hard contact they made with the rough pavement, and Dino was clutching the back of his head with his left hand. Their eyes were wild, and it was clear from their contorted faces that they were in great pain.

Somehow Juan Morales was not surprised as he watched them stumble toward his counter.

"So, did they just hand themselves over to you like a bunch of wimps? Or was it more like trying to capture a pair of bobcats with your bare hands?" Juan asked as casually as possible, but the dig in his voice was plain.

Pedro, his face still twisted in anguish, ignoring the jab said, "Can we get some ice please Juan?"

However, Juan was not done with his ribbing as he reached into the fridge behind him, scooped some ice cubes, and then put them in a clean white towel, one of the many he used to clean the long counter and gave it to the injured man, and said, "I've heard that it's never a good idea to corner a wounded cat because you'll get hurt."

He had warned these two morons to leave this one alone, but did they listen to him? No, so they deserved anything thrown at them – even the ridicule that came with it. They were like a child whose been told by a parent not to play with fire, but does it anyway no matter how many times he's been told that in doing so he'll get burned.

Their other friend, Ernesto Rodriguez, who had also warned them to mind their own beeswax, and was now engrossed in a game of 'Eight Ball' with a new partner, looked up from his table when he saw his two friends teetering toward the counter, and was about to say something when both doors to the main entrance of the pool hall burst open at the same time, and suddenly the place was flooded with at least twenty police officers, weapons drawn, with some of them clad in full riot gear, complete with shields and helmets, like they were ready to engage an enemy so strong that even air support would be a possibility replete with B2 Bombers.

Suddenly the place was quiet as if a switch had been turned off. At least for now, their weapons were pointed to the floor and not at anyone in particular, otherwise more than a few of the patrons would have dove for cover on the floor, thinking that they were about to be mowed down.

One of the men, tall and beefy like the rest of them, more so because of the Kevlar vest under his uniform, strode to the middle of the large room, his service gun, a Glock 19 machine pistol, holstered and on his side, looked around as if searching for someone in particular. He appeared to be in his late 40's or early 50's with a ruddy complexion that seemed to favor the outdoors. From the bars on his shoulders he was a captain, and the tag on the top right side of his shirt identified him as 'Gerrard', Captain William Gerrard, or Willie Gerrard as he was generally known.

This had to have been classified as a high priority bust if it involved a high ranking officer like him.

"Okay, who called it in?" he barked.

Since he was the bartender at the moment, and thus by default the person in charge, Juan Morales cleared his throat, and in as none threatening and polite a voice he could muster asked, "Who called in what sir?"

"We got a call from one Pedro Jimenez that one of the fugitives we're looking for was right here at this establishment, are you Pedro?"

Juan shook his head, looked at Dino and then at Pedro, both of whom seemed to have shrunk in size and pointed. It was after all not a secret.

"You might wanna talk to this gentleman here sir, that's Pedro and I think he's the one who called," Juan said.

The captain's gaze was suddenly focused on the two, who from what the captain could tell, had been at the wrong end of one hell of a beating. One of the men, Pedro's friend presumably, had a towel with ice pressed to the side of his head.

"That would be me sir, I'm Pedro Jimenez," he said meekly.

The police captain narrowed his eyes as he studied the two. He had very strong features, a tight jaw, aquiline nose, and thick eyebrows on an otherwise craggy face. It was obvious from his grooming that he was trying to look younger than his age suggested, but he was obviously losing that battle.

"Gaddammit! What the hell happened to you two?"

Dino said, "We tried to stop them, as law abiding citizens ..."

"Cut the bullshit, where did they go?"

376

The veteran cop knew the drill, these two clowns were trying to be heroes and perhaps carry favor with the police somehow so as to be dealt with kid gloves in any future jam they most likely would find themselves in. They were told specifically not to try and apprehend the suspects or do anything stupid to spook them in any way, but of course they disregarded that warning from the authorities, now here they were, back to square one.

Dino Gonzales, massaging his bumps and bruises on his face while wincing at the same time answered, "We did not see where they went sir." It was true because they were out cold when the brothers made their escape.

Another officer, a sergeant it turned out, stepped forward from the rest of the armed men and stood beside the captain. His name was Jonathan Patrick, a ballbuster if there ever was one. Even though he was in his mid-40's , he looked older than he was with a tight jaw, pursed lips, and a close cropped haircut that could be described as 'dirty blond'. He almost always had a frown on his face, and this moment the creases on his forehead were even deeper this evening, if that was at all possible. And right now his ire was directed at the two nimrods.

"Fuckin' amateurs," he snarled at Dino and his friend.

"Excuse me?" Pedro said as he squinted his eyes at the Sergeant. All they did, as far as he was concerned, was trying to help and they'd gotten their asses kicked while doing so, now to add insult to injury they were taking flack for it? This was bullshit as far as he was concerned.

"You were told to stay put, right?" Patrick fumed, specks of spittle flew from his mouth and onto Pedro's face that he was forced to take a few steps back.

"Well sir," Pedro said defensively. " It happened so fast, we …"

"Do you know if they were driving or on foot?" the cop interrupted, knowing that time was running out, and chastising these men was not going to get them anywhere but they might offer some piece of important information, dumb as they were. And as crazy as it sounded, they did try to help, and in the process got their asses handed to them by two professionals. Had they managed to capture them, they would all be singing a different song right now.

"They may have been on foot, but we're not sure," Dino said, who like his friend was also grimacing in pain. *Those foreigners could surely pack a punch … and a kick*, he thought grimly. *Juan and Ernesto were right, we should have left this one the hell alone.*

"Are you sure?" Jonathan Patrick wanted to know.

Evidently, the captain, Gerrard Williams had decided to sit this one out, and let his subordinate squeeze whatever information he could from the two.

"No sir," Dino said. "You see, we were knocked out for a while and we …"

Williams raised his hand like the traffic cop he once was, stopping him in mid parentheses.

"Save it," he spat and for good measure added, "Nincompoops!"

The two young men were visibly hurt by this, but of course the Sergeant, with affected unconcern immediately turned his back on them and consulted his Captain.

"What do you think sir?" he asked, his demeanor completely different, very much like that of a subordinate speaking to his superior.

The Captain who had since holstered his service weapon scratched his chin thoughtfully and said, "I think they're on foot. The car they jacked was found at

378

an alley about six blocks from here, and based on what these fools told us, I think that would be a fair guess. So alert all the precincts within a twenty mile radius of these new developments, have them set up roadblocks on all major streets and every possible route out of the city. Renew the bulletin, and we should have them boxed in by sunrise."

"Done," Williams said as he snapped a quick salute, and immediately began redeploying and mobilizing his men with the precedence to catch the McDaniels brothers before sunrise.

CHAPTER 44

THE SAFE HOUSE – SOUTH PASADENA, CA.

RIGHT AROUND THE TIME while the two brothers were making their bid for freedom, the mood at the safe house in South Pasadena was anything but pleasant. A day that had begun with the hope of getting rid of what was supposed to have been an easy problem, had instead turned into an unmitigated disaster. Even worse, one of Declan Price's best men, Hector St. John had been killed, and not only that, but the brothers had also gotten away, and were officially in the wind with the incriminating evidence still in their possession.

The two surviving assailants, Reggie McNeal and Miguel Bustamante had managed to get away from the McDaniels' apartment before the cops arrived, forgetting their sworn oath of *never* leaving a fallen comrade behind, as they chased after the brothers, and then ended in a spectacular pursuit that attracted even more police, and then on realizing that, McNeal, Bustamante, and a couple of men they had brought along, manning the vehicle while the three went into the McDaniels apartment, were forced to abandon the chase and head back to the safe house

This was where they were now, and ready to face the wrath of their boss, Declan Price, a man who never complimented success, for it was expected, failure on the other hand was punished severely. The two, McNeal and Bustamante, felt exactly the way they looked – bruised and swollen – the aftereffects of a brutal beating at the hands of opponents who were said to be clueless and naïve. As the two massaged their faces, with ice packs to try and ease the swelling, they wondered at least for the hundred and sixtieth time that day how they had been duped into thinking that the assignment was going to be a cakewalk. Only to be confronted by two young men who obviously had above average fighting skills, and hit like Mack trucks.

How on God's green earth could something so crucial like this have been missed? Miguel wondered again as he pressed the ice pack even harder to his face where a Dumisani McDaniel fist had landed, and had no doubt that his colleague was also thinking along the same lines. They were seated in the living room like two like elementary school kids waiting to be summoned to the Headmaster's office, which in fact was what was about to happen, for their boss was in his office, what had once been a bedroom, where he was right now talking to someone on the phone. There was a large office desk, a landline, fax machine, and a few filing cabinets. Just like the rest of the house, it was sparsely furnished with items that could be left at a moment's notice if they needed to run.

There were two other men at the safe house that day, the hulking giants Reggie McNeal had seen at the Country Club with their boss, who like before were stationed at opposite ends of the living room, their thick arms folded across their chests and silent as carved statues, but kept an eye on Reggie and Miguel. The two were under no illusion as to what awaited them.

The intelligence on the two brothers though accurate to some extent, only went so far. The fact that Sasha and Dumisani McDaniels were skilled in the art of unarmed combat had been missed, and that proved to be fatal at least to one of them. Had they possessed that tiny detail (not so tiny now in retrospect) about the brothers, they would have planned better and thus come better prepared.

However, men like Declan Price thought of themselves as infallible, mistakes were made by others and not them. Reggie McNeal was almost certain that the man was already shifting blame. It was always odd to watch these deflections, because of the strange honesty to them. Reggie, just like his partner in crime, Miguel, had come to believe that they were less a deliberate reaction to failure than an unconscious one. Declan Price, their boss, saw himself as foolproof and both men were proven correct when, a few minutes later, they were standing nervously in front of Price's huge desk.

Their boss was incensed. This, according to him, was supposed to have been a simple snatch and grab mission with the incriminating footage in his possession right now, and none would be the wiser. Now the two African boys were out there, and only God knew what would happen if they somehow leaked what they had to the media. With this in mind, he had no choice but to tell his brother everything. Needless to say, the news was not well received.

"What do you mean they got away with no trace at all?" Declan Price screamed a little later as the two men gave their report.

"The cops were closing in boss, so all things considered we had to bail," Reggie McNeal said defensively.

"My guess is that they're in police custody," Miguel Bustamante added quickly.

From behind his desk, Declan Price stood up so abruptly that his two men were forced to take a few men backwards.

"What?! Are you stupid or just a plain imbecile? If the cops had them in custody, I'd be the first to know." Like McNeal and Bustamante were supposed to know this. "My goodness," he continued. "These two are just a couple of amateurs, ignorant foreigners from the jungles of some African backwater who've never seen a streetlight, let alone tell north from south, and yet they managed to outwit the two of you and not only that, that idiot St. John got himself killed in the process. I can't work with such stupidity!" he banged his fist on the huge mahogany desk as he screamed the last sentence, again his two men took a slight step back.

The two looked at one another and then at their boss. Their look said it all, they disagreed with everything he was saying, and Declan Price was quick to pick on it.

"What?" he asked, "You don't agree?"

"We don't disagree," Reggie said.

"And what's that supposed to mean?" Price seethed as he finally took a seat again.

Reggie said, "Well sir, they fought like tigers, in a way that suggests that they have some sort of training that's world class." He then unconsciously rubbed the bump on his forehead as if to stress the point he was making.

Declan Price retorted by saying, "Skilled enough to disarm and beat up three well trained, special forces veterans, well paid assassins even to an extent of killing one? Are you two telling me that you're pathetic without sounding dumb?"

Yeah, pretty much, Bustamante thought but did not dare say aloud. You were not there and it's easy to call plays in the comfort of your $1000,00 leather chair.

The silence stretched out as the two men avoided eye contact, and Price interpreted that as having made his point.

"That's what I thought," Declan Price said when a reply was not forthcoming. "Now, get the fuck out of my office now, and I'm *not* interested in seeing either one of you alive until the bastards are cold and buried, do I make myself clear?" His eyes were blazing with rage. If he thought the two were expendable, there was no doubt in his mind that he would have had them killed right at that instant.

The two left the room with their heads hung in shame, it had been more than an ass chewing, they were totally humiliated. It was not enough that they had suffered a beating at the hands of the brothers, and the unabashed tongue lashing only added to their humiliation.

Alone in his office after the two left, Price dropped his head on the shiny large table. The anger he had so passionately displayed was really to hide the fear that had been building ever since he got the news that the Genuine Bank Heist, as it was being called by the media, had been caught on tape, and that the damning evidence was in the possession of these two unwitting foreigners.

This was supposed to have been easy, track them down, find out what they knew, and quietly put them out of their misery – after all he believed in the old axiom: dead men tell no lies. When it looked like things were spiraling out of control, he was forced to face his brother, the future presidential candidate, and tell him everything. To say Gilbert Price was apoplectic at hearing this would be a gross underestimation. The man was livid, seeing his ultimate political dream going down the drain. He remembered the call verbatim.

"Do you have any idea what you've done?" Gil Price yelled time and again during their phone conversation.

"I did it all for you Gil," Declan countered, and went on to lecture, "Presidential campaigns are bare knuckle street fights with knives and all."

"And look where that has led us!" the older Price screamed as he did for most of the conversation.

Like every politician, Gil Price knew the peril he was in. Sins of the brother would definitely rub off on him, innocent or not, there was no way he was going to disassociate himself from this scandal if and when it came out, and in this electronic age the news was going to spread like wildfire, because whether he liked it or not he was hitched to that wagon. He was faced with two choices, both of them bad. Gilbert 'Gil' Price could quietly drop out of the race, stating some unknown reason, or he could press on with the risk of the scandal coming out, hanging over his head, and if he was going to chase his White House dream, he would have to join in the plan of eliminating the brothers and retrieving the tape before the 'what you call' hit the fan.

The only redeeming factor, if it could be called that, and let him to choose 'Door Number Two' was that with the ill-gotten gains from the notorious heist, his younger brother had hired the great Justin Miller. A move that sent shockwaves among his staff, and a stab of fear in his potential opponents. After all, the man was known to pull victory from the jaws of certain defeat on every campaign he managed. And if there was someone who could pull Gil Price's fat from the fire, that someone was Justin Miller.

The man was highly sought after unquestionably, and when his brother managed to lure him to the Gilbert Price Presidential Campaign, that trumped any transgression he had committed. Justin Miller heading his campaign eclipsed all that, and it was now about damage control. Up to this point, Declan was certain that the brothers had been handled, so when his two men came back to report that the McDaniels brothers had gotten away, and worse still, Hector St. John had been killed in the botched raid, the older Price had just cause to be alarmed. So far, it had just been the devil's luck that the man could not be traced to him or his brother.

After he collected himself and had his breathing under control, he reached for the phone on his desk, and dialed the secure unlisted number that belonged to his brother – the candidate. And inform him that the genie had left the bottle, and worse still, there was the real possibility that it could not be put back. Basically that the two brothers, Dumisani and Sasha McDaniels were still in the wind.

***

As Declan heard the distant ringing of the phone, he took another deep breath as he braced himself for the avalanche he knew was coming. Normally, this was a conversation that, strictly speaking, would be much better in person, but for now, and following Justin Miller's advice after he had been briefed about the danger the brothers posed, recommended that the candidate and his sibling keep their distance and contact to a minimum, and on a need to know basis. The potential for blowback was unimaginable, and if Gil Price could maintain some sort of plausible deniability the better. Even though all parties knew that such a ploy would be of no consequence once the full story behind the Genuine Bank Heist saw the light of day.

However, little hope of containment and damage control was infinitely better than none at all. The only way they could keep a lid on this is if they knew the brothers from that 'African backwater' called Botswana were silenced and soon, and done so in a way that would not create any waves.

"*Hello?*" he heard the familiar voice of his brother on the other end of the line.

"Blue," Declan said.

"*Monrovia,*" the other party, his brother, said.

The brothers had agreed on a secret code known only by the two of them. If the one calling said '*Blue*' and the other answered '*Monrovia*' their home city, it meant the caller, in this case Declan, was not under duress and that the line was secure.

"Is the line secure?" The younger Price asked by way of greeting. Of course that part had been covered in their coded greeting, but Declan wanted to be on record as having asked that. He knew that his brother, the politician, was thorough like that.

"Of course."

"Good," Declan said, "We have a problem man."

"*I know,*" the Senator barked at the other end with suppressed rage. "*It's all over the gaddamn news,*" he said, referring to the high speed chase and the subsequent hunt for the McDaniels. "*What the hell happened Declan? You assured me that there was not going to be any ripples, now we got ourselves a damn typhoon for Christ sake!*"

"It was the only way we could ferret them out," Declan said warily.

They, meaning Declan Price really, had leaked it to the media through one of the detectives he had on the take that the brothers, Dumisani and Sasha McDaniels were wanted for questioning in connection to the murder of one Hector St. John, bounty hunter (even though this piece of information was conveniently omitted), and former Police Officer with the LAPD after serving two successful tours in the Gulf War with the Special Forces. How long and tight that story was going to hold was, at best, anyone's guess.

"I know that," Gil hissed. "But this thing is starting to stink, and I won't be comfortable unless that tape, or whatever the hell it is, is in our hands. Find them, find them now!"

There was a note of desperation in the politician's voice, something his younger brother was all too familiar with since they were kids.

Declan then asked, "Are you saying that we up the ante and use people in the force?"

Apparently, the Senator's tentacles reached all the way into the United States Army elite – the Special Forces. And he had a marker to call apparently. However, what his brother said gave him pause, an idea.

"I understand they're skilled fighters too G…" he caught himself in mid-sentence. One of the very strict guidelines they had to adhere to was to never, under any circumstances, use the Senator's name while talking on the phone – no matter how secure they thought the lines were. "I wonder how we could have missed that. I mean Christ, you'd think that would be something almost impossible to miss, right?"

This was followed by a long silence on the other end that Declan was forced to repeat himself.

"Right?"

Silence.

"Hey …"

"*How do you catch a Jaguar*?" Gil Price interrupted, and subsequently breaking the silence on his end.

His brother had to think about this one for a bit before he answered, "By hiring someone who has caught a Jaguar before, no?"

"*Exactly*," Gil Price said.

Declan had to wonder where his brother was going with this, but knew better than to push. He could almost see Gil's ill-concealed glee at the other end.

"Is there something I should know?" Again he had to bite his tongue to keep from blurting out his brother's name, but knew he had to cut to the chase of the matter, time was running out and each hour without the McDaniels in their custody was calamity in the making.

"*Yes.*"

"What is it?"

"You'll know soon enough, what I have to tell you can only be done in person," the Senator said.

"Okay, I'm on my way," Declan's curiosity was peaked now. Without being told, he knew that once again his older brother, the Senator and future President of this great country had figured a way out of their dilemma.

CHAPTER 45

WHAT DECLAN PRICE DID NOT KNOW, nor would have guessed in a million years, was that two nights after talking to his brother, a Gulfstream 5, better known as the G5, was about twenty thousand feet above the Pacific Ocean and already in US airspace, and due to land at the Bob Hope International Airport in Burbank in less than five hours, which meant 8:15 am the next morning, completing a long flight from Seoul, South Korea.

The lone passenger, in this luxurious plane, was a drop dead gorgeous Asian woman with an athletic gait that spoke to the decades of physical training that had turned her into a lethal killing machine, many in the dark world of international spy craft had come to know and fear.

This was the assassin Mi Kyong Park.

In light of the McDaniels fiasco, and after the obligatory tantrums, rantings, and insults were dished out, it was time to take a deep breath and think sensibly. The preparations to launch a bid for the Oval Office were well underway, and dropping everything now would be folly as far as the Senator was concerned. In spite of what he had led his brother to believe, he was aware of the brothers and the incriminating evidence in their possession, and there was only one way to stop them before this thing came to light.

There was only one man, Senator Gil Price believed, who could bail him out of this mess his younger brother had dumped on his lap, and that was his Campaign Manager, Justin Darius Miller. The man's reputation of pulling not just one, but two rabbits out of the hat had reached mythical proportions. The fact that Justin Miller hated losing, and was willing to do whatever it took to win, even if it meant getting his hands dirty in the process made him the ideal man, the fixer, so to speak.

The man had, after all, successfully managed two presidential campaigns with both parties at different times, depending who got him first. A third successful bid would be a record, and the man's ego was just too big to not try and be the one to set that record. A first of the kind in the history of the Republic. No one got to where he was without knowing how to sidestep a few landmines along the way.

Without wasting time, Gil Price summoned his campaign manager for a private meeting, minus his younger brother, and laid everything on the table, leaving nothing out, including the Genuine Bank Armored Car heist. However, the Senator was careful not to mention that his $1 Million retainer was paid as a result, and the veteran political campaign manager did not ask. In fact he said very little during the Senator's '*come to Jesus moment*', and if he was shocked he did not show it.

There was a long silence following the Senator's disturbing narrative as the expert campaign manager took it all in. He knew from experience that when faced with a crisis, it was best to not act on the first impulse that comes to mind, and this was a very real and potentially catastrophic crisis. With only one recourse if they were to continue with the race, and that was to eliminate the brothers before the information they possessed became public. That was a given, the only thing was to find them before that happened.

Thus far the brothers had proved to be elusive. That, dumb luck of the highest order, and the kind of grace afforded to idiots and drunks in a fatal crash that always seemed to kill the innocent, had kept them out of reach. Justin Miller thought about it for a while as he stretched his hands, leaned backwards, and rested his head on his dovetailed fingers and gazed for a while at the white perforated ceiling above.

Miller was not known for his patience. In his mind this was the singular trait that had propelled him to such great success. He was a decisive taskmaster who worked people as if they were his serfs. When he committed to a campaign, as he had now with the Price Presidential bid, he wanted nothing but positive results, and compliments to subordinates were unheard of.

In the world of political consulting and campaign management, the man was king – untouchable. No other living person had successfully managed two separate bids for the Oval Office. His ability to orchestrate a campaign had taken on legendary aura in the media and in Democratic circles. His opponents, on the other hand, thought of him as the most underhanded unethical jerk ever to stalk the wings of American politics.

Miller wore this reputation as a badge of honor. In his mind, if his opponents were dumb enough to follow the rules, that was their fault. Any sensible person by definition would have walked away from the Gil Price Campaign with all the baggage it had, but not Jason Darius Miller. Again, as he gazed at the ceiling, he realized the challenge, and the pull to become the first and only person to manage three successful bids for the

White House was just too great. Like Stonewall Jackson, the man did not know the word retreat.

He was a practitioner of all the most underhanded techniques. To him politics was guerilla warfare. Hit and run tactics were the marching orders he gave to his staffers and operatives. '*Go on the offensive*', he had told Gil Price time and time again, and to never *ever* admit any wrongdoing to the press or your opponent.

Now, being a man who also readily engaged the dark side of politics in his 'win at all costs mind-set', he also knew of unsavory characters he could call on to fix a problem, like the major one he now had on in his hands. Miller needed an assassin to track down and eliminate the McDaniels brothers. In this instance it had to be a well-trained hired gun who was foreign, and most importantly not too expensive.

It was a day later, after a fitful night of endless phone calls, encrypted emails when he was led to a freelancer who had once been a top spy for the South Korean Secret Service, the National Intelligence Service (NIS), and this was none other than the deadly Mi Kyong Park. Following a few more protracted phone calls and encoded emails with her handler, a sum of $125,000 was agreed on, with $62,500 wired immediately to a numbered account in the Bahamas, and the rest upon completion of the job.

With all that agreed on, Miss Park was on a G5 Gulfstream that had been sent specially for her in Seoul, South Korea with one objective in mind and that being to track down and terminate the McDaniels brothers quietly, but altogether very thoroughly and in a way that would not point a finger at the Gil Price campaign.

CHAPTER 46

SOUTH KOREA'S PRINCIPLE Intelligence Agency, the National Intelligence Agency (NIS), though not as renowned as its counterparts like the CIA, MOSSAD, MI6, and others just like it could be just as ruthless and sophisticated. They, like the Chinese, used small, highly trained units to carry assassinations around the world in much the same manner as the Americans, the Israelis, the British, the Chinese, and the Russians.

One notable difference though, was that the South Koreans had come to rely upon one unit in particular which also specialized in crossing over into North Korea and smuggle out defectors from that country, and classified information and secrets about that nation's vaunted nuclear program among many other secrets, and share that information, at a price, with her allies in the west.

Within that particular unit was the female agent Mi Kyong Park. Highly trained in both unarmed combat and weapons, Mi Kyong was a force to be reckoned with and an intriguing background to boot. The CIA, MOSSAD, and the British MI6 had been watching her with great admiration and awe over the years.

The product of two South Korean diplomats who were rumored to have been selected by the NIS to marry and reproduce, Miss Park had the perfect background. If there ever was an agent who was perfectly cloned, Mi Kyong Park was that type of person. Born in Los Angeles California, and raised in the upper class neighborhood of Koreatown in West Los Angeles, Mi Kyong had been educated by private tutors, who bombarded her with foreign languages from the time she left diapers.

By age five she began her weapons training, and hand to hand combat that she was a first degree black belt in the Korean martial arts style Taekwondo, and entered the University of Southern California (USC) at the age of sixteen, left it with two degrees at the age of twenty one.

To round out her graduation, she spent a grueling year training with an elite Korean Army outfit. Here, she learned to camp, cook over a fire, cross raging rivers, survive in the ocean, and live in the wilderness for days on end. When she was twenty-four, the INS decided that the lady had studied enough and it was time to start the killing.

What lured in many of her victims was Mi Kyong's stunning beauty, and she was not above using her sexuality and appeal. At five feet nine inches, somewhat slender for her height and toned, she was taller than the average Asian woman and thus would stand out in a social gathering like a bar for instance, where she once sat alone and in less than five minutes, her intended target, a known philanderer who had become cozy with the North Koreans, and was also selling government secrets to them, offered to buy her a drink after she rebuffed previous attempts from others.

He got his throat slit while in one of the men's urinals, where he had taken her for a 'quickie', after making certain that the room was momentarily unoccupied. It had taken an hour to find his body, which had been crammed in a rather small garbage can.

The man's bodyguard, no shrinking violet himself, made the mistake of worrying about his protectee, and went to the men's room to look for him. The deadly Mi Kyong Park was waiting inside the cubicle. They found the bodyguard with his head stuffed down the toilet, which had been clogged and was backing up. The second man, an accomplice of the spy, died seconds later at the table where he had been sitting alone and becoming worried about his missing colleague, and the stunning woman he had left with for a quick one. A waitress, replete with a waiter's jacket, hurried by and without slowing down, thrust a poison dart at the back of his neck.

As killings go, it was quite sloppy. Too much blood, too many witnesses. Escape was dicey, but the 'Fatal Beauty' as she became known in the Intelligence community, got a break and managed to dash through the busy kitchen unnoticed. She then was loose, and sprinting through the alley after discarding her stiletto heel shoes, caught a cab and was safely inside the walls of the South Korean Embassy in Hamburg Germany where this assignment took place. And the next morning she was on a plane to Seoul.

The audacity of the attack shocked the intelligence world. Rival agencies the world over scrambled to find out who did it. It ran contrary to how the Asians, and in particular the Koreans, normally eliminated their enemies. They were famous for their patience, the discipline to wait and wait until the timing was perfect. And like a pack of African Wild Dogs, the deadly *Lycaon pictus*, they would chase with single minded determination until the prey simply gave up.

Many such killings took place around the world. In the far east, in East and Western Europe, the United

States, and in some sub Saharan African countries to name a few. And afterwards the 'Fatal Beauty', the '*Femme Fetale*' retired from government sanctioned killings and went private, becoming a hitman for hire and that was how the deadly Mi Kyong Park, the *Femme Fetale* came in the crosshairs of a campaign manager who would do whatever it took to win – morals be dammed. And that was why, unbeknownst to the two brothers from Botswana, Sasha and Dumisani McDaniels ended up being pursued by one of the deadliest killers known to man in this millennium.

CHAPTER 47

THE DANGER IN THE MIDSUMMER NIGHT was palpable, and felt real to a point that one could reach out and touch it. To be a fugitive from the law in a developed country like the United States can be daunting even for the craftiest of criminals born and raised in the country, with help from friends, like minded criminals, and access to resources that may assist in evading capture. For two young, innocent, and naïve foreigners who had yet to know their way around, to be in that situation was probably as close to the definition of 'true hell' as one could get. Throw in the fact that they were indeed strangers in a strange land, the stress level alone felt like a slow and excruciatingly painful death.

This is because law enforcement in a city like Pasadena, and many like it all over the country, is well trained, financed, highly motivated, and in possession of technological skills hard to comprehend, let alone circumvent unless faced with criminals with unlimited budgets thrown at counter surveillance, and the ability to corrupt personnel high up the food chain, such criminals of course would be Narcos, anything less, not to mention the McDaniels brothers would be considered easy prey.

When Sasha and Dumisani left 'Jerry's Billiards', the pool hall at the corner of Washington and Lake,

398

after disposing of the two goons who tried to apprehend them so as to carry favor with the local cops, the two had only one thing in mind, and that was to leave the country as soon as humanly possible.

Luckily, Sasha had the fanny pack strapped to his waist when they were suddenly attacked that morning. There was no way they could even dream about going back to their apartment. The money Sasha had in his fanny pack they figured, could be just enough to get them to the border, and once in Mexico they could find their way to the airport, where they would purchase two airline tickets to Botswana with one of the two credit cards that had a $10,000 credit limit.

Juan Morales's sobering news about being wanted by the police for murder, meant that public transportation of *any* kind was out of the question. The brothers knew without being told that there'd be plain clothes policemen waiting to nab them the moment they showed up at any bus station, airport, or train station within a hundred mile radius. Even private 'Pay For A Ride' transportation like Lyft and Uber could not be trusted, so Mexico was the only viable option under the circumstances, and that was if they could even make it that far, let alone make it out of Pasadena.

With Mexico being the only option, what was left was to try to make it to the border in San Diego, which was over 100 miles away on foot, or some form of transportation. To say the odds were highly stacked against them would be the understatement of the millennium. In fact it was insane to even contemplate such a feat, but sometimes humans will do the seemingly insane, the impossible – if the insanc or the impossible was the only choice.

They were going to try making it on foot to the San Diego border, this with only Misty's phone as guide, which according to 'Google Maps', was 146 miles from where they were, give or take. According to the information on the App it would take two days on foot, and that was if they walked nonstop, which of course was out of the question, as the odds were totally against them making it that far over terrain, neighborhoods, and places they did not know.

Right now, Sasha and Dumisani were on a quiet unlit street called El Molino that ran parallel to Lake Avenue, a major street with heavy traffic that ran north to south. El Molino ran through mainly a residential neighborhood with palm trees flanked on the sides and at close intervals, like almost every street in Southern California.

The brothers knew what lay ahead. They had at least 148 miles to cover and most likely all of it on foot, and what was worse they had almost an entire police force after them, if that bartender Juan was to be believed, which they did because Sasha had seen the flyer, or APB (All Points Bulletin) then there was no time to waste. It was time to risk it all and run. They took a knee at the point where El Molino intersected with Douglas street, at a place where the street was the darkest.

And then suddenly, they took cover by falling flat on their bellies on the sidewalk, and simultaneously rolled in and under some bushy shrubs that marked the residential boundary of a home that looked to be a mid-side three bedroom house. A black and white police car had in a trice appeared from the south side of El Molino Street. Its headlights were on but most ominous of all was a powerful beam of light mounted on top of the vehicle that would start searching first to the left and then to the right, the gleam was concentrated mainly at dark corners. The brothers knew right away what was happening. The hunt was on and the cops were frantically looking for the McDaniels brothers, who they deduced were on foot and thus not too far from where they were last seen – Jerry's Billiards.

The first cop car was then followed a few minutes later by another, which was most certainly looking in places where the first patrol car may have missed. It was obvious that a massive manhunt was in play, very soon a police helicopter would be in the air and there would be no escaping that. The brothers emerged from their hiding place the moment the last patrol car disappeared around a corner, and were certain that there was no other coming.

"What do we do now?" Dumisani asked as he dusted the grass and leaves clinging to his clothes. "Why should we be running? Let's flag down one of these patrol cars and explain to them what's going on?" he suggested.

His brother was already shaking his head 'No' before he even finished the sentence, and said, "Dumi, didn't you hear anything I said man? We're in deep shit man. These cops probably have orders to shoot us on sight, and you know how trigger happy cops in this country are. Their mantra is shoot first and ask questions later, and let's face it Dumi, you're my brother and I love you but you're black, need I remind you the many African Americans killed by the Police? Cops and blacks don't mix, and I'd take a bullet before I let that happen to you."

Dumisani, suddenly in deep thought slowly nodded and said, "Oh yes."

The fact that we're foreigners makes as an even easier target," Sasha McDaniels emphasized.

"So we're dead meat basically," Dumisani bellyached.

However, that was not the real issue troubling the young man. Over the past few months, ever since he sustained that injury on his wrist during the fight with

Viljeon and his cronies at the Sedia Hotel, Dumisani's dependence to painkillers found him taking more than the required daily dosage, and this continued even after his injury was not an issue anymore. Before leaving Botswana, he had stocked enough pills to make a crack house happy for a month, but now that they had left the apartment with such haste, the thought of grabbing one of the bottles filled with the Oxycodone had not even crossed his mind.

Now he was beginning to feel the familiar dullness behind his eyes, and knew that the 'jonesing' was coming. Add to that, they had over a hundred miles to cover, almost all if not all of it on foot, and not to mention the fact that they had a dogged pursuer on their trail, both who they believed was out to kill them the first chance they got. Plus, the brothers knew that the arm of the law was long and was going to squeeze the life out of them like an anaconda.

Thinking about all this, Dumisani muttered again, "We're dead meat basically."

"Yes, but that doesn't mean we have to make it easy for them."

"So we head for the border?"

"Yes," his brother answered with no hesitation.

As they made the final preparation by studying the route on Sasha's phone, which by the look of things was going to need recharging soon, and also making sure that their rucksacks had the basic supplies intact, Dumisani was suddenly hit by an overpowering sense of melancholy.

"Sasha," he said as he turned to look at his brother with a pained look on his face. "Why did this happen man? Our dreams shattered in less than a minute … why?"

His brother looked around for a moment, and then up and down the street one more time. In spite of all that was happening, all was quiet, with an occasional car driving by after long intervals.

"I don't know Dumi," was all he could say.

"Maybe this was not meant to be," Dumisani shook his head sadly and added, "We should have never left Botswana."

Sasha said, "Yeah maybe Dumi, but what's of paramount importance right now is that we get to the border, and get the hell out this God forsaken place."

It was time to do the improbable of getting to the San Diego border on foot, and without help, while at the same time out maneuvering one of the best trained, well-funded, and technologically advanced police forces in the world - not to mention in terra incognita with nothing but the unshakable trust and belief they had in each other.

Shaking the uncomfortable feeling of not having enough of the narcotic in his system, Dumisani said, "Okay bro," he gritted his teeth with renewed vigor. Let's get cracking, we'll improvise along the way, we're hunters remember? And we've trekked animals over long distances on foot. Any idea how far in Kilometers?"

Sasha was waiting for this, having grown up using the metric system like the rest of the world, he, like his brother, was always converting things like weight and measurements in his head after having arrived in the US.

"That is a little over 200 kilometers."

Dumisani grimaced at the revelation and then gave a low whistle. That was almost the same distance from Gaborone to Palapye, and they'd be doing it on foot. However, according to MapQuest, much of that distance would be mostly through urban areas not bush or jungle, which made the task, improbable as it seemed, much easier all things considered.

"We're going to have to get food and water at some point. I also suggest that we jog trot on opposite sides of every street we take, because together we draw attention." In his mind he said, *Hopefully, somewhere along the way we will be lucky to run into some street dealer who can help me find, what do they call it here? A fix.*

Sasha knew his brother was right because he instantly patted him on the shoulder and they hi fived.

"Right on Dumi."

As Sasha was about to cross the street to begin this incredible journey, his brother grabbed him by the sleeve of his sweater and said, "Sasha, remember for this long jaunt we got to eat man, so let's make it our first priority along the way and at a place that is not very conspicuous."

His brother nodded and said, "You're right, let's say after an easy ten?"

"Yes," Dumisani agreed.

'Easy ten' meant they were ready to jog ten miles nonstop. That they were in tip top shape was beyond reproach, Dumisani and Sasha had trained in every terrain and weather possible except snow, they had even participated in marathons and had been planning on taking part in the 50 mile run at the Antarctica continent, before Sahili and his men threw a monkey wrench into those plans by murdering their parents. So their confidence of reaching the San Diego border unscathed was not as outlandish as it sounded. The only question was if they could make it there before the law and or the bad guys caught up with them.

They then set off at opposite sides of El Molino Street, and began jog trotting south at a steady pace. It was the beginning of an improbable journey. They went on that way that in no time they crossed the famous Colorado Boulevard near Old Town Pasadena.

From here they turned right, and joined Los Robles Avenue, from the GPS directions they had committed to memory, they knew the street stretched another ten miles or so through South Pasadena, San Marino, and Alhambra where it changed into Atlantic Boulevard. It was in Alhambra where the brothers got their second wind, and pushed harder, constantly on the lookout. Whenever they saw a Police Car or anything that looked suspicious, they ducked for cover, and stayed that way until the potential danger passed.

With every step though, Sasha and Dumisani knew they were getting closer to their purpose, and that was reaching the San Diego border at San Ysidro, where they would then cross into Tijuana Mexico. Once here, they'd purchase the two airline tickets, already booked on Air Mexicana, which would fly them to Rio de Janeiro Brazil, where a connecting flight would take them to Cape Town, and from there to Sir Seretse Khama International Airport, and safety. Once home they were then going to contact the US State Department and tell them everything they knew, including showing the copy of the images caught on Dumisani's camera regarding the Genuine Bank Heist. That all depended if they made it to the border safely.

With that in mind, Sasha patted the fanny pack around his waist for perhaps the thousandths time that day. It was their salvation, and he thanked the high heavens, Mr. Selepe the deceased loyal ranch hand, the mother they never met, Naledi, and their departed parents, for he knew they were watching over them to give him the presence of mind to keep the fanny pack strapped at all times. Without it … he did not even want to entertain that train of thought.

CHAPTER 48

HUNTINGTON PARK, CALIFORNIA – 131 MILES
FROM THE SAN DIEGO BORDER – 08:56AM.

THE THREAT WAS FAR AND WIDE. Every black and white, even anything that resembled a police car or a grey van was a possible danger. What they did not know was that their current malady was even worse. There was a formidable assassin sent to track them down. In spite of their current situation and the daunting odds stacked against them, the brothers trudged along. Deep down they knew that their quest was futile, however knowing this that did not mean that they wouldn't try. The brothers would rather die on their feet than be sitting ducks.

As agreed and planned, they jog trotted at opposite sides of the street, avoided highly lit streets wherever possible, and crowds where they would stand out. At some point, so as not to draw attention to themselves, they would stop jogging and then walk briefly before resuming their run. They started their improbable journey at El Molino street, which like Lake Avenue ran north to south. They kept pushing at a steady pace, and thus far were maintaining the pace they vowed to keep of running nonstop for ten miles.

As young men in their mid-twenties and in terrific shape, running had been part of their strict training regimen, thus the task to them was not that all unnerving, but keeping the same pace for over one hundred miles, and over three days because that's how long it was going to take to get to the San Diego border was pushing it a bit. In reality, and considering that this was the peak of summer, fatigue and dehydration was going to be a factor. Dumisani and Sasha were aware of all these obstacles, but they pushed them out of their minds. The brothers had adopted a 'to hell with it mindset' and marched on.

In no time, they crossed the 210 Freeway, stayed on El Molino until the street ended some two miles later, and then they turned right when they got to Colorado Boulevard, and joined Los Robles Avenue, which took them through South Pasadena, the exclusive neighborhood of San Marino, until they reached the city of Alhambra. Each time, whenever they saw something that looked like a police car, or a vehicle deemed suspicious, the brothers would dart behind one of the numerous palm trees that lined up the southern California streets, and were as ubiquitous. At times, instead of dodging behind a tree, they would just hit the pavement and then roll onto the lawn that grew on the side of the sidewalk, or just simply break stride, and appear like any other insomniac out for a night stroll. And then when it was safe again, they would trudge along.

It went on like that all night until they reached Huntington Park in the early hours of the morning. Drenched in sweat, Sasha and Dumisani had covered just under twenty two miles in almost six hours. An almost incredible feat seeing that these were two young men who had absolutely no idea where they were, and only a general idea as to where they were headed.

***

Huntington Park is a city in the "Gateway Cities" district of Southern Los Angeles County. They are known as such, because this is a largely urbanized region located in Southern California between the City of Los Angeles, Orange County, and the Pacific Ocean. The cluster of cities acquired the name because they are situated literally as the "Gateway" between the two counties of Los Angeles and Orange, with the central city of Cerritos located equidistant from Downtown Los Angeles, Long Beach, and the center of Orange County. It is part of the Los Angeles-Long Beach-Anaheim-California Metropolitan Statistical Area (MSA), and has a population of approximately two million.

Named after the prominent industrialist Henry E. Huntington, Huntington Park or 'HP' as it is affectionately known by many of its current residents, was incorporated in 1906, as a streetcar suburb on the Los Angeles Railway for workers in the rapidly expanding industries to the Southeast of Downtown Los Angeles. The main street, of which the McDaniels brothers found themselves, was a major commercial district serving the city's largely working class residents as well as being the retail hub of Southern Los Angeles County.

It used to be, as it was with most cities, an exclusively white community most of its history, Alameda Street and Slauson Avenue, which were fiercely segregation lines in the 1950's, separated it from the black areas. The changes that shaped Los Angeles from the late 1970's, the rapid growth of new suburbs in Orange County, the eastern San Gabriel, western San Fernando, and Conejo Valley, the collapse of the aerospace and defense industry at the end of the cold war, and the implosion of the California real estate in the early 1990's – resulted in the wholesale departure of virtually all of the white population of Huntington Park by the mid 1990's.

The vacuum was filled almost entirely by two groups of Latinos, upwardly mobile families eager to leave the barrios of East Los Angeles, and recent Mexican immigrants. Today Pacific Boulevard is once again a thriving commercial strip, serving as a major retail center for working class residents of Southeastern Los Angeles County – only now targeting a Hispanic public with many signs in Spanish.

Aside from being the commercial business street of 'HP', the east to west running Pacific Boulevard has also been the location for festivals, carnival affairs, and parades. The '*Carnival Primavera*' is held each year for three days across nine blocks of Pacific Boulevard in Huntington Park. The event always features Central American and Mexican food, carnival rides, games and live music. However, at 3:31 am when the brothers finally got to Pacific Boulevard, drenched in sweat and most of all ravenously hungry, the normally busy street was virtually deserted, save for an occasional car driving by. This had been the place they had both agreed on to take their first break.

Among the numerous alleys and small side streets that connected to Pacific Boulevard like arterial veins, they found one with a large commercial trash can that had been pushed to the side of the alley created by two buildings, a clothing store and real estate office of some variety, which were closed now, and found their hiding place where they could lay low for a while, rest, eat, maybe freshen up a bit and continue with their incredible journey, which no doubt was fraught with danger. It turned out to be the perfect spot because across the street from them was a family owned Mexican Restaurant called 'The Sukasa'.

The establishment with white stucco paint and neon signs in Spanish was closed at the moment, and they decided that this was where they would have their breakfast. A quick grub, and hopefully, and surreptitiously get some information on their status as fugitives on the run. It was risky, they knew, but at the same time they did not want to be caught napping. It was 4:17am when they found a place to hide, and the restaurant opened at 8:00 am. Knowing this, the brothers waited. After making sure that the alley was secure with one or two avenues of escape if the need arose, Sasha found a clean card box in the trash bin that he tore at and corners and spread it on the pavement behind the garbage bin, and used it as a makeshift mat to lay on.

The brothers knew the importance of sleep, considering the current situation they were in. They decided to take 45 minute naps apiece which meant when one went to sleep for that three quarter of an hour, the other kept watch. This went on like that until the restaurant opened. They did not immediately enter the establishment, but instead waited a while, as they watched first the owner, a middle aged Hispanic man accompanied by a woman they guessed to be his wife, unlock the front door and shortly thereafter were joined by four more people, the staff obviously, two young men and two young women, all of them Hispanic.

Even from across the street, the brothers, especially Sasha McDaniels, could tell that one of the young women of average height, with long black shiny hair, and luminous eyes he could see even from across the street, was really beautiful. She had to either be the daughter of the owners or the waitress, or both, he guessed that by her clothes. She was not dressed like the other three. Instead, she had on a pair of white shorts, which revealed the shapely legs of a runner, and a lose fitting pink t-shirt with a writing or logo he could not make, because right at that moment, she and the rest had disappeared inside the restaurant. They watched as the lights were turned on and the 'Open' sign displayed.

Dumisani McDaniels noticed her too, but for entirely different reasons. Junkies for some peculiar reason have a homing beacon that which, no matter where they are, can sense another one like them miles away. Dumisani was now dealing with an enemy far deadlier than the one after them, and this foe was coming hard, chewing at his bones like a starving hound. It had been hours since he had taken his last dose of the Oxycodone, and now he was jonesing badly, in need of a fix.

His brother Sasha had yet to notice, but few minutes earlier he thought he saw his brother shaking a bit, and still sweating even though they had stopped running a few hours earlier, and not only that, but Dumisani seemed to be 'out of it' as they said in this country. It worried him at first, but soon shrugged it off and attributed it to fatigue.

Which, Sasha thought, was going to be a problem because they still had over a hundred miles to cover over unknown terrain, dangers ahead they were not even aware of, and here was his brother shaking, sweating, and seemingly not all together mentally. He wondered what was up with that, Dumisani was a tough sonofabitch, again as the American would say, even tougher than him if truth be told, so this new development was a bit worrisome. Hopefully, he thought, the food would do him some good.

Dumisani had also noticed the tattoos on the arms of the young woman who had just walked into the 'Sukasa'. Nonetheless, in that brief moment, from the way she walked, the way her head swiveled from side to side as if on a bubblehead doll, the young man realized that he may have found the solution to his current and pressing malaise.

Yes! He thought triumphantly as he felt the adrenaline surge through his veins.

In no time, Dumisani and Sasha were crossing the main street, which was starting to show signs of life, and were inside the cozy little restaurant. Not surprisingly, the brothers were the first patrons that day. They were hungry, exhausted, a bit disheveled, but still maintained their cool demeanor, as the beautiful young woman they had observed earlier, for totally different reasons, walked up to them with a big smile on her face that emphasized a pair of sexy dimples on her cheeks.

She led them to a booth at the far right corner of the room, well away from the windows and where it was a little darker than the rest of the place. The establishment could seat at least 60 customers. There were a mixture of tables and chairs depending on the mood of the customers. The booths were located on the sides of the wall, and by the windows. The others that sat two, four, and those meant for bigger parties were situated in the middle of the room. On the walls were beautiful paintings of the owner's cultural heritage. Oil paintings of women working the fields, pounding the corn into powder, another with a rolling pin turning the powder into paste which in turn makes the tortilla, the cornerstone staple food of the Hispanic people.

As soon as the two were seated, and placed their backpacks on the floor by their feet, the young lady smiled and said, "Hi, I'm Connie, what can I get you two gentlemen?"

Constanzia 'Connie' Trejo was a twenty two year old Psychology Major at California State University Los Angeles, better known as Calstate LA. She worked at her parents' restaurant during her spare time and on weekends, when she was not bogged down by schoolwork or midterms, which was also a bonus for her parents, Pedro and Leticia Trejo, who happened to be immigrants from El Salvador, and had immigrated to the United States while in their late teens after tying the knot. Just like many immigrants in similar situations, they worked two, sometimes three jobs at a time until they saved enough money to open their own restaurant, the 'Sukasa'. A bistro that served Mexican, Salvadorian, and other South and Central American country dishes, and was thus very popular during lunch and dinner hours, in spite of stiff competition on the main commercial street.

In situations like these, it was usually Sasha McDaniels who would be the first to talk. Of the two, he was the designated 'icebreaker', instead it was Dumisani this time.

"Can we get some water please?"

The two, Connie and Dumisani maintained eye contact that lingered a little longer than normal. The waitress had seen it before – the cry for help. She was not using anymore and was determined to stay clean. It was also why her parents were thrilled to have her working at the restaurant every chance she got. That way, they could keep an eye on her lest she fell off the wagon again, because only God knew how expensive 90 day stints at cocaine rehabs were if paying out of pocket.

Right away Connie knew what her customer wanted, needed, and it wasn't breakfast, at least not at the moment, and Constanzia Trejo just so happened to have what he desired stashed away at some hidden corner in the storeroom that even her parents knew nothing about. She got paid fifteen dollars per hour, but a girl could always use some extra cash, she always told herself.

"Absolutely, two waters coming right away. I'll bring the menus too," she said as she turned to leave, but not before giving Dumisani that reassuring wink and a nod so subtle that Sasha missed it, but confirmation for Dumisani, that "tell" that she had the contraband.

Sasha then asked, "What do you have?"

He wanted to get on with the business of eating and get going.

Connie had already been on her way to get a pitcher of water and two menus, but then stopped turned and backtracked to the booth. Then said in a practiced voice that had done this so many times:

"Our special this morning is the breakfast burrito, huevos rancheros …"

"Sorry what's that?" Dumisani interrupted in spite of himself.

"What's what?" Connie asked with an impish smile on her face. She could tell that the two were not from around here, their foreign accents notwithstanding, but that they were *not* from this particular area, which made her wonder what they were doing in this part of town and on foot no less, the backpacks were the dead giveaway. From the way the black guy was starting to 'jones' maybe he had come out here to score. However she quickly pushed those thoughts out of her mind and concentrated back on what she was doing.

"The huevo ranch, or whatever it is you called it," said Dumisani.

Connie smiled again, revealing a set of healthy sparkling teeth to add to her beautiful dimples and said, "Huevos rancheros, that's egg on salsa served with corn tortillas, I'll also add a chorizo and egg, which is sausage with egg on the side as well."

"Sounds delicious, I'll have that and the burrito," Dumisani said.

His brother added by saying, "Lots of it. We're starving." Following a brief pause, he asked rather hopefully, "You do take traveler's checks now don't you?"

"Yes we do. So two breakfast burritos, and two huevos rancheros with chorizo, all extra coming right up. Anything else to drink beside water? Coffee? Orange juice maybe?"

"Lots of water please and juice," Sasha said. Always the one to speak for both of them.

As she turned to leave to fulfill her order, Dumisani stopped her by asking, "Excuse me Connie, where is your toilet?"

"My what?"

He immediately realized his mistake and corrected himself and quickly said, "Your restroom, the men's room?"

The two made eye contact again, and right away communicated the underlying unspoken message. Dumisani was aware of where the bathroom was, and Connie knew he knew, because the sign was clear for every patron to see the moment they entered the Sukasa Restaurant. This was about something else and they both knew it. *Street dealers and buyers*, Dumisani thought wryly. *We're the same the world over.*

Sasha, who never missed such subtleties, especially when it involved his brother, did not catch any of this. His mind was clearly elsewhere as he kept looking around at the entrance and through the window at the street. There was still danger lurking out there in the street, and he did not want he and his sibling to be caught napping.

"Over there to your left," Connie said as she gestured with her head to the right side of the room, where the bathroom or *banos* were located.

Dumisani gave her a couple of minutes before he got up and went to the 'Men's Room'. The hallway that led to the bathrooms was dimly lit with dark blue painting on the walls, and was empty as expected because as of now at least, there had been no other customers in the Sukasa. The door leading to the men's toilet had a picture of the Greek god Poseidon, holding a pitchfork, painted on it. And the door leading to the 'Ladies Room' had the picture of the Roman goddess Venus on it.

Once inside, Dumisani immediately went to one of the enamel basins, and took a minute to splash his face with cold water. It felt great, and made a mental note to remind his brother to do the same. They both needed it after that long run from Pasadena, and when he stepped back into the tiny corridor she was there waiting for him just as he had expected she would.

"What do you need?" she asked in a hushed tone.

"What do you have?"

"Oxy, ten milligrams, Narcos 10 milligrams, and also heroin, but with that if you need to cook right away, you'd have to do it out back, I can show you where, but just not in here," Connie said again as she looked around to make sure that they were alone.

"I just need the Oxys. How much?"

"$7 each, I got twenty of them, but I can give you all for $5 a pop."

Normally, the street value of Oxycodones was $10 each depending on the dosage, in other words $1 per milligram, some like the tiny blue pill cost $30 per. For

416

someone like Dumisani McDaniels who was new to the country and its street vibes, in other words clueless, he had no idea what a great bargain this was, and the young woman in front of him could have easily burned him if she so chose, but luck was on his side, because Connie rather liked him and his friend. Besides, she said to herself, business was a little slower than normal these days, and if you please new customers, chances they will tell others like them of this establishment – though she hoped about the business and not the illicit trade.

Dumisani nodded and said, "Okay, I'll take all twenty Connie, but I'll have to give you the $100 in Traveler's Checks, will that work?"

Normally, with this kind of trade, she preferred cold hard cash, but then thought 'what the heck?!' especially when she saw that pleading look again in the eyes of this dreadlocked, young handsome stranger with a foreign accent, similar to that of his white friend. She wondered what that was all about, especially since they looked a bit scruffy and frightened.

"Okay, cool that should work," she said.

"Do you have a couple on you right now?" Dumisani asked a bit eagerly, and then quickly glanced around even though there was nobody around in the dimly lit hallway, but was worried nonetheless that his stealthy brother may just silently show up any instant. Such a reaction was the obvious 'tell' law enforcement on the streets always looked for when trying to make people dealing in illegal drugs.

Connie Trejo had anticipated this, so she reached into her pocket of her short pants, and fished out two round white pills, the holy grail for any addict, and then handed them to him

417

"Thanks Connie." He would have hugged her out of sheer delight, but caught himself just in time. "When you're ready," he continued. "Just come by our table, but please make sure that my brother does not notice, or better yet if by chance he leaves the table to come here," he gestured with his chin at the Men's Room.

The young woman frowned, and starred at him with a puzzled look on her face.

"Your brother?" she asked. "The white guy out there?" Connie motioned with her head at the dining area.

"Yes." He was starting to sweat again now, needing his fix.

Connie shrugged as if to say, whatever, as she abruptly turned to leave. She had work to do, like fulfilling the breakfast order the McDaniels brothers had requested.

***

Inside the bathroom, Dumisani was alone as he chucked the two pills into his mouth, chewed them to powder with his strong molars, ignoring the familiar bitter taste and washed them down by cupping the faucet water in his right hand. He was warned, among other things, as was Sasha , that tap water in the United States was not good for human consumption, because of very high deposits of lead in it, but at the moment he could have cared less – not for a boy who grew up on an African ranch, drinking water pumped from a well, and sometimes water from rivers and streams when out hunting or camping as they did with their parents, so compared to that American water was nothing – leaded or unleaded.

Dumisani waited for a few minutes before the familiar feeling of euphoria swept over him like rain after a very long and hard drought. He felt himself again, the guilt that had assailed him for having to resort to a narcotic to feel whole again vanished with the exhilaration that came. With the few more he was expecting from the waitress, Dumisani now felt like he could handle the rest of the jaunt to San Diego – their salvation – and many more like it with maximum ease. The 'high' made him feel invincible, even the fear that had been looming over him like a dark cloud, the thought of being hunted by armed killers and the police deserted him.

Back at the table, Sasha noticed that his brother appeared to be chipper. He was about to remark on that but Instead he asked, "You were in there rather long Dumi, are you okay?"

"Yes, why?"

"I don't know man, you don't seem to be lethargic as you were earlier on." Sasha looked at him closely as if searching for something on his face, not that he suspected his brother of taking some drug, it was just that there was something different, not off, but different, or maybe, he thought, he was reading too much into it. Like any animal sensing danger, Sasha was always alert whenever he was put in a stressful situation – like being hunted by armed men wanting to kill them.

Damn! Dumisani thought. He then made a mental note to himself, to be very careful, the next time he got his fix. This guy, his brother, knew him very well, and picked up on certain nuances other people missed - especially when he was on high alert and tensed – like right now.

To their relief, Connie arrived with two hot platters steaming with huevos rancheros, breakfast burritos, and two wooden bowls, one filled with chips and the other with hot salsa. One of the cooks was trailing behind her balancing a tray with a pitcher of ice cold water, two frosted glasses and a tall glass of orange juice and a plate of Mexican sausages, which apparently she added on her own volition and thought the brothers would like at no extra charge.

"Will that be all gentlemen?" Connie smiled, but her eyes were focused on Dumisani. The two had some unfinished business, and the beautiful young Hispanic woman was reminding him that there was still that small matter of payment for services rendered that needed to be addressed, and Dumisani understood immediately, glad to oblige her.

He looked at his brother, who was just about to attack his food when Dumisani said, "Come on Sasha man, aren't you going to wash your hands?"

This was a habit that had been instilled into them by their parents, mom really, and Sasha, remembering the withering look he would get from her whenever he touched or was about to touch food or even fruit without washing his hands, quickly withdrew them from the plate and blushed, his face then flushed as if he had been caught with his hand in the cookie jar.

"Oh!" Sasha said, and then quickly stood up, and without another word headed in the same direction Dumisani had come earlier on.

Dumisani watched his brother until he vanished around a corner, and then immediately his eyes fell on the fanny pack Sasha had left on his chair, and instantly reached for it and on the inside pocket was a neat stack of the Traveler's Checks. He tore out a $100 leaf, and handed it to Connie who smiled and then winked conspiratorially at the dreadlocked young man as if to say, *nice doing business with you*, and left.

A few minutes later, Sasha and Dumisani were dutifully devouring their breakfast with an appetite that suggested that they were indeed famished. The all night run had obviously burned a lot of their calories, and add to that the food was delicious so much such that they were silent as they wolfed it down.

And so engrossed they were with their meal that they did not notice the two men who entered the Sukasa, and then like the professionals they were, immediately peeled off and parked themselves at the opposite sides of the room. They were both white with barrel chests, closed cropped hair cuts, and dressed in worker's clothes replete with safety vests, which made sense because the city of Huntington Park was home to many factories and construction companies, in short a blue collar city.

However, it was mostly Hispanic workers who normally came at this early hour for a quick grub before heading on out to work. The sight of two white workers, and before them the atypical pair, was certainly something akin to a rare sighting. Connie noticed them instantly of course and so did the staff in the restaurant. She signaled the other waitress, Lupe Salazar, to give her a hand. She then went to the one seated close to the door, while Lupe attended to the other who was seated at a table closer to the wall, and almost diagonally opposite the brothers' booth.

What seemed strange to Connie was that she had, by sheer chance, seen the two men walking toward the restaurant on the sidewalk together through the large window that faced the street, and could have almost sworn that she saw them get out of a black SUV that then drove away slowly, headed west on Pacific Boulevard. The two men obviously knew one another, she observed as she walked over to the patron, coffee jug in hand, to take his order and fill his coffee cup as

421

was routine. Why then were they acting as if they did not know one another the moment they walked into the Sukasa?

She asked him if he wanted a cup of coffee to which he nodded and then recited the breakfast menu in rapid succession. Connie had inadvertently shielded the man's view from the brothers' booth, and the man, as nonchalantly as possible tried to look past her as she listed the breakfast items they had on offer – Connie noticed – but then pretended as if she did not. Something bizarre was definitely at play, and it had to do with her two earlier customers, one of whom she had sold drugs to.

Lupe Salazar noticed their interest in the other two customers too. She brought it up when the two women were in the kitchen to submit the breakfast orders to the restaurant's chef.

"My customer was asking me about the two cute men, the black one and the white one," Lupe said in an off handed sort of way as she stooped in the kitchen's main freezer to extract the frozen bacon the cook had asked for, and handed it to him.

Constanzia Trejo's antennae was suddenly perked up again, something was definitely afoot here, she thought.

"Did you notice his hands?" Connie asked, as she took her eyes from the cook who had smashed a few eggs and was ready to toss them on the gigantic griddle.

"What about them?" Lupe asked, puzzled.

"Lupe, many guys who work in the factories around here, dressed the same way as these two have a certain texture to theirs. Our guests here, looking at their hands, at least my customer's, are smooth like he's never lifted anything heavier than a fork in his life, let alone work in a factory or in construction as their outfits suggest."

Lupe nodded thoughtfully, and now that she thought about it, there was something off about the recent customers. First it was the two slightly disheveled and exhausted young men, one of who was always on constant alert like a tiger with the eyes to match, and fidgeting. And then there were these two new arrivals.

"Connie," Lupe suddenly looked up, ready to give voice to her thoughts. "Do you think those two young men, the black one and the white one could be running away from the police, and the two men who just came in are bounty hunters?"

Lupe grew up in the East Los Angeles barrio where she had seen it all. Drive by shootings between rival street gangs fighting over turf on which to peddle drugs, among other things, two of her brothers were serving long stretches of time at the infamous Corcoran State Prison in Northern California, so Lupe knew a thing or two about bounty hunters without being told.

There was sudden alarm on Connie's face as she pulled out a pad from her pocket, which inside had the itemized check of the brothers' bill for the breakfast, and left the kitchen without another word. Dumisani was the first to notice her as she made her way to their booth.

"This is delicious Connie," he said smiling as he shoved a piece of sausage with his fork inside his mouth. "Thanks for recommending it."

She gave a rather nervous smile as she said, "Thanks."

Sasha immediately picked up on it, but instead said, "Yes, it's true Connie. Can we have some more water please?"

"Yes," she said quickly.

Connie then starred at the brothers as if debating to herself about telling them of her suspicions or not. She knew she could have been mistaken about the two other men. The two young men were now looking at her curiously. This sudden change in her demeanor, even though she tried to hide it, was worrisome.

"Something's wrong." Sasha stated this as a fact, not a question, as he looked straight into her somewhat panicked brown eyes. And Connie, ever so slightly gave a subtle nod.

To hell with it, she thought and then let slip in a harsh whisper, "Yes. I think some men are after you."

Dumisani felt as if he had been kicked in the stomach. Maybe because of, or in spite of Oxycodone in his blood, his training kicked in, and he forced himself to control his breathing, that way his heart rate would not spike and he would be able to relax – notwithstanding the dire situation they now found themselves in.

"What are you talking about?" Dumisani asked as calmly as he could.

"Don't look now," she said. "But those two men who walked in earlier have been checking you guys out without being too obvious about it."

Dumisani stared at his brother who stared back with those gentle but at times intense, piercing blue eyes of his. The look in their eyes said it all: *Christ! They found us, but how?*

Constanza knew she had struck a nerve when she noticed the look too, even though their demeanor hardly changed, something which, in spite of the current circumstances impressed the young woman. It was what they did not say or do that confirmed her earlier suspicions that the two young foreigners were running from something. They did not at once, or at all for that matter, shrug and laugh off her concerns. In fact, if anything, it seemed as if their senses had perked up, like animals detecting that they walked or about to waltz into a trap.

Connie leaned forward and pretended to refill one of the cups with water from the pitcher, which she was doing in fact, and spoke to the brothers in a harsh whisper while trying to be as casual as possible.

"I would suggest you exit through the kitchen, I've already alerted the cooks and the busboys, even those who just arrived, so go. Do it *now* – go!"

Sasha looked up at her and smiled. *Oh, he's good*, Connie thought to herself. Anybody else watching would have thought it was just a patron making regular conversation with his waitress. Sasha was inwardly blessing this brave young beautiful woman, and promising to look out for her if, God willing, this nightmare comes to a happy conclusion, but that remained to be seen. Right now there was only one thing in mind – survival.

"Thanks Connie," he said. "How much do we owe you for breakfast?"

"It's on the house," she said quickly as she turned to leave. There were other customers trickling in, and needed to be seated and served.

"An Angel in shorts," Sasha McDaniels said quietly to himself.

The brothers were left to ponder their dire situation. The beast had shown his face and once again they were caught in his tentacles.

"Okay Dumi," Sasha said to his brother. "How do we get out of this one?"

If these two newest goons thought the McDaniels boys were simply just going to give in, and hand themselves over like a pair of docile lambs to the sacrificial alter, they were in for a huge surprise. After all, these two young men starred down the ferocious Sahili and his gang, and lived.

Dumisani McDaniels, already in tactical mode said, "I'll pretend like I'm going to the toilet Sasha, and then in exactly 45 seconds after I leave, follow. We will meet at the back."

"Okay," Sasha agreed.

What the brothers did not say out loud, even though they were thinking it, was that this could very well be their last stand. If their pursuers could find them when they thought they had, or rather were about to make it clean to the San Diego Border, which was still over 100 miles away, then that meant they had serious resources at their disposal. They could not outrun them. But first things first, they had to make their move, and fast.

Dumisani paused for a beat, picked up his backpack, but he did not sling it over his shoulder. Instead, he opened and peeked into it as he headed toward the john, as if something he had to do or use inside the privacy of the restroom was in his backpack. Sasha, on the other hand, felt the proverbial moment of calm before the storm he always felt before getting into a fight, be it in the ring like when he fought at the All Africa Championships, or a street fight.

Resisting the temptation to glance at his watch to gauge how much time had elapsed since his brother left, Sasha counted to one hundred, got up, picked up his backpack, and headed the same way his brother did.

The two men, Rob McNamara, who was seated close to the door, and his colleague, Luis Bramble, watched the two brothers, their targets really, get up and leave at seemingly timed intervals. However, they were headed the wrong way. The two men exchanged a knowing look that said, *what are they up to*? McNamara made a subtle gesture as he took a sip from his coffee cup and pretended to read the newspaper he was sure to bring along. *Let's wait and see*, he communicated to his partner. They did, but the brothers did not reappear, and after five minutes the two man hunters realized that something was not right, the brothers had sensed danger, and had decided to split.

When they were handpicked for this mission to accompany that 'bitch from hell', the Asian woman, they were warned that these two targets were good with their hands and feet and had to be handled with care. They were not to lose them under any circumstances.

McNamara was the first one out the door after leaving a five dollar note to cover the cost of the coffee, a generous tip. He tried to make his move as casually as possible so as not to arouse suspicion among the rest of the patrons, who were beginning to arrive in droves, including workers whose shifts were starting a lot later, but it was already too late for that. There were customers and staff who had long noticed these men with safety vests, which on them seemed out of place.

Once outside and on the sidewalk, both men looked this way and that for any sign of the brothers. The main street was slowly buzzing with activity as businesses were opening up, and people headed to work in both directions.

"They made us," Luis Bramble said, stating the obvious.

"They sure as hell did," McNamara agreed, his jaw tightened as he clenched his teeth in anger.

They had underestimated the brothers again, and there was going to be hell to pay if they had let them slip through their fingers like the other team did. There was no way they were going to let that happen with them, they were *not* going to botch this one they swore to themselves.

McNamara reached into his pocket and pulled out a device the size of a deck of cards, complete with a screen. It was a tracking device that was already powered up. He studied the screen and nodded.

"They're somewhere in the back, let's go," he said.

Both men unconsciously felt for the slight bulge underneath their safety vests for their stun guns. They were under strict orders to bring them back alive. The two men were told to rough the brothers up if they could, but certainly no fatalities.

CHAPTER 49

THE SAFE HOUSE – SOUTH PASADENA, CA.

THE YOUNG CYBER GEEK, Erick Russell was on pins and needles as he sat at his desk in the living room of the Safe House in South Pasadena. He had been here since the job on that Genuine Bank Armored car had been successfully pulled, and since then he had not been allowed to set foot outside the house until the heat died down. This was basically the nerve center for all their operations and he was to manage whatever crisis, from a technological point of view, from here twenty four seven. The two towering men, Declan Price's guard dogs were also there, and assigned to keep an eye on the young man at all costs and not let him out of their sight.

One of these babysitters, as he secretly referred to them, or 'Moron number one', but had come to know his given name as Luis Bramble had even reminded him on more than several occasions that if he even thought of running, he had orders to shoot him in the kneecaps. A task he was seemingly eager to fulfill apparently because he took utmost joy in describing how much such a thing would hurt.

"Dude, you'll beg me to kill you," Bramble cackled. Apparently, he thought the whole thing was hilarious. "That's how much pain you'll be feeling, and I'll let you squirm on the floor like a worm attacked by ants."

Erick Russell though, had no intention of finding out, so he stayed put. Did as he was told, and pretty much kept his mouth shut and mostly to himself, whenever he was not on the computer hacking away. He was informed that there will be someone coming later that day to spearhead the chase of the McDaniel brothers, whose trail it seemed was growing colder by the hour. Erick would have to find a way to track them down from right here at this Safe House in South Pasadena.

To show that this was a very high priority task, Declan let the young cyber geek know that if there was anything he needed to make his job easier in his quest to tracking down the McDaniels brothers, all he had to do was ask. Erick made his list, and two people he never saw came by got the list, and were directed to a particular electronics and surveillance store in Beverly Hills, and in no time the 'command room', as Erick referred to it, had everything that was state-of-the-art.

There were encryption equipment, counter encryption, satellite surveillance, wiretapping, secure communications, the works. Even with all this, there was no trace of the brothers. Even contacts, highly placed moles within the Altadena Sheriff's Department who were investigating both the Genuine Bank Armored Car Heist, and the killing of one Hector St. John, had nothing new to tell. Not a peek since they were last seen at Jerry's Billiards in Pasadena. That was until the mysterious, extremely gorgeous woman, Mi Kyong Park announced her arrival.

***

When the Gulfstream G5 landed at Burbank Airport at 10:45am that morning, the sole passenger, Ms. Mi Kyong Park was quickly whisked through customs and immigration, using an American passport with an alias making the process even faster, and an identity she used when it came to conducting missions in the continental United States. There was a driver waiting for her in the parking lot in a black SUV with tinted windows.

The drive from the Burbank Airport, also known as the Bob Hope Airport, to the Safe House in South Pasadena took exactly 28 minutes. The chauffeur took the 5 freeway south, connected with the 134 east, which then joined the 210 east from which he took the Fair Oaks Street exit south, which took him to South Pasadena. All throughout the drive, not a word was exchanged between the chauffeur and his beautiful and at the same time intriguing passenger, whose face was covered by dark sunglasses. They were both well trained.

By necessity, Mi Kyong almost never met her employers in person, that was her handler's job, the one who handled the contracts, and negotiations, and only if it was essential. Communication was usually via telephone (secure lines that were not listed) encrypted emails, dead drops, and sometimes through regular mail. There was a good reason for this, for most people who solicited such services of having other people eliminated, were the narcissistic type who liked their problems to be solved in the most permanent way, and did not like loose ends. Sometimes that loose end would be solved by getting rid of the man (or woman in this case) who had made their problem disappear.

431

There were a couple of clients who in the past thought it best to get rid of Miss Park permanently, after she had successfully completed her mission with aplomb, or welched in paying the remainder of her fee that had been agreed upon in advance. This was a big mistake they soon found out, because they were dead usually in less than forty-eight hours after making that fateful decision. Thus far, there had been only two who had attempted to do that, and had met their maker in so brutal a manner that warned those harboring such thoughts that they too would suffer the same fate if they chose to go the same route. Fear was the only thing that kept people honest in this business.

When the black SUV pulled into the driveway of the secluded house in the quiet neighborhood of South Pasadena, Mi Kyong did not wait for her driver to open the door for her, but instead did it herself, and stepped out onto the cobblestone driveway, holding her miniature 'Go Bag' she would not even let her chauffeur touch. She was carrying that in one hand, and a Kate Spade bag hanging from her left shoulder.

Her long hair was pulled back, revealing an oval face with a delicate upturned nose, and a clear almost milky complexion. She had on a long summer dress that clung to her and exposed a nice curvy figure that was sexy enough to make men stop and gawk. The large dark sunglasses on her face fit well with her high cheekbones. Mi Kyong Park looked and felt like the drop dead Southern California summer girl, and certainly not the deadly assassin she was.

In spite of the long flight, the beautiful woman showed no signs of distress, as she led herself through the front door of the hideaway. Apparently, she was familiar with the entire plan of this dwelling, its set up, who was supposed to be there and in what capacity. She entered the living room without knocking, startling the young geek, Erick Russell, who immediately jumped from his chair, which was in front of the desk that was now covered with all the technological equipment, gadgets, and several 17 inch monitors that had all been set up to track their quarry. Declan Price's attack dogs on the other hand, maybe because they had been forewarned about the imminent arrival of this woman by their boss, barely flinched. That courtesy had apparently not been extended to the young man. The two men were seated on the couches at both ends of the living room, watching TV.

"What's the latest so far?" Mi Kyong said without preamble. Her accent was definitely American with a Southern Californian twang, even though the woman was a chameleon and could speak about a half a dozen languages fluently.

She immediately parked herself on the same chair Erick had been sitting on just moments ago. Took out a laptop from her 'Go Bag', placed it on the huge desk, and began to fire it up.

"Eh, nothing so far ma'am," Erick said, wondering, not for the first time who this bossy beautiful Asian woman was.

She nodded and then said, "Have you been able to isolate the calls in the area?"

"Still in the process of doing so," Erick said.

"How long will it take?"

"I'd say at this rate," the young cyber geek said while scratching his goatee, "nine hours or a little less."

"Any way to speed up the process?" Mi Kyong wanted to know. She still had her sunglasses on.

One of the goons, Robert McNamara, known to everyone as 'Bob', was suddenly not focusing on the seventy five inch plasma TV, but instead at the mysterious beauty less than ten feet away, while trying to appear as indifferent as possible. He watched her as she tinkered at her laptop, and at the same time cross referenced what she had on her screen with Erick's multiple monitors on the humongous desk, and wondered what she looked like naked. He doubted she would disappoint him.

"Nine hours is the best estimate we can get at the moment miss …" Erick let the last word trail, hoping that she would help him out by giving her name, no such luck. Mi Kyong just simply ignored him.

"I suppose we will have to wait now won't we?" she said. "Not like we have a choice," Mi Kyong added.

"I agree," Erick said.

He had already pulled another chair and sat next to her, but at as respectable a distance from her as possible. The woman was a beauty, no doubt, but the young man could somehow sense a kind of danger exuding from her that Erick felt that the best thing for him, would be to do his part, basically do everything in his power to be on her good side. Sexy and beauty aside, Erick Russell just knew that this woman could kill him in one deft move. He was going to follow her orders like a good soldier, and stay out of her way as much possible.

"Is my room ready?" She asked without looking up from her laptop.

"Yes." The answer came quickly, but it was not from Erick. It was Bob McNamara, the goon who had been eyeing her from across the room while pretending to watch TV. He was really taken in by her.

Mi Kyong got up from her chair, and grabbed her 'go bag'. Being familiar with the plan of the house and the possible escape routes, she knew where her room was. It was the main bedroom, which had its private shower and bathroom, a few doors down the hallway.

Of course McNamara was more than eager to escort her or give a personal guided tour, but one glance from her, dark sunglasses and all, was enough to keep his butt stuck to the leather couch. A split second later she was gone, and everyone was back to doing their own thing.

Erick Russell had hacked into the brothers' phone company to track the calls received and made from their cell phones and landlines. It was a long and laborious task. So far the young computer pirate had been able to determine that the brothers had left their phones at their apartment. There was one phone though, which they were using it seemed, or at least was in their possession, and with the equipment at his disposal was able to use it as a homing beacon whether it was on or off. He was able to cross reference it with the calls received that morning. The brothers had answered one call that morning, and that was the phone they had in their possession.

It took eight hours and fifty seven minutes for Erick to determine that the phone, which belonged to one Misty Abdul, was in their possession. The last place they were seen was at 'Jerry's Billiards', the information once backtracked was able to prove they had pinged the phone at that location, from there they were able to pick up the route they took, and based on the times the cellphone pinged the different cell towers along the way, Erick was able to tell that whoever had that phone was on foot.

At the moment, which happened to be 5:17am, on his screen it pinpointed their exact location on Pacific Boulevard in Huntington Park, across the street from a business establishment, a 'Mom and Pop' Mexican/Salvadorian Restaurant called the 'Sukasa'. An enhanced search by satellite and he was able to see the location live, which meant sooner or later, he would also be able to see the McDaniels brothers on screen live, and in living color.

He then quickly relayed the information to an already wide awake Mi Kyong Park, who then issued the necessary orders, and then in no time she and Declan's attack dogs, Robert 'Bob' McNamara and Luis Bramble were in the black SUV, with McNamara at the wheel, on their way to Huntington Park.

CHAPTER 50

HUNTINGTON PARK, CALIFORNIA – 131 MILES
FROM THE SAN DIEGO BORDER.

THE BROTHERS, SASHA AND DUMISANI McDaniels,
made a quick exit through the noisy kitchen, amidst a
cacophony of dishes clashing, cooks and busboys
yelling at one another in a language the brothers
thought to be Spanish, but during all this, none of the
kitchen staff batted an eye, or even stole a glance at the
two young men as they made their way through the
kitchen, and toward the backdoor. Apparently, they
had been tipped ahead of time and played their part of
blissful ignorance.

The backyard of the restaurant was surrounded by
a high fence with barbed wire, something the brothers
noticed when they stood at the last step that led out of
the kitchen, and looked this way and that, wondering
which way to go. There was a gate that led to the main
boulevard, and another which led to a long back alley
that went on and on until it joined another main street
the brothers were not familiar with.

The front gate was a none starter because that was
the one their pursuers would expect them to use. The
long back alley was a problem, an unknown in which
they could be boxed in, and they would be trapped with

no visible option of retreat if the need arose. The men after them were armed with guns, and were ready and willing to use them. They, on the other hand had no weapons other than themselves. Their feet and hands, deadly as they were, were no match for bullets.

Their enemies had bungled the first attack, when they ambushed the brothers at their apartment. There was absolutely no way they were going to let that happen a second time. Dumisani and Sasha looked around again for a possible hiding place, they had to find one quickly, because the bad guys, they knew, would be out to find them any minute. There was nothing in the backyard, other than an abandoned car that had been sitting there for decades, old crates of beverages stacked one on top of another about ten feet high, and a huge commercial garbage bin that was surrounded by a rectangular brick wall, six feet high near the south end gate. It was not ideal, but it could work.

"The garbage bin Sasha," Dumisani said in a harsh whisper. "It's our only chance."

Without another word, but in silent agreement, the two rushed to the enclosure housing the garbage bin. They were just in time to hide behind the huge garbage container, with Sasha deliberately leaving the gate to the enclosure wide open, and the one that led to the alley shut, when Bob McNamara and Luis Bramble rushed in the backyard from the main street, stun guns in hand as they spread out and used hand signals to communicate. Not knowing what to expect, they decided to re-holster their stun guns and brought out their Glock 19's which they slowly fitted with silencers as they kept looking around.

With their backs to each other, and their arms outstretched, the two men noticed the back gate at the same time that led to the alley. Their quarry had to have gone that way, they exchanged a subtle nod, coming to the same conclusion.

McNamara said, "They couldn't have gone far, so we go after them."

They lowered their firearms but stayed alert. Both men also had bogus LAPD badges that they were ready to flash in anyone's face, just in case someone dared question what in the hell they were doing snooping around on private property.

Just as they were about to open the gate that led to the alley, the other goon, Luis Bramble, stopped as if considering something.

"What?" his partner hissed in a fierce whisper.

Instead of voicing his thoughts, he gestured with a nod of his head at the enclosure that housed the restaurant's garbage bin they had just passed to the left. It needed checking, was the unspoken message. McNamara nodded his assent, and they slowly and silently backtracked.

***

In their hiding place, the brothers were just about to heave a sigh of relief when they head the fading footsteps soon retrace their steps. Dumisani and Sasha were both cramped in the tiny space between the wall and the huge garbage dumpster, with almost no room to maneuver if it came to that. As they heard the gate to the enclosure squeak open at the hinges, they starred at each other. Again the look in their tired eyes said it all.

It was uncanny, as if somehow the two could communicate telepathically. They were exhausted. Dumisani and Sasha McDaniels were tired of running with no idea where this running would take them, let alone doing so in a foreign country. They were tired of running knowing that they were tired of being tired. The San Diego Border was at least 131 miles away, and they could lie to themselves as many times as they could, but making it to the border on foot and against these odds was fantasy at best, in spite of their formidable individual strengths.

Now here they were, trapped like a pair of mice. This was it, this was their Alamo, their last stand. They slowly but quietly unshouldered their backpacks, and placed them in between them so their hands could be free to raise them in surrender. Dumisani and Sasha sighed as they leaned against the wall in the space created by the enclosure, and the garbage bin.

"Let me see your hands!" Robert McNamara screamed the moment he peeked inside the crevice and spotted the brothers seated side by side, and pointed the silenced Glock 19 at them. He thought he would get better cooperation with that than the stun gun.

The brothers must have hesitated because he shouted again, "Now! Your hands assholes!"

Sasha and Dumisani starred at him blankly, as they slowly complied, and began crawling out of their hiding place.

"That's it," McNamara said, as if he was encouraging a toddler taking its first steps. "Nice and slow."

Right at that moment, McNamara thought he heard a muffled sound behind him, and before he could turn to see what had caused that, the brothers saw him suddenly fly to the side like a rag doll, headfirst and slam against the wall so hard that the gun fell out of his hand and clattered harmlessly to the ground a few feet away. Both brothers knew what could have most certainly caused that – a well delivered flying kick executed by a professional. He tried to get up on all fours, but a kick to the face knocked him over and out, that a few seconds later his unconscious body was on its back facing upward – out cold.

None of this made sense. Dumisani was the first one out and he immediately went on the attack. In his desperation and confusion, he went at the figure in front of him, and his opponent parried his attack like the grandmaster he was. In his drug induced haze, Dumisani tried to go after him again, but the figure grabbed him by the hands, he tried to break free but it was like they were clamped in a vise and pulled him closer.

"You must be Dumisani!"

Say what?! Dumisani's eyes suddenly regained focus and he could scarcely believe what he was seeing. First it was the clerical collar, the black shirt, the pectoral cross dangling from his neck, and then the face that looked very familiar.

No! Dumisani thought. *Impossible, and yet …*

"Uncle Sean Kane?!" asked a now very perplexed Dumisani McDaniels.

He glanced behind his uncle at something that caught his eye. It was the unconscious body of McNamara's cohort Luis Bramble. He, like McNamara were so concentrated on capturing the McDaniels brothers that they did not notice their uncle to who their backs were turned, and he had Bramble exactly where he wanted. All he did was reach at the meaty part of his upper shoulder, in between the neck and the clavicle, pressed hard and he was out like a bulb in less than five seconds, which then made it easier to deal with McNamara, who he saw pointing a gun behind the trash bin, and he could only hazard a good guess as to whom that gun was pointed to and acted accordingly.

"Uncle Sean Kane?!" this time it was Sasha's turn to be as flabbergasted as his brother, as he crawled out of his hiding place.

This was like an episode from the '*Twilight Zone*' it could not be happening, it could not be real, and yet there it was, their long lost uncle, the Reverend Sean Kane McDaniels in the flesh standing tall and erect, very much like their father. In fact it looked like the same person but in two different bodies, except their uncle's hair had once been blond and now it was almost totally white.

"Uncle Sean Kane?" Sasha said again.

"H-how did you … how …" Dumisani, just like his brother, was finding it hard to get the words out of his mouth.

Their uncle, realizing this, said, "It's me boys, I'll explain later, but what we need to do is get out of here right away. We're parked a few blocks away from here. Come on let's go!"

Without another word, the three took off, they exited through the main gate that led to Pacific Boulevard from the Sukasa restaurant backyard, leaving the two unconscious bodies where they were and in no time they were gone.

Pacific Boulevard was already bustling with activity, as the city's downtown area came to life. Sasha and Dumisani, still shocked by this new development kept glancing behind them to see if they were being followed - their uncle noticed.

"Act normal," the reverend admonished. "Don't look suspicious, just act natural."

They both nodded and kept up with the older man's brisky pace.

"How did you find us?" Sasha wanted to know.

The reverend smiled and then said, "Technology son, apparently one of you took Misty's phone and that's how we were able to track you."

Again Dumisani froze. This was unbelievable. Did his uncle just say what he thought he said? And not only that, but he also spoke of her as if he knew her. Dumisani took a step toward his uncle, and then as gently as possible, grabbed him by the arm so he could face him.

"Misty?" he asked. "As in Misty Abdul, Uncle Sean?"

"Yes, your friend Misty Abdul nephew," Sean Kane McDaniels smiled as he clapped him gently on the shoulder, a gesture that was visibly affectionate. In that brief moment, looking into his nephew's wide eyes, he could tell that he was in love with the beautiful young woman who had become his sidekick.

"H-how?"

"She's in the car waiting, and I'll tell you all about it."

It is a strange world we live in, Dumisani McDaniels thought as he unconsciously quickened his pace. The thought of seeing Misty Abdul in the next few minutes was dizzying. Nothing else mattered, the danger obviously still lurking out there and at every corner, capped by the fact that there was obviously a team of sophisticated killers out there after them with cyber capabilities to track them down that defied logic. The fact that their lives could very well be in danger was now of no consequence, what was of great relevance at this very moment was seeing Misty.

***

The brethren, Sasha and Dumisani were in a state of shock as they quickly walked with their uncle to where he said he had parked his car. There were too many questions that needed answers. Here was an uncle they had been searching for all their lives, and more so since their arrival, not a peek, and then suddenly he appeared in of all places Huntington Park, and when they were on the run no less. Talk about great timing.

"Uncle Sean," Sasha said. "How did you bump into Misty?"

They were approaching a busy intersection, so far so good. No one had accosted or even looked at them funny, neither did they see anyone who did not fit – in other words, someone who could be coming after them.

"I arrived shortly after you bailed, it seems. The place was upside down, and right on the floor of your living room, I see this girl lying unconscious, luckily she was coming around and we managed to get out before the cops arrived and found us there. There was also a dead man on your living room floor am sure you'll explain once this is over." It was just remarkable how much he looked and sounded like their dad.

"But she's okay though, right uncle Sean?" Dumisani asked again, anxiously.

"Oh yes," Sean Kane smiled.

Sasha asked, "Uncle Sean, you know what's happening right? We're on the run. Why are these people are after us?"

"You have something they want, and they want it badly, and not surprisingly, they want you silenced."

Dumisani said, "I think we know what they want Uncle Sean."

"Go on," the reverend prompted.

In shorthand, Dumisani told him all they knew. The class project that required him to film everything he saw, felt, and heard on his first full day in the United States, which led them to inadvertently film what turned out to be the Genuine Bank Armored Car Heist.

"So you actually got a chance to watch the contents of what you filmed?" the reverend wanted to know.

"We did uncle," Dumisani said. "But we did not see anything out of the ordinary."

Sasha added by saying, "The thing is uncle, we were there at that supermarket a few days ago, we were right there, but we have no idea what could have happened."

"There was a robbery guys," the reverend said matter of factly. "It happened and you guys must have caught it on your camcorder, and the men after you know it."

They had turned the corner and were walking south toward a car less than a block away, that was parked, like others of the side of the street.

"You probably heard this boys," Sean Kane McDaniels said, "but you see, places like that supermarket you went to, Jones's, and many like it, are high foot traffic areas, lots of cash paying customers and the like. They collect cash by the truckload everyday they'd have to hire someone to make daily deposits, so their bank, Genuine Bank in this case, has custom built armored vans that can blend in with every other car, and come either every day, or every other day to make the cash pickup, and make the deposit on their behalf, and even fill their instore ATMs with cash. So if these cars pick up from numerous stores and such similar places, well do the math."

The brothers nodded their understanding, they knew all this, or at least had gotten an inkling from the news, but having their uncle explain it made even more sense.

"You boys witnessed something, and the people who are behind this know it, and whoever they are," Reverend Sean Kane McDaniels paused for a beat and

445

then continued, "are some very powerful people with connections at the highest level, judging by the ease with which they've been able to trek you down thus far."

Again Sasha and Dumisani nodded their understanding, because, and once again, they knew all this, but decided to let their uncle impart his pearl of wisdom, after all he was playing the brand new role of the doting uncle for the first time in his life and seemed to be enjoying it, plus after all said and done, he did save them for certain doom.

"That is why we need to get out of the country right away Uncle Sean," Dumisani said, he was long past wanting to go to the nearest police station and explain things.

"And that man, that ex policeman we killed in our flat, Uncle Sean, was all self-defense," Sasha added. "That guy, whoever the h.." He caught himself just in time, remembering that he was speaking to a man of God who did not tolerate swear words. "Whoever he is, was a thug plain and simple, a killer, the worst of the kind. It was either him or us. They were not playing games Uncle Sean, they wanted Dumi's camcorder and were ready to kill for it, and in broad daylight to be sure."

He went on to describe in glowing detail the type of weapons their assailants had, and the fact that they were fitted with silencers, it was not to scare them into giving up what they had, Sasha reasoned, they meant to get what they came for and then kill them.

Goodness gracious, Sean Kane McDaniels thought, Broderick was spot on about everything he suspected was happening with my nephews.

"Which is why you got to help us get to the San Diego border at least Uncle Sean," Dumisani pleaded.

However, as he said this, a thought suddenly occurred to him in the form of one beautiful name, yes, Misty Abdul. Any chance she will come with him? He wondered. After all, he was young, rich, handsome and yeah, okay, the US dream did not pan out, but they could have as good a life in Botswana as they would have had here. They …

"That won't do," his uncle's voice broke his reverie. "We're *not* running from this. We're going to face it to the end."

Hearing their uncle emphasize the word *we* meant he was fully invested in their fight, but most importantly, he believed them, which was more than enough. He suddenly felt revitalized.

"How are we going to fight this?" Sasha asked.

Sean Kane McDaniels smiled, it was the type of grin he usually reserved for a congregation, and said, "I have a friend who I served with in the First Gulf War, we were in the Navy's Special Forces, the SEALs, and he was also well versed in Military Intelligence. He will help us figure out a way out of this."

"Is he any good?" Dumisani asked. "Someone we can trust?"

"Oh yes"

"Is he any good," Dumisani asked again.

"How do you think I found you?" the reverend smiled as they approached what the brothers assumed was their uncle's car. He was going to tell them more about Lenny Broderick later.

It was a clean Nissan Altima, but had obviously seen better days. Sean Kane was just about to say something, but froze instead. He looked inside the car again, and then around, then at the other cars parked in the vicinity. Something was dreadfully wrong and the brothers sensed it immediately.

"Uncle Sean?" Dumisani asked with a sinking heart.

"Is this it?" Sasha asked, pointing at the car, as he brushed a strand of hair that had covered part of his face. Something he did when he was nervous.

"Yes." Even though his voice was calm, Reverend Sean Kane McDaniels's face had turned ashen pale.

"Uncle Sean?" Dumisani asked again, but suddenly got it. Misty Abdul was not in the vehicle, in fact, she was nowhere in sight.

"Where is she?" the older McDaniels asked, more to himself than to anyone in particular.

"Who?" Dumisani asked, even though he damn well knew who, and suddenly felt that cold, all too familiar fear rise in the pit of his belly to his throat, almost chocking his voice because it sounded croaked when he said quietly, "Misty?"

"Yes," Sean Kane nodded. "I told her to stay put."

"Maybe she went to get a soft drink or something?!" Sasha offered helpfully, not even presuming to entertain the horrible alternative.

"I doubt it," his uncle said. "I told her specifically to sit tight, besides, I gave her a burner to call me because I have her's …"

"A what?" Sasha asked. "What is a burner?"

"Oh, a prepaid phone you buy and later discard once you're done with it."

Sasha nodded his understanding, so his uncle continued.

"She was to call me if anything out of the ordinary happened, no matter how inconsequential, or if she decided to step away from the car to say use the bathroom or get something to eat, anything, while I went looking for you two."

Sean Kane opened the passenger door of his car, and on the seat was a phone. Not the one he had given

Misty, but a totally different one, and placed in such a way that he would see it the moment he entered the vehicle, or opened the passenger door. A sinking feeling of deep melancholy dawned on the three men.

"What's the meaning of this?" Dumisani asked the moment he saw his uncle pick the phone like it was a hunk of radioactive waste, and raise it to eye level for all to see as he inspected it.

"I wonder …"

As Sean Kane was about to say something, the phone rang, and the reverend had to wonder if they were being watched. He looked at the phone for a moment as he let it ring. The screen said it was from an 'unidentified number', and whoever had left it there for him to find made sure it was on 'Speaker Mode' so everyone could hear.

McDaniels pressed the green 'TALK' button. There was at least a five second pause before a strange metallic voice that was obviously using a 'voice changer' to distort the tone of the caller's voice and accent, emanated from the tiny speaker as if it came from some far dark corner of the galaxy. Sasha and Dumisani who had been facing outward, in case this was some cleverly orchestrated misdirection, stepped closer.

"We have the girl, and if you want to see her alive again, give us what we want or the next time you see her, she will be in pieces. Do not go to the FBI, or the police, or the girl dies. We will be in touch."

His party was just about to hang up, but the reverend quickly jumped in with: "Wait a minute, who are you and what is it exactly you want from us?"

"You know what we want … be ready to hand it over within three hours, we will be in touch. Hold on to that phone."

449

"Wait, who'll be in touch? … you? … where? … how?"

The line was dead.

The brothers looked at their uncle, shell-shocked. The situation had gone from bad to catastrophic or as they would say in the American street lingo: the shit just got real. And why? Because the bad guys, whoever they were, had Misty Abdul.

CHAPTER 51

ARCADIA/MONROVIA, CA–24 HOURS EARLIER.

REVEREND SEAN KANE MCDANIELS knew that to find and save his nephews, he may have to perform deeds that went against his call of being a man of God. He would have to resort to acts of deceit, blackmail, violence, and yes, even murder for this to have a happy ending. He was in a bit of a moral quagmire, but this was different in that it involved family. Dumisani and Sasha, his blood nephews, needed him more than they could have ever needed anyone in their lives.

To justify what he was about to do, McDaniels remembered a verse from the bible that was fitting for this present predicament. It was from the book of Ecclesiastes verse 3:8 – *A time to love and a time to hate, a time for war and a time for peace*. This was a time for war, a war to clear his nephews, and get them back on track of living their American dream.

There was one problem though, the beautiful young woman Misty Abdul. The young lady was brave, no doubt feisty and full of life, a firebrand. The kind that don't start fights, but didn't run from one either. He could not take her with him though. This was going to be a very dangerous undertaking, he knew. Sean Kane McDaniels was a trained former operative during the first Gulf War meaning he had seen live combat, and a one time member of one the Army's best of the best – the United States Navy SEALs, and Misty was nowhere near any of that. If anything, she would most likely get in the way. And yet …

He was in his car when Misty Abdul climbed in through the passenger door and on the seat, where she had been earlier when they drove to her parents' home in Arcadia, and strapped her seatbelt. He noticed that she had changed into something more casual. A pair of loose fitting grey sweatpants, a bright yellow t-shirt with a sports bra underneath even though she did not need one, and her shiny dark hair was pulled back in a long ponytail and held in place by a headband so that not a single strand of hair hung loose on her face.

She looked at the street in front of them through the windshield, and then back at the reverend, when she noticed that he was lost in thought. It was a beautiful bright, shiny, Southern California late summer afternoon.

"Well?" she prompted as in 'well what are we waiting for let's go.'

Silence!

"Father Sean Kane? … hello? … anybody there?" Misty smiled as she snapped her fingers at him.

"I still think this is too dangerous Misty," the man of God said at last. He was still looking ahead through the windshield, and not at her.

"Father Sean Kane, we've been through this already, Dumisani and Sasha are my friends, and I want to help them as much as you do."

"Yes, I understand Misty, but you could get killed and I don't want that on my conscience. Look, I admire your courage and devotion to my nephews, but …"

"Father Sean Kane," she interrupted. "You may think you don't need me but you do."

She looked the older man straight in the eye as she said this, and he could see the conviction in her eyes. This was going to be a tough one he knew, and each minute they were wasting arguing, was a minute not looking for his nephews.

"Oh yeah? How so?" Sean Kane flashed her a mirthless smile.

"Okay, you said one of the things you'll need to track them down is my phone, right?"

"Yes," the reverend agreed, wondering where the exotic looking knockout of a beauty was going with this.

Misty gave a self-assured smile. One where you know that some sucker has jumped headlong into an elaborate trap you set.

"Okay let me ask you this Father Sean Kane, do you know my phone number?"

"No."

"How about my wireless carrier and the make and model of my smartphone?"

"No."

"Then I guess I'm coming then. So please drive, we've wasted enough time as it is."

Father Sean Kane McDaniels had to suppress a smile, as he at last turned the key in the ignition, and heard the engine under the hood roar to life. This young woman was sharp as a tack, and maybe this was God's will, who knew? He of all people knew that The Creator of the universe worked in mysterious ways. He looked at her for a few seconds as if sizing her up. It went on like that until Misty started to feel a little uncomfortable.

"What?" she asked.

He smiled and said, "I think from now on you should just call me Sean, or Sean Kane if you prefer."

Misty nodded, smiled and then said, "Okay Sean, can we now go find your nephews?"

***

The people who were after his nephews, McDaniels figured, were willing to do what it took to achieve their objective. It other words, they were willing to play dirty. From his experience and time with the Special Forces, McDaniels knew that to fight a 'dirty war' you got to form a 'dirty unit' that was more than willing and capable to engage the enemy at their own game. Sean Kane McDaniels would have to play dirty, and for this mission he needed a likeminded and equally trained companion. He knew of such a man, his name was Lenny Broderick, a former SEAL swim buddy and later a martial arts student of his.

He had not seen his swim buddy, as SEAL partners were known, in almost a decade, and his last known address was, as was the Price brothers, in Monrovia California. McDaniels prayed that that had not changed over the years. Right now Lenny Broderick was the only person in the world who had the means and the moral ambiguity of what it took to track down his nephews. As McDaniels sat in his car ready to drive, he racked his brain to recall where his former swim buddy lived. He remembered that it was very close to the San Gabriel Mountains. Where the heck was that place? He asked himself, as he gripped the steering wheel even harder. Misty noticed, like she did everything.

"What's the matter?"

"There's a man, a former buddy of mine in the navy who can help us, but I haven't seen or talked to him in ages," he replied.

"Do you remember where he lived back then?"

"Yes, in Monrovia, close to the mountains."

She suddenly, as if by magic, had a smartphone in her palm, another one she got from her parents' home apparently, and was ready to start searching.

"From as far back as you can remember," Misty said. "Do you think he owned his home, or was he renting?"

"I'd say he owned his home, why?"

"These days you can find almost anyone online if you know where to look. Normally, stuff like home ownership and all pertinent details are public record and easy to dig up."

McDaniels doubted if Lenny Broderick could be found that way. The man was part of Military Intelligence while with the SEALs. A man who had made his fair share of enemies foreign and domestic, in other words, a person who would never make it easy for anyone to find him.

"I don't think you'll find him that way Misty," Sean Kane said.

"Why not?"

"It's hard to explain but trust me, he's not a man who'd have his personal information on a public domain or any other for that matter." He could not go into detail, at least not yet.

Neither did Misty apparently because she did not pry, instead she asked, "But you do have a general idea where his last residence is, right?"

The reverend and former SEAL nodded.

"Okay then that's a start."

They finally drove off and were soon heading north on Baldwin Avenue, passed the Santa Anita Mall

455

on the right and the Los Angeles Arboretum, which was diagonally opposite the mall, on the left. Instead of getting on the 210 East via the Baldwin Avenue Ramp, Sean Kane kept driving north toward the San Gabriel Mountains, which on this late afternoon offered a breathtaking view as the setting sun reflected on the mountain tops.

"I never get tired of this view," Misty said. "It's always had a profound impact on me ever since I was a little girl."

"I can see why," the reverend agreed.

"I suppose one can say I've been fortunate in that growing up in this area the mountains become a part of you," she added.

The reverend simply nodded but said nothing. They were coming at an intersection where Baldwin crossed Foothill Boulevard, a major street that ran east west, and as its name suggested ran parallel to the mountain range. Sean Kane had not been to this part of town in years, but suddenly things started coming back to him, as he turned right on Foothill, and was now heading east.

After crossing Santa Anita Avenue, he slowed down considerably. He knew he was going to have to turn left, but what street was the question. That was crucial in finding Broderick's house. He knew that if he missed the turn that would be it, he may never find it. His mind was searching for something. Something he knew was important. The name of the small street he was supposed to turn on.

"Come on think Sean Kane!" He had no idea that he had said that loudly.

"What was that Sean?"

"Huh?"

"You said *think Sean Kane*. Think about what?"

"Oh, I was …" And then suddenly his face lit up. "Sunset street … that's the name of the street we're supposed to turn on, and I think it will be coming up soon."

They were now in an area where Foothill Boulevard ran through shopping complexes on both sides, a MacDonald's, a 76 Gas Station, a few independent restaurants, and after passing Ralph's Supermarket on the left and a CVS Pharmacy on the right, they came upon a small street that intersected with the main one – Sunset Street.

He turned left, and then a block and a half later made a right on Merchant Street and then a quick left on a small street called El Nido. They were suddenly in a quiet and exclusive neighborhood. The further up they went on El Nido the more Misty realized that most of the homes on this part of town were actually situated on the mountain range, and then ahead of them there was a sign that clearly stated, '*Street End, No Thoroughfare*'. Misty looked at the sign and then at the older man. There was a question coming, McDaniels could tell, and it did not take long.

"Is it one of these homes, because the sign says that's it, we've run out of road."

"No, but just wait and see."

It did not take long, because right at the cul-de-sac there was an obscure dirt road that was very easy to miss, and certainly the type you don't find on a map. It was flanked by trees and bushes that led them to a two storage chalet that was built by carving in the side of the mountain, which somewhat gave it the look of a mini fortress.

There was a gate that led into a small well-kept yard, and inside was a driveway made of gravel that made a semicircular loop that led back the way it came. The reverend stopped at the gate, opened his window, and looked around. All was quiet, save for the sound of crows and other creatures in the shrubs and trees behind.

"This is it," McDaniels said. "Not much has changed since I was here."

Misty nodded. Suddenly, and for no apparent reason, the beautiful young woman felt uneasy, because of the mountains and trees that obscured the rays from the setting sun, the shadow made the place feel as though it was dusk.

They got out of the car, the gate was open and with the reverend leading the way, they walked toward the front door.

"Is anyone home Sean?" Misty asked in a low tone not because she expected an ambush of some sort, but because of the somewhat overwhelming silence and effect of the place.

The older man did not answer. Instead he looked ahead, around, and beyond the house. Sean Kane McDaniels had unconsciously reverted to tactical mode as he felt his former self, the SEAL, returning.

As they silently walked to the front door, Sean Kane noticed, for the first time the tiny garage on the western end of the house, it had not been there before, apparently his friend had added the garage during the years they had lost touch. It was closed, so there was no telling if there was a vehicle in it or not. The curtains were shut so they could not see inside. Normally, he would have asked Misty to remain safely in the vehicle, but he wanted her close to him. The area was unnaturally quiet to a point that the reverend felt something stir in the pit of his stomach. He did not like this one bit, and moreover after all said and done, he was wholly responsible for this young woman's life.

They stepped on the tiny porch with Sean Kane McDaniels still leading the way. There were several flowerpots with plants in them that reflected that the owner took good care of them. McDaniels strained his hearing to try and catch any sound from inside the house, anything to indicate to him that there was someone in the house – nothing.

"Don't move! Stay where you are!"

The voice that sounded behind them was authoritative, deliberate, controlled and it froze them in their tracks, just as Sean Kane was about to knock at the front door. Misty shrieked and dropped her purse, but the reverend, the former SEAL hardly flinched.

They slowly turned, hands shoulder high and barely ten feet away from them was a broad shouldered man, almost six feet tall with curly red hair that was turning grey, particularly at the temples, and a thick grey beard on an otherwise handsome face. He was dressed in a white t-shirt which, despite his middle age, defined his muscular physique and a pair of faded jeans. However, there was a Beretta in both his hands, and it was pointed at them.

His eyes suddenly squinted, as if trying to place the face of the man in front of him, not at the attractive woman.

"No way," he said as he slowly lowered his firearm. "Sean?" the man said. "Sean Kane McDaniels?"

McDaniels smiled and said pleasantly, "Lenny Broderick!"

"Man oh Man!" Lenny said. "I thought they were jerking my chain when they told me that you gave your life to the Almighty."

He gestured at the shirt and collar, holstered his weapon at the small of his back, spread his arms wide and said, "Come here brother!"

McDaniels smiled widely, stepped away from a dumbfounded Misty, and a few minutes later the two men were in a long and tight embrace that seemed to last for ten minutes. A true reflection of the strength of a bond that was created by two men who had been through a lot together. A bond not even the many intervening years could tarnish let alone break.

"How have you been brother?" McDaniels asked with a smile Misty Abdul was seeing for the first time. It was true she reflected, as she studied the two men that SEALs form a bond that is almost like blood.

"How long has it been brother?" Broderick asked as the two men finally broke their embrace.

"Twenty two years."

"Doesn't seem that long," Broderick said as he took a step back as if to reassess his long lost friend.

"Yeah," McDaniels agreed as he looked around and then back at his long lost friend and brother in arms. "But what's with the cloak and dagger stuff right in the middle of the day?"

By that, he meant the reception he and Misty received.

"Sorry about that man. I'm in private and personal security nowadays since I retired from the Navy, and you'll be amazed at the number of people who've tried to break into my home to steal crucial information. Some even posed as girl scouts selling cookies door to door if you can believe that."

Lenny then looked over his friend's shoulder at Misty Abdul as if seeing her for the first time, and smiled.

"Are you going to introduce me to the beautiful young lady reverend?"

He enunciated the word 'reverend' deliberately and the insinuation was obvious. As a man of God who swore to dedicate his life to The Lord, how on earth did you end up with a pretty young lady on your arm?

The necessary introductions were made, and then things turned serious when it was time to explain why they were here. They were in Broderick's cozy living room by this time, and just as they came to the crux of the matter, Lenny Broderick raised his hand like a traffic cop, imploring his friend and former SEAL partner to stop talking.

"I think this is a conversation we must continue in the basement. It's more secure, and I get the feeling you're also going to like what I have to show you," Lenny Broderick said.

They all stood up, normally he would have rather preferred to have this conversation with McDaniels in private, absent the young woman, but he realized that she was just as crucial to this crisis as his friend was. He then led them to a small stairway they had not noticed before at the other end of the living room.

CHAPTER 52

Monrovia, CA – 21 HOURS EARLIER.

THE BASEMENT HAD AN EARTHY, musty smell because the house was built into the side of the mountain. For a small house, at least when compared to the rest in the neighborhood, the basement was huge and soundproof judging from the thick padding on the wall.

That was not it however, the place was what one may call the 'ultimate man cave'. There was a long well-kept desk attached to the wall, which stretched almost halfway around the room, and on it were flat screen monitors, close circuit T.Vs, encryption and surveillance, counter surveillance equipment, and numerous computers, and screens that tracked Lenny Broderick's drones that he had specially made for stalking and shadowing purposes. The room looked eerily similar to Erick Russell's space at the safe house except this one was clearly more advanced. There were also other gizmos Broderick's guests could not make head or tail of.

At the opposite end of the room, across from the equipment, was a long leather couch to which he directed Sean Kane and Misty to sit. This was after he offered them a beverage, which they both declined. It was apparent that the Lenny Broderick spent a lot of time in this basement, which he described as his 'Nerve Center'. He went on to explain to his two guests that he provided top notch security for an exclusive clientele around Southern California, mainly inventions and patents for companies as well as guarding their secrets remotely.

For example, there was a green energy company in Orange County whose owner had invented a prototype generator that worked like a power grid generating electricity, what made this invention unique was that it ran on air. This had the true potential of being a 21st Century wonder that could be key to mankind's over reliance on fossil fuel that could one day be depleted. That particular company had signed a secret deal with the United States Government, who were bankrolling the final stages of this project.

There was no arguing the potential value of this device for it was priceless. Priceless and dangerous for this was something that could cause wars and the people's lives behind it could be in peril. Oil was the blood line of certain Middle Eastern countries like Saudi Arabia for instance. If suddenly, a big buyer of their commodity like the United States ended their reliance on oil, that could spell disaster to the desert kingdom and many other oil producing nations to an extent of which was left unsaid.

Lenny Broderick's security firm was tasked with watching that prototype at its secret location around the clock, and they were ready, at a moment's notice, to react with lethal force if there ever was a breach orchestrated by intruders, or even those whose sole aim was to steal the intellectual property that provided the blueprint as to how this generator operated, he even showed them the monitors that revealed in real time that particular sample called the 'COGAR'. He also went on to explain that part of his job was to keep the people who built it under secret surveillance, to make certain that they did not get cute and start consorting with the wrong people for a price.

After giving a brief overview of what his security firm was about, even though the former SEAL was holding back, and McDaniel could tell, now was not the time to press for more detail. Now was about tracking down his nephews and this was the only man who could help him. However, he knew that in order to get to the crux of the reason why they were there at Broderick's house, he had to endure the dog and pony show until he was ready.

Sensing the reverend's anxiety, Broderick said at last, "Okay, in here we're safe and secure. Nothing any of you say will leave this room. So what gives McDaniels? Seems to me like something's up."

"My nephews are in trouble, and I'm talking life and death trouble," Reverend Sean Kane McDaniels said without preamble.

"You nephews?!"

"Yes, Sasha and Dumisani. They just arrived from Botswana a little less than two weeks ago, I think," McDaniels said.

"Your nephews?" Broderick asked again, his brow twisted as if searching his memory for something he knew was there but could not retrieve.

"Yes, Sasha and Dumisani. You know my brother's sons, the one who …"

Broderick suddenly snapped his fingers as it came to him.

"Yes," he said. "I remember now. I'm so sorry Sean, I read about it online and I remember trying to get hold of you to convey my condolences, but I couldn't find you for some reason. You had fallen off the grid, only to find out later that you were on some religious crusade."

"Yeah, yeah, yeah, all that's true," the reverend said a bit impatiently. Enough already, it was time to get on with why he had come here. He did, and so did Misty Abdul, she did so in glowing detail.

She began by telling the ex-Navy SEAL about her first meeting with the brothers in Botswana, when she and her two friends had visited the country on a Safari, the surprise reconnection via social media, which then of course led to her having a gun to her head when she went to the brothers' apartment the previous morning. A visit she had been looking forward to, but instead got more than she could have possibly bargained for.

"Any idea what these men wanted?" Broderick wanted to know.

He had been listening, without interrupting, for over five minutes as the beautiful young woman with enchanting luminous eyes related chapter and verse about what happened.

"They wanted Dumi's camcorder, and it seemed to me that they were ready to kill for it and I mean that literally. I get the feeling they would have killed us anyway if they got it."

"Why do you say that?"

"Just thinking of the old adage dead men tell no lies?"

Broderick and the reverend nodded their agreement, almost chuckled at the clever wisecrack, but instead urged her to carry on.

Misty went on to explain that she had been knocked unconscious just when, according to her, 'all hell broke loose'.

"And just how specifically, excuse me Sean Kane, did all hell break loose?" Broderick asked.

"Well," Misty said. "It seemed to me that Sasha and Dumisani were not simply going to hand over the camcorder without a fight, and that's when I got hit in the head with the gun butt, or whatever it was, then everything turned black. And when I opened my eyes again, is when I saw Sean hovering over me. I thought I had died and a priest was administering his last rites," Misty added, not trying to be funny.

Broderick listened attentively at the young women's recital, and when she was through, he looked at the reverend.

"And here we are," Sean Kane said. "Now, what Misty didn't mention is that the man my nephews were forced to kill was an ex-cop. So word is out that my boys are cop killers, and you know how that will turn out."

As a matter of fact, the former SEAL knew exactly how information like that would be handled, especially by the lowly beat cops with itchy trigger fingers, who were at times predisposed to shooting first and asking questions after. However, this had been a home invasion, albeit in broad daylight. Obviously, the death of this perpetrator could be classified as a clear case of self-defense. These men were certainly not cops executing a search warrant, they were a bunch of goons carrying out a hit on clueless innocent young men. They were looking to take something that did not belong to them by hook or by crook, and in the process leave no living witness, which was why they came with all that firepower. Why then was blame being placed on the brothers who were currently on the run?

Something was afoot here. There was something major being hidden. As a former Special Ops veteran, Lenny Broderick saw the aftermath of the assault on the McDaniels brothers for what it was, a cover up. The two boys had witnessed something, or were unknowingly in possession of some damning information, and these attackers were sent to make them cough it up. This was exactly what he told his former SEAL swim buddy. There was no way to sugarcoat this, the boys were in mortal danger and that danger was growing every minute.

"That is why I need your help in finding them, and I mean *now*," Sean Kane McDaniels said with much emphasis in his voice.

Broderick was silent for a while, obviously running the numerous possibilities in his mind as he returned to his swiveling chair in front of his numerous flat screen monitors. The flat screen he was seated in front of, was the largest of all the ones that were placed neatly at two and a half feet intervals.

"Let me have your phone number again Ms. Abdul and your network carrier."

Misty provided the information and the former SEAL began working his magic, as the strange characters appeared on the screen. It went on like that for a while. Nothing was said during the time, it was all quiet save for the tapping of the keyboard as Broderick's fingers flew above it at almost breathtaking speed, as he brought to bear his entire hacking skills. He was in the midst of doing just that when he was suddenly hit by a thought that came from left field.

It was so sudden, so unexpected that the former SEAL practically leapt from his chair, as he first swiveled around to face his equally startled guests, Misty in particular, for the reverend hardly flinched, something that spoke volumes about his many years of training. He was obviously well versed in the art of reacting very quickly to precipitous surprises.

"What is it?" Sean Kane McDaniels, cool as a cucumber.

Lenny Broderick did not answer right away, but instead kept starring at his once long lost friend with vacant eyes, so dark brown that they looked like two

467

puddles of used motor oil. He was gazing at his friend, but judging by his look it was obvious that his mind was elsewhere. McDaniels could almost hear the churning inside his friends' head. Misty on the other hand was becoming uneasy.

"What Broderick?" Sean Kane asked again as he sensed Misty's unease.

"Where did you say your nephews lived again? I mean the exact address?"

McDaniels told him and then looked at Misty for confirmation, who nodded in agreement. They were both wondering where the former SEAL was going with this.

Without another word, Broderick swiveled back at his desk, and began working the keyboard again. Suddenly a live satellite image appeared on the large screen. It was the entire area of the McDaniels' brothers neighborhood and the surrounding businesses within a two mile radius. He zoomed in by using a small device similar to a miniature joystick next to his keyboard. He was obviously engaging a satellite more powerful and precise than that used by 'Google Maps', most likely military because the live images were in super hi definition, which made them crisp and precise.

He punched in a few more keys and then in a hoarse murmur said, "Jesus Christ!"

As he swiveled in his chair to face the reverend again, he again immediately realized his indiscretion when he saw the white collar on his neck, instead of a necktie.

"Oh sorry about that Sean."

McDaniels merely made a sweeping gesture with his hand as if swatting away a fly, indicating that the slip by his former swim buddy was of no consequence, there were more important things to deal with right now, and Reverend Sean Kane McDaniels would be the first to tell you that he was no Saint himself.

"What gives Broderick?"

"Did you hear about that Genuine Bank heist?" was the veteran Special Ops man's answering question.

"Yes, it's been all over the news, the gang, whoever they are hit a Genuine Bank armored van, and got away with a little over a million dollars in cold hard cash. Why?"

"The perpetrators," Lenny Broderick continued, "Got away clean. No witnesses, the security cameras were compromised, most likely remotely. A heist that took place in a public area and no one saw anything. A kind of op you and I would have been proud of, and it happened within walking distance of your nephews' apartment."

"So what are you saying?" it was Misty Abdul who asked this time.

"Think about it, a high stakes heist has taken place not too far from your friends' home, Dumisani is a film student I just found out, no, actually TV and Film, and one of the things I was able to find out is that his new school, the one he's about to enroll in, have given its freshmen class, and Dumisani in particular an assignment of filming his surroundings the first few days within his arrival …"

The reverend and Misty exchanged astonished glances. Lenny Broderick being the thorough man he was had hacked into the Art Center's mainframe, and found out all about Dumisani's curriculum. With that in mind, Sean Kane McDaniels sprang to his feet with a frown on his face, not one borne out of anger, far from it, but something else – nothing but unadulterated and naked fear. He could see it now, if Broderick was suggesting what he thought he was, then his nephews were certainly marked for death.

"What are you saying Lenny? The boys, my nephews are witnesses?"

Lenny Broderick pursed his lips thoughtfully and said, "I can't say for certain, but what else could it be?"

Before the priest could answer, the former SEAL continued:

"The boys are in the same vicinity of a very brazen and sophisticated heist, obviously orchestrated by some very powerful people with access to resources that boggle the mind, and then three days later, in broad daylight just as much, the bad guys force themselves into their home with all kinds of firepower, demanding their camcorder. What was on it that they were ready to kill for? I mean Sean, you don't make those kind of enemies when you've been in a new country for a little less than two weeks."

McDaniels suddenly felt his knees weaken as the bile rose to his throat. It took all of his training and then some to not show his feelings to the others, but his former swim buddy and teammate within that unique fraternity known as the Unites States Navy Seals saw the truth by merely looking into his eyes. After all, they had experienced hell on earth together and survived. They hoped they will again, this time for the sake of two innocent young men who had wanted nothing other than to start a new life, in a new country known for making your dreams come true after they themselves had experienced their own version of hell in the country they were born.

"Lenny," McDaniels said in a tone filled with dread. "Can you help me find my nephews, and I mean right away before these people do?"

The former SEAL nodded slowly.

"I've installed a software in the phone that they have, Misty's phone to be precise, to work not only as a homing device but as a bug as well, you will be able to track them down and also hear them even when their phone is off. Just do me a favor, when you leave here, get a throwaway phone and call me the second you have it and that way I'll have the number. Once you're done with it, destroy it right away."

He then raised a cautionary finger and said, "Just know this Sean Kane, if I can find them, so can they."

He did not have to spell it out to them, and to Sean Kane McDaniels in particular that time was of the essence and they had to get moving right away.

"Thank you blood brother," Sean Kane McDaniels said.

The two men stood and met at the center of the basement and hugged.

"Good luck, now go find your nephews," Lenny Broderick said.

"I appreciate all your help."

As they broke from their brief but brotherly embrace Broderick said, "Don't forget to get that burn phone first chance you get. And the moment you make contact, hand your phone to Misty and use her's."

The reverend nodded. Broderick then turned to Misty Abdul, his hand outstretched for a handshake. Instead, the beautiful young woman did an amazing and totally unexpected thing, she ignored the handshake and hugged him instead, to show her utmost gratitude.

"Thanks for all your help Mr. Broderick," Misty said with a smile.

"Lenny," he said almost out of breath as he recovered from the jolt of electricity that ran through his body, "Call me Lenny, Misty."

"Okay, thanks Lenny," she obliged him.

At last the spell was broken and soon all three were climbing up the stairs that led from the basement and into the cozy living room.

"Call anytime you need me, McDaniels, I will be watching you every step of the way, and once again make sure you get me the number of the burn phone you get right away," Broderick said as he watched his friends get into the reverend's Nissan Altima to fulfill the second phase of their dangerous undertaking.

McDaniels simply nodded his consent as Broderick watched them from his porch as they drove away. The former SEAL did not like the odds faced by his former partner among the 'Frogmen'. The way things stood, McDaniels and his sidekick stood no chance against whoever it was who was coming after his nephews.

It was time, Lenny pondered, to get proactive. His honor required it, his training allowed that, and lastly his loyalty to his former swim buddy demanded it. This man had once saved his life, and it was time to reciprocate.

Like everyone else, Lenny Broderick had heard of the 'Genuine Bank Armored Car Heist'. It was a precise takedown that had been executed by professionals with Special Forces training most likely. The shot taken at the driver through that tiny crevice, and most likely from a moving vehicle, and the downing of the computers tasked with operating the surveillance cameras minutes before the takedown, and back in operation, minutes after the heist spoke volumes of their depth and power.

Now that he had a chance to look at it for the second time, thanks to McDaniels' visit, he had a hunch that the theft and the attack on Sasha and Dumisani, two young men he had yet to meet, was somewhat connected. Yes, he was grabbing at straws, there was no strong evidence, actually scratch that, none at all to link the two, just a hunch. However, it was hunches that made or broke them in their world.

This is what their instructors had taught them during their gruesome training to, among other things, trust their instincts.

He went back to his basement, and was soon in front of his console. Broderick then brought up the biographies of the detectives investigating the robbery, and the two charged with the attack at the McDaniels' residency. As he dug deeper into their backgrounds and hacked into their personal lives, the one named Daniel Frazier caught his interest. He dug deeper, and it was like peeling an onion in that one thing led to another and he started seeing a path. A path that led right back here in Monrovia California, in the form of a potential presidential candidate, Gilbert Price and his brother Declan.

"Jesus H. Christ in heaven and your mother Mary," the former SEAL murmured to himself. And then added disingenuously, "Sorry reverend Sean Kane, but I'm sure you'll understand."

He had opened pandora's box, and from what he uncovered, the only person he could bring into the loop about what he had unearthed was detective 'Danny Boy's' partner, Rick Chavez. Broderick thought him a straight shooter. What he needed now was someone within the law enforcement fraternity, and so far this man Chavez was someone he thought he could trust, at least for now, and to a point.

CHAPTER 53

THE FIRST STOP Sean Kane McDaniels and Misty made was at a Walmart Super Store off of Mountain and Myrtle Street off the 210 Freeway in Monrovia. Here they got a couple of top of the line burn phones, and he gave the other to Misty, just to be on the safe side, more was never bad in situations such as these he had long found out.

The moment they were in possession of the phones they had them fired up and ready, after purchasing at least a month's worth of minutes, even though he doubted they were going to need that much. The way McDaniels saw it, it was better to have more and not need them, than need them and not have them. He then contacted Broderick, who immediately went to work, and almost immediately he was able to hear his nephews talking. On the small screen of his phone and Misty's, he also saw live images of them and where they were at that moment. It was surreal as it was breathtaking that for a moment the reverend could hardly believe his eyes and ears.

Ain't technology grand, he thought to himself.

They were at a place, he observed, a small restaurant called the 'Sukasa' in Huntington Park, about twenty six miles away from where they were. The reverend felt the adrenaline turn to icicles in his

474

blood as it ran in his veins, the moment he heard his boys' voices and images emanating from the screen and tiny speaker of his burn phone. He almost blasphemed, but caught himself before one of the words he had long ago sworn not to utter left his lips.

When they were finally back on the 210 west, the Altima was moving as fast as it could under the circumstances. Broderick had warned his friend that if they could find the brothers, so could the bad guys, thus it was a matter of who was going to get to them first. Sean Kane would have preferred to step on it, but now was certainly not the time to get pulled over by some overzealous California Highway Patrol Cop for speeding. Instead he kept his speed five miles above the legal limit of 65 Miles/hr.

They were past the Lake Avenue exit when Misty Abdul sighed and asked a question Sean Kane McDaniels knew was coming any moment.

"Sean," she said as she turned in her seat and as far as her seatbelt would allow. "Who is that man, Lenny Broderick, what's his story?"

The priest, the vicar, Sean Kane McDaniels focused on the tarmac ahead, wondering how much he could tell her for some of it was still classified information, but he knew he had to tell her everything about his acquaintance and himself. The beautiful young woman had so far earned his full trust.

"You've heard of the United States Navy SEALs, yes?"

Misty nodded and said, "Yes … well sort of."

"It's a fraternity in the army, or more specifically the United States Navy. The acronym stands for Sea Air and Land. A highly trained unit of commandos who are sent on highly secretive, delicate, and for the most part very dangerous missions. The Bin Laden raid for example was conducted by a special unit within the

SEALs called 'SEAL Team Six', the best of the best, and the selection process into this elite unit is brutal, with a sixty-eight percent dropout rate."

He went on to tell her more, and could not stop, especially about the SEAL selection process. Concisely, the reverend continued by telling Misty that it was human nature, for example, to seek shelter, to either stay warm or dry or cool depending on the conditions. SEALs on the other hand were an exception to this rule. Knowing that they could be called upon at any moment, they took it upon themselves to train in the worst possible conditions. It was why, McDaniels emphasized, they had to endure *'Hell Week'* during their selection process.

During this time, candidates were deprived of sleep for days on end and marched continuously into the cold surf of the pacific at all hours, in soiled sandy uniforms. Most of them could handle the physical torment, the academic rigors were challenging but not overtaxing, and the verbal assaults from the instructors was for the most part ignored. It was the cumulative effect of all these however that got to the SEAL candidates. By the time *'Hell Week'* arrived they were already in a weakened state.

Their bodies were sore, their nerves were frayed, and then the very bedrock of mental stability was yanked from underneath them. They were robbed of sleep and warmth. And when the body is deprived of these two *basic* necessities, individuals begin to do strange and unpredictable things. This was when most men broke and rang the bell, signaling that they were dropping out.

To the average citizen, waking up a group of young men by slamming metal trash can lids together at 2 am was cruel enough, but after you added in the fact that the men had just gone to bed 30 minutes

476

earlier, and had not been allowed more than an hour of sleep in three days, it seemed downright inhuman.

But the SEALs weren't just looking for anyone. There was nothing nice or normal about warfare. It was mentally and physically exhausting, and was all done without the comfort of a bed, a hot shower, and warm food. Most important, it was unlike any other job for one plain reason – *you couldn't just quit*. If you were working for an airline, he told her, and you got sick of throwing heavy suitcases around, you could at a moment's notice walk away from it all. If you didn't like your boss at work you could easily quit.

In the world of the SEALs, the reverend went on to explain, there was no quitting, because quitting usually meant that you had to die or someone else did. That, more than anything else, was what '*Hell Week*' was all about. The men who ran the Naval Special Warfare Center in Coronado California, needed to find out *who could take it*, because in the world of Special Operations or 'Spec Ops' to some, quitting was not an option.

The reverend went on to explain that before he found 'escape into the cloth', he too had been a member of this elite unit and so was Lenny Broderick. In fact he and the Hi Tech wiz were members of the same SEAL training class. They trained together, and were swim buddies. SEALs were usually trained in pairs, and the two men, McDaniels and Broderick were paired together.

When Iraq invaded neighboring Kuwait, a move that sparked the first Gulf War, the coalition forces of Britain, France, Germany, The Netherlands, and the United States sent their Special Forces Commandos behind enemy lines to infiltrate Iraq. One such team were the SEALs, a team which McDaniels and Broderick were a part of.

Their sole purpose was to scour the Iraqi Desert in what was called 'Scud Hunts'. Their mission being to hunt and destroy Iraqi Scuds which were for the most part camouflaged, and moved from one point to the next via a Scud Transporter Erector. In order to provoke Israel into entering the war, Saddam Hussein, the Iraqi dictator, had ordered his troops to fire scud missiles at the Jewish Nation, with the hope that if they entered the fray, that alone would break the coalition forces by forcing the Arab Nations to abandon the NATO troops and join Iraq, or at the very least stay neutral.

On one of those missions, Broderick and McDaniels got separated from the rest of their colleagues, and had to hike the desert on foot, evading Iraqi patrols along the way, and when they managed to commandeer a vehicle from some locals on the way to their farm, the incident was reported to the local police, who in turn informed the army and two attack helicopters were deployed.

The moment their vehicle was spotted, it was hit with a missile, but miraculously the two men were spared, which McDaniels would later attribute to providence, but Lenny Broderick was badly injured and McDaniels had to carry him on his back, hiking the rest of the way, twenty eight miles through the most hostile and enemy infested terrain, until he reached the Syrian border and safety for this was friendly territory.

An extraction team was then dispatched to rescue the two men. Sean Kane McDaniels had fulfilled the time honored code of the United States Navy SEALs of never leaving your comrade behind, alive, dead, or wounded. It was during this second phase of his journey, with a half dead colleague on his back, armed with only a pistol, a bag of iron rations, and one canteen of water when McDaniels had an epiphany.

He felt the presence of God in that desert. Only the Lord, he believed, could have given him that superhuman strength to hike that desert. And after the war, when he requested an early honorable discharge from the Navy, the request was granted with a Congressional Medal of Honor for valor in the face of incredible odds. He then joined the Ministry and became an ordained Minister, a warrior of God.

Lenny Broderick followed soon thereafter, the moment he reached state side, and fully recovered from his wounds, and with his pension, savings, and a GI Bill started a security consulting business. He became successful in ways not even he could have imagined in his wildest fantasies. However, the former SEAL knew and never forgot that he was alive today and living the good life because of one man, Sean Kane McDaniels the priest. And he made a personal promise to himself that if ever the time came when his savior needed his help, he would be there for him.

This was one promise he intended to keep and more. So when one day his former swim buddy unexpectedly showed up at his doorstep to solicit his help in finding his nephews who were on the run, the man was more than happy to reciprocate.

CHAPTER 54

HUNTINGTON PARK, CALIFORNIA – 131 MILES
FROM THE SAN DIEGO BORDER – 11:38 AM.

WHEN THE ALTIMA PULLED ONTO Pacific Boulevard in Huntington Park, Sean Kane McDaniels was already in hyper tactical mode, as he felt his old battle instincts return. It was not something he willed or wished, it just came like the rising sun or a flame of fire coming alive from ash. It was his training he knew as a former SEAL and as a martial artist. Misty Abdul was seated on the passenger seat next to him, smartphone in hand, which as they got closer to where Sasha and Dumisani were apparently, the images and the voices emanating from the tiny speaker and screen became more and more crisp.

The young woman could hardly contain her excitement, it was very surreal.

"They're getting ready to leave Sean," she said in a harsh whisper as if afraid of being overheard. "They've seen someone or something that has spooked them and are ready to bail."

"Oh no, they found them," Sean Kane said in despair.

"There's a small street coming up," Misty said.

Without another word, the reverend turned left on an obscure street that ran north to south, and was hard to miss because it intersected with the busiest street in the city. He checked his heartrate and took several breaths to bring it under control as Misty watched him curiously.

He did not have a weapon, only surprise, which he knew could beat the strongest. McDaniels looked at his reflection in the rearview mirror, fixed his hair and the priestly collar on his neck so no one could miss it. The reverend knew that with the collar displayed in the manner that it was, no one, least of all his enemies would expect such a man to initiate physical violence. The unfortunate would be victim would certainly hesitate when faced with this, and that hesitation would be all he would need – hesitation will make your worst nightmare come true.

"Okay Misty," Sean Kane said, "please stay here while I go get my nephews."

She opened her mouth to protest, but the priest shot his arm out forestalling any argument. He had been expecting that, resistance from his young confederate, and it was time to set his foot down and show who was really in charge. After all, he was trained for such things Misty was not. From what he and his former swim buddy were able to gather, and Misty Abdul knew for she had been on the receiving end, was that these men they were about to encounter were stone cold killers.

"No Misty, it's best that you stay put. There's a good, no a better than even chance, that things could get hairy out there, and I'll need you here in case we need to make a quick getaway."

The older man could tell that his unwitting sidekick was still not totally convinced.

"I still think I can help Sean Kane, you'll probably need me out there." Misty was looking around as she said this, and McDaniels thought he knew what it was that was making her a bit apprehensive. It was the neighborhood, he realized.

"You'll be fine Misty. Just stay in the car and hold on to that phone. You're in a public place so you're safe, just stay here don't leave even for a second, just text if you need to – no calling in case I'm in a situation where stealth will be imperative."

At last the young woman nodded in agreement. Seeing this, McDaniels played his 'Ace' in the hole by saying, "Besides, there's a chance that one of the goons may recognize you and blow our cover, so it's best if you kept out of sight."

"Oh yes," Misty agreed as she at the same time felt a bit foolish for not realizing the obvious sooner. "I did not think about that. You're right, I'll stay here. Good luck."

And before she could stop herself, Misty leaned over to the preacher as he was opening his door and kissed him on the cheek.

"Please be careful Sean Kane, and bring them back safe, especially Dumi."

The reverend, Sean Kane McDaniels turned and looked straight into those beautiful haunting bedroom eyes, there was a small smile that was creeping from the corner of his mouth. He was about to ask why Dumisani in particular, but realized instantly that there was no need for that. The answer was clearly in her eyes.

In no time, McDaniels was on his way. He had Misty's second smartphone in his palm as he said a silent entreaty to the Maker of the Universe. On the small screen he could tell that his nephews were at least less than a block away, and it looked like they were on the move. He took a deep breath and quickened his pace.

In no time McDaniels was at the back gate of the Sukasa Restaurant, and was just in time to see Bob McNamara and Luis Bramble snooping around, teasers in hand. It was obvious what they were looking for, or more to the point *who* they were looking for – his nephews. The former SEAL braced himself. He was going to take out Bramble first, he was closest to him and most importantly, his back was to the preacher. The men were obviously not expecting any resistance let alone an ambush. And that was what they got, a well-executed surprise attack. It was over in no time, and it was time to reunite with Misty Abdul and get the heck out of dodge.

***

In spite of the reassurances bestowed on her, Misty Abdul could not help feeling uneasy. The sensation started creeping in like the steady flow of a slow moving muddy river. It began soon after Sean Kane McDaniels left to go find his nephews. After the older man left, Misty felt as if a warm protective blanket that had been shielding her from the biting cold had been rudely and unceremoniously yanked off of her with no warning.

It was a bright, lively southern California mid-summer morning and the area was bustling with activity. People were up and about, driving up and down the small street, and others were on foot on the sidewalk. She took in her surroundings once again, there seemed to be nothing suspicious at all as no one seemed to pay her any mind.

As the minutes ticked by, the tension began to wear off and she began to relax at last. She then rolled down both windows, Misty was seated now at the driver's seat as instructed. She then closed her eyes briefly and took in a deep breath of air. They were not too far from the Pacific Ocean and thus Misty thought she caught a tiny whiff of the salty air that came from it.

At that moment she noticed a young Asian woman walking toward her on the paved sidewalk. She had long shiny dark hair and was dressed in a long cream white summer dress, and in spite of the large sunglasses covering her face, Misty in an off handed sort of way could tell that the woman was quite pretty in fact.

She appeared to be a tourist of some sort because she had a camera in one hand, the kind most common with Japanese holidaymakers, and in the other she had what looked like a map. She was looking around as if searching for something. The lady passed the car as she headed south on the sidewalk, but immediately stopped and backtracked a few steps until she was a few paces from Misty's half open window. She unfolded the paper she was holding, and starred at Misty, who was on high alert now.

The lovely Asian woman's glossy lips parted to form a smile, and Misty was immediately at ease.

"Excuse me miss, sorry to bother you," the stranger said in an accent that told Misty that the woman was certainly a foreigner. Her thick accent and the fact that she was Asian, the stranger was what some Southern Californians derogatorily referred to as 'FOBs' – 'Fresh Off The Boat'.

"Yes?" Misty said.

Even though she was at ease, she still watched the woman closely. Something did not feel right, did not pass the smell test, but she was comforted by the fact that they were, as the reverend had said, in a public area with too many eyes watching, so she felt safe even though something, some sixth sense told her there was something not quite right about this woman.

"Well, my friend and I think we took the wrong turn off of the freeway. We're trying to get to Venice Beach," the woman said.

Wow, they're way off, Misty thought, because Venice Beach was at least twenty miles southwest from where they were.

"Oh, that's way off miss," Misty said, suddenly eager to help and chalking her suspicions to unnecessary paranoia. "You may have to probably get back on the 110 freeway and …"

At that moment, Misty heard a sound from behind, the clicking sound of her passenger door opening, and before she could react, a man she had never seen before was in the car seated on the passenger side seat, and jabbing a long black object she quickly realized was a gun fitted with a silencer poking at her ribs. It was *DeJa'Vu*!

And before she could move, let alone utter a sound, the Asian woman stepped forward and casually leaned through the open window, her face barely a foot away from Misty's who was forced to recoil a bit, but for the damn gun poking at her ribs.

"Now miss Abdul," the woman said softly but firmly and in a voice devoid of the thick accent she had heard earlier. "Be still and behave yourself."

Misty was thunderstruck! They knew who she was, and if they did, that meant they knew all about what she and the reverend were up to. So much for the element of surprise. It was them who had been stunned by a crafty opponent, it had been them who had been caught napping every step of the way. Now she looked like an animal caught in a trap. Misty was hoping, *no* willing that someone would realize what was going on and come to her rescue. No such luck. This was a kidnapping job handled by professionals.

Her bowls turned to water and her knees felt like jelly as the man beaconed with his weapon, ordering her out of the vehicle.

"Nice and slow," he said. "Any funny business or if you look sideways you will lose a kidney. Nod if you understand."

She did. And the lady gently took the phone she had in her hand as the other goon prodded her on the small of her back with the business end of his silencer, urging her to keep walking. In no time, they were leading her to a black SUV, but before they left, the Asian woman, Mi Kyong Park left a generic cellphone on the driver's seat, which Sean Kane McDaniels and his nephews would later find.

The moment Misty was in the backseat of the SUV, she was sandwiched by yet two other rough looking men she was also seeing for the first time, and a black hood was placed over her head. The man who had pointed the gun at her assumed the wheel, and Mi Kyong sat on the passenger side. After the assassin broke open Misty's phone and threw away the parts in different garbage cans by the road, she gave the order to the driver, and the SUV drove away, headed west on Pacific Boulevard.

CHAPTER 55

THE BOYS LOOKED AT THE EMPTY CAR, the phone and then at their uncle. They still had their backpacks shouldered like two regular college kids between classes. The one Dumisani had contained the camcorder, *his* camcorder that had sparked this entire fiasco.

"They have taken Misty boys!" Sean Kane McDaniels said, stating the obvious.

"I gathered that," Sasha said. "The question is how do we get her back, and how did they figure she was with you Uncle Sean?"

The man of God had to think about this for a moment. All along he had been operating on the assumption that he had the upper hand in the surprise department. They, whoever he was up against, had no idea who he was and his relation to the McDaniels brothers, or so he thought. Now the tables were turned and Misty Abdul's life was in danger. The stakes couldn't have been any higher, because they involved a totally innocent woman, a woman he had been solely responsible for. She had trusted him implicitly and he had let her down. The thought alone made him sick to the stomach in a way he could have never imagined. For a man who never had kids, it felt as if Misty was the closest thing to the daughter he never had.

He stepped away from his nephews, and took out one of the burn phones he had purchased from Walmart and called Lenny Broderick, and told him all that had happened.

The former SEAL listened patiently, and when he was through there was a very long silence that stretched for almost a minute. The pastor patiently waited him out. Lenny Broderick, besides being a very skilled combatant during his active duty days, the man was also a thinker. Every move, every mission was always well thought out and planned.

"Okay, here's what we're going to do brother," Broderick said at last. "Play along, do as they say, let them think they have you boxed in, and there is absolutely no retreat for you and your boys. In essence what you will be doing is buying time for me to organize a massive counterattack that will end all this."

"How?" McDaniels asked, suddenly very interested in knowing what his friend was up to.

"I've been digging up some very crucial information since you left, something is shaping up, and I'm beginning to see a picture coming together. This is bigger than the heist by the way and has far reaching repercussions. Seems to me that your nephews stumbled into something large with political implications, and I'm not talking simple state politics, I'm talking the White House, 1600 Pennsylvania Avenue my friend."

Sean Kane McDaniels was thunderstruck, not certain he was hearing his friend correctly.

"What are you saying Lenny? That the president of the United States or someone close to him is involved?"

"Not quite, I'm talking campaign funds. You know these days running a campaign, especially the ultimate one costs a fortune, right? And fundraising is a pain in the posterior, right?"

"Right," the man of God concurred again.

"Well, like I said a picture is beginning to form, but I've told you more than enough already," Broderick said, inching back a little. "This line is secure, but I can't take that chance of telling you everything I've uncovered thus far on the line, not with the way the stakes are at the moment. I'll fill you in later and in person hopefully, right now what's of paramount importance is getting the girl back safe and sound."

"You got that right."

"So, like I said before, play along, do as they say and update me the second after they make contact again. I got you brother and I won't let you down."

"Never thought you would," the older McDaniels reassured his friend.

"One more thing," Broderick said before ending the call. "I think there is a dirty cop in the Altadena Sheriff's Station, a detective named Daniel Frazier. He is in charge of the team that is looking for your boys, and he's been feeding them chaff so they look elsewhere while he buries the truth. He's doing this at the behest of someone I'll tell you about a little later once I confirm and cross reference the facts that I have so far. His partner though, Rick Chavez, is a good cop and definitely on our side. Anyway, I've got to end this call brother and get back to work. But remember, play along when they call, and let the boys know that's important."

The pastor nodded even though the other man could not see him, and then pressed the 'END' button.

Again, his nephews looked at him for answers. He was the leader now. Dumisani seemed to be taking the news of Misty's obvious abduction the hardest of the two it seemed, Sean Kane observed. All of a sudden the young man was sweaty and jittery, like he was jonesing, but instead chalked it up to the stress. Dumisani was indeed jonesing, he desperately needed another dose of the Oxys and was waiting for their backs to be turned to him so he could quickly, but unobtrusively pop a couple in his mouth and chew them.

Sasha on the other hand was still seething over this unexpected turn of events, and that it had come to them from left field.

"But uncle Sean, how could they have known of your involvement?" Sasha wanted to know.

"I can't say for sure Sasha, but somehow they managed to figure out my connection to you two. If they were able to do that, it also means they know my background, my military training and service before I gave my life to the Lord. Look son, we're dealing with a highly sophisticated bunch of individuals, and unfortunately this is about to get worse before it gets better."

They were still standing by Sean Kane's Sedan, waiting for the call about making the exchange. There was no point hiding now. The enemy had them, to use the cops' parlance, mugged and numbered.

"Why is it about to get worse Uncle Sean?" Dumisani asked.

He had surreptitiously swallowed two Oxys and they were starting to work their magic. He was not jittery anymore nor was he sweating. His uncle noticed the sudden night and day change, and knew something was up with his nephew. They would have to deal with that eight headed monster later.

"You heard what they said right?" Sean Kane asked, "if we contact the cops or the FBI they will kill her. So we will have to assume that they will kill her, but we …" the reverend sighed and then rubbed his tired eyes, and looked around. He was then silent for a while.

"What is it Uncle Sean?" Sasha asked.

"That tape these people want is very important to them, and I'm talking life and death important. And it's our only leverage. It's the only thing keeping Misty Abdul alive, the only thing keeping *us* alive. And we cannot under any circumstances cede that advantage."

The brothers nodded solemnly as Dumisani unconsciously held the backpack containing the camera even tighter. On the other hand, sitting around and waiting for things to happen was certainly not an option nor was it in the McDaniels DNA – the McDaniels men were ready to fight back.

"Okay!" Sean Kane clapped his hands together once, apparently having reached a decision. "Come on, get in the car boys, we need to get out of here and be on the move. We need to find our girl, basically be ready the moment these goons make contact."

Moments later, the Nissan Altima was headed west on Pacific Boulevard. The reverend was trying to put himself in his enemies' shoes, and thus took the same route he presumed they would have taken for the simple reason that it led to the nearest major freeway. He knew that they were going to take Misty Abdul to some place remote, most likely far from prying eyes, and possibly not easy to access by vehicle without being spotted miles away.

The Harbor Freeway, the 110, and the likeliest of the escape route, ran north/south. From there, Sean Kane knew it was anyone's guess. His plan was to already be on the freeway the moment the kidnappers called again. He had already given Lenny Broderick the specifications of the phone they had left, and he knew that his friend was at the moment feverishly

491

trying to break its encryptions and use it to their advantage.

They rode in silence as he connected to the 110 South, and it went on like that until they joined the 405 Freeway North, one of the busiest, if not *the* busiest interstate in Southern California. The three men were still consumed by their own thoughts, when their uncle finally broke the ice.

"Boys," Sean Kane McDaniels said at last, "I'm so sorry that I did not make it to the funeral."

Dumisani, who was seated in the front seat next to his uncle, turned to face his brother in the back seat. The two exchanged that familiar look that communicated their thoughts, which said, *Are you kidding me? Your brother and sister in law are murdered in cold blood by marauding poachers and all you can say is sorry you couldn't make it?* They expected more from a man of God, after all death and the afterlife were supposed to be his specialties.

"Yes, we understand Uncle Sean," Sasha said at last, as if placating him in a way.

Any resentments the brothers may have felt toward their uncle was forgiven the moment they saw that assailant McNamara flying sideways, after being struck by their uncle who had come looking for them and had rescued them right in the nick of time. They were on the 405 Freeway heading north now, and the traffic was not as bad as it normally was on this late morning.

Sean Kane sighed and then said, "Just know that your father and mom were very wonderful people, I loved them dearly and when the time comes I will honor them properly by …"

He was suddenly interrupted by a sound that froze all three men in the car. It was the shrill sound of the phone the abductors, Misty's abductors, had left for them. The black phone had been by his side in a cup holder and in plain view for exactly this reason, and within easy reach the moment it rang. Sean Kane snatched it and immediately pressed the green 'TALK' button of the generic phone.

"Yes?"

After at least five seconds that same disguised voice sounded at the other end.

"Hand the phone to the black brother," the command came again without preamble.

"What?"

"Do it now or the girl dies!"

The reverend, cool as ice, turned to his nephew.

"The kidnappers want to speak to you. Now, remember stay calm no matter the provocation," he said before handing the phone to Dumisani. It was obvious that they figured him to be the weakest link of the trio. "Remember," his uncle added quickly, "the main objection is getting Misty back safe and sound. Keep that in mind at all times."

Dumisani nodded, he could care less about the camcorder and what it had. Hey, if it meant exchanging the damning evidence in exchange for Misty's life, and letting him and his brother be and in peace to pursue their American dream, he was willing to make that deal. However, even as he thought it he knew it would not be that easy. The young African man, just like his Caucasian blood brother had a lot to learn in the cold, harsh world of murder, armed robbery, deception, and ruthless ambition that the people who never wanted their secrets see daylight, also espoused the same of those who knew about them.

This was why Sean Kane McDaniels had sought the help of his former SEAL buddy, for exactly such a scenario of fighting fire with fire when and if the time came.

Dumisani took the phone from his uncle, turned it on speaker, and then braced himself for the storm he knew was coming.

"This is Dumisani McDaniels, the black brother. What is it?" he said this in as calm a voice as he could muster, but mainly to conceal the nervous ring in his tone.

"Is this the negro?" the camouflaged voice emanated from the tiny speaker.

"Yes, I already told you, this is Dumisani McDaniels the negro, where is Misty?"

"The recording and your camcorder or the girl dies."

"I think you've made that clear at least five times and honestly it is getting boring."

"Oh, you wanna get cute now jungle boy?" the voice mocked.

"No, I don't want to get cute, I just want to know that Misty is okay. Can I speak to her?"

"Why?"

Are you kidding me? Dumisani thought to himself.

Aloud he said, "Look, you want something from me, you have my friend and I just want to make sure that she is okay."

"She's okay."

"I'm supposed to just take your word for it?"

"Not like you got a choice now do you?"

The car suddenly slowed down and Dumisani looked up to see that they were hitting a part of the 405 Freeway where traffic was becoming thick, and slowing down rapidly. They were in a place called Westwood. The Wilshire exit, according to the signs, was 4 miles away. Sasha and Sean Kane were listening silently at the conversation – spellbound.

"Actually I do," Dumisani retorted.

Now was the time to lie, to bluster, to blitz, push things a bit and show these people, whoever they were, that he was not scared, that they were *not* scared.

"*Is that right?*" the annoying voice mocked again.

"You see, if you keep playing these games or hurt Misty in any way shape or form, my brother and I will just drop this tape and camcorder at the nearest police station and disappear *after* we tell them all we know."

His uncle and Sasha gave him quizzical looks as if you say *what are you doing?* Or more precisely, *are you out of your mind?*

"*You do that,*" the voice said in a calm and yet menacing way and made more so by the disguise, "*I'm going to start by slicing off her ears, and then her pretty lips. You can guess where I'll go from there if you keep fucking with me! And I won't even kill her, I'll let her live the rest of her pathetic and miserable life as an ugly mute everyone will run from, including you.*"

The bluff backfired, for now Dumisani was frightened by the kidnapper's words, as his imagination ran wild.

He took in a deep breath and said, "Okay, okay … don't do anything stupid. I'll give you the damn tape, just please let her go."

There was a brief pause on the other end of the line before the voice sounded again. "*Good … I had an inkling that that would jog your intellect a bit. Malibu Canyon Park in one hour … alone, we will be watching you. Keep the phone with you at all times, I'll call you when you get there with the next set of instructions.*"

"Assuming I go along, what guarantee do I have that you will let Misty go?" Dumisani demanded.

"*None, that all depends on you and if you follow my instructions to the letter.*"

"What? Did you say Malibu? What is a Malibu?"

"You heard me, Malibu Canyon Park in Calabasas in one hour, now get your ass in gear now or the broad loses an ear, I can start now so you can hear her scream, yes?!"

"No, no, no ... don't do that, I'll do as you say, I just wanted to make sure that I got the name of the place right." Dumisani was horrified.

"Good, and to the two of you listening in on this call," the voice continued, *"I see you anywhere near the area, I will mail you her eyeballs. One last time, if you involve the cops, the FBI or any John Q law and order type, you'll find out what a hot date my men are, and once they're done, we will inject her with the HIV just for good measure."*

The line went dead.

These people are animals, Sean Kane McDaniels thought as he shook his head in despair.

CHAPTER 56

THERE WAS A STUNNED SILENCE in the car after Dumisani's chilling call with Misty Abdul's abductors. The vehicle was now crawling along the 405 Freeway north as traffic got thicker. Sean Kane McDaniels took out a Bluetooth earbud, activated it with his phone and then inserted it in his left ear, away from his nephews' view. Apparently his party on the other end, Lenny Broderick, was on standby because the connection was instant.

"Did you get all that?" the older McDaniels said by way of greeting.

"Got it all, and like I said play along," Broderick said on the other end.

"Play along? "Sean Kane McDaniels asked incredulously. Apparently the reverend was having second thoughts about this part of his friend's strategy, especially after that unsettling call. "My nephew will be out there alone, exposed, with no back up and not to mention in a foreign land." He glanced at Dumisani as he said this, and then back at the road as he negotiated his way through the now heavy traffic.

"My brother," Broderick implored as he resorted to the SEAL code when addressing a close colleague you've been to hell and back with. *"Do you trust me?"*

"That's not the point Lenny you ..."

497

"Brother, do you trust me?"

"Of course," McDaniels said.

"So trust me when I say play along, I will not let you or your nephews down."

The reverend wanted to ask his friend how he was going to accomplish that, but then thought better of it and let it go. He then hung up without another word, placing his trust and faith, and that of his nephews in a man he himself had once saved a long time ago. Sean Kane McDaniels knew that gratitude, just like the beauty in women, fades as the years go by. He had not stayed in touch with Lenny Broderick in decades, and when he did it was only because he had gone looking for him, however he had no choice now but to have faith. It was similar, he reflected, to jumping over a cliff with the hope that there was a net somewhere at the bottom to hold you.

He was silent for a while as he pondered over the phone call with his friend. It was obvious that the ex-SEAL was planning something he had to keep as close to the chest as possible. Now though, was the time to deal with the immediate problem at hand.

The pastor then faced his nephews.

"Okay," Sean Kane McDaniels began as he unconsciously fingered the cross dangling from around his neck. "As we decided earlier, it is obvious that we're dealing with desperate pros here. They're going to kill the girl, am sorry Misty, because any which way you slice it, she's a witness, but we're *not* going to let that happen."

The brothers nodded their agreement. By now traffic had eased up a bit, and Sean Kane was driving the Nissan along the 101 North. This was the freeway that was going to take them to the Malibu Creek Canyon Park.

498

"Okay uncle Sean," Sasha said. "Why only Dumi though and not both of us?"

Sean Kane sighed and said, "They figure he's the weak sister, I mean that figuratively, and he'll be easier to deal with. Well, that's their first mistake."

Dumisani asked, "Shouldn't we notify the police now that we know exactly where they are and where they are holding Misty?"

"My guess is that whoever we're dealing with is well connected with a mole within law enforcement. They will know the moment we make contact and move to some place we don't know and now Misty will be in real danger, so we will have to play this one close to the vest boys, but don't worry Dumi, Sasha and I will be close, and come get you the moment the need arises."

The two brothers shared a more than puzzled look, as the Altima cruised along the 101 north. They were in the nicer part of West Los Angeles County as they drove past the cities of West Hollywood, Sherman Oaks, Woodland Hills, Tarzana, and were now approaching Thousand Oaks. However, Sasha and Dumisani were too caught up in the here and now that they did not appreciate the beauty around them, even though they were in a part of town they had never seen before.

"And just how are you planning on coming to my rescue Uncle Sean?" Dumisani wanted to know.

His uncle glanced at him and then smiled.

"Dumi, do you trust me?" the reverend echoed his former SEAL buddy Lenny Broderick.

"Yes of course, but Uncle Sean that's not what …"

"Trust me Dumi, when I say we will not let you and Misty down."

A sign by the side of the freeway said the Malibu Canyon Park was less than ten miles away. They all noticed it at the same time and fell silent. The moment of truth was upon them. What the three men did not say, but was at the back of their minds was that this could very well be it for them. There was a very good chance that they may all end up dead.

***

Established in 1974 and opened to the public in 1976, the Malibu Creek State Park is a state park that preserves the Malibu Creek Canyon in the breathtaking Santa Monica Mountains. It covers a vast area of 8,215 acres from below the Malibu Lake in the west to Piuma Road in the east. It follows the creek down to the Pacific Ocean, and includes the Adamson House and the creek's mouth in the Malibu Lagoon at the beach. Tapia Park has recently been incorporated as a subunit of the park. It includes natural preserves: the Liberty Canyon which is 730 acres, the Udell Gorge 300 acres, and the 1,920 acre Kaslow Preserve.

The land that is now Malibu Creek State Park was once inhabited by the native Chumash people for millennia. These are a native American people who historically inhabited the Central and the Southern Coastal regions of California, in portions of what is now San Luis Obispo, Santa Barbara, Ventura and Los Angeles. The Chumash were most famous for their redwood canoes, which they used to travel the coastline for hundreds of miles. By the 1860's a few homesteads existed, including the Sepulveda Adobe, which still stands today.

Don Pedro Alcantra Sepulveda was a California pioneer homesteader, who had built his home in 1863 in what is now the Malibu Creek Canyon Park. Because of its vastness on a landscape of over 8,000 acres, the scenery is truly spectacular as it is dramatic with jagged peaks, stunning canyon vistas, oak woodlands, rolling hills, world class hiking trails, and chaparral-covered slopes. And after a good rain the namesake Malibu Creek comes to life. The park is something of a miracle when one considers how little has changed since the Chumash inhabited the area 5,000 to 10,000 years ago.

A number of feature films and television series have been made in this location from as far back as 1913, when Hollywood was coming into itself. The 1968 movie '*Planet Of The Apes*' was shot here with a magnificent set constructed specifically for this movie along the banks of the Malibu Creek. The 1958 movie '*The Defiant Ones*' starring Sidney Poitier and Tony Curtis was among many more that were shot here, including classic TV shows like '*M.A.S.H*', and '*Tour Of Duty*'. The park is still used occasionally for filming.

Two and a half miles due west, and very much visible from a trail along Goat's Butte is two mountain peaks, and between them is an old barn that was constructed to house cattle and horses that were used in a western feature film that was shot almost entirely at the Malibu Creek Canyon Park in the mid 1950's. Even though the forest has reclaimed most of the surroundings, making it hard to negotiate the trail leading to it, the barn is still very much intact, well hidden, and not well known by many to be there. A perfect place to conduct activities one did not want seen or heard.

It was also a perfect place to hide Misty Abdul, which was exactly what her kidnappers were doing as they waited on the McDaniels brothers, Dumisani in particular, to make the exchange.

**

Moments later, after they saw the sign that informed them that the Malibu Creek State Park was a few miles away, the Nissan turned left and onto a dirt road that went on for two miles until they arrived at the entrance. The three men looked around while in the car without a word. All was quiet, there was not a single soul or vehicle in sight, which could only mean one thing, their enemies had made certain that the park was deserted, devoid of potential witnesses. It was also reasonable to assume that they were being watched.

Dumisani and Sasha saw something else. The place for as far as they could see, was eerily similar to the landscape of their parents' ranch in Maun, right from the rolling countryside, the forestation and the mountains. The brothers then looked at one another, and agreed without uttering a single word. It was hard to believe this was a landscape in Los Angeles County and not home.

The reverend glanced at his watch, 2:49PM. The abductors had demanded that they be on site in one hour two and a half hours ago. Sasha had asked about that, if being late wasn't going to put Misty in danger. The reverend, who was somewhat well versed with such situations in his previous life, scoffed and told his nephews that besides traffic being a pain in the proverbial behind in Los Angeles, something the kidnappers were well aware of, in order to wrestle some of the control back, it was necessary to not follow through on things you can easily get away with without pushing your luck.

He was about to open his mouth to say something to break the ice and the inevitable tension, when instead the ringing of the generic cellphone did it for him.

No one needed to tell them that they were being watched, because there was absolutely no way this could have been a coincidence. They stared at the phone in the cup holder for a second, and then at Dumisani, who following a brief hesitation grabbed it, and pressed the green 'TALK' button.

"Yes!" Dumisani said in an icy voice he was using mainly to cover his nervousness.

The now familiar metallic voice said, *"That's far enough. Now get your late ass out of that car and walk due west the rest of the way. Tell your friends to turn around and head back to the freeway, and not stop until they get to Pasadena. Someone will be watching them to make sure they're doing exactly as instructed."*

Dumisani felt a cold chill run down his spine as he realized that he would be going into an unknown operation naked, in other words alone and with no back up.

"Whoa! Whoa! Slow down there whoever you are, wait a minute how … " Dumisani said almost frantically but determined all the same to maintain control.

"What?" was the curt interruption.

"How is Misty and I going to get back home?"

"Just worry about you and her coming out alive," was the ominous response. *"And that will be up to you if you follow my instructions, which you're not doing now are you? So I'd suggest you get going right this minute. I'll say this once and only once, hold on to that phone and follow the path and don't deviate unless I tell you to."*

The line went dead and Dumisani immediately looked at his uncle and then at his brother, who both nodded, indicating that they too heard every word.

"Yeah," Sean Kane McDaniels confirmed, "we heard it all."

"Okay," Dumisani said, "but what I'm I going to do Uncle Sean? I'm totally disorientated, I can't tell east from west or north from south, let alone find my way through some canyon."

Sean Kane nodded thoughtfully and said, "Hold on."

He tapped the Bluetooth earbud and waited a few seconds before the connection was made, long enough for him to notice that it took a little longer this time.

"Uncle Sean what's .." Sasha was about to say, but his uncle raised his hand to silence him, apparently he was not aware that his uncle was making a call because he was on the side of the car where he could not see the Bluetooth.

"Yes brother, I heard it all," came the voice at the other end of Lenny Broderick. *"They think no one else can hear them because they have a highly sophisticated jammer that can discourage any eavesdropping within a half mile radius. That's why your connection to me was a bit delayed at first, but now we're good, but let's air on the side of caution and not stay on the phone for too long."*

"But like I told you before, my nephew will be all alone man," Sean Kane said almost in a whisper, not because he did not want his nephews to overhear his conversation, but the overwhelming tension in the vehicle at that very moment.

"Yes, I get it all brother, the problem at least for them is that they think no one can hear them and don't know that I'm on to them and that I'm at least ninety percent sure of their endgame, just do as I say and I think we will be fine."

The reverend knew all this, and was getting a bit impatient at what he saw as his friend ducking the immediate problem at hand.

"Okay that's all fine and good, but how about my nephew?"

"Just tell him to do as told, just as you should."

The line then went dead, Sean Kane then looked his nephew in the eye. It was the moment of truth.

"Alright Dumi," he said, "this is a State Park, follow their instructions and you'll be fine. We will not be far behind."

"But uncle Sean, they want you to turn around and head back to Pasadena, which means they'll most likely have you followed. So how are you going to watch my back?"

The priest smiled, very much like someone who knew something others did not.

"That's what they think," he said.

Sasha added by saying, "As for the bush Dumi, don't worry about it, it's nothing compared to what we're used to."

Dumisani smiled, not because what his brother said was reassuring, but to hide his nervousness, something he did not want the two men to see.

"Right on Sasha," he said as he gave him the thumbs up, the universal sign to show that everything was okay.

It was time for Dumisani McDaniels to leave and go find Misty Abdul, and the unknown. The three men got together for an impromptu hug, and their uncle said a prayer.

He concluded by saying, " … and watch over your son as you have O Father in Heaven."

Dumisani opened the door, got out, and shouldered the back backpack that had the camera. The weather was dry and hot but the young man barely felt it as he held the cellphone, the lifeline to the kidnappers, but most importantly to Misty Abdul, the woman he had fallen hopelessly in love with. He could not even begin to imagine how terrified she must be at the moment. The young man took a few deep breaths to calm his heartrate before he turned to face his brother and uncle one more time. This was going to be difficult, facing the unknown alone.

"Stay calm Dumi, no matter the situation, remember Misty is the main objection," Sean Kane McDaniels said.

"I won't let anything happen to you," Sasha added for good measure.

Dumisani smiled, albeit nervously and raised his fist. His brother did the same, a signal to one another although somewhat subtle communicated a lot. It said, we've been in a jam before that we got out of, hopefully, we will get out of this one as well.

At last he turned to leave and Sasha and his uncle got into the Altima, and as instructed, drove off. The last image Dumisani saw of his uncle was of him tapping the Bluetooth earbud in such a way that if someone was watching their exit, say through a high power pair of binoculars, that person would think the reverend was brushing off an errant strand of hair. However, Dumisani McDaniels knew better and the thought gave him solace. His uncle was communicating with the mysterious man on the other end on a line that was supposedly blocked in this area. This gave him a sense of calm that helped dispel the naked fear that was now dangerously close to spilling over and out of control.

And the last thing Dumisani McDaniels could afford was letting his fear get the best of him. Fear he knew was a feeling like any other, like getting cold for instance, it was a matter of controlling it. The martial arts had taught him that a long time ago, now he was going to need that training and much more if he and Misty were going to survive this, now he was on a quest of not saving his life, but that of a woman who he was not even sure she felt the same for him, and most importantly he was going to fight for his and his brother's American dream.

CHAPTER 57

As Dumisani followed the path into the interior of the park, he could feel the danger in the air with every step he took. The danger was unmistakable as it was real this time because with every step he took he was getting closer to it, this time alone and not with his brother as it would normally have been ever since they were kids. In short Dumisani felt naked without Sasha to watch his back. Once in a while he would be startled by a Deer (the park had many of them) that would take fright, and scamper into the surrounding forest, or a rabbit here and there. It seemed as if these animals were everywhere.

He stopped and looked around. All was quiet except the singing of birds, and the sound of insects. The heat, even though twilight was only a couple of hours away, was still almost unbearable and he did not realize why until he took off his sweater and tied the arms to his waist. That was when the phone rang again, the only other thing he had besides the backpack with the camera. He did not have any weapons, because it was agreed upon earlier that he would most likely be frisked the moment he got to his destination.

Even though Dumisani McDaniels did not carry a weapon, he was a weapon. The thought alone gave him yet another surge of adrenaline. However, something else was happening. It began with the dullness behind his eyes, followed by a dry throat and lips. Soon that sensation was going to be followed by blurry vision, nausea, sweating, and if left untreated at that point, diarrhea, fever, and the dreaded chills.

"Yes!" Dumisani said the moment he pressed the green 'TALK' button.

"*Having fun yet?*" the metallic voice mocked.

If they, or whoever it was, behind that voice was intending to piss Dumisani off, that person was doing one heck of a job. Add to the fact that he was almost 'jonesing', the young man fought to keep his anger in check. The path was now cutting through thick forest, and looked now like a meandering tunnel.

"You know," Dumisani said as he wiped his sweaty brow with the back of his hand, and at the same time avoided branches that seemed to block him from moving forward. "This is getting a bit irritating, where am I going and when do I get to talk to Misty?"

As he ventured deeper and deeper into the park forest, the path kept looping around and at times it looked as if he was retracing his footsteps, making him wonder how on earth Sasha and their uncle were going to find him. Their enemies were cunning, no doubt, they had picked their rendezvous point, wherever it was, very well.

"*In about twenty minutes at your current pace, you will see an abandoned barn that has not earthly business in the middle of a park. It was an old movie prop that ...*"

"Hey, hey, moron, I don't care about all that okay? How do I get Misty back and ..."

"*Keep walking!*"

The line went dead. However, during that brief exchange the kidnapper had said something subtle but telling nonetheless, and in such a way that Dumisani almost missed it. '*In about twenty minutes at your current pace …*'

How did they know his current pace to a point that they could time his arrival? Jesus! He thought. They were watching him somehow. This worried the young man from Botswana but he trudged on. In retrospect he should not have been surprised. This type of thing, kidnapping and luring their loved ones, Misty in this case, to some forgotten corner of a large state park was obviously not their first rodeo. They had done this type of thing before, and were thus familiar with every corner and unknown areas of the park.

There was a particular section where the foot path dipped into what looked like a mini gorge as he approached the two mountains in the west, he could also smell the salty air, which told him that the Pacific Ocean was not very far away. The path was flanked by overgrown bushes and trees, making it hard to negotiate his way through and constantly having to parry away the branches that were temporarily blocking his sight and path. Meanwhile, the dullness behind his eyes was getting worse and his vision was blurring. Somehow Dumisani felt he was getting closer to his destination, something that accelerated his heartbeat and with it the stress. He reached into his pocket and fished out two Oxys, threw them into his mouth, and chewed them to dust before he washed them down with a swig of water from the bottle he had in his bag specifically for that purpose.

"Mama watch over me," Dumisani muttered to himself.

The 'Mama' he was sending the entreaty to, asking that she watch over him was not Natalie McDaniels, the woman who had raised him like she did her own, and never once had she failed in that duty. No, it was to a mother he never met, the mother who gave him life, Naledi Moletsane, for in African culture, especially Southern African they believed in the power of their ancestors – something his white brother nor his white parents would never understand - for it was rooted like code in the black African's recessive gene.

The foot path began its gentle upward climb, and when he broke free from the bushes, he saw it right in front of him – the barn. It looked old, dilapidated and abandoned. Nevertheless it was still intact. It appeared as if the area around it had been cleared at one time, but whoever had been using it left, and the forest came back as it always does, reclaiming its place. The vegetation that grew as a result was different from the rest of the area, making it well hidden.

Dumisani stopped, frozen in awe as he looked at the barn that was now about fifty yards away. It had been built using flat planks that evidently had been coated with copper boron azole to discourage attack from termites, which explained why it had survived the decades virtually intact. From where he was standing, partly hidden by the surrounding trees and bushes that fringed the pathway, Dumisani guessed the dimensions to be fifty feet long and forty wide. The double doors that marked the entrance, one of which was damaged with gaping holes suggested that the barn stood facing south.

He felt the opioids. Powdered oxycodone produced the best high, he was finding out very quickly, because that defeated the manufacturers time release additives. It was the familiar feeling of euphoria, followed by that, as was befitting the present scenario, confidence and invincibility. There was, however, a slight nagging feeling he could not shake. The place was the proverbial needle in a haystack, hard to find unless you were given specific directions to follow. The question now was *how* were Sasha, his uncle, and the mysterious man, his uncle's confidant, going to find him?

Dumisani stayed rooted at the same spot for a while, watching the barn. It was surrounded by tall grass almost five feet high that almost covered the place entirely. All was silent, he looked to see if there was any person moving about but there was none. The whole thing was eerie. He felt the blood flow through his veins as he imagined Misty Abdul inside the place, obviously scared senseless. And what was her crime? He asked himself again. It was for knowing the brothers and nothing else, and now she was being held against her will and God knew what else they were doing to her, the abuse she was most likely enduring at the moment. Just the thought alone started to replace the feeling of euphoria to that of unabashed anger. Somehow he had to find a way to end this.

He was pumping himself up, psyching up for the final steps of his quest, when he felt movement to his left and then to his right, and before he could react, Dumisani was immediately and roughly shoved to the ground with both arms pinned to his back while one of the assailants had the pleasure of stripping the backpack that had the contents of all these troubles, and proudly display it before his eyes. The squat man did not dare look inside as per instructions. Nonetheless, the speed and precision of the take down and capture was nothing short of spectacular.

All in all it had taken less than five seconds, for Bob McNamara and three of his cohorts to accomplish that. Enough time for the old Dumisani, not the one currently high on opioids, to have sensed them before they made a move, assessed the danger and deal with it accordingly. However, this Dumisani McDaniels's senses were now dulled by a mind- and mood-altering drug that was slowly taking him to a road of ruination.

He looked up and around at the four men now starring down at him.

One of them was, like the rest of them, well built with toned limbs and a body that betrayed the fact that he ran five miles an hour every morning, and worked out like a fiend. He was Asian and his name was Ulysses Chiba, the other man, their leader most likely, was Robert 'Bob' McNamara. They were all dressed in camouflage, which made them blend completely with their surroundings, and their faces were painted green and black. Perhaps the last part was a bit overkill and totally unnecessary, especially since they were going after one man at the moment who was a foreigner no less, and had never been to this park or any other like it in the United States. The capture of Dumisani was remarkably easy and being honest with himself, the young man knew why.

The Dumisani McDaniels not under the influence of amphetamines or any other mood altering stimulant, would have with his incredible sixth sense prevalent among highly trained martial artists, sensed their presence long before they took him down and reacted accordingly, and not be led to the barn like a lamb to slaughter. The four men had MP 5 Sub Machine guns slung across their chests, and a bulky Automatic in a nylon holster at the hip of each and every one of them. With all this firepower in display, perhaps it was prudent that Dumisani did not react physically, or so he told himself. The young man tried to focus as he braced himself for what lay ahead as he was silently lcd to the barn.

CHAPTER 58

AFTER ONE OF THE MEN roughly shoved him through the double doors of the barn and into the interior, Dumisani immediately took in his surroundings. The place was pitch dark with just a few rays coming in from the setting sun, via small chinks here and there. The floor was hard, and upon further observation, he realized that it had been covered with cement that had been plastered in years after the barn had been built, if stories that this was a place where a movie production company kept its cattle and horses were accurate. There were areas on the floor where the cracks had widened so much such that weeds grew in them.

The place had been abandoned for decades no doubt, but by the look of things, the debris that had become a part of it had been cleared away recently. As Dumisani's eyes became accustomed to the gloom, he looked around to see that there was nobody near him and the four men who had brought him in had taken advantage of his moment of confusion to silently step out, and stand guard outside. Surprisingly, his backpack with the camera still in it, had been left at his feet.

Now this was strange, the young Motswana thought to himself, as he slowly picked up the backpack and placed it on his shoulder. He then starred ahead. In the dark, at the far end was a section above the floor as wide as the barn and about ten feet from the floor where bales of hay had once been stored when the place was still in use. On the left were built in ladders that were used to get to the loft. Upon closer inspection, Dumisani thought he saw a figure, a human figure, sitting on a chair.

He took a few steps forward. The figure looked like it was tied to a chair. Another closer look, his eyes now totally adjusted to the gloom revealed the fact that it was Misty Abdul!

"Misty!" Dumisani screamed in spite of himself.

He broke into a sprint, but before he could cover the distance between him and her, Dumisani felt something tug at his upper right ankle, which made him stumble and fall face first to the floor.

He was still on the floor, more stunned than hurt, when he realized that he had not been alone in the old shed all along. There had been someone in the dark right beside him, and it had been that someone who had tripped him.

As he looked up again, Dumisani saw someone appear from the dark corner of the hay loft ahead of him, and when the figure stood by Misty, the place suddenly lit up, most likely the electricity was powered by a silent portable generator from outside. The first thing he instantly noticed was a bound and ball gagged Misty Abdul. Her once well-turned-out hair was now disheveled and a trickle of blood was visible on both corners of her mouth, and a bright red welt below he left eye, confirming Dumisani's worse fears in as far as her captors handling of her. He studied her clothes for any sign that they had done more than slap her around and let out a huge sigh of relief. Misty was a very beautiful and attractive woman and male kidnappers were not known for their restraint. In spite of all that had been done to her, the young woman still looked very pretty.

The anger that surged through his body though was none like he had ever felt before. He fought to suppress it for Misty's sake, losing his cool would not help matters one bit, if anything it would most certainly compound the problem. The man standing next to her was well dressed, albeit casually, in a nice fitting two piece jeans jacket and a matching pair of pants, together with a face, and on it a well-trimmed mustache that revealed the fact that he took his grooming way too serious for a man, like he put way too much in it than was necessary.

The man smiled as he noticed the look of genuine confusion on the young man's face. He went on to put his hand on Misty's shoulder, and Dumisani thought he saw her flinch at the moment of contact.

"So good for you to join us Mr. McDaniels," Declan Price said as if he was a greeter at one of the world renown Las Vegas casinos.

"You got what you want from us, now let her go," Dumisani demanded as he looked around.

Two more people suddenly appeared at opposite ends of what used to be the hayloft. One of them was an Asian woman with shiny shoulder length black hair. She was stunningly beautiful Dumisani McDaniels quickly noticed. She was holding a phone similar to the one the kidnappers had left for them to communicate with. Making the young man realize that she was among the goons he had been talking to all this time.

She was dressed in loosely fitting light grey cotton sweatpants and a matching top, but coolly dressed as she was, that did not take away from her beauty, nor was it easy to associate that somewhat chilling metallic voice with that pretty face. Let alone the fact that her gaze was piercing, and by choice it seemed, as she followed him with her eyes.

The other man was someone he was now familiar with unfortunately, Bob McNamara. A man he was seeing now for at least the third time, the first being at the Sukasa Restaurant and as recently as a few minutes ago, as part of the welcoming committee.

"You know what I love about this place?" Price continued as if what Dumisani had said was nothing but hot air. "Nobody can hear you scream for miles on end."

The threat was completely unveiled and Dumisani heard it loud and clear. He unconsciously took a couple of steps and in his peripheral vision, saw two men emerge from both sides. One of them was Ulysses Chiba, eager and ready for a fight it seemed, Dumisani noticed that too. However, his main disquiet was Misty Abdul.

"Who the hell are you people anyway, and why don't you just leave us alone?"

"Take five steps forward and gently place the backpack on the floor, and then step back five paces," Price said, again as if he had not heard a word Dumisani had said.

Dumisani hesitated, as he looked around. On realizing this, Declan Price placed his hand behind Misty's neck and squeezed hard. The beautiful young woman's eyes bulged as she tried to scream which was reduced to a sift muffle behind the red ball gag.

"Do it now boy or watch me snap her neck like a toothpick," Price said in a soft and yet ominous voice.

Dumisani immediately did as he was told, and quickly stepped back to where he had been standing earlier on.

"Thank you!" Price said in a voice that was anything but. He then stepped forward, and continued

517

by saying, "Young man, or shall I say *boy* from now henceforth, when I tell you to do something, don't make me repeat myself, okay?"

Dumisani merely stared at him without saying a word.

"I said, do you understand?"

His question was met with yet more silence, as Dumisani remained defiantly mute. The truth of the matter is that right this instant, he did not care whether he lived or died, but one thing he was certain of was that if this was it, he Dumisani McDaniels was going to die fighting and on his feet.

One of the men to his right chuckled, and was joined by his counterpart to Dumisani's left, it was one big joke, very funny even though Dumisani failed to see the humor.

"He's got balls, you gotta give him that," the one to his right, Ulysses Chiba, said. He was Asian but his accent revealed that he was born and bred in the US.

Declan Price's smile then turned mirthless and said, "Oh, you're counting on your uncle and your brother to come to your rescue aren't you?"

Yes he was, but of course that was not something he was willing to confirm or deny, instead he looked up at his tormenter in astonishment. Declan laughed outright now when he saw the look on the young Motswana's face.

"You really thought we were going to let those two leave, head on out to Pasadena and tell their story? No way in hell we were going to allow that loose end to mess things up for us."

Jesus Christ, these have got to be the most talkative criminals in history, they're revealing more than they should, Dumisani thought.

He took a step forward and said, "What have you done to my brother and my uncle you two faced lying snake," Dumisani fumed.

"We had them followed then pulled over by the California Highway Patrol, except that it is not a real CHP car that will be pulling them over and they were too dumb to know the difference, and then they'll be taken into custody for some trumped up traffic offence, but of course they will not be taken to the police station. They'll end up in some corner of the nearby forest, and a bullet into each one of their heads the problem will be solved. The holes have already been dug, but don't worry, you'll be joining them soon. But first, we're going to have some old style gladiator like fun."

"That was not the deal!" Dumisani yelled.

"Deals get modified all the time Mr. McDaniels," Declan Price flashed that annoying smirk again, very pleased with himself.

"Just let her go, you got what you want and she had absolutely nothing to do with this," Dumisani besought knowing very well that his plea was futile.

Dumisani was about to say more, but froze when he saw another player appear from somewhere in the dark behind the hayloft, and stop right beside the bound Misty and Declan Price. He was white too, well dressed with nicely cropped salt and pepper hair that put him in his late 40's to early 50's. As he got closer to his cohort Declan Price, Dumisani recognized him instantly but found it hard to believe what he was seeing.

"Jesus Christ!"

"Not quite," the newcomer retorted with a smile that was eerily similar to that of the other man standing next to him.

"Jesus Christ!" Dumisani exclaimed again. "Senator Price!"

"Yes," Gil Price said, still amused at the young man's stunned look.

"Senator Price?!"

"The same."

Dumisani was in total shock now. This was beyond outrageous. Why was this man even here?

"Oh, so you know who I am?"

Things suddenly came full circle in Dumisani's mind. The Genuine Bank Heist, the aggressive nature in which they then tried to silence the brothers, not to mention the seemingly limitless resources that were at their disposal.

Instead of answering, Dumisani was finally putting things together, "So this is what it was all about, the Genuine Bank Heist that is … campaign funding."

Normally, this was the type of information he would have rather kept close to the chest. It was the kind of knowledge that could get him killed, but knowing that this was most likely the end of the road, Dumisani McDaniels was past the point of caring.

The Senator and his brother exchanged a puzzled look. It was obvious he had hit a nerve and he enjoyed their look of discomfort. The amphetamines made him push even harder.

"It was wasn't it? You needed money for your presidential campaign, and in doing so robbed that armored van and murdered that innocent man, didn't you?" Dumisani smiled with ill-concealed glee. He was suddenly enjoying having the upper hand, even though he knew it was just temporary.

"What are you talking about jungle boy?" Declan Price asked, trying to cover.

Even Misty's eyes were wide with astonishment as these revelations came to light and more so that they came from Dumisani McDaniels. She was amazed and impressed in spite of herself.

"Yeah," Dumisani smiled. "My brother and I may be from Botswana but that does not mean that we are stupid."

The senator looked at his brother and then at Mi Kyong Park, who had not even for a split second, taken her eyes off Dumisani like a trained attack dog ready for its master to give the word to pounce, and go for an intruder's jugular vein.

"Make it quick, no more loose ends," Senator Price said to his brother as he turned to leave. Apparently, he preferred to keep his hands clean and let the others do the dirty work.

"But you said you wanted to be entertained first Gil," Declan said to his brother in a low voice so the others would not hear him.

"Right, but I have to make sure that the other brother and that damn uncle of theirs are taken care of right away. It has to be done right Declan, it must end tonight!" the Senator said with finality.

Declan nodded, and watched his brother leave via the back door. Senator Gilbert Price was tired of all these screwups, this entire stupidity that had been going on lately. He could not understand why the simple task of getting the camcorder from the brothers, and kill them thereafter could have been so hard and unnecessarily complicated. Not to mention the fact that they were forced to part with $50,000 to hire an assassin to clean up this mess that could have been easily handled. And now, to make matters worse, he had taken the great risk of coming out in the open and be directly involved, in the process forfeiting the golden politician's 'get out of jail free card,' and that being plausible deniability. Of course all that would prove moot once the brothers, their uncle, and now the girl were silenced permanently.

Now, as long as they were above ground, it meant his plans were out in the open. That McDaniels kid was right when he said the Genuine Bank Heist proceeds was all about campaign financing. Who else had he told? Was the nagging question now, which was why he had to personally see to it that the other two McDaniels men, right now on their way to Pasadena, or so they thought, had to be neutralized, only then would he be able to sleep like a baby.

Senator Price was thinking all this as he exited the barn via the back entrance, where an assistant was waiting on a four wheel Doom Buggy that had an extra seat for a passenger, waiting to take him back to his vehicle waiting at the parking lot. He kept checking his phone to make sure that he had not missed the all-important call he was waiting for, to let him know that Sasha and his uncle the Reverend Sean Kane McDaniels were no longer a threat.

***

By now the sun had dipped behind the Santa Monica Mountain range, which meant that darkness was setting in quickly. And with night, the predators of the forest and the two legged kind came alive. Inside the barn it felt like night already, and so with the fading of the natural light, so did hope. Dumisani knew he was now on his own, Sasha and his uncle, if what he heard was true were as good as dead or just about. The feeling of loss and rage sweeping through him was at the moment indescribable, but he knew if he had even a prayer of getting him and Misty out of this alive, he would have to keep his personal feelings in check.

McNamara and the other man, Ulysses Chiba were now closing in on Dumisani from both sides. He was still focused on Misty and Declan on the hayloft, so he felt rather than saw them in his peripheral vision. The mysterious Asian woman had not moved from where she had been standing, nor had she uttered a single word. There was something about her that worried the young third degree black belt from Botswana, though he could not pinpoint exactly what it was. It was the eyes most probably. Beautiful as they were, they were cold and calculating, like the dark eyes of a man eating Tiger shark.

Dumisani McDaniels had been around killers before, Sahili and his gang for one, and he could see the same look in the beautiful enigmatic woman as he did in those marauders. Beautiful as she was, the woman was no eye candy, the woman was a killer that much was clear. Why else could she be here and also direct the conversation that lured him here?

"Could you at least free up Miss Abdul?" Dumisani pleaded, knowing very well what the answer was going to be.

"Not before we have some fun," Price smirked. Oh, how Dumisani wished he could slap that self-serving grin off his face!

"What are you talking about?" Dumisani asked, even though he knew exactly what. The man was a fan of cockfighting, but with humans. He felt the two men closing in.

"Ulysses?"

"Yes sir!"

"McNamara?"

"Yes sir!"

"Make it hurt!" Price ordered. The time for talking was over.

Dumisani flexed his arms, cracked his knuckles, and assumed the proper fighting stance. He then threw a glance at Misty Abdul and saw tears flowing down her cheeks. That and the gag made him want to scream in blood red rage. The beautiful young woman did not deserve any of the suffering that she was being subjected to. That said, the youngster knew he had to focus on what was about to happen – a fight to the death.

He was going to take on two men well versed in the martial arts at the same time. As they approached, circling him like two predators about to attack, Dumisani faced Ulysses Chiba first and then Bob McNamara. They were smirking, apparently eager to tear the young African to smithereens with their bare hands.

"You and your white brother disposed of one of my best men," Declan said, "and incapacitated another, let's see you do the same to Chiba, a natural born killer, and McNamara one of my best. Let the games begin!" He clapped his hands together twice as if he was refereeing a mixed martial arts bout in Las Vegas.

Even through her gag, Dumisani could hear Misty shriek as she looked on in sheer terror. These men were going to kill Dumisani with their bare hands right in front of her. She tried to close her eyes to avoid at least not watching the horror unfold in front of her, but for some reason she just could not get herself to do that.

The two men let out a blood curdling *kiai*, the war cry synonymous with the martial arts at the same time as they attacked Dumisani from both sides so as to confuse him, but he had long anticipated such a move so he took a step forward, and swiftly performed a graceful forward somersault, followed by another in such a way that the two side flying kicks from the assailants hit nothing but air, and a split second later the two bodies clashed and they both fell to the ground, more humiliated than hurt.

Dumisani did not wait for them to get back on their feet, before he executed a backward flip and landed next to Bob McNamara, and immediately leapt high in the air, his right knee bent, and landed with every ounce of his force on McNamara's chest, feeling the immediate collapse of a couple of his ribs or more. Bob McNamara howled in agony and realized that the scream of pain itself was excruciating. He then gagged and coughed, still lying on his back. He coughed again with his palm covering his mouth, and when he withdrew it to look at it, there was blood. It meant one of his broken ribs had punctured his lung.

He rolled over, got on all fours, and then started crawling to the other side of the barn. Every movement, it seemed, caused too much pain. This meant that Robert McNamara was out of the fight before it even started. Dumisani had removed him from the equation so swiftly and efficiently that even Declan Price, who was still watching the whole thing unfold safely above on the loft, was grudgingly impressed not only with the speed with which he had managed to accomplish that, but the grace and effectiveness with which the McDaniels brother had done it. It was true what he had heard about these unusual siblings – they were good. And once again they had underestimated them.

Dumisani now faced Ulysses Chiba, the Japanese American mercenary. Of the two, Dumisani had pegged him to be the better fighter, which was why he had to get rid of McNamara right away. A two against one fight is never a fair fight no matter how good you were. Forget the stuff you see in the movies, for those were well staged and carefully choreographed fights. Street fights on the other hand are more abstract, disorganized and most importantly there are no rules – anything goes, fair or unfair.

Which was why when Dumisani and Ulysses Chiba finally engaged is a fierce fight, they fought silently in a deadly ritual older than time, and each knew that only one of them would come out of this one alive. To conserve his strength, Dumisani McDaniels fought defensively, letting the attacker initiate while he would retreat two steps back whenever Ulysses would unleash a barrage of kicks and punches, most of which hit nothing or were easily blocked or parried away, and then stand his ground and wait for another assault to come from the Japanese fighter.

When after a few more round house punches and kicks from Ulysses found nothing but air again, Dumisani heard his opponent's breathing become more rapid at last, and knew the moment he had been waiting for had finally arrived. *Time to end this*, the young man said to himself and saw his chance when they began circling each other again, mainly for Chiba to catch his breath. Dumisani then quickly feigned like he was going left, Chiba bit, and he jumped high in the air and executed a front flying double kick, the *mae tobi geri* or *tobi mae geri*, where the left foot feints and then the right snap kick catches the opponent on the chest, face, or belly since it was unexpected. And from a master martial artist like Dumisani McDaniels whose speed had been breathtaking thanks to years of training, this was what in boxing was equivalent to the knockout punch.

That was precisely what happened to Chiba. The blow, a front snap kick, landed on his chest and sent him sprawling to the floor. As he struggled to his feet, Dumisani performed a jump spin kick which landed on the jaw, and was about to go for the kill when he felt a heavy blow on his back that not only made him feel as if his lungs had collapsed and emptied of oxygen, but sent him flying almost ten feet away and landing on his belly.

Two incontrovertible facts hit him at once. The first being that he had not felt the attack coming, his senses were dulled by the drugs evidently and second, from as far back as he could remember, and for as long, he had never been hit that hard before. He was slow in getting up as he fought to suppress the bile rising up his throat, and when he did and turned, he saw Mi Kyong Park the beautiful Asian woman who had given him pause calmly gazing at him, one foot in front of the other, her fists up at chest level and poised in the classic martial arts stance.

Somehow she had leapt from the high hayloft almost ten feet, and landed softly and gracefully on the floor, then delivered a perfect but strong flying side kick, the *yoko tobi geri*, to his back. Unfair because his back was turned? Absolutely, but so is life. It then occurred to Dumisani that just as he was putting the Japanese fighter, Ulysses Chiba, out of his misery he thought he heard Misty screaming through her gag, but mistook her cries when in fact she was trying to warn him that the woman was about to attack.

Dumisani was slow in getting up, wondering if he had a broken bone or two in his back. The pain was excruciating.

"Fuckin bitch!" he managed to say as he spat a gob of blood from his mouth, where a Ulysses punch had landed earlier in the fight. "You ought to be ashamed of yourself, attacking me while my back was to you, coward!" he continued. His eyes were full of rage and now renewed hatred.

Mi Kyong just stared at him coldly, and in a way that dared the young master to engage her in yet another fight to the death. Just then he felt rather than saw Ulysses Chiba struggle to his feet, but a lightening back kick from Dumisani to the chest put him out for a long ten count. It was now him versus the unknown assailant standing in front of him.

Dumisani once again twisted his neck this way and that, to ease the kinks he felt coming. The two circled one another like two hounds ready to slug it out. Mi Kyong's hair was tied in a ponytail he noticed, and immediately reached behind his back, held his long dreadlocks in one bunch, and then pulled one lock and used it to tie the rest of them in place. He had forgotten to do that in his fight with the American Japanese mercenary and almost paid the price. He was not going to make the same mistake again.

Something else was happening though as he eyed his opponent. The dullness behind his eyes was returning, the shaking of his hands and legs soon followed. He tried to blink the itch behind his eyes, and with it the dullness but that only made matters worse. Misty noticed the sudden change, and became alarmed as she wondered what was wrong with him. But then again, somehow, Misty Abdul had that sinking feeling that she knew what it was about, but tried hard to push the troubling thought her mind was leading her to, and that being the man she had long fallen in love with, the sweet, kind, and extremely handsome African boy was a drug addict.

Dumisani reached into his pocket, and without looking fished out a few Oxys and immediately threw them into his mouth, in a move so fast that no one except a wide eyed Misty noticed, her wildest fear confirmed. And as been the habit, chewed them to dust and with the some of the blood still in his mouth, swallowed them. It was at that moment when Mi Kyong Park attacked.

The assassin spun forward, and in a move so swift that Dumisani McDaniels, with all those years of training behind him, getting his black belt with Sasha at age 15, champion of his weight class at 17, did not anticipate the speed and ferocity with which she covered the distance between them, and not only that delivered two quick reverse punches to the chest before he had time to block or parry either one of them.

Dumisani staggered backward before falling on the seat of his pants. *Damn this woman is good*! Dumisani thought. He countered with a deadly front kick of his own, but Mi Kyong stepped back and while his leg was way up, she too kicked but aimed under his knee and the point of her shoe caught him in the fleshy area, the pressure point, sending pain up his entire leg from the hip to his toes. The pain was numbing as it was sickening, so much such that when he placed his foot on the floor, he could hardly feel it.

With the adrenaline still pumping up through his veins, he managed to kick again, but this time with his left leg but Mi Kyong intercepted the attack with yet another of her own, and identical to the first. This time her strike caught him on the inside of his left knee. Yet another pressure point, and just like it had been with his right leg, the excruciating pain shot up his left leg like it had caught fire in the inside and right into his marrow. And then like a condemned building about to be demolished with depth charges, Dumisani stood still for what seemed like a ten count, when in reality it was close to half a second, and fell to the floor standing straight like a tree in the amazon forest after meeting the business end of an electric saw.

The sight was almost comical, but to Declan Price it was because he howled with laughter and the relief that finally the brother, one of them at least had finally met his match. Misty on the other hand was horrified because it looked like Dumisani, try as he may, could not get on back up on his feet. He rolled this way and that in complete agony. Mi Kyong Park stepped forward and placed her foot on his chest and stepped hard.

"Be still Mr. McDaniels," Mi Kyong said in a perfect American accent as she increased the pressure. "To be quite honest, I expected a lot more from you. I thought you were going to be a much worthier opponent. Now look at you, a couple of not so hard kicks and here you're groveling on the floor – pathetic."

The embarrassment of having being bested so easily, and by a woman no less, was more than he could handle, as he felt the Oxys beginning to work their magic on him. Mi Kyong applied more pressure as she read the expression on his face. Suddenly, like cold ash and within it a live amber suddenly sprinkled with gasoline, Dumisani felt his strength return, as his eyes suddenly popped open like a pair of saucers on his face that made the assassin pause for a brief second, enough time for Dumisani to roughly swat her foot with all his might, making her stagger backward as the young Motswana stylishly flipped to his feet like a wounded leopard ready to wreak havoc.

The fight was on, this time with a more ferocious and seemingly rejuvenated Dumisani McDaniels. However, Mi Kyong Park matched Dumisani's savagery with her own. She was nimble as she was quick, but with his burning rage, Dumisani was able to back her up toward the wall with a rapid kicking combination, and when he saw an opening, he delivered several roundhouse punches, the first which she was able to elude by stepping back with Dumisani's fist grazing her chin. The second caught Mi Kyong on the shoulder, which spun her around and enabled him to grab at her sweater so that he could pummel her on the face. The moment he did that, she stepped forward, hooked her leg behind his and swept his legs from under him.

Dumisani was still holding on to her sweater as he went down, and instead of letting go, he held even tighter. Her sweater ripped and as opposed to breaking her fall, Mi Kyong went down with him, falling on top of Dumisani. For a moment they wrestled on the floor, rolling this way and that like a pair of intertwined spitting cobras entangled in a fight to the death. The woman was strong, there was no doubt about that. However, what prevented this from being the ultimate beat down it should have been from the onset, and with Dumisani McDaniels on the receiving end of it, is that the young man was well versed in the Brazilian style martial arts, Gracie Jiu Jutsu.

This was a form of fighting well suited for the unpredictability of street fights. Dumisani was familiar with this type of system, but unfortunately so was his opponent, and to make matters worse she seemed better than him, for she countered every move he could throw at her. For instance, at one point, he had her left arm in an armbar lock, a position if say this were a professional bout, and Dumisani had her locked in this position inside the ring mixed martial arts fighters called 'The Octagon', she would get out of it by simply tapping the canvas three times thus submitting to her opponent, and giving him the fight.

Instead of yielding though, the beautiful killer somehow reversed into Dumisani's hold and before he knew it, she was sitting astride on his torso, torn sweater and all, and began pounding him mercilessly with her fists. At first, even though his back was to the floor, he was able to block the first few punches to the face. But she then changed tactic and began hitting his chest, stomach, face and then back on the face. The blows were punishing as they were sickening, because Mi Kyong was putting her entire 108 lbs. behind every punch.

As he felt his strength leaving him, Dumisani in one desperate move, heaved his torso to the left and Mi Kyong fell to the side, and he rolled in the opposite direction before quickly springing to his feet and faced his assailant, and assumed the horse riding stance, the *Kibadashi*, as he prepared for her next assault. She was ripping her sweater off, exposing her bare torso, except for a black sports bra she had on inside.

Dumisani's ears were ringing, but even through the din inside his head, he could hear Declan Price and the rest of his cohorts, including Bob McNamara and Ulysses Chiba, cheering her on to finish him off, something they themselves could not do. His face was bloody and his lips were swollen, but still the young master would not back down – never! He charged forward with double front flying kicks that hit nothing, because the woman just stepped aside and executed a couple of quick rapid punches to the kidneys that caused Dumisani to bend forward, as he staggered backwards again, and fought to keep his footing.

The *coup de grace* was when Dumisani McDaniels, now severely weakened and barely able to stay on his feet, turned to face her, his last stand apparently and assumed the proper fighting stance, when Mi Kyong Park let out a mirror shattering *kia*, spun forward and delivered a high flying side kick to the chest that caught Dumisani square on the chest, knocking the wind out of him and sent him flying across the five feet space between him and the wall at the western side of the barn through which his body crushed through the old rotting planks, and landed outside amid the debris – out cold!

Mi Kyong squeezed through the opening that was created by the impact, in doing so she had to pry some of the planks loose in order to get through. She was intent on finishing the job yet furious with herself, for this one had taken much longer to put down. This Dumisani McDaniels was not the pushover she had imagined him to be, okay not a pushover per se, but certainly not as tough as he had turned out to be. He had been a worthy opponent no doubt and no coward certainly. There was something about killing cowards that Mi Kyong found distasteful.

These were the thoughts going through her head as she stood triumphantly over the fallen Dumisani, and looked down at him once again. He was helpless as he lay still, unconscious. It was now time to end this once and for all and collect the remainder of what was owed to her. Mi Kyong thought this as she lifted her right leg, and turned it in such a way that when she brought it down with lightening quickness, her side thrust kick would be like a hammer crushing Dumisani's larynx, throat and the vertebrae bones beyond such that the young man would first drown in his own blood, before he succumbed to the blunt force trauma.

"*Adieus* Mr. McDaniels," Mi Kyong said as she was about to unleash, with all her might, the finishing blow.

Her foot was halfway to Dumisani's throat when Mi Kyong was suddenly lifted off her feet, into the air and her body was flung some ten feet away like a rag doll, by a powerful side flying kick, the deadly *yoko tobi geri*.

"Get away from my brother tramp!" Sasha McDaniels howled after delivering the kick.

He then watched Mi Kyong Park tumble and roll before she struggled back onto her feet, dazed and confused. It was dark now, and through the light that came through the opening made by Dumisani when he went through the wall, made it possible for Sasha to see what the beautiful woman had done to his brother. There was pandemonium everywhere as suddenly the place was alive with men with guns dressed in SWAT uniform, and others she did not recognize through her confused state. They were in actual fact men from Lenny Broderick's security team to the rescue.

Sasha knelt beside the fallen Dumisani, horrified at what he was seeing. Both his eyes were swollen, one of them, his left, was almost shut and his lips were thick as sausages.

"Dumi? … Dumi? …" Sasha called out to his brother, his eyes were glassy with tears and an indescribable rage that made him shake, but knew he had to control, lest he ended up like his brother or worse.

Dumisani slowly began to regain consciousness as he managed to open one of his swollen eyes and began to focus on the hazy but familiar white face that was staring down at him. His bloody, chapped, and swollen lips parted slowly in what passed for a weak smile. Wasn't he in the same exact situation months ago back home, lying on the cold floor of the Sedia Riverside Hotel in Maun? He thought weakly as he tried to place the face looking at him with great concern.

"W-what t-took you s-so long Sasha? P-please h-help Misty, they … they h-have her t-tied up t-to a c-chair m-man …"

"Don't worry about that man, it's being taken care of as we speak. First I got to teach this bitch a lesson. Don't move!"

He turned to face the beautiful Asian woman and at that moment he felt Dumisani's hand get a good grip on his, and then he faced his brother again.

"J-just b-be careful Sasha, t-that girl is g-good …"

His brother just smiled, tears and all, and patted him on the shoulder then squeezed his hand, an intimate gesture between two people who spent their whole lives together, casual as it would have been to any observer it was not so to the McDaniels boys, because what he was telling his brother without saying the words out loud was, *worry not my brother, I got this. Not just for you, but for me as well.*

As Sasha McDaniels sized her up, it was hard to imagine that beautiful face and perfectly shaped body was capable of inflicting so much pain, injury and suffering on another human being. Again Sasha fought to control the rage that was threatening to erupt like suddenly active volcano that had been dormant for decades. Now was not the time to have emotion dictate what he was about to do, for what he saw was not the screaming beauty, but a monster.

"Oh, you're going to pay for this woman!" Sasha, the other young master, and arguably the better fighter of the two said in a low but menacing voice that somehow gave Mi Kyong Park, a seasoned and world renown killer pause.

To cover her newfound apprehension, she simply nodded at Sasha and smirked, the truth is, she should have not done that, because that's what really did it.

CHAPTER 59

THE FULL SCOPE OF LENNY BRODERICK'S plan began to reveal itself to Reverend Sean Kane McDaniels, when he and Sasha were back on the 101 Freeway south, and supposedly on their way back to Pasadena. They were barely a mile away when the reverend heard the beeping on his Bluetooth earpiece indicating that there was an incoming call.

"Yes?" he said by way of answer as he tapped the device in his right ear.

"Okay, stay at your current speed, do not go over 55 miles/hr.," Lenny Broderick instructed.

The reverend did not answer, and the uncomfortable silence went on for a while until his party was forced to prompt his old friend.

"Sean Kane? ... buddy?"

The reverend sighed and then said, "Lenny, I think it's time you laid all your cards on the table and tell me your entire plan from A to Zinc, or else I'm gonna turn around right this minute, and go abet my nephew with or without your help. And by the whole plan I mean *everything*!"

Like every good soldier, Sean Kane McDaniels felt that now was the time to know the big picture, and what he was faced with, the strength of the opposing army, the location of enemy scouts, their supply lines and reinforcements if any, and go over contingency plans in case he had to make a tactical retreat. In battle, he knew that if you were confronted with an unknown enemy you had to take these precautions in case you also had to make contingency plans on the fly, not be fed information one bite at a time as his friend was clearly doing.

Broderick sighed and then said, "*For your own good Sean it's better …*"

"Everything Broderick, or am turning around right this instant."

The lines were drawn and the former SEAL at the other end knew it. He sighed again in resignation, knowing that it was a reasonable request.

"*Okay, I …*"

"Wait!" Sean Kane interrupted, and looked at his nephew seated on the passenger side. "Am gonna put this on speaker so that my nephew Sasha can listen in." This was said in such a way that the matter was not up for debate.

That is why he did not wait for Broderick's to respond and instead disconnected his Bluetooth earpiece and connected the auxiliary cord to his phone, and then the other end into the car's stereo so that Broderick's voice could emanate from the speakers.

"Okay Lenny, we're all ears. Let's have it."

Sensing that if he dwelt too long on the subject they'd be wasting valuable time, Lenny Broderick cut right to the chase, also there was still the issue of coming to Dumisani McDaniels's aid, the poor kid was out there on his own and would be needing their help like right now.

"*Here's the deal Sean Kane, and I swear to you one swim buddy to another, I'll tell you more once this is over, but what I can tell you right now is that my security company, to add to what I told you at my house, also specializes in counter surveillance particularly the kind that involves industrial espionage, and I mean that on the high end. There're fifteen men under my employ, all of them former military, and by that I mean special forces vets. Some in my group, myself included, specialize in hi-tech spying as I told you earlier at my house. You see, after you and Misty left, I was able to dig in deeper. I'm talking wiretapping, hacking, passive and active surveillance, the works. I then dispatched two drones after you left, one to follow you when you went looking for your nephews, it's still high above you."*

Uncle and nephew gasped at the news and Sasha instinctively peeked through his window and up in the sky, as if searching for the drone in question. It finally made sense to the reverend finally why it seemed the former SEAL was with him in person every step of the way.

"Wait a minute, did you say a drone?" Sean Kane asked incredulously.

"Yes, and please Sean let me be quick but brief," Broderick said with some irritation at being interrupted. *"We don't have much time as it is. I'm watching you right now via drone, and the second one I had it track Dumisani."*

"What?!" Sasha and his uncle exclaimed at the same time.

"Is my brother okay?" Sasha wanted to know, he was beyond anxious.

"I last saw him entering a barn about five minutes ago. Not to worry my men are already deployed and closing in. What's of paramount importance right now is that a fake California Highway Patrol car is closing in on you."

Lenny Broderick must have sensed the immediate tension in the car because he quickly added:

538

"Don't worry, we're going to take care of that one too."

"How?" was the expected question from the priest.

"In precisely a mile and a half you will come to an overpass where a switch will take place ..."

"What switch?"

Broderick went on to tell them that a car similar to the one the reverend was driving, a Nissan Altima, same make, model, color and even license plate. In other words an exact replica, was waiting under the overpass that would take their place the moment they overtook it, and whoever was in the decoy, presumably Broderick's men, where to lead the fake CHP car to an exit where a number of police cars, who had already been alerted and members of the real California Highway Patrol, would be waiting for them. Some would be in unmarked cars and the rest in the official black and whites that were to light up the moment the Altima gave the signal, which would be the flashing of the headlights twice. The way it was set up was in such a way that the culprits would have no other recourse but to surrender without a fight.

Broderick went on to inform his former SEAL buddy that the moment the switch with the other car was made under said overpass, to turn around and hightail it back to the Malibu Creek Canyon Park, where at the entrance they will be met by two of his most trusted men, Randy Ironside and Paul Hanna, who were going to silently lead them to the barn where Dumisani was last seen.

The phone conversation ended just as they were approaching the overpass in nearby Calabasas across the 101 freeway Broderick had warned them about. By this time, Sasha's jaw had loosened to let in some of the fast fading sunlight into his partially opened mouth, scarcely believing what he had been hearing. This man, whoever he was, his uncle's friend was truly one of a kind. He was astonished at what this man could put together, and set in motion just to give the McDaniels more than enough to fight back.

As they drove underneath the overpass, both men saw a Nissan Altima parked under the overpass, right next to the freeway and almost concealed by the shadow cast by the overhead beam, and as uncle and nephew glanced at the car, they noticed two men seated inside, for their dome light was on for their benefit most certainly. Sean Kane McDaniels almost smiled when he noticed that the driver and the passenger were both white, but the similarities did not end there.

The driver was older with aging blond hair, a black short sleeved shirt with a white clerical collar and cross, and the passenger was a young dirty blond with broad shoulders, dressed from what they could tell at a quick glance, a black sweater. In other words a Reverend Sean Kane and Sasha McDaniels double. Once again, the lengths to which Lenny Broderick had put all this together was nothing short of miraculous.

The entrap Altima did not start moving until they were almost out of sight, and then uncle and nephew took the next exit, looped around and as instructed, began heading the opposite direction, which meant that they were now on the 101 north. Had the situation not been significant, as in life and death portentous, the reverend would have laughed out loud when he saw the decoy Altima being lit up by the fake CHP car. The Altima had its signal on, indicating that they were getting ready to pull over at the next exit where they were being led into an elaborate trap – again just as Lenny Broderick had intended.

It was dusk by the time they got back to the Malibu Creek Canyon State Park, and for Sasha it was like returning to a sight he only saw in his deepest darkest nightmare. For some reason, the surrounding forest seemed monstrous, like a dark hairy beast and within its belly, somewhere in the darkness was a brother he loved more than life. It pained him to no end that Dumisani was out there vulnerable and was at the moment needing him.

The moment the Altima pulled through the entrance, Sean Kane turned off the headlights and as before, following Broderick's instructions drove the vehicle to an almost obscure part of the park, and away from where hikers and campers normally parked their cars. The moment he did so, and following a fifty count, the two men stepped out of the car on high alert, and looked around waiting for a possible attack, but none came and then took a different route from the one Dumisani had taken over an hour and a half earlier. Officially, the park was closed at this time of day, but this of course did not apply to those who were willing to flaunt this rule.

According to the mastermind, Lenny Broderick, Dumisani had gotten to the barn in question using a pathway that headed westward, which then meandered back south to its destination. It was when the two McDaniels men were at a section where the trail was like a tunnel within the thick vegetation, when out of nowhere the two former Special Forces men they had been warned to be on the lookout for, Randy Ironside and Paul Hanna suddenly appeared out of nowhere like forest sprites.

Since the McDaniels had been expecting them, they were not unduly startled as any person would have. Besides, the current situation was already tense for none of them ruled out an ambush from the enemy. Ironside and Hanna looked very much like the Special Forces veterans they were, as they stood waiting for

Sasha and Sean Kane on the trail ahead of them, and not hand-picked members of a private security firm.

Even in the dark, Sean Kane McDaniels could tell that the machine guns the two men were carrying, were the Colt Model 733 of the M16 family. They were clad in camouflage fatigue, the type used by the navy SEALS with green paint on their faces. Their chests were bulged because of the Kevlar vests within, and instead of the cross cropped haircuts prevalent among army personnel, theirs was long and tied up in ponytails. All this was backed by the Heckler and Koch sidearm. In truth, with all this firepower, and it was safe to assume that the other men hidden around the forest were just as armed, McDaniels could not help but think that this was like bringing a bazooka to a knife fight, but his thinking was it was better to be staggering under heavy armor than none at all.

The introductions were brief, punctuated by brief nods all around, before the two men Ironside and Hanna led the way by jog totting silently along the path with the two McDaniels men easily keeping pace. Sasha McDaniels, his heart fluttering, felt the adrenaline surge once more through his veins. For a moment he imagined how it felt to be part of some of the most spectacular special ops takedowns the world has ever known. The raid at the Entebbe Airport in Uganda, the Bin Laden Raid at a compound in Abbottabad Pakistan, and many like it. In a way going to rescue his brother felt very much like it.

As they approached the barn, coming in from the north, one of the men, Paul Hanna who was leading the line suddenly froze to a standstill, and raised his right hand and made a fist. Sean Kane McDaniels had earlier on warned his nephew of this particular maneuver, and what to do when it happened. The three trained veterans, including the priest collar and all, immediately took cover by diving to the side among the tall grass. Sasha, very impressed, followed after an awkward pause.

There was no immediate danger however, Hanna just wanted to pause briefly and hold a short conference before they engaged the enemy. When the two vets turned to face them, Sasha noticed for the first time that they were wearing night vision goggles, which he soon realized was the reason why they negotiated the crooked trail through the forest with such ease.

Hanna asked everyone to take a knee, and when they did, the former Ranger with the United States Marines flipped the night vision goggles on top of his head. Sasha also noticed that he had an earpiece mike in his left ear. Obviously, it was how he was getting feedback and live play by play instructions from Lenny Broderick.

"The others will be joining us in precisely one minute," Paul Hanna announced. "And from here we will split into three groups where we will flank the target from three sides, and wait for word from up top."

"How long will that take? Getting word from on up as you put it?" Sean Kane McDaniels wanted to know. "After all, my nephew is in there and not to mention a kidnapped young woman whose lives are in peril as we speak," he added after a brief pause.

The other vet, Randy Ironside fielded this one by first nodding, a gesture the McDaniels could see even in the dark.

"One of our guys watching the place saw two men leaving the barn on a couple of dune buggies just a few minutes ago. One of them looks very much like United States Senator Gilbert Price, according to our man."

For a moment, the reverend thought he had not heard him right, and that he was hearing things, after all this had been a strange last few days ever since he found out that his nephews, still new to the country, were on the run. Could it be that the Senator, a possible United States Presidential candidate was involved? What else could explain why he had been here at the scene of a possible crime?

"Say that again?" Sean Kane's harsh whisper was raised a tad. "Are you sure?"

"As sure as I'm kneeling beside you right now." Ironside said. Like his colleague, he had also flipped his night vision goggles to the top of his head.

The priest suddenly felt a stabbing fear at the pit of his stomach, as an abrupt troubling thought hit him hard. He must have made some sound to voice that fear and discomfort, because Hanna suddenly looked up at him.

"What?" Hanna asked.

"My nephew and this young woman Misty Abdul are inside that barn and have seen the Senator," Sean Kane McDaniels said in between gritted teeth.

"And?" Ironside asked, still not catching the drift.

"Do you think they will just let them walk out of here to tell their story? That man is running or is about to announce that he will be throwing his name in the hat to run for president of the United States. Do you think he will allow anything even remotely resembling a scandal to taint his image?"

Ironside and Hanna exchanged a look that said, *You know what? The preacher man is right*. Still on one knee, Paul Hanna tapped his earpiece and turned away from the other men so that he could speak privately. The other men assumed that he was relaying news to his boss that the situation was actually far worse than they anticipated, after what the reverend pointed out.

Sasha meanwhile was like a Pitbull on a leash fighting to break free. His brother was in that barn less than twenty meters away for Christ's sake! Not to mention Misty. Why were they not storming the place right this instant? He wondered.

His uncle, the Reverend sensed a change in the young man's demeanor. He was unusually quiet at this moment he thought. Sean Kane knew that by now, and from what he had gauged in the little time he had known him, was that he was not one to stay subdued. He would have thrown in his two cents by now. What concerned him now, even in the dark, was the way in which Sasha was studying the barn and grinding his teeth at the same time as he did so. A habit he had come to notice about his nephew whenever he was agitated and about to do something.

Sean Kane was about to ask one of the men they just met a question when the still night was shattered by a loud noise, a loud shriek to be exact, coming from inside the barn. And suddenly, the western side wall broke open, creating a large hole out of which a body came flying out like a rubber doll that had been thrown by a petulant child. The shattering of the aging plywood and the sound that followed as a result froze the men momentarily.

Soon afterward, through the light that now came from the hole created by the body that had hurtled out of it, a woman in loose fitting sweatpants, a spandex sports bra, and dark hair tied in a ponytail stepped out of it to follow him. It was clear from her posture and demeanor that it was she who had initiated the attack. And the person being pulverized, trounced in fact was Sasha's brother, Dumisani McDaniels.

It was all Sasha could take, and before his uncle or any of the two former special forces men could react, let alone utter a word of caution, or warning or even physically restrain him, Sasha was on his feet and like a gazelle sprinted toward the barn at an incredible, and yet stealthy speed. Perhaps because he grew up on a ranch whose vegetation was very similar to this one, Sasha McDaniels negotiated the terrain by leaping over shrubs, avoiding rocks and bushes as he propelled his powerful legs forward with what could only be described as grace.

"Damn!" Paul Hanna said beneath his breath

"Move in!!! Move in!!!" Randy Ironside yelled in his mouthpiece.

Suddenly, Sean Kane McDaniels, now on his feet, saw about fifteen men in all in three groups of five rushing in at three sides of the barn, as their figures disatouched themselves from the surrounding forest. Past experience from countless operations had so long ago imprinted into their brains that it was always the norm to a point of almost being a prerequisite that no one operation goes as planned.

These were men who were trained to adapt to any situation, and have a contingency plan in case anything went wrong, like a brother who throws caution to the wind, and rushes to the aid of his sibling before the command to do so was given. By the time the reverend and the two other men, Hanna and Ironside were joining the other men as they rushed toward the barn, Sasha McDaniels and Mi Kyong Park were already engaged in a deadly and yet spectacular hand to hand combat that was breathtaking to watch.

CHAPTER 60

TWO THINGS CAME TO MIND as Sasha McDaniels faced off with the deadly woman who had just pummeled his brother to a pulp. Number one, she was good and by that it meant above average good to a point of being as deadly as a wounded leopard. The second being that in order to beat her, let alone stand a chance, Sasha knew he had to keep his anger check. Rage, he had been taught by his master, his father, was a fighter's worst enemy because it distracts you from your true intent, which is to defeat your enemy.

Seeing his brother on the ground again, badly beaten and bleeding, a brother though of a darker hue, but with whom he shared a bond thicker than blood nonetheless drove him to near insane fury, however Sasha fought to contain it as he deliberately took deep breaths to lower his blood pressure. The two circled one another, locked in a death stare. The woman was a knockout, there was no doubt about that, and had piercing dark eyes of a killer that was undeniable. Meanwhile, there was pandemonium all over as Hanna, Ironside, and their colleagues overwhelmed and subdued Declan Price and his men.

They did this by using strip shaped charges on three sides of the barn to blow holes through the walls, and as the stunned men who had been glecfully watching the fight between first Dumisani and Mi Kyong Park and suddenly his brother coming out of nowhere, were still trying to comprehend what was going on was when Hanna and Ironside's men exacerbated the confusion by detonating flash bang grenades, and then it was over in no time. That's because the flashbang grenades are less lethal explosive devices meant to temporarily blind and disorientate an enemy's senses.

Reverend Sean Kane McDaniels burst into the barn soon after Hanna and Ironside pretty much had everything under control, while Price and his men lay on the floor with their hands secured behind their backs with plastic ties. Price was raving like a mad man about his rights, and how these men were nothing but paid mercenaries who had no right to arrest him or his men, let alone make a citizen's arrest.

Hanna and his men just ignored the ranting man, as Reverend McDaniels looked around, and then up at the loft where he spotted Misty Abdul still tied to a chair with a ball gag in her mouth. Her eyes awe-stricken when she recognized him, and then suddenly welled with tears of relief.

On seeing her, the man of God looked around and spotted a ladder that was fixed to the side of the loft. It looked new, suggesting that it had been recently replaced.

"Hang on Misty," he said. "I'll be right there."

As he rushed to the ladder and grabbed hold of the first rung to start climbing, a man no one had seen, suddenly appeared from the dark area under the loft by the ladder where he had been hiding. One of Declan Price's lackeys most certainly. He was brandishing a huge knife whose large blade was glimmering from the overhead light. The reverend spotted the slashing movement from his peripheral view at the last possible second, and took a step back then delivered two lightening quick strikes. The first disarmed him as the blade fell harmlessly to the floor, and the next was a series of quick blows to the stomach, ribs, and solar plexus then ended it with a round house kick to the chest that sent him sprawling to the floor where he lay still, and down for a long count.

However, the last expression on the attacker's face before he was subdued was one of utter shock at seeing a man with a ubiquitous priest's collar and a cross dangling from his neck , well versed in the ancient art of the martial arts. And not only that, but the priest hit like a Mack Truck.

When he finally got to Misty, he looked around again to make certain that there was no other person hiding elsewhere in the loft, and waiting to spring yet another surprise attack. He then carefully looked under Misty's chair to make certain that it was not booby trapped – it was not. He then quickly but gently untied her, and also took the uncomfortable ball gag out of her mouth.

"Oh thank you Sean Kane," Misty said and immediately broke down and fell into the reverend's arms sobbing.

He then quickly inspected the young woman for any signs of any outward injuries, besides the ones he could see, the bruise on her cheek that showed she had been slapped several times, and possibly also back handed on her mouth, because there was a dry trickle of blood running down from the corner of it she seemed oblivious of. Other than that, and in spite of what she had experienced, Misty Abdul was fine and beautiful as ever. The priest only worried about the mental scars for now.

He gently helped her to her feet, which were wobbly at first, until she was strong enough to take a few more steps on her own toward the ladder.

"Are you alright?" he asked after she stumbled a bit.

"Y-yes Sean." She then looked around and then down at the commotion that seemed to be under control finally, after Declan and his cohorts were gagged. "Dumi?" Misty wondered aloud when she did not immediately see him. "How is Dumi?"

"He's okay," he said quickly, sparing her the details because in truth Dumisani McDaniels was far from okay. "I need to get you out of here."

As he led her to the ladder, she suddenly turned to face him and said, "Did you know that Senator Gil Price is involved? I saw him."

"Yes," Sean Kane affirmed.

"He left with Dumi's camera not too long ago, what's going on Sean?"

"Yes, I know Misty but he was intercepted just as he was getting into his car."

"And there's that awful woman who was fighting it out with Dumi and …"

As if on cue, the reverend was interrupted by a shriek from outside the barn, a reminder that Sasha McDaniels was still fighting it out with the assassin, Mi Kyong Park and holding more than his own. There was another sound growing louder in the distance. At first it sounded like continuous thunder which then turned into the sound of rotor blades.

The reverend heard it too and immediately glanced at his chronometer and smiled. He had been expecting it.

"Right on time," he said as he looked at the more than bewildered young woman. Now he knew she had more than enough questions to ask that would last all night, but right now was certainly not the time.

"What?" Misty asked, already her lower lip was trembling, expecting the worst for some reason.

"Lenny Broderick has come through yet again."

"What's going on?" Misty asked again.

Her questions were going to have to wait, because by now they were climbing down the ladder with Misty right behind the priest, who then quickly raced outside the barn. Misty followed closely behind him keeping up with the grace and light footedness of youth. She once again gasped as she witnessed Sasha and the Asian bombshell still engaged in a skillful, and yet ferocious altercation.

She looked to the side and then for the first time noticed Dumisani lying on the ground, barely conscious and rushed to his aid without saying another word. She first knelt by his side and then sat on the dirt and thereafter curdled his head in her lap. Misty looked up at Sean Kane who was distracted by the fight between his nephew and the deadly Mi Kyong Park.

"He needs medical attention Sean," she implored.

"Hang on Misty," the priest said instead with an upraised arm among amidst all the chaos around.

By now, Sasha and Mi Kyong Park were fighting it out like two roosters in a duel to the death, with neither of them having the clear upper hand. What was clear to those watching in awe, including the captain, was the indisputable fact that the two fighters were kickers, because the aerial display was simply spectacular. With both of them hollering with every attack, they would clash in the air when each executed a flying roundhouse kick that looked like a pair of inharmonious spinning blades.

At one point both fighters fell to the ground, and then got up quickly then circled one other to catch their breath, before going at it again. Sasha suddenly changed tactic and began relying more on his hands. The woman, his opponent Mi Kyong Park, he finally realized was lethal with her kicking combinations, the plan was to neutralize that strength.

Sasha McDaniels felt that to do this, he would have to resort to the true and tested ultimate street fighting style, Grazie Jiujutsu the art that focuses, among other things, taking your opponent to the ground, controlling one's opponent, gaining a dominant position and using a number of techniques to force them into submission via joint locks or chokeholds. As the two continued circling each other, still breathing hard, Sasha began thinking quickly wondering how he was going to get her to the ground. Mi Kyong Park, was like a Black Mamba - Africa's deadliest snake.

And just like a Mamba, she was incredibly swift and dangerous. A Black Mamba's bite can kill a fully grown bull elephant with one bite. A grown man can die within an hour if he does not get immediate medical attention. With this in mind, Sasha had to act quickly and in doing so had to force the issue. He rushed her when she least expected, and Mi Kyong was about to lash out just as Sasha stopped abruptly and then smiled, a move that forced the assassin to launch an attack.

He had succeeded in baiting her, so when she kicked, he managed to parry her foot, and immediately sweep her legs from under her just as she stumbled backwards, and the moment Mi Kyong hit the turf with her back, Sasha was on her like in an instant. For a while the two wrestled on the ground like two antelopes caught in a rope trap. That was when Sasha was able to perform an armbar submission, as he was about to twist her arm to the back, Mi Kyong, apparently familiar with the move, reversed the hold and was about to apply the same technique on him, when he lifted his leg in the air while on his back was to the ground, hooked it on her back and used his other leg to grip her in a scissors like hold on her belly and squeezed.

By now there were brushes, leaves, dirt and all other debris blowing in their direction and everywhere as the two helicopters from the Sheriff's Department began their descend, preparing to land. Meanwhile, as all this was going on, Sasha McDaniels squeezed as hard as he could. Mi Kyong tried clawing, pinching, biting – anything she could to free herself from this death grip. The mistake she made, which in all fairness was unavoidable, is that she had to breath, and by breathing that meant her belly detracted, when she did he squeezed even harder until he felt her weakening.

The moment the birds landed and the doors opened immediately, members of the Los Angeles County Sheriff's Special Weapons and Tactics, commonly known as SWAT poured out. Soon thereafter, they secured the scene and in the process relieving Hanna and his men. A paramedic was also among them and began immediately attending to both Misty and Dumisani. On witnessing these developments, and after making sure that Mi Kyong was subdued for he had kept squeezing her into a pretzel until she was unconscious, Sasha then rushed to his uncle's side.

The two men embraced for the first time with Sasha letting tears of joy and relief flowing down his cheeks. It was over. At long last it was over. Thank God almighty, the young man thought.

"My swim buddy Lenny Brodcrick came through my boy." The reverend Sean Kane McDaniels gave voice to his nephew's thoughts as he patted him on the back.

553

A little later, the leader of the SWAT team, clad in black like the rest of his men with a riot helmet to boot, and brandishing a machine gun in both hands, came over to where the two men were standing. The name displayed on the top right side of his jacket identified him as 'RAMSEY'.

"Excuse me gentlemen," he said. "It's Reverend McDaniels, right?"

"Yes."

Since his back was turned, Sasha whirled to see the stout but strong looking man standing beside them.

"Captain Derrick Ramsey with the Los Angeles Sheriff's Department," he introduced himself as he stretched his arm for a firm handshake.

"Pleased to meet you captain, this is one of my nephews, Sasha McDaniels," he gestured at Sasha and continued by saying, "The other is over there, Dumisani McDaniels being attended to by the paramedics."

Ramsey turned to face the direction at which he was pointing and then looked back at the reverend, who could immediately read confusion on the other man's face even in the semi darkness.

"Oh, you mean your niece?"

"No Captain Ramsey that's my nephew's friend, Misty Abdul."

The captain looked at Dumisani again and then at Sasha and their uncle, was about to say something but then thought better of it and then shrugged as if to say 'whatever', before he said, "The detectives will have questions for you two."

"Not a problem captain, I would like to talk to them too, and so will my brother," Sasha said as he massaged a bump on his forehead. "You may also want to question her too," Sasha indicated, as he pointed behind him with his right thumb without turning.

"Who?" Ramsey asked, perplexed, after he followed Sasha's direction.

"Her," Sasha said as he turned to face where he had left the unconscious Mi Kyong and immediately froze.

The woman was gone.

CHAPTER 61

TWO AND A HALF WEEKS LATER.

A WATERFALL STARTS WITH BUT ONE DROP, and what you have after that is one of the world's seven wonders in the Victoria Falls, so goes the gist of an old African saying. It all started like a soft murmur when a reporter hard by picked up some unusual chatter coming from the Malibu Creek State Park, and it snowballed from there. The reporter, one Kimberly Reeves who sometimes freelanced for the Los Angeles Times just so happened to be at the right place at the right time.

The McDaniels story was the kind every reporter worth his or her salt dreams of stumbling upon, because it had all the juicy ingredients anyone can think of. Murder, robbery, kidnapping, and political conspiracy at the highest level. It started innocently and casually enough. Kimberly Reeves, two years removed from UCLA's School of Journalism, just so happened to be in nearby Thousand Oaks visiting some friends, and was getting into her car, a beat up Toyota Camry with fifty thousand miles past its scheduled oil change, when she heard the commotion over the police band radio she had in her vehicle, and was ready to head back home to Tarzana when she decided to go and investigate.

Just like cab drivers, reporters and journalists, both paper and digital, have the police band radios in their vehicles. Cab drivers use them primarily to avoid traffic jams when going to pick up or drop off a fare. Reporters on the other hand need it for the one thing that is the lifeblood of their profession – information that leads to news. Sometimes for the tall plain looking twenty six year old brunette, the calls on the police band could be a source of free and great entertainment, particularly the domestic calls. The same held true for cab drivers on long and slow nights.

With a racing heart, Kimberly Reeves drove north on the 101 Freeway toward the Malibu Creek State Park, wondering what she was going to find when she got there. Like everyone else, Kimberly knew that the state park was closed at this time of day. What was worse was that this was a dark moonless night, and right in the middle of a forest, and she would be alone with no one to watch her back.

The thought alone was enough to cause some apprehension for the young reporter, enough to have her consider turning around and head back home, as she approached the main entrance to the park. Kimberly Reeves was armed with nothing except her camera, notebook, and miniature recorder. However, curiosity matched her fear as she stepped out of her vehicle and into the dark night. Kimberly immediately heard the unusual sounds coming from the northern side of the park, and the light in the midst of the pitch darkness.

Normally, she would have been frightened to step out alone in the dark and into the forest in unfamiliar territory to begin with, but somehow the usual feminine fear of the dark deserted her as she followed the sound and the light in the distance. Later, she could not tell which of the many possible paths she took, but presently, she found herself at a small opening in the forest, and the old barn.

This was where Kimberly Reeves was treated to a strange sight, and subsequently broke wide open a story of a lifetime that shook first Southern California and later the world to its core. It took a while to make sense of what was happening at first as she looked around, not knowing where to start. There were members of the Los Angeles SWAT team all over the place, and inside what looked like a dilapidated and abandoned barn, what it was doing here was another story. However, inside the barn were several men lying face down on the floor, and cuffed with what looked like snap ties behind their backs. What on earth was going on? The young reporter wondered.

After showing her press credentials, she tried to speak to the man in charge, Captain Ramsey and his men, who as expected were tight lipped. Their excuse was that they could not talk to any member of the press on or off the record, without first getting permission from their media relations department. That and the standard '*can't comment on an ongoing investigation*' was what stymied her with the law enforcement men. However, as Captain Ramsey gave this statement, he winked at her and then gestured at four individuals at the opposite end of the clearing not too far from the grounded helicopters.

The four individuals were surrounded by what looked like paramedics, in essence what the captain was telling Kimberly was that these were the people to talk to. And this was where the reporter hit the motherload. To further add more credibility to her story, she found out that there was a reverend involved. She turned on her miniature tape recorder, and let the three men including the lovely woman Misty Abdul tell their story from beginning to end.

Midway through her interview, when Kimberly realized just how huge this story was, she excused herself and stepped a few feet away out of earshot and used her cellphone to call the *Los Angeles Times* Front Desk to put in a request for two things: the first being to reserve the front page of next edition's publication, and the other to send a camera crew to record this monumental event.

It only expanded from there on. Other newspapers and television stations, including 24 hour cable news networks like CNN followed suit, but by then Kimberly Holly Reeves was way ahead of the pack. This was her *'White Bronco'*, her *'Mount Rushmore'*, her *'Driving Miss Daisy'* all rolled into one. With its typical aggressiveness, and an unlimited budget, the *Los Angeles Times* serialized the story into three parts, and the story of the McDaniels brothers and their uncle was milked for all its worth.

In the following days it seemed, no one could talk of nothing else. For a while the brothers were besieged over and again that for a while they could not leave their apartment, and at their uncle's request, Lenny Broderick had a few men camp out unobtrusively in front of their building to keep an eye on them. Sasha and Dumisani were never told that there were men watching them to make sure they were safe.

Something else was happening as the story broke, and that was the Genuine Bank Armored Car Heist and with it the brutal killing of Martin Anderson. Thanks entirely to footage taken by Dumisani McDaniels, the mystery as to who was behind the robbery and the murder was solved. The who scheme was blown wide open the moment the arrests were made at the Malibu Creek State Park.

The instant Declan Price was implicated, the entire carefully laid plan of sending Gilbert Price to the

White House fell apart like pieces of dominoes. With the media doing all the leg work by digging deeper and incessantly, they basically did the work for the detectives, and in particular one Detective Rick Chavez and his team which included Chelsea McClintock. This was after his other partner, Daniel 'Danny Boy' Frazier, was also Implicated after having been found out to have been on the Price payroll, and had tried to pull all stops into having the only two unwitting witnesses, the McDaniels brothers, killed while in the Pasadena and Altadena area.

Some like the hacker Erick Russell, decided to distance themselves from the oncoming storm by turning state witness before even asked to do so. He did this by surrendering to the authorities the minute word reached him that his boss Declan Price had been arrested. With Russell as a cooperating witness, and a willing one at that, proved to be the death knell, because he was able to provide the detectives with information on how they had planned and executed the 'Genuine Bank Heist' including their ability to hack into the Jones' Supermarket computer mainframe, and disable the surveillance cameras in and around the store twenty minutes before and after the robbery.

Arrest warrants were then issued by a federal judge and this gave the story even more oxygen, as if it did not have enough already. The story remained on the headlines for a while longer and in this era of cable news TV the narrative just simply refused to die, especially when footage of the Price brothers, now certainly public pariahs, in handcuffs became available, the airwaves just went ballistic.

A week and a half later, Sasha and Dumisani were walking south down Lake Avenue, when they came upon a newsstand at the corner of Lake and Woodbury Avenue. They were both wearing baseball caps and decked on dark sunglasses, but their attempt at a disguise fooled no one. They still got curious looks of recognition every now and then, because their faces and their story had been flashed all over the news bulletins and newspapers. They were receiving daily requests for interviews from *Good Morning America*, *60 Minutes*, and the like. Of the two, Sasha McDaniels as expected seemed to be enjoying the attention the most.

Both brothers did however walk with noticeable limps because their bodies were sore and bruised, thanks in large part to that deadly encounter with Mi Kyong Park, who as of yet was still in the wind and mostly forgotten because the focus of the case had taken on significant meaning the moment Senator Gilbert Price was implicated. Not surprisingly, Sasha and Dumisani did not even bring her up in their discussions except to wonder who she was, and where their enemies had found her for the woman was incredibly talented, and clearly the toughest opponent both of them had ever encountered.

They then stopped and quietly read the headlines of the major newspapers.

'U.S. SENATOR, DECLAN PRICE LINKED TO GENUINE BANK ARMORED CAR HEIST ...' was the headline of the *Los Angeles Times*, by Kimberly Reeves. The part they could glimpse read: *Thanks to two brave brothers from Botswana and their uncle, one Reverend Sean Kane McDaniels ...*

Next to it was the *USA TODAY* with the bold headline: PRICE INDICTED!!!

The Pasadena Star News: AFRICAN BROTHERS, SASHA AND DUMISANI McDANIELS HELP BREAK OPEN MYSTERY BEHIND INFAMOUS HEIST!

The Los Angeles Tribune: REAL LIFE HEROES, MEET THE 'BLOOD BROTHERS' SASHA AND DUMISANI McDANIELS!

The brothers shared a glance and smiled, before reading what they could catch from the article, which was under the byline of some writer they did not know about, but it was as with many others, shared with Kimberly Reeves. It was obvious that the young reporter's star was rising with every minute and every day that passed – and most importantly, so was her stock. This was something that could very well propel her to her first Pulitzer and priceless notoriety in the same way that Carl Bernstein and Bob Woodward did when they broke the Watergate Scandal story.

It read: … their uncle, the Reverend Sean Kane McDaniels, himself an exponent of the martial arts, just like his nephews, and a former United States Navy SEAL with the help of a friend who owns a private security firm based in Monrovia California, and Detective Rick Chavez of the Altadena Sheriff's Station together with his new partner were able to crack the case wide open. The use of modern day gadgets that would make James Bond cringe with embarrassment and spy crafts such as drones, tracking devices hidden in ordinary cellphones …

Sasha and Dumisani looked at one another again then turned and resumed walking. They knew the story more than any journalist put to cover it. It was just that, and even though they did not want to admit it loudly, they were enjoying the attention and celebrity status this case had garnered. They were headed to a different supermarket this time, which was located at the corner of Lake and Washington called 'Food 4 Less'. Currently the idea of going back to the Jones' Supermarket was not appealing at all. This, in spite of the establishment's repeated attempts of giving them groceries for free for one month, thanks in no small part to their unwitting role in exposing the criminals behind that brazen heist that had left one person dead, and close to $3 Million dollars gone.

For now at least, Sasha and Dumisani were content to walk the almost mile and a half from their apartment to '*Food 4 Less*'. They also knew the possible commotion they would cause the moment they set foot in that supermarket, but were willing to endure and possibly bask in it.

After a long silence Sasha said with a goofy smile, "You know Dumi with all this hullabaloo going on I've decided to up my plans."

"What plans?" Dumisani wanted to know, still facing the long pavement on the sidewalk ahead. It was obvious that his mind was elsewhere for he was lost in thought.

"My plans of opening a *dojo* with an after school program for troubled youth."

Dumisani nodded silently. It was just like his brother of course to find opportunity in everything. As they walked, Sasha could not help but keep that million dollar smile on his face, anticipating the press conference he was going to hold the moment he was ready to cut the ribbon to mark a new beginning in the next chapter of his life. He even drew up a list of people he was going to invite for that grand opening. A list of invitees that included Constanzia 'Connie' Trejo, the waitress at the Sukasa Restaurant and Juan Morales at Jerry's Billiards. These were two people who saw fit to help two complete strangers who owed them nothing, when they were on the run. They had also made peace with Mrs. Virginia Perry and paid for the repairs to the damages they caused to her car.

He was still smiling in anticipation as he turned to face his brother, and instantly the smile vanished.

Something was wrong with Dumisani. This was odd because there was so much to be happy about.

"Okay Dumi, what's going on with you man?"

"Nothing, I'm fine," he lied.

"No, you're not!" Sasha said as he gently grabbed his brother by the shoulder so he can look him in the eye.

"You've been quiet, moping and sad the last few days. What is it man? Still homesick? Missing mom and dad?"

Dumisani did not answer, and for the first time in a very long time eye contact with his brother was hard.

"It's not only that Sasha," Dumisani admitted at last.

"What then?"

They were now at the section of Lake Avenue where the road intersected with Howard Street, and it just so happened that right at the corner were the offices of a small weekly newspaper called the *Pasadena/San Gabriel Valley Journal*, whose founder and editor in chief was Joe C. Hopkins and his wife, the publisher and managing editor Ruthie Hopkins. Coincidentally, the paper had also run a story of the McDaniels brothers in one of their weekly circulations. It was late afternoon Sunday and the offices were closed, so they found a shade under a big tree by the fence that leaned over and onto the street. It was still midsummer, so both young men sighed with relief as the shade from the tree cut off the scorching rays of the midday sun.

"It's Misty man. I haven't heard from her since. I've tried calling, texting, everything - not a word." He shook his head as if even he could not believe this was happening.

Sasha nodded slowly and then at last said, "Perhaps she needs time to herself Dumi, you know to recuperate mentally and otherwise, after all that she's been through, I would think that is to be expected."

Dumisani began grinding his teeth in deep thought.

"Or maybe she doesn't want to see me anymore," Dumisani suggested. Just the thought alone was worse than death. He had fallen hopelessly in love with that Persian American woman.

His brother's attitude on the other hand was, just suck it up, there are plenty other fish in the ocean, but he dared not voice it. Dumisani it seemed was crawling deeper and deeper into some sort of cocoon he could not explain. As yet, Sasha did not know of his brother's drug use, which was spiraling out of control with each day, and was becoming harder to control let alone hide.

"Give her time Dumi," Sasha said soothingly, "she will come around."

"But tomorrow is the big day Sasha. I told her, no I asked her to be there and that would mean a lot if she showed up."

Sasha nodded but said nothing for a while as he gazed at the cars driving up and down the busy street.

"Maybe uncle Sean Kane knows. Ask him tomorrow when he comes to get you."

The following day was the first day of school for Dumisani McDaniels at the Pasadena Art Center College of Design. Of course his case was now well known, and the school, in an unprecedented move, had arranged for him to speak at its gigantic auditorium and thereafter screen the film that was supposed to have been his class assignment, but had instead become a piece of media history very much like the Rodney King beating tape.

Undeniably, Dumisani was very nervous about the big event, and in his mind he would have felt better if

Misty Abdul was right at the podium by his side during the 'Q & A' session that was sure to follow.

An hour later, they were on their way back from *Food 4 Less*, where they went about shopping for groceries, and managed to accomplish that task without drawing much attention. As they walked back to their apartment, Dumisani began feeling that familiar pain and dullness behind his eyes, which prompted him to unconsciously pick up his pace. He could not get to his stash of Oxys soon enough.

***

The Art Center College of Design was founded in 1930 in downtown Los Angeles as the Art Center School. In 1935, Fred Archer founded the photography department, and Ansel Adams, an American landscape photographer and environmentalist known for the black and white images of the American West was a guest instructor in the 1930's. Then during and after World War 2, Art Center ran a technical illustration program in conjunction with the MIT of the west coast, the California Institute of Technology, better known as CALTECH.

In 1947, the post war boom in students caused the school to expand to a larger location in the building of the former Cumnock School for Girls in Hancock Park neighborhood, while still maintaining a presence at its original downtown location.

The school began granting Bachelor and Master's degrees in arts in 1949, and was fully accredited by the Western Association of Schools and Colleges in 1955. In 1965, the school changed its name to Art Center College of Design. The school went on to expand its programs, which included a Film and Television

566

program in 1973. A program that, among other things, attracted a young African boy from rural Botswana to its campus, and with him a story that was to be remembered and retold for years to come.

The school moved to the hillside campus in Pasadena in 1976. It was designed by modernist architect Craig Ellwood, and stands on property that stretches over 175 acres and overlooks the grand city of Pasadena from its location on the hills in the west. This was what Dumisani McDaniels, his uncle the Reverend Sean Kane McDaniels were looking at, the beautiful hillside campus of the Art Center College of Design, as they drove up the paved road uphill the next morning for Dumisani's highly anticipated first day of school.

Their uncle had arrived early that morning to take his nephew to school on his first day. The story was still running in the papers and the 24 hour cable news, but for the first time it was showing signs of slowing down. The reverend on the other hand had a live in quarters with fellow parishioners at the Fuller Seminary also in Pasadena, and there was even talk of him taking up a temporary teaching post while in between his missionary work, which was set to continue after he made certain that his nephews were safe and settled. What the brothers still did not know was that for now and in the foreseeable future, Lenny Broderick's men from his security firm would be keeping an eye on them at no charge at all to the reverend, who had made sure of that arrangement.

As of right now, Mi Kyong Park was still in the wind, and based on what the reverend witnessed that woman was a killer - beautiful as she was. So it was with little or no resistance from his former SEAL swim buddy in keeping an eye on the reverend's nephews, which under the current environment he felt was the most prudent thing to do.

Now, as they pulled up to the parking lot, Sean Kane looked over to the side at his nephew. He was dressed in a pair of tight fitting jeans, a nicely pressed beige long sleeve shirt and tie, and a maroon jacket.

"Ready?" the reverend asked with a wide smile.

"Yes uncle Sean Kane," Dumisani nodded with a nervous smile.

The Art Center College of Design's auditorium had a capacity of 600 and word was that it was at the moment packed to the bream, with many others on their feet as they waited in great anticipation for the intended speaker. Sasha, who was seated at the back of the car, leaned forward and patted his brother on the back in a way that was so affectionate that words were not necessary.

"I'm proud of you son, both of you in fact, and I know your parents are."

"Thank you uncle." He looked around, the parking lot was packed. The way one usually is when there's an important event taking place, and it just so happened that *he* ,Dumisani McDaniels, was the special event taking place.

"Still no sign of Misty?"

"Give her time," his uncle said. "She was traumatized remember? And may want to lay low for a while."

"I understand," Dumisani said, even though he did not because he choked on the words as he said them.

This was supposed to have been the greatest day of his life, the mark of a new beginning and in his mind Misty Abdul was supposed to have completed the picture.

There was a long silence in the car before it was time for Dumisani to leave. The way the event was arranged was that Dumisani was to meet a certain Professor Peyton Weaver, who was in her early 50's, and taught Journalism at the college. That meant she, like everyone else that morning, had read all there was about the McDaniels brothers and when she found out that Dumisani was set to attend her school, the lady just went through the roof, and took it upon herself to be at the forefront of officially welcoming the young man to the Art Center College of Design.

Thus it was little wonder that she was waiting for him at the entrance, all five feet three inches of her and full of spunk.

"Dumisani McDaniels?" she said with a wide and inviting smile when she noticed him walking toward her.

She was dressed in a two piece pin stripe business suit with a matching blouse within, and her hair was knotted into a bun, Professor Weaver had the image of an archetypical professor even though looking at her Dumisani had to wonder whether the image had created her. There was also a touch of makeup on her face for she was cognizant of the fact that there were going to be cameras in the audience, not to mention the fact that there was television crew from the local station, ready to film the historic occasion of a Freshman student giving a presentation of his unusual assignment.

"Yes, and you're Dr. Peyton Weaver I presume?" Dumisani said with his arm outstretched for a handshake.

"Indeed, pleased to meet you Mr. McDaniels, and welcome to our school."

"Thank you Dr. Weaver, and it's just Dumisani please, or Dumi if you prefer."

"We're pleased to have you as part of our student body. I'm certain you'll find life here at the Art Center

College of Design to be very exhilarating," she said as she flashed him one of her best smiles. Very much like a college coach after landing a highly sought after high school football recruit.

"It's my greatest pleasure professor. I just want to be the best I can be and follow in the footsteps of my father," he reflected.

"Good answer Dumisani. Are you ready?"

"Yes." He then heaved a heavy sigh, this was it.

They could hear the buzzing coming from the auditorium even from where they were.

"Can I get you anything before we go?"

Dumisani took a moment before he gave an answer. He casually reached into his pocket, and thereafter made a quick decision, especially in anticipation of what was about to happen and that being speaking in front of a crowd of eager people, many of them intellectuals.

"May I have some water please and use the bathroom?"

"Certainly. Wait right here and I'll be right back."

Fifteen minutes later, Dr. Peyton Weaver was standing at a podium on the huge stage in front of a microphone. Dumisani was out of sight, standing behind the stage curtains temporarily obscured from the audience as he waited to be introduced. He was now wired and ready to talk.

After the audience was finally settled, the professor made a subtle gesture that had obviously been prearranged, and Dumisani emerged from the shadows and the place erupted that it took a while before everyone was quiet again. The flashlights from the sea of cameras was incessant and so was the filming.

"And here he is ladies and gentlemen," Dr. Peyton Weaver said amidst the drama. "Mr. Dumisani McDaniels, who will also let us watch the film he shot that's been on the airwaves lately the world over. What you probably don't know is that every first year student admitted to our school is supposed to submit a short film he or she made the first day of class, and this ladies and gentlemen was Mr. McDaniels, or Dumi's, if you prefer, first assignment."

It took a while for the thunderous applause and hollering to die down yet again.

"The film as you know, caused a seismic change in our political landscape, particularly when looking at the next general election, but most importantly it went far in giving justice to a family who had a loved one so brutally taken away from them – ladies and gentlemen, Mr. Dumisani McDaniels."

This time the applause was accompanied by a standing ovation that did not subside until Dumisani took to the podium, and raised his hand in appreciation. All this was beyond overwhelming, and he could not stop the tears from running down his cheeks.

"Thank you Dr. Weaver, and thank you everyone. My name is Dumisani McDaniels, I was born and raised on a ranch in Maun Botswana, together with my brother Sasha by two parents who loved us more than life."

At that moment he looked at the audience, who were spellbound and hanging on every word, as he searched for his brother and uncle. He found them somewhere in the middle, and squinted his eyes just as he was about to continue speaking. That was when he saw something that spiked his blood pressure and made him gasp slightly.

No way! He thought to himself. Totally forgetting the microphone at his mouth.

"Misty?!" he blurted out, wide eyed. "Misty?!" he said again. "Is … is that really you? Oh my God!"

Sensing an opportunity to add even more spice to an even more dramatic occasion, Peyton Weaver, a seasoned journalist first and professor second, quickly stepped to the podium beside her soon to be brand new student, and followed his gaze into the audience. Misty Abdul saved her the trouble by tentatively standing up from her chair. She had been sandwiched between the Reverend Sean Kane McDaniels and his other nephew. They both wore goofy smiles on their faces, revealing the fact that they had enjoyed playing Dumisani like a fiddle.

Dr. Weaver covered the microphone with her left palm and then eagerly whispered in Dumisani's ear.

"It's Misty right?"

"Yes, Misty Abdul."

The professor then smiled, gestured at the beautiful young woman who was dressed in a pair of beautiful summer baggy pants, and a blouse with spaghetti stripes at the shoulders. Even from that distance, Dumisani could tell that her shoulder length hair had been permed, and her beautiful face had a touch of makeup, which Dumisani knew had been to cover the bruises that were on her face.

"May you come forward Misty," the professor invited with a welcoming smile on her face.

Heads swiveled and jaws dropped to the floor, as the drop dead gorgeous exotic looking beauty made her way to the stage like she belonged. Her timidity and shyness vanishing with each step that by the time she climbed up on the stage, spread her arms for an embrace as she rushed toward Dumisani, the six hundred plus men and women in the audience was again in raptures. They were, right before their own eyes, witnessing a real life Hollywood ending to a story that had gripped the headlines for nearly the past two weeks.

"Misty? W-what? H-how?"

The young man from Maun was beyond thunderstruck, and before they both knew it they were in each other's arms, locked in a hard suffocating embrace as their lips met and exploded into a passionate long kiss, flashing cameras and an applause on top of that.

"You didn't think I'd miss this for the world now did you?" Misty said in her throaty voice as they briefly broke from their embrace to look into each other's eyes, seemingly oblivious of the others, the hundreds of pairs upon them some of them, especially from the women in the audience teary with joy, envy, and some outright jealousy, but not the kind that would cause someone to move to the extreme of wanting to end the fairytale romance, but the kind that wished it had been them instead.

"Thank you Misty. Thanks for coming," he said breathlessly amid the applause and cheers. The Genuine Bank Heist hero had found love right in front of them.

***

Later that afternoon, Dumisani and Misty were walking eastward on Colorado Boulevard, hand in hand, this was when Misty hit him with, "Dumisani, I know you have a drug problem and the sooner you deal with that, the better it will be for both of us."

She had stopped, turned and looked him in the eye to make certain that there was no mistake in what she was saying.

The young man was too stunned to speak. His first instinct had been to deny the accusation as this was the standard operating procedure for every addict, but

Dumisani loved this woman way too much to lose her just when he had found her. So he nodded slowly, eye contact was almost impossible, but when he led her to a nearby Italian restaurant where they were soon seated at a table for two, he told her the whole story, leaving nothing out. He was in treatment at the Huntington Memorial Hospital, also in Pasadena, that very night. A procedure that was going to take a week and after that the slow but steady road to recovery, at a thirty-day lockdown facility in North Hollywood.

***

Right around the time when Dumisani McDaniels was having his moment in the limelight, a young pretty Asian woman donned in dark sunglasses and a hat together with a forgettable outfit like any other traveler, was checking in her luggage, one medium size suitcase, and using a passport with a different name than the one she used when she arrived in style via private plane a week earlier.

This time, Mi Kyong Park was traveling low key, commercial and not even First Class. She was riding economy, and basically kept her head down, keeping as low key as she could. The heat was still on she knew, and Mi Kyong knew that she was possibly a person of interest from the authorities who may want to ask her a few questions she did not want to answer. So the key was to get out of the country as quickly as possible.

Mi Kyong had avoided capture because of two incontrovertible facts. Sasha McDaniels, the only person to beat her in a fight got distracted by the arrival of the Sheriff's SWAT team, which gave her a chance to escape by rolling on the ground until she was hidden by the bushes, and from there made her escape. The second was her survival training in the forest which gave her the ability to elude capture.

From there she was able to make her way to the Pacific Ocean Beach, where she was able to steal a car that belonged to a lone surfer still out at sea, and from there made her way to a Safe House in Korea Town no one in the Price organization knew about.

It was here where she lay low, licking her wounds, and after purging anything that might link her to Declan Price and his men, she planned her getaway. As the huge jumbo jet, Qantas Air levelled off after take-off at the Los Angeles International (LAX), with Sidney Australia as the destination, the assassin was able to finally reflect. There was still that small issue of payment, money owed to her. She expected the remainder of her fee that was to be deposited into her offshore account within 48 hours. There was also the matter of the man who beat her, the other McDaniels brother, Sasha. She would have to bide her time, regroup and come back to avenge that one beat down.

For Mi Kyong Park, this was personal, and could not under any circumstances let that one go. Not now, not ever. She was going to come after Sasha McDaniels, and this time she will be better prepared both mentally and physically.

THE END

Author's Note.

THIS IS A WORK OF FICTION, more so than ever, nothing in the preceding five hundred plus pages happened to me or to anyone that I know or heard of in my entire life. It was all a product of my imagination. Names, locales, incidents, save for certain historical facts and names is all made up. Any resemblance to actual persons alive or dead is purely coincidental, and real places and names in instances that could not be avoided are used fictitiously. Once again, it was a pleasure letting my imagination run wild and taking creative license on a lot of facts, especially where research was required, but overlooked, meaning that it was hardly a priority because that's where my creativity came to play. That said, it was a wonderful ride as I sincerely hope it will be for you the reader.

Sebati Edward Mafate,
Monrovia California, USA.

Acknowledgements.

WRITING IS A VERY LONELY ENDEAVOR, especially when you're not a very well-known writer without a huge fan base like your more established counterparts, which is why every morsel of attention your work garners, a pat on the back, constructive criticism here and there, a suggestion from someone who took time out of their busy day to read your work, is very much akin to an oasis in the Sahara, which is why MS. Faith Christa Ntuli leads the pack of the people I am most indebted to. Her unbiased feedback, after proofreading the manuscript and editing was priceless, and to be quite honest I have no idea what I would have done without her, because '*Thank You Faith!*' does not even come close to suffice. Her help was just priceless, there was also Zoe Isaacs who also helped in that regard, Hugh Molotsi, for his unending support, Mpho Mapoulo, Aurelien Henry Obama, the one person whose determination to see any endeavor he undertakes to the end is like something I have never seen, Imani Archibald Seboni, MmaKgosi Keloneilwe, Maria Vaughn, my daughter Ulani Edith Mafate and her indirect encouragement, Dineo Motsamai for her 'never say die' attitude, Raymond Mafoko, Sebata Mpho Mokae, Adam Masebola, John Moreti, Aubrey 'The Great' Kekana, Cassius Latlhang, Anita Miles, and many others that it would take pages to mention them all, but were instrumental in making '***Blood Brothers***' come to life is something I'll carry with me for as long as I am alive.

Once again, thank you so very much for your encouragement and for believing in me and in the story.